# A Ballad for Slayers & Monsters

# ALSO BY RITA A. RUBIN

*Of Knights and Books and Falling In Love*

# PRAISE FOR A BALLAD FOR SLAYERS & MONSTERS

*"With a cast that you'll love to root for and an array of dazzlingly dangerous monsters, this is a fantasy that will sweep you off your feet."*— **Laura R. Samotin, author of *The Sins On Their Bones*.**

*"A gripping tale of magic and adventure, of family and finding love in unexpected places."* — **Amy Marsdon, author of *We're All Monsters Here*.**

*"Adventure, sapphic romance, vampires, and dragons? Sign me up. A Ballad for Slayers & Monsters is packed with a little bit of everything I love in a book, making for an engaging and thrilling story with compelling characters. With unique worldbuilding, a quick-paced plot, and some good ol' enemies-to-lovers, this is a must-read for lovers of fantasy...and vampires."* — **T.L. Morgan, author of *Silver Blood*.**

*"Rubin's debut into sapphic fantasy is not to be missed. This tension-filled, adventure-brimming novel has me on the floor, not to mention that the expanse of internal conflict and well-rounded characters, including the antagonist, just kept me reading. If you romanced Karlach, Shadowheart or Lae'zel in 'Baldur's Gate 3', you will absolutely fall in love with A Ballad for Slayers & Monsters."* — **Quinton Li, author of *Tell Me How It Ends*.**

*"A Ballad for Slayers and Monsters is a refreshing and exhilarating addition to the sapphic fantasy genre, filled to the brim with explosive action and fierce monsters at every turn. But at its core lies the unforgettable story of Kas and Claudia, whose perfect chemistry left my heart bleeding and soaring all at once. An incredible tale of loss, love, and a badass sword-wielding lesbian."* —**S.D. Simper, author of the *Sea and Stars* trilogy.**

*"A Ballad for Slayers and Monsters is nostalgic dark fantasy for fans of 'The Witcher' and classic TTRPGs, and a fun addition to the sapphic vampire romance genre."* — **Vesper Doom, author of *The Binding of Bloom Mountain*.**

# A BALLAD FOR SLAYERS & MONSTERS

RITA A. RUBIN

# CONTENT WARNINGS

- Violence
- Blood and gore
- Sexual references
- Sex scenes
- Brief mentions of past suicide
- Brief near drowning experience

# PROLOGUE
## TEN YEARS AGO

IT WAS the eve of Kasanna Lelvinare's twelfth birthday when the monsters came.

It was a frigid night, with winter only around the corner, but Kasanna could not have been warmer or more content. She sat in the parlour of the Lelvinare manor, located outside the city, Veldenier, surrounded by the rest of her family. Wrapped up in their beloved voices and presence.

Her father, Lord Lelvinare, was seated at the head of the long table, regaling her older brothers, Lorenzo and Julus, with the war time tales of their ancestors. Kasanna's elder sister, Alvera, was crocheting a doily by the window seat, while also keeping an eye on the little ones, Ria and Givann, who were playing with their toys on the bearskin rug. The beast it had come from had been hunted by her father.

A fire crackled and burned in the hearth of the adjoining lounge room, filling the air with a comforting warmth and keeping the outside chill at bay.

Kasanna herself was seated beside her mother, Lady Lelvinare, on the reclining couch, resting her head on her mother's shoulder and listening to her as she read from one of Kasanna's storybooks, instead of one of the tomes about the Saints Lady Lelvinare so often liked to read to her children.

Strands of her mother's long, red hair—the same colour as Kasanna's own—hung loose down her shoulders, tickling Kasanna's nose. Her mother's voice was so soft that she felt as if she were in danger of nodding off at any moment.

" . . . and the valiant Slayer Lyar plunged the sword, *Velane,* straight through the foul dragon Morvelth's heart. Ending the scourge of the dragons once and for all."

It was a pleasant end to a pleasant day, soon to shepherd in one full of joy and celebration. All in Kasanna's name.

Little did Kasanna realise that the idyllic world she had lived in since the moment she was born into it, was about to shatter like a crystal cut glass dropped onto flagstone.

A sound came from the lounge. Like something heavy falling to the floor.

Lorenzo was the one to get up to see what had made the noise that had captured all of their attentions.

The last Kasanna saw of her gentle, and attentive brother alive, was of him standing in the shadowy archway, his back to her.

A shadow seemed to detach itself from the rest in the other room. Moving with a speed Kasanna could hardly hope to keep track of until it reached her brother, tackling him to the floor.

There was a person crouching on top of Lorenzo. Their face almost completely shrouded by a mane of dark hair.

Before Lorenzo even had the chance to struggle free, the stranger lifted a hand with nails as long and sharp as some sort of forest creature's and clawed open his throat. Blood spilled, spraying the air and quickly pooling on the floor. Lorenzo went still and the stranger began *drinking* the spilled blood, as if it were water and the stranger dying of thirst.

The screams that erupted were deafening to Kasanna's ears. Especially her mother's heart-rending cry. *"Lorenzo."*

Two more strangers stepped into view. They all wore ragged clothes, to match their unkempt hair. Despite this, one of the first things Kasanna noticed about them was how beautiful they were. Their features were as fine as a marble statue's. Their skin was pearl grey and their eyes gleamed red like rubies. Their pointed fangs were a pristine white.

Kasanna had read enough stories to realise who—or *what*—these strangers were.

Vampyrics.

"*Monsters!* How dare you enter my home," her father bellowed. He pulled down one of the decorative swords that hung on a nearby wall and advanced upon the vampyrics.

But he never stood a chance. Kasanna's father was a tall man with wide shoulders. Always able to heft Kasanna or one of his younger children into the air with ease. She'd always thought him the strongest man in the world.

And yet the lone female vampyric tore his head from his neck as if he were made of a flimsy sheet of parchment.

One by one, Kasanna saw her family fall to the barbarity of these monsters.

She saw Julus's jaw ripped off by the vampyric that had killed Lorenzo. The little ones, Ria and Givann, picked up by their ankles and thrown against the brick wall. Could do nothing but watch on as the vampyric with a rusted axe, split her sister Alvera nearly clean in half. Spilling not just blood, but glistening entrails onto the floor with a wet sound that Kasanna thought would never leave her memory.

Shock and fear held her still. It left her oblivious to anything but the carnage around her. She barely even noticed when her mother lifted her up and fled from the parlour.

Kasanna could hear her mother sobbing, yet that did little to slow her down as she raced into the lounge, toward the hallway, which would take them to the foyer and then the front doors. Where they could escape—

They never even made it into the hallway. Kasanna was thrown from her mother's arms, landing hard and awkwardly on the stone flooring in front of the fireplace. She screamed as a horrid pain lanced down her arm from her shoulder.

When she struggled with herself into a sitting position, she saw her mother, struggling in the arms of the axe-wielding vampyric.

"Put me down! *Put me down!*" Lady Lelvinare cried. She was being held with her feet off the floor.

The vampyric sniffed at her neck. "This one smells delicious." He ran his tongue over blood-drenched lips. "Can't wait to have a taste."

"*Mama!*" Kasanna screamed, reaching for her mother, even though she was powerless to do anything.

Her mother's gaze was frantic. Agonised. The face of a woman who had just lost everything she held dear, but for one, and was desperate to see it saved. "Kasanna. Run. *Please, run—*"

The vampyric sunk his fangs into her mother's neck.

She went slack in the vampyric's hold, her eyes going wide as blood began to trail down her neck to stain the collar of her lavender dress.

Kasanna had once read a book where death was described as a light going out in one's eyes. And that was exactly how Kasanna would describe it as she watched the life ebb out of her mother, and the colour drain from her skin with each drop of blood the vampyric took.

Once he'd had his fill, the vampyric dropped Lady Lelvinare's body onto the floor like a discarded sack of grain.

He sighed like a man who had quenched a powerful thirst. "Just as I expected . . . delicious."

The other two vampyrics had come to join their compatriot. All three of them were covered nearly head to toe in the blood of Kasanna's family.

"Looks like there's only one little mouse left," said the female vampyric with a grin that would've sent chills down anyone's spine. Her eyes were all red now, no whites to be seen, and the skin around them had turned the colour of ash.

But Kasanna's attention stayed focused on her mother. Her body lay twisted. Her once pristine dress, now stained with her own blood. And her eyes stared unseeingly at Kasanna. All of the warmth and love in that gaze had vanished.

Her mother was dead. All that was left was her corpse.

And that was finally enough to break Kasanna.

A sound wrenched free from her throat. A long, drawn-out cry. So harrowing, even to Kasanna's own ears. It was giving voice to all of the anguish and terror roiling within her like a stormy sea. She screamed so hard and so long that it *hurt,* and she thought she might die from the pain of it.

"Enough of this," growled the dark-haired vampyric. "Just kill her already. She's making my ears hurt."

The vampyric who had just killed Kasanna's mother, moved towards her. Stepping over the body with his axe dripping red.

Kasanna could not be sure what exactly possessed her to move as she did. Perhaps it was some instinctual part of herself taking over. Or her grief hardening into anger and a desperate need to survive.

As the vampyric drew closer, reaching down for her, Kasanna whipped around and grabbed the iron fireplace poker from its stand by the hearth. She lunged out with it, its sharp tip catching the vampyric's outstretched hand.

With a shout, the vampyric wrenched away from her, gripping his now bleeding hand against his chest.

Kasanna staggered to her feet, breathing hard, as the dark-haired vampyric howled with laughter. "A human child actually managed to wound you!"

There was a murderous look in the axe-wielding vampyric's red eyes as he fixed them on Kasanna. "I'm going to cut you wide open—"

Before he could finish that sentence, Kasanna had stuck the poker into the fire behind her and used it to fling burning debris up at the vampyric.

And that was how Kasanna discovered the disastrous effect fire had on vampyrics. As soon as the embers and burning bits of wood made contact with the axe-wielding vampyric, he caught ablaze as easily as an oil-soaked rag.

He let out a terrible scream, dropping his axe as he flailed and stumbled back into the dark-haired vampyric. Just that brief contact was enough for him to catch fire as well.

It took no time at all for the fire to spread. It caught on her mother's prized embroidered rug, crawling up the wooden centrepiece table, and trailing across the floor until it could climb a bright path up the heavy, red curtains. Very soon the entire room was lit up, the air furnace hot and filled with the acrid stench of smoke.

The two male vampyrics had been lost in the fire, but the female launched herself at Kasanna, screaming like a banshee and hoisting Kasanna off her feet with a strangling hold by the neck.

Her eyes were wild, her elongated fangs on full display, only inches away from Kasanna's face. Kasanna had thought her beautiful when she had first laid eyes on her. Now, however, she simply looked like what she was. A monster.

Kasanna lifted the poker and swung it until its sharpened tip pierced through the vampyric's temple. Blood poured and the resistance of sinew and bone made Kasanna's insides lurch sickeningly.

The vampyric dropped her with a screech. Letting go of the fireplace poker, Kasanna stumbled behind the vampyric and pushed her with all her strength, sending her hurtling headfirst into the fireplace.

Kasanna didn't wait around to watch her light up the same way her cohorts had. Instead, she turned tail and fled through the burning lounge. Past the ashes of the other two vampyrics.

Past the scorching body of her mother.

The fire had already made its way into the hall, snaking up the walls and across the ceiling. Consuming the body of a servant left by the staircase. Part of one of the beams collapsed in a fiery heap almost right on top of Kasanna. She stumbled, but quickly regained her footing. Racing towards the tall oak doors at the end of the hallway.

She swung them wide open, ignoring the burning in her palms when she gripped the door handle and bolted outside.

The freezing outdoor air was a shock after the sweltering heat she'd just been trapped in.

Kasanna ran down the stone steps and onto the pebbled pathway that bisected the front gardens of the manor house.

She did not stop to watch as the fire clawed its way outside through shattered windows and the opened front doors, pouring smoke into the night air as it worked to consume the Lelvinare manor's exterior as well.

She did not stop when she almost fell over the body of one of their guards. His stomach ripped open and spilling blood and ropey insides onto the pathway.

Kasanna kept running. Through the gardens and down the snowy hilltop her family's home was perched upon. The only thought coursing through her mind was that she needed to get away. Needed to get as far away as possible from the burning wreck of the only home she had ever known. From the terrifying monsters who might still leap out at her from the darkness at any moment.

Away from the place she had witnessed her family die.

She broke through the tree line of the woods that stood nearby her home. Woods that her parents had always expressly forbidden her from entering alone.

Kasanna had no destination in mind as she tore blindly through the woods. *Run,* a voice in her head urged her on. *Run.*

The snow was painfully cold against her bare feet. She felt the pointed edges of rocks and sticks hidden beneath stab painfully into the soft soles of her feet. But still, she did not stop running.

It was a cloudless and moonless night and Kasanna could hardly see her surroundings.

Which was how she came to tumble down a sharp drop in the earth.

Her body impacted harshly on juts of rock. A cry tearing from her lips each time as pain as she had never known before bloomed in her shoulder, her elbows, collarbone, stomach, knee, and ankle. And there was nothing Kasanna could do to slow or stop her descent.

It only came to a halt when she landed in the water of a gushing river below.

Kasanna felt as if her body was being pierced by thousands of ice-tipped knives as soon as she hit the water. It swept her away and fought to keep her head below its violent currents.

"Help!" Kasanna cried out before the water washed over her head once more. The battle to keep her head above the water was one she was swiftly losing.

Panic tightened like a cold fist in her chest each time she was submerged in the pitch-dark water. Every time her lungs screamed for more air.

*"Help me!"*

Then, she was falling again. Through a spray of water that stung her eyes and deafened her to all other sounds but its roar. And this time, when she fell through the water, her head collided with something hard, and the world went black.


Wakefulness came back to Kasanna in fragments, coming and going like the gentle ebbing of a wave along the shore.

The first thing she became aware of was of a white, plastered ceiling above her, cracked in places and stained from water leaks.

The next was that she was lying on a narrow bed and that her body was *throbbing* all over. When she tried to sit up to get a better look at her surroundings, the pain that spiked through her almost robbed her of breath.

"I would not move around too much if I were you."

Turning her head against the pillow, Kasanna found a woman she had never seen before, standing in an open doorway, carrying a wooden platter of food and a water pitcher. She had soft, copper skin and long, dark hair pulled into a knot at the back of her head. She was dressed in a red tunic, dark trousers, and boots.

"You've got yourself quite a few bumps, bruises and broken bones," said the woman as she brought the tray over. Setting it down at the foot of Kasanna's bed, before taking up a seat on the chair at her bedside. When she folded her arms across her chest, Kasanna noticed much of the skin of the woman's forearms, bared by her rolled up sleeves, were littered with scars.

"W-Who are you?" Kasanna asked, her voice cracking from disuse. "Where am I?"

"My name is Tsurra of Lyancoso, and we're at an inn called the Lilac and Tulip in Brai."

Brai. Kasanna was sure that was a village not far from Veldenier.

"You've been asleep for a while now. I was passing through two days ago, when I noticed you lying on a riverbank," Tsurra of Lyancoso told her, as she picked a roll of bread off the tray, tore off a piece and popped it into her mouth. "I thought for sure you were dead. You were white as a sheet and soaked to the bone and looked as if you'd been trampled by a diavol."

"A . . . what?"

"A type of monster. Nasty pieces of work. Anyway, I thought I'd be having to bury you. But remarkably, you were still breathing. Brai was the closest village I could bring you to be looked at by a healer."

"T-Two days?" said Kasanna. "I've been here for two days?"

"Aye."

So it had already been two days since that night. Ludicrously, she thought, *I've missed my birthday.*

But perhaps that was for the best because what kind of birthday would it have been? She would not have been awoken by the excited squealing laughter of Ria and Givann. She wouldn't have had Lorenzo and Julus there to muss her hair and tease her that she would be an old hag soon. Nor would her father and Alvera be there to present her with gifts and warm embraces. Her mother would not have had the servants bake Kasanna's favourite sponge cake with strawberries and cream.

Because they were all dead.

As clear as a summer sky, Kasanna could still see how each of them looked when they died. Her mother's unseeing eyes. Her father's head ripped from his shoulders. Alvera split in two grisly halves.

An ill feeling washed over Kas. Her stomach heaving as if she had filled it with spoiled milk. She tried to sit up, despite her body's violent protests.

The unfamiliar woman leaned forward, pressing her back against the pillow. "I told you not to move."

"You. What exactly are you?" Kasanna demanded. "A warrior? I see you carry a sword with you."

Tsurra did not hesitate to answer, "I am a Slayer."

Anger bubbled up in Kasanna's chest, as hot as the tears that spilled from her eyes.

"Then why didn't you save us? Where were you? You could have killed those monsters. And then they wouldn't have—my mama and my papa—none of them would have . . ."

The words were choking her. She couldn't breathe, couldn't continue speaking. All she could do was cry in a way that shook her battered body painfully.

"Easy, girl." Tsurra was leaning over her now, a worried set to her brow. "Breathe. You need to take a breath."

But Kasanna wasn't sure she could. She did not think this grief would ever release her from its cold, dark claws again.


"Do you have any other family I can send word to?" Tsurra asked of her the next day. "Aunts or uncles?"

Kasanna shook her head despondently. Even though in truth, there was her grandparents, her mother's papa and mama, and her father's sister, who lived on an island. They all would've made the journey to the Lelvinare manor two days ago for Kasanna's birthday celebrations but would have instead been met with a burnt ruin and the discovery that Lord and Lady Lelvinare and their children were all dead.

Except for Kasanna.

Tsurra sighed, leaning back in her chair. "I'm sure there are people who would want to know that you live. Especially if your family was as influential in Veldenier as you say. And I cannot keep you at this inn for much longer. I'm a Slayer not a doctor, and one more night here and I'll be almost out of coin—"

"Then take me with you," Kasanna said.

Tsurra cocked a dark eyebrow. "Pardon me?"

"You Slayers have a base somewhere, don't you? A place where you rest and train new recruits?"

"Aye. The Slayers Keep. But it's not a physician's clinic to bring any stray child to. If I were to bring you there, you'd have to be—"

"Wanting to become a Slayer?" said Kasanna. "Good. Because that is what I want."

Tsurra looked taken aback, her brown eyes widening before her face settled into a frown. She was silent for a while. Kasanna could tell she was mulling over her words.

"You've been through a terrible ordeal," Tsurra said. "Especially for one so young. It's not impossible to believe that you are not thinking clear—"

"No." Kasanna's voice came out stubborn; harsh. "No, I'm not—My whole family is dead. My home has probably been burned to the ground. I would have nothing to return to. I would have nothing to live for. But becoming a Slayer could give me that, couldn't it?"

"Being a Slayer is a far cry from being a Lord's daughter."

"Well, I'm not a Lord's daughter. Not anymore."

Tsurra was gazing at her like Kasanna was a puzzle that needed careful deliberation before she could even attempt to solve it. Kasanna hoped she was doing a decent job of keeping the desperation she felt off her own face. Kasanna was a stubborn girl, she'd been told so many times over the years, sometimes fondly, sometimes in chastisement.

She was also a child of wealth and was used to getting what she wanted.

But bed bound as she was with a bruised and broken body, there was little she would be able to do if Tsurra decided to decline her request and walk out the door.

*Please, do not let her walk away from me,* she sent a silent prayer to any Saint that would listen.

Finally, Tsurra spoke. "To become a Slayer, one has to endure years of long and rigorous training. It won't matter who you were before you come to the Slayers Keep, you won't receive any special treatment. Because the monsters you face will not offer you any. They might even send you to an early death. Are you sure that's what you want your life to be? Hunting monsters and dancing with death?"

Kasanna did not hesitate.
"Yes."

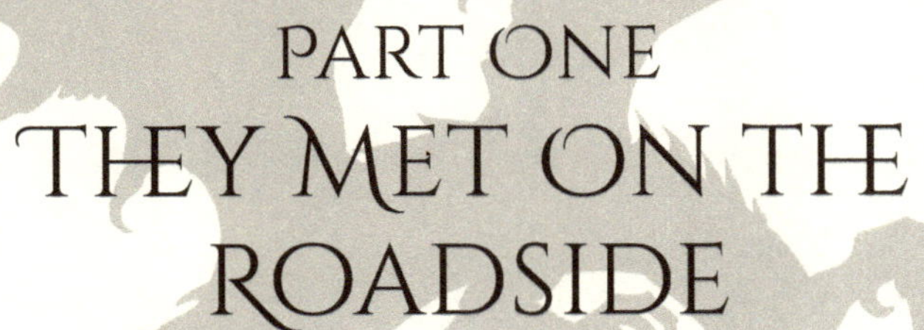

# PART ONE
# THEY MET ON THE ROADSIDE

# CHAPTER I
# KAS

MONSTER SLAYING WAS ARDUOUS WORK. It was not something for the idle of spirit or faint of heart.

As Kas of Veldenier knew all too well.

The rays of the late afternoon sun were harsh on her back as she rode along the winding road of the countryside. Her horse, a blue roan gelding, galloped hard, with no sign of tiring. It spoke to his breeding as a Slayer's mount, he had more speed and stamina than an ordinary horse.

It was not long before Kas left behind the yellow fields of wheat and paddocks of sheep and bovine, and was riding through sprawling green hills, and tangles of forestation. The road they were on became less well-travelled, more overgrown with weeds and grass.

It was a familiar sight when travelling through Murdo, one of the eight provinces of Vil Tresar. Murdo was also known by another name—*No Man's Land*. Of all the provinces, it was the smallest and the most uninhabited. It was mostly made up of farmland and dense forests. There were no major towns or cities. No high priests or priestesses oversaw the needs of the few people who did live here, and no sintiarns to govern them. Those people were left to fend for themselves.

She hadn't long been out in the wilds when Kas spotted something near the side of the road. She gave the reins in her hands a hard tug and brought her horse to a halt, before leaping out of the saddle, the soles of her boots hitting the dirt with a heavy thud.

Lying in the tall grass, surrounded by fat, buzzing flies was a cow.

The remains of one, at least.

Kas knelt by the bottom half of the unfortunate animal to get a better look at it. Judging by the sprawl of its legs and scattering of blood and innards in the grass around it, Kas would say that it had been dropped from higher up. She also noticed scratches that were deep and long, along its hindquarters. Scratches that could have only been made by some incredibly sharp claws.

Or talons, to be precise.

Kas straightened up from her crouch and returned to her gelding. After heaving herself back into the saddle, she spurred him onwards once again.

She thought to herself, not without some satisfaction, *we are definitely headed in the right direction.*


The night before, Kas had been enjoying a dinner of simple fare in a secluded corner of the inn of a small farming village, when she'd been approached by a man.

As she tended to when approached by strange men—especially in places where they were likely to be intoxicated—she'd placed a relaxed hand on the hilt of one of her swords, propped up against the wall beside her, which had almost stopped him in his tracks. The man hadn't looked like the type to cause trouble, however. He was a short, thin man of middle years with a timid expression on his weather-worn face.

"P-Pardon me," he said. "But you're a Slayer, ain't ya?"

"Who wants to know?" asked Kas.

"Me. Please, I need yer help."

Kas gestured for the man to take the seat opposite her. "What is your problem?"

The man sat and started explaining. "A nasty old beast has taken to raiding our farms as of late. At first it only went after our livestock, then 'bout a week ago, it got a woman, Old Lilda while she was walkin' through the fields. I saw it come down from the sky and snatch her up with my own eyes. And three days ago, it came back and went after me boy." The man's voice cracked. "I ran at it with me shovel and somehow managed to fight it off and rescue my son. Though it didn't leave us without a few scrapes and bruises." He rolled up the sleeve of his tunic to reveal a ragged bandage wrapped around his forearm, spotted with dried blood.

"What sort of monster is it exactly?" Kas asked him. "You said it came down from the sky."

"I ain't too sure, I'm afraid. But it's a great big, frightful-lookin' thing. 's got black feathers like a crow and a big beak, but the body looks more like a great big cat."

"Must be a gryphon, then." Gryphons had to be one of her least favourite monsters to hunt. They were large, brutish things and were perpetually cranky. That they could fly often made them all the more difficult to slay.

"So what say you, Miss?" the man said. "Will ya not help us?"

Kas finished off the last of her drink. "I can help. But my services don't come for free."

"Whatever the price, I'll pay it. If it means ridding us of this monster, and making our home safe again, then I'll gladly give ya all the coin I own."

And that was how Kas came to be tracking the gryphon of No Man's Land.

Fortunately for her, the task was made easier thanks to this gryphon being so messy with its food. She found several more animal carcass pieces, all in various stages of decomposing, that must have been dropped while the gryphon was carrying its meals back to its nest. Gryphons were also notorious shedders. More than a few times, Kas spotted black feathers as long as her forearm, tangled up in grass and bushes or lying in the middle of the road.

It was only as Kas drew closer to the mountains did she hear a cry split the air. It sounded like a bird of prey, only deeper and scratchier.

More monstrous. She knew all too well that it was the cry of a gryphon.

She steered her horse beneath the cover of a copse of trees, just in time to see a black shape circling in the sky up ahead. It went around a couple of times before she saw it go in for a landing on a rocky peak, disappearing behind the trees that surrounded it.

*That must be where it's nesting.*

Kas dismounted and gave her horse a firm pat on his sweat-dampened withers. "You did good, Bod, bringing me all the way out here," she murmured. He answered with a twitch of his tail. "Now you wait here and keep out of sight."

She didn't bother tethering him to a tree. She knew Bod would stay where he was until she returned, and if he did need to run, he would find her later. She grabbed what equipment she needed from the saddlebags.

Her two silver swords were already strapped to her back in their scabbards. She fitted her crossbow alongside them and slipped a handful of arrows tipped with silver into one of the pouches in her belt. Lastly, she tucked a worn-looking, leather gauntlet into her belt. On the palm of the gauntlet, a rune was inscribed, shaped like a triangle with a swirling pattern inside.

Once she had everything she needed, Kas set off for her trek up to the peak.

The climb wasn't too long or too taxing. Kas was hardly even out of breath by the time she reached the top. Which was a good thing, as she would need every bit of energy she had to face this monster.

Keeping low to the ground, Kas finally got a good look at the beast she was hunting.

Just as the farmer had described, it was covered in black feathers, yet it had a body more reminiscent of a lion, with a long cat-like tail that swayed from side to side. It even had a mane of longer black feathers covering its neck. It had to be one of the largest gryphons Kas had ever seen. Easily double the size of Bod, meaning it must have been an old one.

The gryphon had its back to her and was standing in the large nest it had built for itself out of branches and leaves and what looked like scraps of clothing and clumps of animal fur. It appeared to be busying itself with eating. The snapping of its beak and sounds of ripping flesh audible even from this distance. All around the gryphon's nest were bones and the rotting remains of its victims. Mostly livestock and forest creatures, but Kas did spot what appeared to be a human arm by the gryphon's tail and wondered if it had belonged to that Old Lilda the farmer had mentioned.

She watched as the gryphon tore off a large chunk of meat and swallowed it whole.

*All right, time to get to work.*

Kas drew her swords from the scabbards at her back. The low hiss of scraping metal caught the gryphon's attention.

Its head snapped in her direction, giving Kas a perfect view of its haggard, bird-like face. Its hooked beak was smeared with blood, and its slit-pupiled, yellow eyes found her instantly.

Kas smirked. "Hello, beasty."

The gryphon let out a piercing cry. It stood on all fours, flapping its massive wings once before it charged towards her.

Kas stood her ground, holding her swords at the ready. Only at the last moment, when the gryphon was almost upon her, did she move out of the way. Dodging to the side and swinging one sword so the tip of the blade caught the gryphon in the side of the neck.

It was hard to see what sort of damage her sword did because of its thick, feathered mane, but her blade came away with blood and the gryphon screeched and stumbled.

Even if Kas hadn't been able to seriously wound it, just the touch of silver against its flesh would be enough to cause it hideous, burning pain. It was the effect silver had on all monsters.

It spread its great, black wings and took to the sky.

As the monster wheeled around, Kas dropped her swords, and pulled out the crossbow at her back. She went to load it with one of the arrowss, but the gryphon didn't allow her the chance.

It came careening towards her quicker than she would have anticipated. With a powerful blow from its taloned foreleg, Kas went to the ground and her crossbow flew from her hands, landing a few feet away from her.

*"Shit,"* she hissed, as she scrambled to her feet and dove for the crossbow.

Once again, the gryphon beat her to it.

In one moment, Kas was reaching for the crossbow, and in the next she was being hoisted off the ground by her leg and carried into the air.

Short strands of her red hair whipped into her eyes, buffeted by the wind that grew stronger the higher the gryphon carried her. Her blue scarf nearly unravelled from around her neck. Kas knew what was happening. Sometimes gryphons liked to drop their prey from great heights, as a way to kill—or at least seriously injure them enough that they wouldn't fight back—before eating.

She had to think fast and find a way to free herself from the gryphon's talons while they were still close enough to the ground that a fall wouldn't kill her. Probably.

Kas reached for the gauntlet tucked into her belt and pulled it onto her right hand.

"Oi, you ugly prick!" she shouted above the wind.

The gryphon turned its head to look down at her. Its eyes narrowed, almost as if her name calling had actually offended it.

She thrust her gauntleted arm out, open palm pointed at the gryphon. There was a flash of light and a plume of fire erupted from the gauntlet and into the gryphon's face.

The monster screamed at the scorching heat and released its hold on Kas. Sending her plummeting to the earth.

Kas fell toward the tops of the trees that grew around the gryphon's nest. All she could do was shield her face with her arms as she broke through the canopies. She felt the stinging bite of leaves and twigs against her exposed skin as she fell, before she was finally able to catch herself on a sturdy branch. She stayed hanging from it, suspended only a few feet above the ground, and allowed herself a moment to catch her breath.

A shadow fell over her only seconds before the tree canopy burst apart above her, and the gryphon was tearing towards her. Half its face scorched, and its beak opened in a shrill cry.

With no other choice, Kas let go of the branch and fell to the ground. Landing hard on the rocky floor.

Leaves rained down on her as the gryphon worked to free its large body from the treetops. Kas scrambled out of the way just in time to avoid being crushed by a falling branch.

She found herself in the gryphon's nest, standing in the rotting remains of one of its meals. But she paid that little care. Instead, she looked about for where she had dropped her crossbow and sighted it only a short distance away.

Kas heard the loud impact of the gryphon crashing to the ground as she raced for her crossbow.

A few sprinting leaps and Kas gathered up the crossbow, found it undamaged, but missing the silver arrow she'd been about to load into it. She hurried to retrieve another one, because when Kas looked over her shoulder, it was to see the gryphon lunging toward her.

Kas loaded the arrow, lifted it against her shoulder and took aim.

But she didn't release the trigger straight away. Instead, she waited until the gryphon drew closer. Closer. Closer.

*Now.*

Kas released the trigger and the silver-tipped arrow cut through the air and buried itself in the gryphon's chest.

The gryphon's body lurched. A screech tearing its way from its throat.

Kas ducked as the monster soared over her head.

And then crashed to the ground, near the rocky ledge.

It lay in a large, feathered heap, screaming and kicking feebly at the air. Kas could already see blood beginning to spill from where the arrow had gone in.

Kas stepped around the injured creature to retrieve one of her swords. With the long, silver blade in her hand, she came to stand before the gryphon. It was dying, the life slowly bleeding out of it. Yet it still had the energy to stare up at her with baleful yellow eyes.

It opened its deadly beak and let out one last defiant cry.

Kas lifted her sword and swung down.

It was a clean and quick end. Unlike what the gryphon would have given to those it had already killed.

Kas wiped some of the blood from her blade on the dead gryphon's feathers. It didn't rid the weapon of red entirely—she'd need to give it a proper rub down with an oiled cloth for it to be truly clean. But it did the job for now. She slid it back into its scabbard and turned to retrieve the other sword.

As she did, Kas peered at the gryphon's nest and noticed what she had not before. That nestled amongst the forest litter, bones, and half-devoured carcasses, was a white-shelled egg.

Approaching the nest, Kas lifted the egg, its weight only putting some strain on her arms. It could have almost passed for a chicken's egg, had it not been larger than Kas's head. Its shell was also far too white and pristine. It looked as if it had been carved out of stone.

However, Kas knew better. What she held in her hands right now was an unborn gryphon chick. A creature that would grow to be as vicious a beast as its mother. A monster that would take Saints knew how many lives.

Contempt curled in Kas's chest as she gazed at the egg.

Tucking it under her arm, Kas stepped past the trees and towards the ledge, staring down at the drop below, the protruding rocks and hard earth that awaited below.

Kas held the gryphon's egg with outstretched hands, before allowing it to fall.

CHAPTER 2

# KAS

IT WAS near sundown when she returned to the farmer's house and tossed the gryphon's head onto his doorstep.

The man looked as if he had seen a sunrise for the first time, while his wife wept—although Kas was unsure if they were tears of joy or horror at the sight of a monster's severed head in front of her home.

"Thank you. *Thank you,*" he told her profusely, the smile never leaving his face. "Hold on a moment. Let me go get your coin."

The neighbouring villagers had gathered around to stare at and whisper around the head of the gryphon. One dirty-faced boy poked it in the eye with a stick.

"Did you kill that monster all by yourself?" A small girl had wandered over to where Kas stood alone by the broken fence.

"Sure did," she said.

"Is that the biggest monster you've ever killed?" asked an older boy, Kas assumed to be the girl's brother. They had the same straw-coloured hair.

She considered for a moment, twirling her wyvern's tooth ear piercing. "No. I had to slay a giant last winter in Novicra. That was much bigger."

"What about a dragon?" asked the girl, eyes wide and bright. "Have you ever killed one of those?"

"Don't be stupid, Clemen," her brother scoffed. "Everybody knows the dragons have been gone for thousands of years."

The girl glared at her brother and gave him a hard shove that nearly knocked him off his feet. The pair of them turned their attention to kicking and yelling at each other.

The boy was right of course, a dragon had not been seen in Vil Tresar for centuries. Not since they were sealed away by the first Slayer, Lyar. Unfortunately, sealing away the dragons hadn't also put an end to the monsters they had created. Which was why Lyar of Rosille had created the Slayers, a guild dedicated to hunting monsters. But where once Slayers had done their jobs for of duty alone, they now did it for the promise of coin. One couldn't survive off appreciation alone, after all.

The farmer finally returned and placed a grubby brown coin pouch in Kas's hands. "Here it is. Your reward. You've more than earned it."

Kas undid the pouch and counted twenty crowns. "This is quite a lot." It was certainly more than she'd been expecting. Especially from a farmer who looked as if he and his family could barely afford the dusty clothes on their backs.

"Aye. It's four month's pay that is. But it was a big task I was askin' of ya. You put yer life on the line for a stranger like me and came through. So, yer owed a decent reward."

The farmer's three children had all come outside now and were taking turns at hitting the gryphon's head with sticks. Pretending they were the ones slaying the monster that had terrorised them.

One of them was a boy with shaggy hair. The left side of his face almost entirely covered by linen bandages. The son who had almost been taken by the gryphon.

He was unsteady on his feet, and when he went to take a swing at the gryphon's head with his own stick, he lost his footing and fell backwards.

The farmer's wife rushed towards him, gathering him up in her arms and scolding him gently for being careless with himself.

The sight brought back a memory of Kas's own. Of a much younger version of herself, weeping over a scraped knee after tripping in the gardens while running after her older brothers. Of her mother, with her kind face and long red hair, lifting Kas into her arms and soothing her with soft words and kisses to her cheek.

Kas dug into the pouch, taking out a handful of crowns and tossed the rest back into the farmer's hands.

"I wouldn't even know what to do with all these crowns," she said nonchalantly. "I'll take this much. You keep the rest."

Without waiting for a reply, Kas turned and walked out onto the road, where Bod waited, and got back into the saddle.

As she rode away, into the waning sunlight, the farmer and his family watched her go.

"That right there is one brave and generous soul," the farmer said to his children. "Take a leaf out of her book, my dears. And live your lives with the same honour and integrity as that woman."

✳ ✳ ✳

*"DRINK! DRINK! DRINK!"*

Kas slammed her empty tankard on the tabletop before her opponent had even finished drinking.

A cheer went up around them and Kas raised her arms in victory. "Thank you! Thank you!" She turned her attention to the man with the sandy blond hair, who sat at the table across from her. "I believe I won this round."

The man had a miserable frown on his face. His cheeks were flushed red from the ale. "This round, and the last two rounds." He fished around in his pockets and produced three gold crowns which he reluctantly handed over to her. "Fuck, my wife's going to be pissed with me."

With a satisfied smirk on her face, Kas pocketed the coin. "I'm sure she will be. But that's not my problem now, is it?"

The man grumbled something under his breath.

Her grin widened. "Care for another round?" she asked, lifting her tankard, and waggled it teasingly.

"I don't think so"—the man stood from his seat on unsteady legs—"I lose anymore coin and my wife'll have me sleepin' with the pigs."

"Would anyone else like to take up the challenge?" she asked of the group that had gathered around to watch her drink others under the table.

But it seemed that none were as willing to risk their money as the last man was. Which was fine. Kas had already amassed herself a nice little fortune from tonight's drinking games. She'd almost made up the coin she had returned to the farmer.

The small crowd around her table was dispersing and Kas felt a touch on her shoulder. She looked up to see the young serving woman with honey-blonde hair and a freckled nose.

"That was quite impressive," the woman said. "And amusing to see some of these men taken down a notch."

"Taking men down a notch is one of my favourite pastimes," said Kas with a wink.

The serving woman's smile turned a touch flirtatious as she collected Kas's empty tankard. "Another drink?"

"Oh, why not?" Kas held one of her newly won crowns out to the woman. Their fingers brushed deliberately as she took it and then departed for the bar.

Now left alone and without a drink to occupy her, Kas's attention strayed around the rest of the tavern, cast mostly in shadow but for the pools of candlelight here and there.

There weren't as many patrons as one might expect of a tavern in a more populated village. Many of those who had eagerly participated in Kas's drinking games had already left. She spotted only three by the bar. Sitting at a table nearby was a large man getting told off by his wife. Something about him staring at her sister's ankles. In one shadowy corner, a young minstrel plucked a few strings lazily on their lute.

Finally, her attention snagged on the conversation happening between two travelling merchants at the table behind hers.

"Cousin of mine in Lucedel told me there had been sightings of a vampyric."

Kas felt her fingers twitch where they rested on the table. Just the mere mention of the blood-feeding monsters sent an unpleasant chill through her veins.

"Lucedel? A big town like that? Are you sure your cousin was seeing things right?"

"Well, it would make sense though, wouldn't it? All those people living in Lucedel would mean plenty of food for a vampyric."

*Indeed,* thought Kas. She scratched idly at a dent in the tabletop with a blunt fingernail. Lucedel. She'd certainly been there over the four years she'd spent travelling Vil Tresar but couldn't say it was a town she had frequented. If Kas remembered correctly the town was somewhere to the south of Verillino province.

*It would probably be close to a week's ride from here. But it's worth investigating if Lucedel really does have a vampyric problem. In the morning, though. After I've sobered up.*

Riding on horseback with a hangover was never fun.

The sound of something metallic striking the floor snatched at Kas's attention. She turned in her seat to see the serving girl had dropped her tray and was being grabbed at by a bald, and clearly drunk, man across the room.

"C'mon, darlin'. Come sit an' talk for a bit!" he said with slurred speech.

The woman tried to release her arm from his hold. "Let me go, please. I'm working."

But the man still did not take his hands off her.

Kas felt a spike of hot anger. Before she knew it, she was striding towards them until she could grab the drunken man by the same arm he was using to keep his hold on the serving woman.

"Pardon me, good sir," said Kas. "But I believe she asked you to let her go."

"Eh? And who the fuck are—*Saints' balls!*"

The man yelped as Kas applied no small amount of pressure to the grip she had on his wrist. Leaning in closer, she said in a low voice, "Let go. Now."

He did as he was told and once the serving woman was free, Kas released her hold as well.

"Are you all right?" she asked of the woman, and received a nod in return.

"You damn bitch. You coulda broken my wrist!"

The drunk man leapt from his chair and swung at Kas. His fist was easy enough to side-step, and when the man's hit didn't land, he wound up stumbling into a passerby carrying two full tankards.

The man carrying the drinks tripped, spilling his beverages onto the woman who had been scolding her husband before ending up in her lap. The woman shrieked and her burly husband shot up from his chair and grabbed the other poor man by the front of his tunic. "Oi, what do you think you're doing, you mangy maggot?"

He didn't even wait for an answer before ramming his fist square into the other man's jaw.

Like oil to a flame, that first act of violence was enough to spark a whole wave of it. Friends of the man who had spilled his drink rushed to his defence with yells and waving fists. Punches were thrown and tables were overturned. Shouts went up and drinks and food were spilled. A chair went flying across the room. It was chaos and Kas was just drunk enough that she felt no compunction about getting involved.

Someone wearing an eyepatch came at her from behind with a club. She ducked, restrained them by their club-wielding arm and punched them in the nose.

She then whirled around to face the man who had been making advances toward the serving woman. Kas caught one of his punches with her palm but was too slow to block the one aimed for her midsection.

There was barely any strength behind the man's hits, and the only thing that blow managed to do was knock her off balance. She fell back against one of the tables behind her, spotted an unharmed drink, downed it in two long gulps and then threw the empty tankard at the head of an oncoming attacker, knocking him out cold.

Everything turned into a bit of a blur after that. It was only when the large man who had been accused of ogling his sister-in-law's ankles grabbed her around the middle and threw her hard enough that she went stumbling right out the front door, did some clarity return to her.

"Fucking hells," Kas groaned. She sat up after having landed in the dirt on her back and rubbed at an aching shoulder.

After giving her spinning head a chance to settle down, Kas got unsteadily to her feet. She could still hear the muted sounds of the brawl happening inside the tavern. Then she heard the distant rumbling of thunder, promising rain. She briefly considered stepping back inside the tavern . . . until a chair came crashing through one of the windows.

*Hm. Maybe not.*

Making an effort not to trip over her own feet, Kas turned and walked away from the tavern.

THAT WAS how she later found herself lying in a mound of hay, sharing a stable stall with Bod. Listening to the sounds of rain on the rooftop, and the soft nickering and huffing of other horses in their stalls.

"Well, this is cosy, eh, Bod?"

The roan responded with a loud huff from where he stood beside her. Little more than a hulking black shape in the darkness.

"I'm sorry. I know you were looking forward to having a stall all to yourself tonight."

A hoof stamp.

"I'll try not to take up too much room." Kas shifted onto her side. "And you try not to shit too close to my head. Deal?"

Silence. Kas closed her eyes and tried to find sleep on the prickly hay beneath her. Her wet, dirty clothes stuck uncomfortably to her body, and the unpleasant stench of horse and damp and manure permeated her nostrils.

The thought came to her unbidden right before sleep claimed her.

*What would your family say if they could see you now?*

# CHAPTER 3
# CLAUDIA

THE CALM, quiet night air was broken by a loud crack that echoed through the woodland.

As if born out of thin air, a young woman, with hair as white as starlight, fell to the ground. Alongside her, an amber-eyed wolf with fur as dark as pitch.

The woman, Claudia, pushed herself up from the ground. Her breathing was laboured with exertion, her hair, clothing and every part of her was dripping with water. Her muscles were weary and sore.

But now was not the time for rest.

On her feet, Claudia took a moment to take in her surroundings. She was standing in the midst of a forest. Where exactly, she could not say. One thing Claudia could be sure about, however, was that she was far away from her pursuers.

She adjusted the brown satchel around her shoulder and placed a hand on the intricate, gold hilt of the rapier sheathed at her side. The familiar pattern of roses carved into the metal pressed into her fingertips.

"Come, Wolf," she said to her four-legged companion and made her way through the trees.

Her mind was still racing from her recent escape, and her heart still thundered in her chest. If she closed her eyes, she could still see herself back at the castle, sneaking through the shadowy halls and down into the long-abandoned sewer. She could still see the vampyrics coming after her as clouds of black smoke as she and Wolf were pulled down the rushing river.

They had come so close to being captured.

It didn't take long before Claudia reached the edge of the forest, where she was greeted by a small farmhouse. With clothes left out on a washing line.

Claudia was all too aware of the drenched clothing clinging to her body. While she was not at risk of taking ill because of the cold, wet fabric, she was incredibly uncomfortable in them. The shoulder of her blouse rubbed unpleasantly against the still raw gash in her skin. With a chilly night such as this one, Claudia's clothes would not be drying any time soon.

She could see the glow of a candle in one of the windows of the house and smoke rising from the chimney. Claudia could hear the sounds of movement and talking from inside the farmhouse—sounds that could not have been audible to anyone without her hearing—but there did not appear to be anyone outside. She decided to take her chances. She could move without making even the slightest sound, after all.

She took a plain, green tunic and a pair of brown trousers before moving back to the cover of the trees to peel off her soaking clothes.

All the while, she hardly took her eyes off the satchel lying in the grass at Wolf's feet while she changed.

An irrational part of her was worried that it would disappear. That someone, or something, would drop down from the trees and snatch it away.

A noise like something moving through the ferns had Claudia's head snapping up, and eyes scanning the forest in front of her feverishly. Every muscle in her coiled for action.

But there was nothing there.

Wolf whined.

"You're right, Wolf," she sighed, as if he could hear her thoughts. "I'm being ridiculous. Serisa and the others would never find me so quickly."

The trastere stone had made sure of that.

Wolf blinked at her. His eyes seemed overly bright in the dark. She was thankful to have him here with her. It was thanks to him dutifully bringing those heavy, rusted keys from their hook that Claudia had even managed to get out of her locked cell.

Claudia hissed as a sharp pain shot up her arm from the bracelet of raw, pinked flesh around her wrist. She had a matching mark on her other wrist as well. Another remnant from her time spent in that wretched dungeon.

Shrugging on the tunic, which was a size too large on her willowy frame, Claudia finished dressing, and tossed her wet clothes into the underbrush. She gathered up her sword and her satchel, holding it close.

*Serisa may not find me yet, but that doesn't mean nothing else might.*

# CHAPTER 4
# SERISA

Serisa's night had started off just fine. It had promised to be a quiet, uneventful night before what was to follow in the morning.

But now she stood on the pebbled bank of a river, bending to pick up a small shard of what looked like some kind of violet-coloured glass. She held it between a clawed forefinger and thumb, scrutinising it in the moonlight.

She knew it was the remnants of a trastere stone. A magical stone that could transport one great distances upon being shattered.

Serisa scowled. It had been foolish of her not to go through Claudia's belongings. Perhaps they would not be in this position now if she'd had more foresight.

"It appears," came a voice from behind her, "that she climbed out from the river, then used the stone to get away."

"Yes," Serisa drawled, flicking the stone shard into the rushing water. "I surmised that myself. It figures that if she cannot use the same powers we can, she would make do with enchanted objects."

The river they were standing before was connected to the same one that flowed beneath the castle. Further downstream was a waterfall Claudia must have used to get this far.

Serisa turned to face Ves, her oldest friend. She was tall—at least a head or two taller than Serisa—and heavy-set, with dark, reddish hair that fell short and straight around her jawline to one side and was shaved on the other. Her skin was pearl-grey, her ears pointed and her eyes the brightest of reds.

Just like Serisa.

Just like all vampyrics.

"Hmph," Ves snorted. "Even we can't travel as far and fast as a trastere stone."

"You're right about that. Well, Ves, I don't suppose you have a trastere stone of your own hidden somewhere on your immense person?" she asked the other vampyric.

Ves's upper lip curled, showing a hint of fang. "Unfortunately, no."

Although Serisa had already expected the answer, a pulse of frustrated anger flared inside of her. Her hand went up unconsciously to curl around the cracked, amethyst amulet that hung from her neck. A reflexive gesture.

But then Ves said something that tempered her ire somewhat.

"I do, however, have our would-be dungeon master waiting for you back at the castle."

Serisa smiled and there was nothing pleasant behind it. "Then let's go see him, shall we?"

THE CASTLE WAS an old structure that had likely once belonged to the bygone kings and queens of Vil Tresar. For the past few decades, however, it had been home to the vampyric clan of Salvaclare. Serisa's clan.

Although they were somewhat diminished in numbers these days.

The castle sat nestled in the lonely mountains that bordered Salvaclare's west and the neighbouring Belicari province. It was an arduous trek up the mountain that no human would make lightly. Making the old castle an ideal lair for vampyrics.

Upon arriving at the castle, Serisa and Ves made straight for the throne room, which lay beyond a pair of towering double doors. Once it might have taken two human guards to open one door, but a vampyric could open them with one effortless push.

When Serisa lived here, the castle had always been kept in immaculate condition. The floors were polished, dust was scarce, and everything was in its place. Now, it seemed the others had let the castle go in her absence. Wisps of spiderwebs hung in every nook and cranny. A few windows had been shattered and bloodstains gone brown adorned some of the carpets. Once, Serisa might have felt saddened to see the home she had been born in brought to such a derelict state.

When Serisa and Ves stepped into the throne room, they found a small gathering of five other vampyrics standing near the dais at the other end of the room. Behind them were stained-glass windows that stretched from floor to towering ceiling, casting patterns of shadow and faintly coloured light across the floors.

One vampyric was being held in the restraining grip of two others, Orna and Larnaz. Orna was a female vampyric with silver hair so long it almost reached the floor. It also covered much of her face so all that was visible was one red eye and half of a mouth curled in a perpetual frown. Larnaz, was a male vampyric with impressive sideburns and a build that almost rivalled that of Ves.

"He was found trying to flee through the courtyard," Ves explained at Serisa's shoulder.

"Really?" Serisa said, then to the restrained vampyric, "Interesting, Ticone, that you try to flee right after Claudia escapes. Could this have been some sort of scheme the two of you concocted while you were alone in the dungeons, supposedly keeping an eye on her?"

Ticone shook his head frantically. Scraggily bits of brown hair fell into his wide, fearful eyes. "No, there was no collusion. I swear, Serisa."

Between one blink of an eye and the next, Serisa was directly in front of Ticone, a hand clamped around his neck. "Then how in the hells did she manage to escape?" she hissed. "Not only that, but how did it manage to escape your attention long enough for her to sneak through the castle and *steal the remnant?*"

"I-I don't—know," Ticone gasped. Slivers of blood were beginning to spill where Serisa's long nails pierced his flesh.

"Don't you dare lie to me."

"It-It's true! I . . . I fell asleep."

Serisa released him. If it wasn't for the two other vampyrics holding him, he probably would have sagged to his knees as he sputtered for the breath she had momentarily robbed him of.

"Passed out more like," she snarled. "I can smell the alcohol on you."

Vampyrics could not eat or drink anything but blood, lest they be vilely sick. Even a sip of water, they could not keep down. However, drinking the blood of an intoxicated person had the same effect on them as if they drank the alcohol themselves. Serisa knew Ticone liked to feed from intoxicated humans so he could experience the strange delights of drunkenness for himself. He must have done so only recently.

He didn't deny it. He couldn't.

"But—" He sputtered. "I—th-the keys were on the wall by the door. I d-don't understand how she could have gotten them!"

"It was probably that pet wolf of hers," Ves put in. "I knew we should have killed that thing."

Serisa released an aggrieved breath. "I could almost forgive such a foolish mistake, Ticone. But I'm really . . . not in the mood."

Her hand came out in one fluid motion that was almost too quick for the eye to see.

And Ticone's neck was severed from his body.

Blood sheeted the stone floor, and the vampyrics that had been holding onto him allowed his headless body to fall.

Serisa flicked off some of the blood coating her hand.

"Was that wise?" Ves wondered. "Our clan is already diminished enough as it is."

"We're not in such dire straits that we need to hold on to a liability like him," said Serisa.

She was well aware the Slavaclare vampyric clan was not what it once was. When she left six years ago, this castle had been home to twenty of them. But it seemed that in Serisa's absence, many clan members had decided to venture out and go it alone. Now all that remained of one of the greatest clans of vampyrics in Vil Tresar was all here in this room.

"And?" said Larnaz. His black doublet was stained with Ticone's blood. "What do we do about Claudia?"

"Why, nothing of course," Serisa said, wandering past him to climb the dais and drape herself over one of the old stone thrones, crossing her long legs over an armrest. "We will simply wait for Claudia to return with the remnant whenever she feels like it."

There was a pause among the vampyrics.

"Really?" Larnaz asked.

He was just quick enough to duck the empty vase Serisa aimed at his head. The shatter as it broke against the floor rang out across the throne room.

"Of course not," Serisa snapped. "Why even bother asking such a stupid question?"

It was Anirea, a vampyric woman with yellow hair tied into two, long plaits on either side of her face, adding a child-like air about her, who spoke up next. "Then, what is your plan, Serisa?"

"Now that's a better way of asking. What we're going to do is find her, of course." Serisa leapt up off the throne. "And I already know just how we're going to do that."

As she strode down the dais, she said, "Ves. Orna. You're coming with me." She didn't need to look behind her to see if they were following. She knew they would. "Larnaz and Anirea, you wait here at the castle. And perhaps when we return, all will be as it should."

There was no further discussion after that. Serisa swept from the throne room with Ves and Orna in toe.

"Do you plan on telling us where exactly we're headed?" Ves asked her after some time as they made their way through the vast castle halls.

"Absolutely not," said Serisa cheerily. "It's more fun if it's a surprise, my dear Ves."

# INTERLUDE
## FIVE YEARS AGO

A YEAR.

That was how long Serisa had been wandering across Vil Tresar in search of her father.

And longer still since she had last seen him. Since the night he had fled the castle, leaving behind his clan. His wife. And even his daughter.

But her mother was dead, and whatever else had been between them, Serisa knew they had loved each other. At least until . . . well, she tried not to dwell on that unpleasant matter. What did matter now was finding him and telling him of her mother's passing.

He needed to know.

And Serisa needed to see her father again after these long years spent without him.

Her search had finally brought her to a small town called Brai in Amiro, one of the western provinces. It was not far from Veldenier, one of the most illustrious cities the continent had to offer. Yet Serisa found Brai to be a rather seedy little town. Every single building seemed to be in some state of disrepair, and the townspeople seemed no less unpleasant.

There were men engaged in a drunken brawl outside of a tavern. A window opened and a woman tossed a bucket of brown slop onto the ground, only narrowly missing Serisa as she walked past.

Serisa had heard that many settlements in this province had fallen into disrepair and disrepute after the Lelvinares were slain. It seemed the new owner of these lands was not so generous with their fortune. She found it hard to believe that her father might be in a place like this, but she was not about to disregard what the vampyric clan of this province had told her when she visited them a month ago. Not when she had no better leads.

Serisa kept to the shadows and empty alleyways as she skulked through the town. Her hood was turned up, shielding her head against the rain that showed no signs of stopping any time soon. She turned a corner, heading down another narrow alley, when she was brought up short by the sight of two figures, entwined together against the brick wall of the back of a building. An awning overhead shielded them from the downpour.

There was no mistaking what they were doing, and if not for the rain, Serisa thought the sounds of their lovemaking would have been much more obvious.

She would have kept on her way, hardly sparing the couple a second thought, had she not noticed that the woman, who had her back against the wall, was looking at Serisa over the man's shoulder with a pair of rich, cat-like, amethyst eyes.

Serisa knew of only one creature that possessed such eyes.

The succubus lifted her hand to the man's other shoulder, and even over the pelting rain, Serisa heard her utter a, "That's enough, Thamuel. Go back inside."

Without any hesitancy or an utterance of protest, the man stepped away, fixed himself up, and disappeared through the nearby doorway.

"It's rude to interrupt someone when they're in the middle of a meal, you know?" the succubus said, with not an ounce of shame for her mostly uncovered state. She pushed some of her long, auburn hair off her bare shoulder.

Like vampyrics, succubi were humanoid monsters, yet unlike Serisa's kind, they often differed greatly in appearance. Some had fair skin, while others had dark. Some grew horns on their heads while others had tails or cloven feet like a goat's. One thing they all had in common was their eyes.

Another thing they had in common was that both succubi and vampyrics fed from humans. Although while vampyrics fed on their blood, succubi fed on their lust.

"Perhaps you should think of taking your meals in private then?" Serisa said.

The succubus grinned as she began to readjust her clothing—which consisted mostly of a thin green dress with a plunging neckline. "It's no matter. I only wanted to get one last feed in before I left this place for good."

Serisa watched the succubus reach for a cloak that looked as though it had been tossed carelessly atop the barrel next to her.

"Before you go, there's something I might ask you," said Serisa.

The succubus's amethyst gaze raked Serisa from head to toe consideringly. "I suppose I could go a quick round with you. I can't say I've ever been with a vampyric before."

Ignoring the succubus's flirtations, Serisa forged ahead. "I'm looking for another vampyric said to be living in these parts. Anor of the Salvaclare vampyric clan?"

The succubus paused while in the middle of buttoning up her grey cloak. "Ah. I knew Anor. Are you his wife?"

"Daughter. And you said you *knew* him? Is he not in Brai anymore?"

"No. He's dead."

The blunt words struck her like a blow to the back of the head. She was almost surprised she did not lurch with the impact, or stagger with how the ground suddenly felt shaky beneath her feet.

When Serisa spoke, her voice somehow came out steady. "How? When?"

"In the winter. A Slayer took up residence just outside of town. Someone put out a contract for Anor, and—" the succubus shrugged one shoulder as if to say *'and that was that.'* "I was there when he rode into town one morning, carrying Anor's head. Which is why I'm getting the hells out of Brai. Tonight. The last thing I need is the resident Slayer coming after me because someone got their knickers in a twist about my sleeping with their husband."

Lifting her hood up, the succubus stepped out into the rain.

As she brushed past Serisa, she paused long enough to say, "I would not stay here too long, if I were you."

The succubus was gone, leaving Serisa standing soaked and alone in the middle of the empty alleyway.

Blood began to drip onto the pavement, mingling with the rainwater. It stemmed from the wounds in Serisa's palms, where her claws pierced her flesh as she curled them into trembling fists.

Serisa found the Slayer's cabin, hardly even a mile north of Brai. It stood in the middle of a small patch of woodland, by the side of a well-trodden road.

It was no difficulty for Serisa to find her way inside. However, she was left disappointed when she soon realised there was no one there.

But she was not about to leave. Serisa would wait as long as she needed to for the Slayer to return. While she did, Serisa could not help but take a look around the home of a *Slayer*. Of the one who murdered her father. Even when she saw the trophies of slain monsters on display all throughout the cabin, some morbid curiosity propelled her to keep looking.

Not only that, but Serisa felt a strange pull towards this place. Something urged her to delve deeper into the house, and stranger yet, she found she could not resist the desire to do so.

Downstairs she saw the mounted head of a diavol on the wall above the fireplace. Its bear-like jaws opened in a permanent snarl, and mounted on either side of it were two wyvern heads. The shaggy, black pelt of a werewolf lay on the floor.

The second floor was made up of a landing that splintered off into two rooms. There she found more mounted heads; ghastlies and imps and even a cave troll.

The pull inside her also grew stronger, like a compass with a spinning needle, she found herself wandering into the room to her right and discovered it to be what could only be the Slayer's bedroom.

A wave of revulsion filled her at the idea of standing in so intimate a place. But she could not bring herself to leave. She felt like a fish caught on a fisherman's lure. She recognised it and loathed the idea of it. Yet still she was helpless to do anything but let herself be reeled in.

There was curiosity, too, however. What was it about this Slayer's home that had such an effect on her? What was behind the voice calling out to her? Begging her to come closer?

Before she even realised it, Serisa had made her way across the room and was standing before a wooden chest of drawers. Kneeling, she pulled open the bottom drawer and started tearing through the clothes folded away inside. She felt desperate to uncover what was hidden beneath, though she couldn't say how she *knew* there was something there.

And sure enough, underneath all the clothes was what Serisa could only think to describe as the scale of some creature.

It was long—the same length perhaps as Serisa's elbow to her wrist —and was shaped somewhat like the blade of a dagger, with one end tapering into a sharp point, while the other was jagged and looked like it had been torn off of whatever it had come from. It was the colour of a red so dark, it was almost black and had a sheen to it like armour.

*This* was where the pull had been coming from. This was what had been drawing her further and further into the cabin, like a flame drawing in a moth.

And it drew her in still, compelling Serisa to reach out and take the scale into her hands.

As soon as she did, images flashed before her eyes, as quick as lightning strikes. She saw fire. So much fire. The terrified faces of humans as they fled from some unseen horror. The visage of some winged creature she had never seen before. It turned its head toward her, regarding her with eyes like fire encased in glass, before opening its maw, lined with rows of sharp teeth, and issued a roar that Serisa *heard* and felt in her bones.

The visions came to an abrupt halt, leaving Serisa gasping. She gazed down at the scale still in her hands feeling both awe and bewilderment. What exactly was this thing? And what kind of creature could it have come from to have shown her such vivid visions?

*Well, whatever it is,* she decided, *I'm certainly not about to leave it here.*

So Serisa tucked the strange scale into the bag at her belt and left the room. She still had yet to hear the Slayer return, and she was still curious to know what the one, as of yet, undiscovered room of a Slayer's home had to offer.

Crossing the landing, Serisa passed into the second room and found the small space lined with glass cabinets full of . . . bones. Mostly skulls. She recognised two as belonging to giants just from their size alone—they looked as if they would reach up to Serisa's waist. There was another that looked like an alderbeast, long and deer-like, with bits of lichen and moss still clinging to the bone. There were countless, fist-sized skulls of imps. The flat-faced skulls of ghastlies and three with the hooked beaks of gryphons.

She wandered around the room until she came to one cabinet that was empty, except for the lone skull on the top shelf.

Serisa's blood ran cold at the sight of it.

It looked exactly like a human skull, the only thing marking it as other were the thin, needle-tip fangs.

*"I was there when he rode into town one morning, carrying Anor's head."*

A maelstrom of rage and sorrow eddied inside of her. She had already known, but seeing it with her own eyes was—

A sound downstairs alerted her to the front door being opened. A broad-shouldered man with a shaved head and a puckered burn scar on one side of his face, walked in carrying the carcass of a slaughtered doe.

Serisa barely gave him any time at all to walk inside before she attacked.

If there was any doubt in her mind amidst the haze of her anger, that this man was even a Slayer, it was dispelled by his lack of terror at being ambushed by a vampyric in his own home. That and the quick reflexes he used to grab her by the shoulders before she could pounce on him. Using her own momentum against her, the Slayer threw her out the door, where she landed heavily in the wet grass and mud.

Having dropped the deer carcass, the Slayer only had enough time to draw a shortsword sheathed at his hip before Serisa threw herself at him again.

Her movements were fast and brutal. Driven by every ounce of her ire. Her all-consuming need to see the Slayer's blood coat the ground and for his head to roll.

The Slayer aimed a killing blow at Serisa's throat. She halted it by grabbing the man's wrist and snapping the frail bone beneath.

He cried out but did not relent. Already he had another blade in his uninjured hand stabbing it at Serisa.

Serisa felt as if she were moving through a fog, and it had little to do with the rain. Her mind was clouded, and her body seemed to be moving only by instinct. Raging through her head were thoughts of her father dead. Dead for so long without her even knowing about it, and all because of this Slayer, who kept pieces of the monsters he killed around his home like ornamentation.

A vision of the vampyric's skull, her *father's skull*, flashed before her eyes, acting like oil poured over the flames of her fury.

*Tear him to shreds,* a dark voice whispered to her. *Bleed him. Gut him. Rip his life away like he did to your father.*

The Slayer was a strong opponent. But Serisa's vampyric speed and strength and her burning need for retribution were what gave her the upper hand, which was what she needed in the end to be able to pierce her claws through the Slayer's chest. All the way through until her hand came out through his back, dripping with blood and viscera.

As the Slayer hacked on his own blood, Serisa felt the murderous haze drift away. To be replaced by a kind of calm. A satisfaction in knowing she had now avenged her father.

The feeling was shattered, however, by something sharp sliding into her side and *burning*.

Serisa jerked away from the Slayer, allowing his body to fall to the ground. Protruding from her body, just above her hip was the hilt of the Slayer's dagger. She could not contain the scream that wrenched itself from her throat as she pulled the blade out, and she knew from the way it felt as though fire was carving through her flesh that the dagger was made from silver.

*Of course it would be. What Slayer wouldn't carry a weapon made from silver?*

The blood was coming thick and fast down her leg, staining her clothes red. Even with the silver no longer in her body, she still felt as if she were being scorched from the inside.

Her knees buckled and her vision swam.

She would not die here. Perhaps, if she could make it back to the Amiro vampyrics—

Serisa's physical form melted away, and she turned to a cloud of roiling, black smoke and took to the sky, blending in with the night and soared through the rain. Over grassy plains that soon gave way to the treetops of a dense and sprawling forest.

A white-hot throb of agony sent Serisa hurtling towards the ground. Her now corporeal form broke through boughs of trees before she landed in a painful heap on the forest floor.

She tasted iron in the back of her throat before she heaved up blood on the grass.

Weakness fell over her like a cold shroud. Her body would not respond to her feeble attempts to move. To get up. To find safety and healing.

A numbness followed and soon she could not even feel the pain of her wound any longer. Her consciousness slipped away slowly but surely.

As it did, Serisa thought she might have spotted something coming towards her through the trees.

But whether she really wasn't alone, or it was a simple trick of the mind, she did not know. Darkness had already claimed her.

# CHAPTER 5
# KAS



"THE PRICE IS TOO LOW, I'm telling you."

"And I'm telling you, I'll not hand over a single crown more than I've already given you."

Kas's temper was beginning to feel as frayed as a rope that had been rubbed too long and too harshly against rough brick. She'd been arguing with this academic in Grevande—a city in Noviscaro province—for what felt like an age. It didn't help that Kas was tired, sore, and covered in foul-smelling ghastly blood that had been baking in the hot afternoon sun during Kas's ride into the city.

She was now standing outside the gates to the Grevande University, an impressive, castle-like structure of brown brick and mortar, arguing with one of its professors who had hired her yesterday to take care of a monster problem at his recently purchased estate.

"Do you see that?" She pointed at the open bag of four severed ghastly heads—almost human in appearance, except for the withered, grey skin, slit nostrils, milky white eyes, and jagged teeth—on the cobblestone between them. "Those are the heads of *four* ghastlies. And you'll find another two in your front yard when you return home.

That's four more than what you told me had attacked you at your gate, this morning."

"Well, perhaps more showed up after I had gone." The academic pursed his thin lips. His round cheeks flushed red with indignation. "Are you calling me a liar, good lady?"

*Yes.* "No. I'm simply saying that having to slay more monsters than was anticipated means I'm owed an extra amount."

"What? You expect me to hand over twenty or even thirty crowns? Do you wish to bleed me dry?"

Kas took in the expensive make of his brocade and feathered hat. She also thought of his large house on a wide plot of land with the neatly manicured garden. She doubted thirty crowns would lighten his purse strings by much.

"Then perhaps next time you should hire some run of the mill mercenary to handle your monster problems for you," she said, allowing her irritation some freedom. "Although they might be cheaper, there's no guaranteeing they'll actually get the job done for you."

The man huffed; his lips curled into a sneer beneath his wispy blond moustache. "Or perhaps I'd be better off working with a man. They might be more reasonable to negotiate with. Unlike a woman."

"Excuse you?"

"I wonder, are you by any chance in the middle of your cycle?" he whispered that last word. "Perhaps you should return to me in a week's time to offer an apology for this little hassle when you are more emotionally—"

Kas had him by the collar. Her other hand curled into a fist that she had every intention of slamming into the man's weaselly face, hopefully bending his nose and breaking his spectacles, when a hard, authoritative voice called out.

"What's going on here?"

Coming towards them from down the street were a pair of stony-faced city guards. Their silver-plated armour glinted in the noon-day sun and their white cloaks were long enough that they nearly dragged along the ground behind them. Both guards carried silver-tipped pikes and wore the golden rose medallions of the Saints at their chests.

Kas released the professor and took a step back from him as he began spluttering indignantly.

"This—This *woman*," he hurled the word as if it were an insult, "has done nothing but harass me, trying to make me pay her more than the agreed upon price for her services. It's a robbery!"

Kas snorted. "Hardly. But you know what? You can keep your money. All of it." She threw the meagre coin pouch back at the professor—hard enough in his middle that he let out a little *'oof'*. "I'll just take this"—she hefted the sack full of ghastly heads, tossing it over her shoulder—"and be on my way."

"Yes," said one of the guards, clearly fighting the urge to pinch his nose against the stench. "That might be best."

Kas stalked off before her bubbling temper could force her to say —or do—anything that could get her into real trouble.

It wasn't long before Kas regretted not taking the ten crowns that had been offered to her. She sold three of the ghastly heads to a merchant whose stall was filled with an assortment of other strange bits and pieces, such as a frog skeleton riding a wooden horse, and a portrait of one of the old kings that had been painted over to look as though he was sticking out his tongue.

She'd only made five crowns off the exchange and had simply given away the last ghastly head to a pair of young children who seemed thrilled to be able to play with it—at least until a woman Kas assumed to be their mother appeared from one of the nearby houses to shriek at them about touching dead things. Kas had quickly made her exit then.

Five crowns had been just enough to buy her a night at the inn with food and drink.

Now, Kas sat in the common room of *The Ruby Lion*, silently bemoaning the two crowns she had left in her purse and drowning that sorrow in a cup of Wyvern's Breath Whiskey.

*The Ruby Lion* was exactly what one would expect of a city inn. The common room was wide and open and dimly lit to suit the ambience.

Swaths of coloured silk decorated the ceiling. A bard sung some jaunty tune up on the stage at the head of the room, where a group of men and women dressed in billowy silks danced.

Kas was seated at one of the tables closest to the stage. She caught the eye of one of the dancers; a woman in sheer, purple silk, with much of her dark skin and thick curves on display. When she realised Kas was looking up at her, she winked one of her kohl-rimmed eyes.

The dancer's attention earned a small smile from Kas's lips, but it still did little to lift her spirits. Tomorrow she'd have to set out looking for jobs she could take to replenish her coin. But finding such work for a Slayer wasn't always so easy. It wasn't as if every second person had a monster they needed Kas to slay. Kas had been at this job for three years now, since she first turned eighteen, and there had been many a time where she had spent months wandering from place to place without finding a single soul that was willing to pay her to kill a monster.

*I should have just taken that bastard's ten crowns,* she thought sourly, and not for the first time that evening. *Damn my pride to the hells. And damn that professor prick, too.*

Kas finished off her venison and downed the last of her whisky, all while entertaining thoughts of how satisfying it would have been to punch that haughty expression of the man's face.

So deep in her fantasies was she, that Kas hadn't realised that the bard and the dancers had finished up, until the dark-skinned woman in the purple silks had taken the seat opposite her.

"Mind if I sit here?" she asked.

"Of course not," said Kas. "Although I'm not sure my permission was really necessary. Seeing as you're already sitting down."

"It's the principle of the thing." The woman pushed some of her curled black hair off her shoulder. "My name is Riovanna, by the way."

"Kas of Veldenier."

"Mm. And you're a Slayer, aren't you?"

"What gave it away?" Kas asked with an upward quirk of her lips.

Riovanna's dark eyes seemed to glitter with a new delighted

interest. "You Slayers all seem to have that look about you. Battle-scarred and travel-worn."

"Have you met many Slayers, then?"

"I have. My uncle owns this inn, see. Has so for as long as I can remember, and over the years I've crossed paths with countless Slayers that have stopped by here." Her painted lips pulled into an alluring half-smile. "I've never seen your face around here before, though. And believe me, I'd remember if I had."

"You don't see many women with scars like these on my face, right?" said Kas, referring to the long scar that carved a diagonal line across most of her right cheek. Starting from the bridge of her nose and ending just above the edge of her jaw. A remnant of the first contract she had taken on her own as a fully-fledged Slayer.

The other was smaller and cut across the right side of her mouth. She'd received it on the night her family was killed, though she couldn't remember how exactly.

"I meant more because of your astonishingly attractive looks, actually," Riovanna laughed, a bell-like sound.

Kas chuckled. "I know. I only wanted to appear modest."

Riovanna laughed again. She reached out across the table, covering the hand Kas had rested there with her own. "You know," she began, "I'm free for the rest of the night. Maybe you and I could go somewhere more . . . private? And you could tell me all about your exciting adventures as a Slayer."

By the look on the other woman's face, Kas thought that talking wasn't the only thing Riovanna had in mind.

Kas answered, "I would love to."


After secluding themselves in Kas's room upstairs, she and Riovanna spent two pleasure-soaked hours together. Having Riovanna in her arms and being able to lose herself in the other woman's body was just the kind of distraction Kas needed from the miserable day she'd had.

They didn't spend their whole time together having sex, however. Afterward, they lay in bed, the sheet loosely tangled around them. The silhouettes of raindrops on the window marking their bodies as Riovanna traced Kas's scars and asked about each one.

"Where's this one from?" The tips of her fingers slid along the long, thin scars on Kas's right shoulder.

"An imp that had invaded a poor old woman's cellar."

Then to the circular scar on the inside of Kas's left shoulder. "And this one?"

"Caught a diavol by the horn," said Kas, toying with a lock of Riovanna's hair. "Somehow, I managed to free myself before it could pierce all the way through."

"Here?" A touch to the burn scars on her forearm.

"Wyvern."

Next Riovanna's hand travelled further down along Kas's torso, stroking as she went, and raising goosebumps along her flesh. Her hand came to a rest at the long, pinkish scar along her hipbone. It was one of the more serious-looking scars that decorated Kas's body. Even though it was years old, it carved an indent into her skin.

"What about this one?"

"A vampyric," Kas said in a more subdued tone. She'd been sixteen at the time and just starting to be allowed to accompany the more veteran Slayers on the contracts they took. That one was supposed to have been an easy one, as contracts went. Travel to a nearby farm and dispatch a small pack of ghastlies that had been eating livestock. But when they arrived, during the night, it was to find that the ghastlies were gone and a vampyric had taken their place.

All the memories of the night three vampyrics had broken into her home and butchered her family came rushing back to Kas. The sight of those blood-red eyes and elongated fangs had caused Kas to freeze and had given the vampyric an ample opportunity to strike at her. The wound had been bad enough that Kas had been in real danger of bleeding out. Thankfully, Caisus—the Slayer she had been travelling with—had brought her back to the Slayers Keep in the nick of time. Kas remembered awakening in the Keep's healing room, surrounded by the scent of eucalyptus and the sound of Tsurra shouting. It was the first and only time she had heard Tsurra sound so fearful.

Riovanna pulled away from Kas slightly so she could stretch, lifting her arms above her head. Kas's eyes were drawn to the movement. The lit candles by the window limned her brown skin in a colour like dark honey.

"The life of a Slayer sounds so exciting," the dancer sighed. "Scary, but exciting. How dull someone like myself must seem by comparison."

"I'm sure you must have your thrilling moments," said Kas.

"Hardly. All I do is work. During the day as a waitress and in the evenings as a dancer. Waiting for the day I can save up enough to move out from under my family's roof."

"You don't get along with your family?"

Riovanna shrugged a shoulder, examining a painted nail. "They're not horrible to me, if that's what you're implying. But there comes a time where you want to escape their stifling presence. Especially when your youngest siblings are still screaming children."

Kas said nothing. She felt a sudden flare of irritation at Riovanna for seemingly taking her family for granted. Followed by a spear of that familiar melancholy whenever she felt lonely for her own family.

*What I wouldn't give to spend just another moment with my screaming younger siblings.*

Riovanna pecked a kiss on Kas's cheek. "I wish we could enjoy each other's company all night long, but I start work early in the morning, and must be heading off."

"Let me walk you home," Kas offered. Any newfound annoyance she might have felt wasn't enough for her to allow Riovanna to wander the streets alone so late at night.

"Well, aren't you chivalrous?" The dancer laughed. "I have walked home on my own at night before."

Kas got up from the bed and began hunting for her clothes that were strewn all over the floor.

"And I still insist."

# CHAPTER 6
# CLAUDIA

Claudia kept her head up and her hood low as she strode through the winding streets of Grevande. Even though it was well into the night and rain came down in pelting drops, meaning the streets were almost deserted, Claudia still preferred to draw as little attention to herself as possible.

She'd been worried that arriving in the city at such a late hour would mean being unable to purchase the supplies she needed. She had been turned away from one merchant stall who was unwilling to do business with her even though the man had yet to start packing up his wares. It was only thanks to a kindly old woman, whose shop had been across the road, taking pity on Claudia, that she was able to procure the things she needed.

Still, she didn't want to linger in this one place for too long. Claudia kept her steps brisk, splashing through puddles that had formed in the cobblestones as she went, until she passed through the gates of the city, over the bridge across the gorge that scarred the earth outside Grevande. From there she approached a nearby forest.

It was there that Claudia found the dapple-grey horse where she had left it, tied to a signpost on the side of the road. It was a risky thing, to leave a horse unattended by the side of a quiet road. Anyone could come along and decide to claim it for their own.

But Claudia had left something in place to deter any would-be horse thieves.

There was rustling in the underbrush, and as if he had materialised from out of the shadows, Wolf stepped out to greet her.

The horse bobbed its head agitatedly at the appearance of Wolf, but calmed when Claudia rubbed a hand up and down its broad neck. The horse had only been with them for a little over a month now and still grew anxious by the presence of Wolf.

"I'm sorry," Claudia said, running her fingers through Wolf's thick, rain-dampened fur. "You had to wait here all this time and couldn't go out to eat anything."

Wolf licked at the underside of her wrist with a soft tongue.

"But here." Claudia reached into the satchel at her hip. "I brought you something."

She pulled out a paper-wrapped parcel, which Wolf took to sniffing at immediately. Unwrapping it revealed slices of dried rabbit meat. She took two and gave them to Wolf, who crunched them between his teeth eagerly.

While Wolf enjoyed the food, Claudia began transferring some of the supplies from her satchel to the saddlebags at the horse's hindquarters. There was only one item she left in the satchel. One she would not—could not—part with for even a moment.

Claudia heard it even before Wolf started to growl.

Something approaching them from the forest at her back.

Beneath her cloak, Claudia reached for her rapier. She drew the blade out with a slow hiss of metal just as the newcomer finally came into view.

It was a person, much of their body concealed by a long, purple cloak. Beneath the hood, Claudia could make out a feminine face with ghostly-white skin and tendrils of dark hair.

Beside her, Wolf kept his head low, and hackles raised, and soft growls rumbling from his throat. Claudia raised her sword, the tip directed at the cloaked stranger.

"Come any closer and you will find yourself skewered on my blade," Claudia warned. "Or mauled by my friend here."

The stranger seemed unconcerned with Claudia's threats. Lipless mouth stretched into an unnerving grin. "Ah, there she is," said the woman, her voice was a rasp. "The one carrying the prize that calls out like a siren song."

Claudia lifted her sword higher, her other hand going to her satchel. "Who are you? Did Serisa send you?"

"Don't know a Serisa. All I know is I can feel it calling to me. It belongs with me."

"And what makes you so confident that you'll even be able to take it off me?"

Wolf's growls grew louder, and her horse reared, whinnying its panic.

"Them," said the stranger.

From out of the darkness of the forest, more figures emerged. At first Claudia might have thought they were ordinary men, but that assumption was quickly dispelled when Claudia saw them for what they really were.

They were corpses—*moving* corpses.

All were in varying states of decay. Some still had their full head of hair and looked as if they had only been dead for a week or two. Others looked as if they had been in the ground much longer. Their skin was shrivelled and peeled away to reveal bone. One was even missing its jaw, leaving a grey tongue that looked like a spoiled cut of meat lolling sickeningly. Filthy scraps of clothing clung to their skeletal frames, or some wore nothing at all.

They carried weapons as well. Swords, and hatchets, and even one with a headman's axe.

The cloaked woman—the necromancer, Claudia now knew—sat back on the grass, while her collection of undead moved to surround Claudia.

*Well,* she thought with grim amusement, *this certainly isn't how I expected the night to go.*

The corpse with the missing jaw let out a rattling howl, before it lunged.

57

## CHAPTER 7
# KAS

THE RAIN HAD STOPPED as Kas made her way back to *The Ruby Lion* after walking Riovanna back to her house in the district by the city gates.

The hour was also growing late; the streets emptier and quieter than they had been when she first arrived at the inn. Which was why Kas was able to hear it as clearly as she did.

The sound of horses screaming.

Coming from the stables near the gates.

*Bod.*

She expected to find the stables ablaze, to hear the shouts of *"fire!"* or even to find it under attack by some monster. Yet when Kas did reach the stables, she saw nothing out of order. No monsters or miscreants in sight and the only flame came from the lit lantern hung in the entrance. But still the horses inside stomped their hooves, snorting and screaming with terror.

Kas could see the old stable hand standing in the middle of the row of stalls, seemingly at a loss for what to do about the frightened animals.

Over the sound of the panicked equine, Kas heard the nearby

howling of dogs. A small black cat rushed out of the stables and past her feet, its fur standing on end and making a pitiful yowling sound.

Something was terrifying the animals of the city. But there was nothing in sight that could possibly be causing this. Kas knew of only one creature that could terrify animals like this, even from a distance.

It seemed a necromancer had come to Grevande.

# CHAPTER 8
# CLAUDIA

CLAUDIA WAS THROWN BACK against a tree. The impact knocked the breath out of her momentarily, but it was hardly enough to slow her down.

The corpses congregated upon her. The closest one swinging at her with its hatchet, intending to bury the edge of it into her skull.

While the corpses moved with a speed and agility one wouldn't expect of a dead thing, Claudia was still much faster. She dodged to the side, the hatchet leaving a scar upon the bark of the tree instead of on her flesh.

Her own weapon didn't miss. When she swung her sword at the corpse's head, cleaving it in two, no blood spilled as the corpse stilled and toppled to the ground.

But it was no time of reprieve for Claudia. The rest of the corpses were still surging towards her, swinging their weapons, and grasping for the satchel at her hip.

She sliced through the delicate tendons that still held one corpse's skeletal arm to the rest of its body. The arm and the rusted shield it held fell and Claudia cut through its midsection.

She spun out of the way of the next corpse rushing her. Grabbing it by the back of the skull, she threw it face-first into a tree. The force of it was enough to cave in its already disintegrating face.

The next oncoming corpse did not even get the chance to engage with Claudia. Wolf leapt onto its back, pinning it to the ground and proceeded to maul it while the corpse could only struggle feebly.

Apart from it all, sat the necromancer. Her arms outstretched before her, fingers twitching like a puppeteer jerking the strings of its marionettes. That was when Claudia noticed the corpses she had felled only moments ago, already beginning to stir to life.

None of them would stay down until the necromancer was taken care of.

Readjusting her grip on the hilt of her sword, Claudia launched herself at the necromancer.

Before she could reach the woman, something barrelled into her, knocking her off her feet and pinning her onto her back. Her sword skittered from her palm, as both her hands were pressed into the dirt by the corpse's vice-like grip.

Above her was the corpse whose head she had severed down the middle. Grisly bits of dead skin and tendon hung along the edges where Claudia's sword had cut through. She thought she could even see the grey, fleshy lump of a brain peeking out of the gaping hole at the side of its head.

Its weight atop Claudia was surprisingly strong. Yet not strong enough to keep her down for long. She surged up and clamped her teeth around the corpse's throat.

The dead flesh against her tongue and thick, congealed blood seeping into her mouth was the vilest thing Claudia had ever tasted. With a sharp jerk of her head and the tearing sound of skin and sinew and the snapping of bone, Claudia tore the corpse's head free of its shoulders.

Its body slumped to the side and Claudia was free to get back on her feet, releasing the corpse's head and spitting the blackish blood from her mouth.

Pain tore through her hip.

Claudia cried out and staggered to her knees.

That was when she saw the shaft of an arrow sticking out of her side. It had pierced her right above her hip.

She also saw the corpse with a bow in its skeleton hands, standing beside the necromancer.

"You should be more aware of your surroundings," the necromancer said in a gleeful rasp. "And here I thought your kind was hard to sneak up on. That's right. I know, even though your looks are deceiving."

Claudia bared her teeth—her fangs—in a hiss. She tried to stand but her knees buckled with the pain that speared through her.

The arrow needed to come out. But she didn't think she would have the time. Already, the corpses were moving towards her with their quick, jerky movements and hollow howls and groans. Ready to make her into one of them. Ready to take the satchel off her. To take—

The night lit up and the air around her turned scorching. A torrent of fire snaked through the air around her. Claudia would have felt a fissure of fear at the sight of it, had she not watched as, like some great serpent, it caught up the necromancer's corpses one by one. Leaving her unscathed.

Once all the corpses had been reduced to nothing more than ashen husks, the fire vanished, and Claudia saw who it was that had come to her rescue. A tall man—no, not a man, Claudia realised, a woman— dressed in dark clothing, except for a blue scarf, and with short, red hair that she was sure would have been more vermillion in the daylight.

Was she a sorcerer? Claudia didn't see an amulet anywhere on her person. She did notice the woman wearing a leather gauntlet on one hand, a fiery glimmer winking out on its palm.

"My darlings!" the necromancer wept wretchedly. "What have you done to my darlings?"

Before the necromancer could even think to flee, now that her reanimated corpses were gone, the red-haired woman took a silver throwing knife from her belt and let it fly from her hand.

The blade went through one of the necromancer's hands and her wails of despair turned to those of pain as she was forced backwards and pinned against a tree.

The woman strode straight past Claudia until she reached the necromancer, yanking the knife out of her hand and grabbing her by the front of her cloak so she could throw her to the ground.

"I always thought you necromancers were creepy bastards," said the red-haired woman. "Using the dead like toy puppets. But I thought you lot had more sense than to just parade your twisted magic around outside a city like this."

Claudia felt something bump against her shoulder and saw Wolf. He was sniffing at the arrow still stuck in her side. His upper lip curled in a snarl.

The necromancer's hood was in enough disarray that a rictus grin was visible on her gaunt face.

"We all take some risks for the prospect of riches, no?" said the necromancer.

"What?" the red-haired woman asked.

"This girl carries something precious. Something powerful. And I doubt I'm the only one who can feel it. Who craves it." An ugly cackle left her throat. "She won't stop being hunted. Not unless—"

Her words turned into a gasp, then a gurgle.

Claudia's sword was stuck through the necromancer's throat.

The red-haired woman started, looking up at Claudia, who stood over her shoulder, with wide, green eyes. She clearly hadn't heard Claudia's approach.

"Why did you do that?" the woman demanded as Claudia pulled her sword free of the now dead necromancer.

"So I will have one less enemy on my trail now."

The woman stood, she was taller than Claudia, and considerably wider in the shoulders. "She could have given you more information."

Claudia returned the woman's glare. "I already know all I need to. You're the one who should stay out—"

She stumbled. A wave of dizziness overtook her.

Claudia supposed that was to be expected. Now that she'd taken the arrow out, her blood ran freely. *Saints,* she cursed, *I thought it might have started to heal by now.*

Darkness crept over her vision.

The last thing she saw was the red-haired woman's scarred face, looming over hers with a look of concern and . . . horror.

Even so, Claudia's last delirious thought before she fell into unconsciousness was,

*She's beautiful.*

# CHAPTER 9
## KAS

Kas was leaned against the wall by the window, arms folded and scrutinising the figure on the bed.

The white-haired woman was still dead to the world. Upon bringing her back to her room at *The Ruby Lion*, Kas had seen to the arrow wound that had felled her. By the loss of blood alone, Kas had surmised that the arrow had gone in deep, and she doubted that the woman would have helped things by pulling it out as she did.

But where Kas had been expecting to find a ragged wound that would likely need stitching and cleaning and bandaging, she had instead found one that looked as if it were already beginning to close over. As if it were days old and not an injury of only minutes ago.

The woman's form was partially hidden in shadow, as was the rest of the room. The lone candle Kas had lit by the window only doing enough to keep the room from being shrouded in complete darkness.

*Did I really see what I thought saw?* she wondered. *Did she truly have fangs?*

Kas kept repeating the image in her mind, of the pair of needle-like teeth in the woman's mouth just before she collapsed. Of course, she'd checked for herself—once she'd shooed away the black wolf that growled at her when she tried to get close—but if she really did have fangs, they'd retracted by the time Kas could take a look.

Maybe that should have been enough to put Kas's suspicions to rest. To assure her that it had only been some post-battle figment of her imagination.

This woman didn't even look like a vampyric, and Kas was all too familiar with what those particular monsters looked like. The woman's skin was fair, not the pearl-grey of a vampyric. Beneath her curtain of hair, her ears were round and human, not pointed like a knife. Her fingers didn't taper off into claws and a lift of her eyelids had shown irises that were a pale, ice-chip blue. Not red like blood.

She looked entirely human.

And yet there was still something about her that nagged at Kas. A gut feeling that she wasn't what she appeared to be. The wound that already looked as though it were healing was proof of that much.

*"Always trust your gut feelings, girl,"* Tsurra had told her many times over the years. That advice had yet to lead her astray once.

At the hollow of the woman's throat, Kas noticed a circular brass pendant with a star engraved upon it. The pendant was held there by a black felt ribbon around the woman's slender neck.

Despite her misgivings, Kas could not deny that the strange woman had an impossibly lovely face. High cheekbones, long, silvery eyelashes and bow shaped lips coloured a delicate pink. She looked like one of those classical paintings or storybook princesses renowned for their beauty, come to life.

Had Kas met her under different circumstances, she might have tried to woo her.

Outside the window, she heard a distant, mournful howl that must have come from somewhere beyond the city. Could it be the black wolf from before?

A sound from the bed drew Kas's attention back to where the woman was coming awake. It was one of those slow, muffled awakenings at first, until consciousness seemed to hit the young woman like a slab of stone. She made a muffled shout as she tried to sit up, only to be jerked back into place by the silver manacles securing her wrists to the headboard. Manacles that Kas had put there.

"About time you woke up," said Kas. "I was afraid I might end up having to sleep on this window seat. In case you haven't noticed, my height would make that very uncomfortable. I'd probably end up with a cramp in my neck for days."

The woman's pale blue gaze looked overbright in the half-shadow as she cast them furiously in Kas's direction. "You," she hissed accusatorily. Kas supposed that was fair enough. She was chained to a bed and Kas was the only one in sight who could have been responsible for it. "Let me go this instant."

"Not until you explain a few things." Kas left her position by the window and crossed to the side of the bed.

The woman's body tensed almost imperceptibly as Kas drew nearer and she never once took her eyes off of Kas. The woman reminded her of a caged, wild beast. Loathe to show any fear of her captor, but not completely able to hide the anxiety of what might become of her.

Kas reached out to pull on the strips of cloth she had tied to the woman's wrists, so the manacles didn't touch her skin directly. She felt the woman's barely contained flinch and knew what she would find before she even saw it.

Kas saw the edges of pinkish weals braceleted the fair skin beneath the cloth, like skin spent a little too long beneath the sun's heat. Marks that certainly had not been there before.

Kas felt a mingling of vindication and anger. So, she had been right about the woman.

"You know I've never seen a person react this way to contact with silver," she mused. "Monsters, yes. Especially monsters such as vampyrics."

The woman's lips tightened. She looked as if she were considering her next words carefully. "You're a Slayer, aren't you?"

"And you're a vampyric."

This time the woman's—the vampyric's—lips curled into something between a smirk and a snarl. "Only half."

This gave Kas pause, her brows knitting together. "Only half? What does that mean?"

"It means that I'm no full-blooded vampyric. I'm also half-human. In case you hadn't noticed my distinct lack of any vampyric characteristics."

The way she spoke that last part gave Kas the distinct impression that she was mocking her earlier words about sleeping on the window seat as someone of her height.

Dislike curdled in Kas's chest. "What's to say this isn't just some enchantment to help you blend in?"

"I can assure you, Slayer"—the vampyric's smile turned a touch sultry—"This is all natural." She winked.

*Oh, wonderful. The vampyric tied to my bed is trying to seduce me.* Kas turned to take her place on the window seat again. Arms folded across her chest, she fixed the vampyric with a glare.

"Let me just be clear that the only reason I haven't decapitated you yet, is because I'm curious about that incident I stumbled upon earlier between you and that necromancer," Kas said. "She said enough before you killed her to make me believe that something is afoot. Explain. Or I'll take the cloth off your wrists and let that silver melt your skin down to the bone."

The vampyric didn't seem to need any more convincing. Taking only a moment before she started to speak. "Very well, then. My name is Claudia of Trulio, and I am of the vampyric clan of Salvaclare. Or I was. Our clan's been quite splintered since the death of our former clan head and the disappearance of her successor six years ago."

Kas didn't miss the odd note that entered the vampyric's voice. Something like barely concealed sadness. She chose to ignore it and let the vampyric continue.

"Little over a month ago, Serisa, the head of the clan, returned to the castle. She said she had important things to share with those of us that remained. What she had to say was that she had uncovered the remnant of the dragon, Ombral."

If Claudia hadn't already had Kas's full attention before, she certainly had it now. Mentions of dragons tended to have that effect on most.

The giant, terrifying beasts of centuries past. The story went that seemingly out of the blue, six dragons, Kovkan, Avazdrin, Ombral, Rorsyl, Nalzaar, and the most ferocious of all, Morvelth, came to Vil Tresar. The winged behemoths intent on claiming Vil Tresar as their new homeland—and enslaving the humans who already lived there.

How long exactly their reign of terror lasted, had been lost to time. What was known for certain was that Lyar of Rosille, and an unnamed sorcerer had been the ones to defeat the dragons. Not by killing them—except for Morvelth, who was slain by Lyar—but by sealing them away, trapping them beyond a magically constructed gateway. That gateway could still to this day be found upon the mountain the dragons had made their stronghold, known as *Va Serote*.

It was said that Ombral—the most cunning of the dragons—had foreseen their fate and left behind a part of herself—a remnant—that would act as a key to free them once again. The remnant had been lost long ago. Even the Slayers never knew what had become of it.

Hearing now that Ombral's remnant was supposedly in the hands of a vampyric was not how Kas wanted to discover its whereabouts.

Claudia did little to temper her worry by saying, "Serisa told us that she planned on using it to free the dragons."

"Your clan leader wants to let the dragons loose upon the world again? Is she mad?"

*But what else could be expected of a monster?* thought Kas immediately after she spoke.

Claudia's face was turned away, so Kas could hardly see her expression. "Serisa is . . . much changed since I last saw her. It seems that she truly desires nothing more than the destruction of humankind. To see them suffer under the tyranny of monsters far greater than any of us living could possibly imagine."

"And the rest of your clan was in support of this idea?" asked Kas, though she already knew the answer.

"I'm sure you're well aware of the kind of sentiment most vampyrics hold towards humans," said Claudia. "They don't think they would do too badly under the rule of dragons. They think they might even live as kings. I was the only one to oppose Serisa's plan. In return Serisa beat me and had me thrown in the castle's dungeons."

"And what made you so eager to oppose the rest of your clan?"

"I am half-human." Claudia made an attempt at a shrug. "I suppose it's left me with a soft spot for them."

Somehow Kas found it difficult to believe that a vampyric—even a half-vampyric as this one claimed to be—felt anything more for humans than humans did for a pork sandwich.

"I was trapped in those dungeons for—I'm not sure how long exactly," Claudia went on. "Until I was able to escape with the help of my companion, Wolf, who stole the keys from the one who was supposed to be watching me while he was indisposed. After I was freed, I went straight to Serisa's rooms, found Ombral's remnant and fled. Since then, I've been on the run, not only from the vampyrics of my own clan, but from monsters who seemed drawn to the remnant."

Kas took a moment to absorb all this. If dragons were the originators of the monsters they knew today, it would only make sense if those monsters felt some sort of pull to a remnant of their creators.

"So you have the remnant now?" wondered Kas.

Claudia nodded to where her satchel sat slumped against the wall near Kas's feet.

Taking that as permission, Kas bent down and started rifling through the worn travelling bag.

She paused when she found a small, crystal-like object that appeared as though it was made out of violet glass.

*A trastere stone. Those are quite rare.*

Though Kas noticed it was damaged with a chip in its surface.

"Try not to pry through all of my belongings," Claudia said. "Or is being a snoop synonymous with being a Slayer?"

Kas grit her teeth against the annoyed retort she wanted to hurl at the vampyric. But she decided it wasn't worth it. She dropped the stone where she had found it and instead reached for the longish object wrapped in an old cloth.

She held it out to Claudia and when the vampyric didn't say anything, Kas took it as the answer she needed.

She set it on the floor and unwrapped the cloth until it revealed what at first glance appeared to be some kind of hiltless dagger. But Kas quickly realised that it was not. It certainly had the appearance of a blade, with one edge sharpened into a point. Upon closer inspection however, it was clearly a piece of horn or a hardened scale. A red-black colour that caught the candlelight in a way when Kas picked it up the way a piece of metal might.

It also wasn't lost on Kas that in her hands, she now held a piece of a *dragon*. One of the first known monsters. Beasts from the storybooks she used to read as a child and in the great tomes she had studied during her lessons at the Slayers Keep.

"Now," said Claudia, "I've told you all that you need to know. Will you let me go now? This silver is growing uncomfortably warmer by the minute."

Still holding the remnant, she turned back to Claudia. "And just what were you planning to do with this? If you really want to keep it out of the wrong hands, why not destroy it?"

"Don't you think I've tried that? I'm a half-vampyric, I could break these chains if they were not silver and then throw this bed at the window to make my escape. But that remnant is unbreakable."

Kas glanced back down at the remnant in her hand. Dragons were said to have been covered in scales as impenetrable as the thickest of armour. No blade had ever been able to so much as draw blood from them.

Except for one. In the vast library of the Slayers Keep, where Kas had spent countless hours learning about monsters and the history of the Slayers, the sword that had once belonged to Lyar of Rosille was mounted proudly on a wall. *Velane,* the Dragon's Bane. The story went that its blade had been forged out of a rock that had fallen from the stars. That it had taken Lyar a day and a night to forge it. It was the only known weapon capable of piercing through a dragon's armoured flesh. The sword Lyar had used to slay Morvelth.

Surely *Velane* would be able to destroy this remnant.

"I'm going to take this to the Slayers Keep," Kas decided. "There's a weapon there that could destroy it." She returned her gaze back to Claudia. "And I'll let you go," she said it with reluctance, "so long as you promise to get as far away from Grevande as quick as you possibly can."

The vampyric arched a snow-white brow. "You expect me to just let you take the remnant?"

"I don't need you to *let* me do anything."

"Your Keep is in Almora, yes? That's at least a month and half's journey from here. How do you think you'll handle that while being hunted by my—my clan and all manner of monsters, all by yourself."

"I am a Slayer. I can handle myself against monsters."

"But you're no all-powerful being. Take me with you. The two of us together might mean less of a chance in this quest ending in death or with the remnant stolen."

Kas almost felt like laughing at the absurdity of the suggestion. "Me? Take on a fucking vampyric as a travelling companion?" she sneered. "And to the Slayers Keep? I think not."

Claudia sighed. "I didn't want to have to do this, but if you refuse my offer, I'll just have to scream until every person in this inn comes running and I'll say that you kidnapped me and threatened to do terrible things."

The vampyric woman's expression was smug as she looked up at Kas.

Kas felt her own harden. The dislike from before rising into her throat, hard as a knot. "And if I told them you're a vampyric, they'd try to finish you off themselves."

"Who do you think they're more liable to believe?" Claudia looked positively delighted now. In a wicked sort of way. "You, an almost brutish-looking specimen with your swords strapped to your back and that impressive scowl on your face? Or me, the frightened, very *human*-looking young woman chained to the bed?"

As unwilling as Kas was to admit it, even to herself, Claudia made a good point. No one who looked upon this woman would believe she was a vampyric—Kas almost couldn't believe it herself. The last thing she needed now was to be hunted down by city guards and thrown in prison because of a monster with a pretty face and a devious mind.

Kas dragged a hand down her face, muttering into her palm, "I hate your face."

Glaring down at the vampyric, Kas leaned over her—and had the pleasure of noting the trepidation that watered down Claudia of Trulio's arrogant smile, as she did so—and pulled out the key to the manacles.

"We leave at dawn."

CHAPTER 10

# SERISA

It was the dead of night when Serisa, Ves and Orna arrived outside of the yawning mouth of a cave hidden deep within a forest.

"Ta-dah," Serisa announced in a sing-song voice, as if she were presenting her companions with some wonderful gift.

They did not seem overly enthused.

"Are you going to tell us now what we're doing here?" asked Orna in her usual monotone.

"You've both been so patient, so I suppose you deserve a reward, but first." Serisa motioned them to follow her as she entered the cave.

Inside they found themselves in a damp tunnel, with roots reaching down from the ceiling like spindly fingers. Serisa could hear the scuttling and clicking of insects and vermin that had made their homes here. Anyone without a vampyric's keen sense of vision might have had difficulty navigating through the near pitch-blackness.

"I came here once on my travels to find my father," Serisa explained. "I'd heard he might have come into contact with a strega who lived in these parts. By the time I found her however, my father had long since been gone."

"A witch?" said Orna. "We're visiting a witch?"

"Claudia used magic to disappear with the remnant. So I say we use magic to find her."

"Are you truly willing to make a deal with a strega to get the remnant back, Serisa?" Ves asked her.

Serisa paused to look over her shoulder at Ves. "Of course I am. I thought you would be too, Ves? Isn't this what you want as well? To see them all burn for what they did to your son?"

She didn't miss the flinch that stole over Ves's stony features. As it did every time her son was mentioned. He had only been a child when humans, out of their hatred and their fear, had robbed a mother of her child.

"Of course I want that," said Ves, and Serisa knew there would be no more debating her plan.

Finally, the tunnel ended and opened up into a wider space. Lit by candles scattered about the place. Bunches of herbs hung from the ceiling alongside the thicker and longer roots that grew down to brush the floor. Strange talismans made from animal bones hung from the walls.

The stench of dirt and death clung to the air.

A large cast-iron cauldron sat in the middle of it all and beside it a wooden benchtop, spattered with dark stains that Serisa knew to be blood. Beneath the benchtop, Serisa spotted a crate and hanging out of the crate was a small, human arm with the little chubby fingers of a child.

Most monsters tended to make meals out of humans, but stregas had a penchant for feeding on children. Often luring them from their homes with trails of sweets and songs laced with magic.

"*Ooh,*" came a voice that sounded at once like a child's and an old crone's. "Do I have some visitors to my humble abode? What do three vampyrics want with little old Brucca?"

"We'd like to ask for some help," Serisa answered the disembodied voice. "And I'm willing to make whatever payment is necessary."

"Oh, I remember you with the raven hair. You came to Brucca's cave once looking for your papa who had already gone far, far away."

"Yes. That's right."

Out of one of the shadowy nooks in the furthest corners, Serisa spotted movement and she felt Ves and Orna tense beside her as into the light stepped a figure no taller than Serisa's hip. One might be forgiven for thinking it was a child, but the longer one looked, the more readily apparent it became that this was no child.

The strega, Brucca, had a squat body beneath a tattered brown shift and disproportionately long, lanky arms. Her skin was the greenish colour of mould, and her face was no more pleasant to behold, with one eye so much larger than the other it looked as if it was in danger of popping out of its socket at any moment. Her nose was long and crooked, and its shape reminded Serisa of a carrot. Her lips were also far too wide and when they split into a grin as she approached them, revealed rows of small, pointed teeth.

"Hmm, and what is it you need my help with now raven vampyric? You weren't willing to make any deals for Brucca's help last time."

"Different circumstances call for it," Serisa explained. "Someone stole something very valuable from me. I want it back as soon as possible and to not have to waste my time scouring the continent looking for her."

"I see, I see." The strega twirled a wispy bit of white hair around a disjointed finger. "You want Brucca to use magic to find her for you."

Serisa nodded.

Brucca made a considering sound. "Sounds easy enough. Wait here, blood-drinkers."

The strega hobbled off towards a collection of crates and clay jars by the cavern wall and began rummaging around through them. Finally, she pulled out a human skull from one of the crates. It was missing a few teeth, and a crack traced a jagged path from its nasal cavity over to its eye-socket.

The strega caressed the skull with unsightly fingers and began to mutter to it in a guttural tone, speaking words Serisa could not understand.

An ominous green light gathered in the air around the skull in the strega's hands. As her strange muttering continued, Serisa heard what sounded like heavy breathing echoing through the cavern. It took her a moment to realise the sound was coming from *the skull.*

The skull's jaw cracked open, and its breathing sounds morphed into a tortured howl.

"Bloody hells," Ves cursed, while Orna clapped her hands over her ears.

Serisa, meanwhile, found she could not look away.

"Hush, hush." Brucca cooed to the skull, as if it were a crying child. "There's a sweet thing," she said as the skull's howls quietened to horrible gasps. "Your name was Marlot, yes?"

The skull drew in a rattling breath. *"Y-Yes . . . You killed me . . . cut open my stomach for . . . trying to save . . . my . . . boy."*

"Brucca remembers. He was a delicious piglet."

The strega wandered back over to her vampyric guests and held out the speaking skull to Serisa.

"Go on," she instructed, "Tell Marlot who you are seeking."

Serisa took the skull into her own hands. "I am looking for Claudia of Trulio."

The skull made a choking sound. *"Claudia . . . of Trulio . . . in . . . N-Nescoro. N-north of . . . here."*

Brucca chuckled unpleasantly. "Listen to dear Marlot. Will not lead you astray. Will lead you to your little thief."

Serisa looked at the skull, satisfied. "Perfect. And . . . in return? What would you have from me?"

The strega smiled in that chilling way that showed off her tiny teeth. "Little old Brucca won't ask for payment. Can sense it on you, raven vampyric. The love. The loss. You're going to set the world on fire because of it. Brucca would like to watch it."

Serisa flinched at Brucca's words. It was more than a touch disconcerting to think that the strega might know what was in Serisa's mind. And in her heart. She fought the urge to touch the broken amulet that rested below her collarbone.

Brucca cackled manically—it sounded like bones clacking against each other—as if she could sense even that about Serisa.

Passing the skull into Ves's hands, Serisa raised her chin, steeling her expression and her mind. "Thank you for your help," she said with forced civility. "It is . . . much appreciated."

Brucca only continued to laugh, until the unnerving sound of it was bouncing off the walls. When Serisa, Ves, and Orna headed back through the tunnel, the sound of the strega's laughter followed them too.

Serisa did her best to drown it out as they made their way back to the outside world. Instead, she chose to focus on the speaking skull they now had in their possession, and which would lead her to Claudia. To Ombral's remnant.

This time, Serisa did allow her fingers to drift up to the sorcerer's amulet around her neck.

*I will find you, Claudia,* she silently vowed. *I won't allow even you to stand in the way of avenging those I have loved. And lost.*

# PART TWO
## THE SLAYER AND THE MONSTER

# CHAPTER II
# CLAUDIA

TRUE TO THE Slayer's word the night before, she and Claudia started their journey bright and early the next morning. Setting off for the Slayers Keep in the alpine regions of Almora province. To get there, they would have to leave Nescoro, head north and cross into Verillino, one of Vil Tresar's largest provinces.

"Why not just use that trastere stone of yours to get to the Keep?" the Slayer had questioned her. "Save us the journey."

"It was damaged in my escape from the castle," Claudia explained. "I would not trust it to take us to our exact destination. It might just end up dropping us in the middle of the ocean."

Still, Claudia decided to keep the trastere stone on her person after that conversation. The middle of the ocean sounded more appealing than what Serisa might do if she caught up to them.

When they arrived at the stables to fetch the Slayer's blue roan, Claudia was pleasantly surprised to find her dapple-grey horse awaiting them as well. Apparently, the Slayer—Kas of Veldenier, as she had introduced herself—had found it in the middle of the road when she brought Claudia back into the city.

And of course, Wolf had joined them once they were some distance out of Grevande.

"You keep a wolf for a pet?" Kas of Veldenier asked her, eyeing the black wolf loping alongside their horses.

"He's not my pet," Claudia said a touch defensively. "And I don't keep him. He's free to come and go as he pleases."

"So you don't keep him around as some sort of convenient snack?"

"*No.* If I'm hungry I'll eat the bread and dried meat I have in my pack. And if I'm thirsty, I have a water flask."

Kas gave her an odd look. "Vampyrics can't eat food or drink anything other than blood."

"Really? Whoever would have thought? Certainly not me," Claudia deadpanned. At the Slayer's scowl, she added, "Full-blooded vampyrics can't consume anything that isn't blood. But I'm half-human, I can eat and drink just as you do. So have no fear, Slayer, you won't awake in the night to find my fangs in your neck."

"I'd cut through *your* neck before you even got the chance." There was real threat behind those words.

Claudia only regarded the other woman with a cool look before returning her gaze back to the road ahead of them. Wolf was now nowhere to be seen and Claudia tried not to feel too discomfited by his absence.

She could always flee the Slayer's side. Take the remnant out from under the woman's nose with her inhuman speed and continue her journey alone. It could be so easy. But Claudia had had plenty of time to think on it during the night, and came to the conclusion that it might be beneficial to take on a travelling companion—especially one that was well versed in killing monsters.

It was not until later in the day, after they had stopped for some food and to water their horses, and now trekked along a quiet road, snaking through a field of tall grass and red poppies, did Kas speak to Claudia again.

"How does one create a half-human, half-vampyric? You weren't really a human that was turned, were you?"

"Really?" said Claudia, amused. "I would have thought that a Slayer of all people would know that humans being turned into vampyrics is just a myth."

Vampyrics, like most monsters—aside from werewolves who were infected, and wraiths who were cursed in death—were born, not turned. The notion that humans could somehow be turned into vampyrics, was nothing but a fallacy concocted to make vampyrics seem even more frightful—or alluring, depending on who one asked.

"Yes, I do know that," snapped Kas. "But I've also never known there to be such a thing as a vampyric who's half-human. So perhaps I'm questioning some things."

"Well, you'll be pleased to know that your Slayer education didn't lead you astray. It's quite impossible for vampyrics to turn humans."

"Then what are you? Is this some new sorcery? Were you created out of some kind of experiment?"

"I'm no experiment. I was created the same way you were," Claudia explained.

"What do you mean?" asked Kas.

Claudia laughed. "Oh dear, did no one ever explain to you where children come from? Must I be the one to enlighten you?"

Claudia very much enjoyed the flustered look of annoyance that overcame Kas's face.

"Of course I fucking know where children come from," Kas said. "So your parents were—?"

"My mother was a vampyric, and my father was but a simple human farmer from Trulio," said Claudia. "He was a kind man, my father. He was out in the woods one night, searching for one of his lost sheep when he had a fall and injured his ankle. That's where my mother found him. Although apparently, she'd had her eye on him for some time already."

"And why was that?" The Slayer sounded genuinely curious.

"He liked to sing. Oftentimes he would do so while working out in the field, and my mother was a great lover of music."

Kas snorted. "A monster a lover of human arts?"

Claudia couldn't say she quite liked the derision in the Slayer's voice. "Is that so hard to believe?"

"In my line of work, I often see firsthand exactly how monsters regard humans and anything we create. We're just food or playthings. Especially for you vampyrics."

"A vampyric can't help the way they were born. They cannot help needing to survive off blood any more than you can help needing water to live. And vampyrics may be monsters, yes, but that doesn't mean that's all that we are. We're not all mindless bloodthirsty fiends just as not all humans are belligerent fools, hungry for wealth and sex."

"Right. If you say so." Kas could not sound more unconvinced. "Anyway, you were saying about your father and your vampyric mother who was stalking him?"

Claudia grit her teeth but decided to continue. "My mother found my father and brought him back to the safety of his home. And she returned every night to tend to him while he healed and in return, he would sing for her. They fell in love and from that love I was born. My mother was already married at the time, so they had to keep their affair a secret, and I was raised by my father for most of my childhood. My mother's husband did find out eventually and he tried to kill my father and I when I was only a babe, but my mother stopped him. I was told he disappeared after that."

"Hm? Oh, are you finished?" said Kas. "I'm sorry, I'm still a bit hung up on the fact that your father fucked a vampyric."

"Oh, do shut up," sighed Claudia.

"Who was eating who, I wonder?"

Claudia glared and Kas returned it with an impish grin. Claudia was tempted to go back on her word about keeping her fangs to herself if it would keep the Slayer from speaking such things about her parents.

She didn't deign to tell the Slayer any more than she already had, after that. She did not speak of her father stolen away by plague, and her distant mother taken by her grief. She said nothing of her years living as an outsider in the Salvaclare vampyric clan. Nor of the one person who had made those years bearable.

"Well, I've told you a bit of my past," Claudia said instead. "Don't you think it's fair that I know some of yours?"

Kas's face shuttered. Any hint of mirth disappearing like a loose pebble swept away by a river's current. "No."

They returned to their not-so-companionable silence.

* * *

AFTER TWO RATHER UNEVENTFUL days of travel, they wandered through a town by the name of Feldania. Kas had insisted it was a quiet town and passing through would be nothing more than a shortcut to the border of Nescoro.

However, upon entering the town, Claudia quickly discovered that it wasn't as quiet as Kas had said, and that the main streets were filled to the brim with people. The crowd seemed to stretch on as far as the eye could see.

"The fuck is this?" she heard Kas groan.

"So much for your quiet little short cut," Claudia couldn't help but remark.

Kas didn't reply but the look on her face let Claudia know she probably had a few choice words for her on the tip of her tongue.

They were forced to dismount and lead their horses by the reins as they weaved through the crowd to try and make it to one of the less-crowded side streets. They earned a few grumbles as they passed, muttering something about them blocking their view.

*What view?*

But Claudia didn't have to wonder long. A cheer went up just as she noticed the doors to the tall, white building across the road from them open, and out stepped two guards in silver plated armour and white capes, shortly after followed by a woman in white robes, with gold embroidery and an elaborate, white headdress. At the front of her robes, she wore a gold medallion that winked in the sunlight. Even though she stood too far away to see it, Claudia knew that the rose symbol of the Saints was engraved upon that medallion.

The tiered, white building with tall, arched doors and frosted windows, was a Prayer House, a place of worship for the Seven Saints. Most towns and cities across Vil Tresar had one. And Claudia knew that the woman in the white robes and headdress could be none other than Divine Rollisenia. The head of the church of the Seven Saints and—to an extent—of Vil Tresar.

Once Vil Tresar had been ruled by kings and queens, and the provinces had been segregated into kingdoms. During that time, wars between kingdoms were commonplace.

Tired of the endless wars that starved and killed them, the people of each kingdom rose up, one by one, to overthrow their rulers. These monarchs and their families either suffered the fate of public execution, a life of imprisonment, or exile. The then small religion of the Saints had risen up in the chaotic aftermath of the revolutions, to restore stability to the continent. Since then, the church, and the women they called upon to be their Divines, had been recognised as the leaders of Vil Tresar.

Flanked by her guards, the Divine, a portly woman Claudia could only assume to be Feldania's high priestess, by the less elaborate white robes and much smaller headdress she wore, and a man who must be the town's sintiarn, all descended the Sanctuary steps, toward an awaiting gilded carriage. Already people were beginning to throw white roses onto the road before the carriage horses.

"Wonder what the Divine's doing all the way out here?" she heard Kas wonder aloud.

A kindly old woman, with a red patterned scarf wrapped around her brown face and holding a basket of white rose petals, answered, "Why Divine Rollisenia is on her pilgrimage."

Of course, the pilgrimage. It was something the acting Divine underwent every ten years. A journey across Vil Tresar to offer blessings to her people. These pilgrimages usually lasted a year or even more.

The last time the Divine had made her pilgrimage, Claudia had been young enough that the memory of Divine Rollisenia riding through Trulio was a blur. But she remembered clearly enough the white of the Divine's horse. She remembered watching from high up on her father's shoulders, and the Divine as having looked much younger and graceful then. Now Claudia could see the lines of age on Divine Rollisenia's face, and the hunch of her back.

Kas and Claudia finally turned into a laneway just as the Divine and her companions reached the carriage. Claudia relished being free of the oppressive crush of other people.

Not that this laneway was completely empty either. Young children rushed past them to join the crowds on the main street, staring at Wolf with a mixture of awe and trepidation as they went. A scattering of vendors still stood about hawking their wares. One man tried to entice Kas into looking at all the different necklaces he had hanging off one arm, but she merely grunted at him and kept walking.

He turned his attention to Claudia. "What about you, my dear? That pendant around your neck looks quite old. Perhaps you'd like to trade for something shiny and new?"

Claudia touched the tips of her fingers to her brass star pendant. "Thank you. But I'm afraid this one holds some rather . . . sentimental value. I'll not part with it."

As they moved on Claudia noticed a slight youth, perhaps no more than fourteen or fifteen years rushed past them, bumping into Kas along the way.

"Oh, apologies, miss," said the girl. She had umber skin and wore the ratty clothing of someone who likely had no home to call their own, complete with a dirty woollen cap over messy black strands that ended around her jaw.

"Watch where you're going," Kas said not unkindly.

Of course, she hadn't noticed what Claudia had. Hadn't noticed those deft hands reaching into places they shouldn't.

As the girl went to pass Claudia, she reached out and brought the thief to a halt with an iron grip on her arm.

"That doesn't belong to you," Claudia said calmly.

The girl's surprise morphed into defensiveness. Her eyes were of a different colour. The right was a dark brown while the left was pale green. They were both narrowed at Claudia. "I don't know what you're talking about."

Wolf took a step closer to the girl and growled, his upper lip twitching into a snarl.

"I'm asking you nicely," Claudia tried again.

"And I'm telling you to let me go."

"Not until you drop what you took." Claudia could break the girl's arm, if she really wanted to. Crush the bones of her wrist to dust and *make* her drop what she stole. Instead, she applied just enough pressure to the girl's arm to make her cry out.

"Ouch! All right, all right, there's hardly anything in there anyway." With her free hand, she threw the coin purse she'd had up her sleeve at Claudia.

It hit her harmlessly in the chest and fell to the ground.

"What in the hells?" Kas was at Claudia's side, bending down to pick up her stolen coin purse.

People nearby were also beginning to take notice of the commotion.

"As a Slayer I would have thought you'd be more aware of your surroundings," Claudia chided and released the thief.

Instead of bolting, like she would have expected, the thief stayed in place, gazing up at Kas with wide eyes. "You're a Slayer?"

"Hey, I know you!" A gruff-sounding man in a butcher's apron approached the thief from behind and grabbed her roughly by the back of her jerkin, almost lifting her off her feet. "You're the little shit that stole a leg of lamb from my shop the other day."

"I think you're mistaken," said the thief, but the look on her face suggested the man was anything but.

"No. I don't forget a face. Or this." With his free hand, the man tore the girl's woollen cap from her head.

What was revealed was that sticking up from amongst the thief's head of unruly hair, were a pair of triangular points, covered in brown fur. Cat's ears.

A few gasps went up from the people who had gathered around them to watch what was going on.

*The girl's a werecat,* Claudia realised. A human that could shape-shift into a cat. Like werewolves, werecats were the product of an infection. Unlike werewolves, werecats could shape-shift at will and didn't lose their senses to animalistic rage while in their shifted forms.

Despite being one of the less dangerous monsters, werecats were still considered monsters.

Claudia cast a covert glance at Kas, who was watching the werecat and the disgruntled man with a furrowed brow.

The man sneered down at the thief. "You know what the punishment is for thieves once they're caught?"

The thief struggled harder, but the man's grip was strong. Claudia thought she even caught a flash of fear on the girl's face.

And so she should be.

Claudia was only just beginning to debate with herself about whether or not it was a wise idea to intervene, when she noticed the thief's body begin to change. Her limbs began to shorten and the brown fur along her ears began to spread along her face and arms.

Soon enough the man was no longer holding a girl, but a large, wild-looking brown cat with a bushy tail.

The cat twisted itself until it could rake its claws along the hand holding it captive.

The man yelled out, dropping the thief who streaked past them as soon as her paws hit the ground, leaving the clothes she had been wearing in a heap. People who had gathered round shouted and leapt out of the way as the werecat raced past them.

The thief climbed up a nearby stall and disappeared onto the roof of a neighbouring building.

"Saints," growled the man. "I almost had her!" He charged past them and down the side street beside the building the thief had climbed.

"Well, that was . . . entertaining," said Kas drily. She took her horse by the bridle and began leading him down the street.

"You're not going to hunt down the werecat?" Claudia could not help but ask.

"A werecat child with a penchant for thievery is a bit below my paygrade."

Claudia scowled but said nothing more and they continued through the streets in silence.

If they had thought they'd seen the last of the werecat thief, they were proven wrong. Claudia and Kas were barely out of Feldania and back on the open road when the girl seemed to appear from out of thin air to walk alongside their horses.

"So, we meet again," she greeted them with a grin that showed off a hint of feline canine. A new cap was back on her head, covering up her ears. She was also dressed now in an oversized jacket over a butter-yellow shirt and grey trousers that looked as if they had been torn off at the knee.

"Shouldn't you be off somewhere running away from angry butchers?" asked Kas.

"Or robbing people?" Claudia added.

Kas gave the girl a threatening glare. "Try snatching anything off me again and you'll regret it."

"No need for threats. I'm not here to steal anything, only to ask a favour."

"What kind of favour?"

The girl moved until she was standing in front of their horses, bringing them to a halt. "She said you were a Slayer." She pointed from Claudia to Kas. "You are, aren't you?"

"Yes?" Kas's voice had an uncertain edge to it.

"Great! Then take me with you. I've decided that I want to become a Slayer."

Kas stared down at the thief in disbelief. "Seriously? A werecat wants to become a Slayer?"

"What's wrong with that?"

Kas nudged her horse around the girl. "I don't know what you think Slayers are, kid, but we hunt monsters. And *you* are a monster."

"But I'm not!" the thief protested, running to keep up with Kas. "Not really. I mean I have cat ears and I can turn into a big cat, yes. But I'd hardly call that a monster. It's not like being a werewolf or a vampyric."

Claudia allowed herself a private little smirk.

"Besides," the thief continued, "it's not as if I was born this way, or I asked to be like this. One day I was walking home from school and some stupid older boy decided to pick a fight with me and while I was trying to get away, he bit me. Then I got sick and now I'm a werecat. If anything, *I'm* just a victim."

"But that's just it," Kas said. "You were turned by a werecat who clearly wanted to pass the disease to someone else. Maybe you'll get that same urge one day. I've seen it happen not just in werewolves, but in werecats like you. And did you know that not everyone who gets bitten survives? You were one of the lucky ones—if you even want to look at it that way."

"I—" Claudia noticed the thief's bravado was waning.

"You might attack someone one day like how you were. And maybe they won't survive. Maybe you'll end up robbing someone of their friend, their parent, their child, and then what? Are they going to have to put a monster's bounty on a *Slayer*? Are you going to be hunted down by your comrades?" Kas brought her steed to a halt so she could fix the thief with a cold look. "Being a Slayer isn't for the likes of you. You're better off continuing to steal for a living."

The thief didn't follow them after that. Once they were far enough away, Claudia allowed herself to look over her shoulder and saw the girl still standing in the middle of the road, looking small and alone.

For a moment, Claudia felt as though she were looking at her past self. At the girl she had been after her father died and she had arrived at the Salvaclare vampyrics' castle. A place that was cold and strange and where she was unwanted.

Claudia felt sympathy in her heart for the young thief.

And a deep, dark resentment for the red-haired Slayer riding ahead of her.

# CHAPTER 12

## KAS

Kas and the vampyric made camp in the woods that night. For the first time in a while, the air was cold enough that Kas got a fire going. She already knew that being only a half-vampyric meant that Claudia was not as intolerant to sunlight as other vampyrics—who could turn to ash at the slightest contact—but Kas had yet to learn how she behaved around fire.

When Kas asked her, Claudia had responded with a withering glare and two syllables, "I burn."

Kas did not bother with a cutting response and simply let the matter lie. However, she didn't fail to notice that while Kas sat close to the heat of the flames, Claudia kept more of a distance. *Interesting.*

Kas took a bite from her meagre dinner of dried pork and a hard slice of bread crust, as she fed another stick into the fire. The flames flared and crackled.

The food she had with her was starting to dwindle. It wouldn't be long before she'd have to buy some more.

*With what, Kas? You're flat fucking broke remember?*

The thought soured her mood.

"Did you need to be so harsh back there?"

Her mood soured further when she heard the vampyric's voice. It was the first time Claudia had spoken to her in a while.

"What do you mean?" Kas responded, her mouth full.

"With the werecat girl in Feldania. You couldn't have let her down with a gentler touch?"

"All I did was tell her the truth. A monster has no place being a Slayer."

Claudia's eyes glittered in the firelight. Though Kas could have been forgiven for thinking they were really sparks of anger. "She was a child," the vampyric hissed.

"But she was still a monster," seethed Kas. "She will always be a monster. She'll always pose a danger."

"So why didn't you kill her when you had the chance? If she's such a danger."

Kas shrugged and began licking the breadcrumbs and salt from her fingertips. "Why should I have? No one offered me any coin."

Kas knew the words were untrue even as she spoke them. But she was hardly about to reveal to Claudia that she had felt some sympathy for the werecat thief. That a part of her—a foolish part—rebelled at the thought of slaughtering the girl like any other monster.

*Even if it's a child, it's still a monster. And all monsters do is ruin lives,* she reminded herself.

Claudia's lip curled with disdain. She'd stopped petting the wolf's head resting in her lap. "That's all that matters to you? You'll kill anything, even a child, as long as there's money in it for you?"

"If it's a monster, then yes. That is what being a Slayer entails, after all."

"Listening to you speak is almost beginning to make me understand where Serisa is coming from."

"Careful there." Kas put a hand on the hilt of the silver sword on the ground at her side. "Or maybe I'll start to think you're a threat."

The wolf lifted its head to regard Kas and there was something menacing in its amber eyes. As if it understood her and did not like what she was saying one bit.

Claudia's gaze was as cold as winter winds as she stared Kas down. "Do you really wish to learn firsthand what kind of threat I can be?"

Kas was aware of Bod behind her stamping his hooves nervously. Always sensitive to the mood shifts around him.

Neither of them moved and neither of them took their eyes off the other. Only the cracking of the fire and the jumping of the shadows it cast broke the still quiet.

Kas was almost tempted to let the simmering tension between them boil over. Pick up her sword and end this farce of companionship with the half-vampyric.

She'd fought vampyrics before. She knew she could take Claudia.

She had a brief vision of pushing her sword through Claudia's heart, taking the dragon remnant, and continuing to the Slayers Keep on her own as she so wished to do.

Kas took her hand away from her sword.

"I won't fight you," Kas conceded. "Not tonight. But don't think it's not because I don't sorely wish to."

Claudia's lips tilted into a half-smile, though there was no warmth to it. "I wouldn't expect anything else."

* * *

ALMOST A WEEK LATER, they were finally drawing close to the border into Verillino. They travelled along a narrow, barely trodden road that snaked through a dense forest of old, gnarled trees and thick grass that would reach a grown man's knees.

Mist blanketed the forest, turning the still air damp. Thick enough to make it difficult to see more than ten paces in any direction. At one point the black wolf trotted ahead of them and Kas lost sight of him completely.

Kas had to admit, she was beginning to find the forest difficult to navigate. But it was not the first time she had travelled through these parts, and she liked to think the map in her head was just as reliable as one on paper.

They reached a fork in the road that was familiar to Kas, though there was no signpost where she was sure there should have been one. *Maybe it got knocked down?*

There was no signpost, but there was a statue that looked as if it had been carved from one of the trees, directly in front of them. It depicted the bust of an old woman, face framed by a headscarf and holding a rose against her neck. Salbane, the Saint of Protection.

It should have been reassuring to see a miniature shrine to a Saint out here—especially one such as Salbane. But something about seeing the carved, expressionless face in the midst of the dense fog was eerie.

"Well? Which way now, Slayer?" demanded Claudia, pausing alongside Kas at the fork. "Don't you know these parts?"

Scowling, Kas pushed some of the wet hair from her eyes before finally making a decision.

"This way," she said, steering Bod down the east road.

Kas was certain the road would bring them to a village or even the old farmer's hut, she remembered from her last journey through these woods, where they might be able to ask for lodgings for the night. But the further it went on, growing more serpentine and leading them further through denser forestation, Kas's confidence that she knew where she was going was beginning to wane. A growing feeling of unease started to settle like a lump in the pit of Kas's stomach.

It was a while later before Claudia finally announced, "We are lost."

"We're not lost," said Kas, purely because she felt she *had* to disagree with anything Claudia said.

"We are. And we're going in circles."

"I wouldn't go as far as to say—"

"Look where we are, Slayer."

Kas did look and her heart sank. Because Claudia was right. *Damn it.*

They were back at the fork in the road. The same one with no signposts and the wooden statue of Saint Salbane.

"What the fuck?" was all Kas could bring herself to say, pulling Bod to a halt in the middle of the crossroad.

"It looks like you don't know these parts as well as you thought," Claudia noted.

Claudia's voice was like taking a flint to the fire that was Kas's easily lit temper. "Well, if you're so all fucking knowing," she growled, "why didn't you speak up earlier? Or better yet, why don't *you* lead us out of these bloody woods?"

"I never claimed to know the right direction we should go in. Perhaps if you hadn't been so insistent that we make a detour into that village yesterday so you could trade for some crowns, you would not have gotten so turned around like this."

Kas blinked incredulously. "You're blaming me?"

Claudia daintily lifted one shoulder in a shrug. "*You* are the one leading us to *your* Keep."

"Just shut up and let's keep moving."

"So you can get us even more lost?"

"Oh, eat shit, will you?"

"How mature of you."

"Who said anything about wanting to be mature? I just want to insult you."

Claudia's glare was cutting. "Instead of being childish, maybe you should—"

She went silent, her gaze going from Kas to the mist beyond the statue of Salbane, at the same moment her wolf started growling. His head also turned in the same direction. It was like watching a pair of predators catch a whiff of some new prey.

Or was it another predator?

By now, Kas could also hear the telltale signs of something moving through the forest; the rustling of ferns, the crunching of leaf litter. And it was drawing closer.

Kas reached for one of her swords at her back, placing careful fingers around the hilt.

"A human," she heard Claudia whisper, even as she noticed the vampyric reach for her gold-hilted rapier.

Even if it was a person, that knowledge did little to ease Kas. Humans could be as dangerous as any monster.

Whoever it was had drawn close enough that Kas could make out the shape of them through the mist. Coming towards them from between two trees directly in front of them. "Halt," she called out. "Who goes there?"

"No one that need frighten you," a light, feminine voice replied. "Just a peasant woman, out foraging for food."

"Come show yourself then," ordered Claudia.

Indeed, it was a woman who stepped out from the mist and trees. A very ordinary-looking one at that. She looked around the same age as Kas, with light, freckled skin and flaxen hair pulled up beneath a damp bonnet. She wore a long moss-green skirt that would have blended in perfectly with their surrounds if not for all the fog. She was also carrying a wicker basket of what appeared to be berries and roots.

Kas's hand fell from her sword. "I'm not sure it's such a wise idea for a woman alone to announce such a thing to strangers."

The woman smiled shyly. She had a pretty smile. "Well, you asked, and I did not want your first impression of me to be as a liar. Also, I could hear you talking about being lost and I did not think I would be in any danger from the pair of you."

"A foolish assumption to make," Claudia said coolly.

The woman's pretty smile faltered, and Kas felt like kicking the vampyric.

"Oh!" The woman jumped back a step as Wolf approached her, sniffing at her skirt, but still growling. "That is a very large—it is a dog, isn't it?"

"He was fed too much as a pup." Kas was close enough that she could shift in the saddle and catch Wolf's rump with the toe of her boot. He gave her an almost affronted stare, but backed away from the young woman, nonetheless.

Kas ignored the angry look Claudia sent her way and focused her attention on the newcomer.

"What's your name? Do you live around here?" she asked. "Is there any chance you could show us the way into Verillino?"

That smile was back. "My name is Innora, and I do live around here, but I'm afraid I can't help you with reaching Verillino."

"Why is that?"

"There is something strange happening in these woods. Has been for a while now. I fear it may be some kind of—of curse."

"A curse you say?" said Kas.

Innora nodded. Her eyes darted about nervously. "It's not something I wish to talk about too much out here. My home is not far from here, if you come with me, I could explain more about the evilness I believe has befallen the woods."

"I'm sorry, but we don't have time to investigate curses," said Claudia.

Innora didn't take her eyes off Kas. Her expression was pleading. She even looked as if she were close to tears. "You are a Slayer, aren't you? Please, I beg you for your help."

Claudia was right, they really did not have the time to get sidetracked by such matters as trying to lift a curse.

However, Kas was a Slayer, and she could not leave an innocent like Innora to suffer through whatever darkness was happening here.

"Lead us to your home," Kas instructed. "We'll talk there and see what can be done."

Innora looked relieved and turned back the way she had come, urging them to follow.

"What are you doing?" Claudia hissed. "We need to be making our way to Verillino. Not stopping to help every young maiden who bats her pretty eyes at you."

"As you so helpfully pointed out earlier, Claudia, we are lost." Kas jumped down from Bod. If they were going to be travelling off the beaten path, then it was better to do so on foot. "Talking to Innora and finding out more about what is going on here may be our only way of leaving these woods." She added, "And when exactly have I stopped for a woman who batted her eyes at me before now?"

When Claudia continued to sit on her horse, looking irritated, Kas merely shrugged and took hold of Bod's reins. "All right. Don't come with me. Have fun wandering endlessly through the woods."

She turned and followed after Innora.

It wasn't long before she heard an aggrieved sigh and the sound of boots hitting the ground.

Innora had a quick stride, despite her long skirt and the uneven terrain. At times Kas feared she would lose sight of her through the grey fog.

But as they walked, the woman hummed a song that Kas was unfamiliar with. At times she switched from humming to singing.

*"Little lamb wanders too far from home*
*Into the dangers of the gloam*
*Ghastlies, and werewolves, and strega, and wraiths.*
*Little lamb cries*
*Little lamb screams*
*Little lamb will never again open in his eyes."*

"What a charming song," she heard Claudia mutter.

It was not a long walk, and soon enough they arrived at Innora's home, a cottage with a thatched roof in the middle of a clearing. There was smoke drifting from the chimney.

"You can leave your horses by the well," Innora told them. "And your . . . dog."

The inside of the cottage looked to be made up of a single room. Kas could see a narrow bed in one corner and a tiny kitchen with a cooking hearth by a window on the other, where a pot hung over a low fire. Straws of hay dusted the floorboards, and beneath that Kas noticed patches of lichen and moss.

Innora was speaking to Claudia. She had already set aside her basket of roots and berries and was holding her hands out to the satchel at Claudia's hip. The one with Ombral's remnant inside.

Claudia clutched the satchel closer to herself. "I'd prefer to keep it on me." The look the vampyric gave Innora was enough to cow the young woman.

*Saints,* Kas thought and then to Innora, "Don't mind her. She's just very particular about her belongings."

Claudia sniffed. "I also don't like my time being wasted." She brushed past Kas and Innora, stepping further inside.

"Why are you such an arsehole?" Kas said under her breath.

"Well?" Claudia spoke, supposedly not hearing Kas at all. "You were going to tell us more about this dark magic you think is plaguing these woods, I believe?"

"O-Oh, yes. Please have a seat." Innora gestured to the table and chairs in the middle of the room. Once they were seated, she asked, "Would you like something to eat or drink?"

"I would like some explanations," Claudia answered.

Kas kicked her leg beneath the table.

The stare Claudia gave her was murderous.

Kas merely smiled. "As I said," she told Innora, "ignore her. Please tell us about the forest. Why do you think it's cursed?"

At her kitchen bench, Innora began cleaning the mushrooms from her basket. With the mist blocking much of the sunlight outside, the light inside was quite dim. The fire in the hearth was the only source of light, though it did little to clear the damp from the air.

"It all started near a fortnight ago now," Innora explained. "Unusual storms and an unusual fog. These forests used to be easy to walk through once. But now . . . it's like a maze. You aren't the first travellers I've seen pass through, only to get lost. And at night it is the worst. There are . . . *things*, moving in the dark. Making terrible noises. Some nights I—I fear for my life."

"Do you have any idea what might have started these odd happenings?" Kas wondered.

Innora shook her head. She set down the knife she was using to cut the mushrooms and wiped at her eyes. "No, I-I have no idea. I am just—I have been so frightened for so long now I—"

Kas rose from her chair and crossed over to the weeping woman. She placed a hand on Innora's shoulder. "It's all right," she told her softly. "We'll figure out a way to help you."

Innora looked up at her with watery eyes and managed a tremulous smile. Her eyes were quite lovely, Kas realised. They were a striking hazel, with a ring of lighter green around the pupil and a much darker shade circling the outer iris.

Innora placed a hand on the one Kas had on her shoulder, sending a pleasant hum through Kas. "I'm glad you're here," she murmured.

Kas wondered if Innora's lips were as soft as they looked. She imagined that if she were to touch her lips to Innora's it would be like kissing a flower petal. She wanted to—

The door shuddered violently, startling them all.

The banging was followed by the sounds of growling and nails scratching against wood. Wolf.

Innora cried out, bringing her hands up to her ears. "Please make it stop!"

"It's all right," Kas reassured her, even though she herself suddenly felt a bit strange. Her head felt clouded and her eyes heavy-lidded, as if she had just woken from sleep.

The wolf continued his scratching.

Turning to Claudia, Kas said, "Can't you shut him up?"

"I find it odd," said Claudia, ignoring Kas and staring impassively at Innora, "that you say you have been living in fear of the woods for a fortnight now, yet when we met, you were out foraging all alone."

"Well, you can't expect me to starve out here, can you?" Innora countered.

"And you were *singing* as you brought us here."

"Can you fault me for doing what I must to try and keep my spirits up?"

"Enough," Kas said to the vampyric.

Wrinkling her nose, Claudia readjusted her satchel. Bringing it to sit more comfortably on her lap.

"Are you sure you do not want me to take it from you?" Innora asked. "I could put it on my bed just over there."

"I believe I told you no the first time."

Innora sighed, exasperated. "There's no need to look at me as if I were a thief, Claudia. I'm merely trying to be courteous."

Claudia stiffened at the same time Kas did.

Carefully backing away from Innora, Kas said, "She never told you what her name was."

Innora stared at her with those round, hazel eyes, and soft parted lips.

And smiled.

# CHAPTER 13

# CLAUDIA

CLAUDIA HAD KNOWN something was strange about the woman and the stories she spouted about the woods being cursed. Claudia had known that there had to be more to her than what she was allowing them to see.

She hadn't known how right she was until she saw that smile.

It was not the smile of the demure, frightful young woman they had met in the forest. No, this was a slow, curling smile that seemed to stretch unnaturally wide for such a doll-like face. It was a smile that sent an unpleasant shiver down one's spine just to look at. It made her look . . . like a monster.

"Well," said Innora. "I suppose the charade could not have gone on forever. Still, I was rather enjoying this little game of pretend."

Her voice grew deeper as she spoke, and that was not the only change in her. Innora began to grow in height, until she stood taller than Kas and her frame widened, stretching her clothes until they looked like they would tear at the seams. Her fair skin darkened to a reddish-purple, bulging veins appeared beneath her skin. It looked as if there was a horrible infection raging through her entire body.

Her pretty blonde hair came loose from its knot and clumps of it fell from her head, leaving only straggly bits of black hair around her now bloated, wart-covered face.

*A strega,* Claudia realised. *Of course.*

It was not only Innora who had changed her appearance, but the room they were sitting in, as well. Instead of the cosy inside of a lived-in cottage, it now looked as if it had been long abandoned and claimed by the woods instead. Moss and lichen overtook much of the walls. Roots protruded from the floor and twisted, leafless tree branches had grown through the windows.

The table stayed as it was, only now Claudia noticed that in front of her was a plate of some sort of stew with the rotting half of a child's face. Maggots writhed in a milky eye. With a gasp, Claudia pushed herself away from the table and heard something crunch beneath her heel. Looking down she saw fat worms and large black beetles scuttling around in the dirt. Claudia kicked at a centipede wriggling over her boot.

Outside, she could hear the horses screaming, and Wolf's guttural growling.

"There was no curse on this forest," Kas was saying. "Only strega magic. *Your* magic."

The strega cackled. "Very astute of you. Though it certainly took you a while to catch on, didn't it? Tell me, was my human disguise so very alluring?" With a grin that showed off her small, pointed teeth, the strega ran her overly large hands over her own body, slapping her hip and laughing some more.

Claudia was behind the strega in a blink. Her rapier in hand and at the ready to cut the witch's head from her shoulders.

The floorboards beneath Claudia burst apart. Thick roots shot up and tangled themselves around Claudia. They twined themselves around her legs, arms and body and even her sword, holding her aloft in the air.

Claudia, who possessed strength enough to tear a tree from the ground with her bare hands, could not break free of these *damned roots.*

"Don't you know how rude it is to sneak up on your hostess?" The strega smirked at Claudia over her shoulder.

Claudia bared her fangs in a snarl.

Kas had both her swords out and was lunging at the strega. More of those gnarled roots burst up from the floor. Yet Kas must have predicted the strega would summon them again after she had already used them on Claudia.

Kas threw herself to the side, out of the way of the grasping roots. She was back on her feet in an instant, ready to hack into the strega— until she was jerked back.

Another root had sprung up from behind and wrapped itself around the sword in Kas's right hand.

Before Kas even had a chance to let go of the sword, the ground beneath her feet shifted to close over her boots. Kas tried to free herself, but the now watery ground held on hard. Little by little, it began to pull her down further. She was already almost to her knees in it.

Now they were both trapped.

"And here I thought a Slayer and a vampyric might provide me with more of a challenge!" crowed the strega. "You were right, however. That little trick of getting you lost in the forest was all my doing. Tricking you into following me to my home was certainly easier than trying to capture you. And more fun, as well."

"What for?" Kas ground out. "Do we look so delicious?"

The strega made a considering noise. "I admit, you don't look too unappetising. Though the white-haired one looks like she has hardly any meat on her. But no, I brought you here because of that . . ."

Claudia felt something creep over her shoulder. At first she thought it was a snake. Instead, it was only another root. Its end curled around the satchel strap on her shoulder and lifted it over her head.

Claudia struggled in vain as her satchel was taken away and handed over to the strega, who made a blissful sigh when it was dropped into her hands.

"I felt it the moment you entered my wood," said the strega, as she dug around inside Claudia's satchel. "The power. The feel of something . . . *magnificent.*"

She held Ombral's remnant in her palm now. Peeling back the cloth to gaze at the broken scale with a hungry kind of wonder. "So this must be it? The fabled remnant of the dragon Ombral. The key to freeing the dragons," the strega mused. "I wonder, if I were the one to use this to free the great dragons from their prison, do you think they'd give me a reward?" Her smile was hideous, and Claudia found herself once again trying to get free of her bonds.

Kas, meanwhile, was sinking further and further into the floor, almost up to her waist now.

"Or maybe I should try selling it for a pretty treasure? Well, I suppose I can decide what to do with it after I've dealt with—"

A dark streak shot through the open window behind the strega, latching onto her face.

A shriek went up from the strega as Claudia realised the dark shape now clawing and biting at the strega's face in a frenzy, was an oversized brown cat. The fur all over its body standing on end.

Following through the window soon after was the easily recognisable shape of Wolf. He leapt at one of the strega's outflung arms—the one clutching the remnant—and sank his teeth into the bruise-coloured flesh.

The cat and Wolf were proving distraction enough that the strega's spell on the roots and the floor binding Claudia and Kas fell away.

Claudia dropped to the floor just as the strega finally grabbed hold of the large cat and flung it off her before using a spell to throw Wolf off her arm as well.

But no sooner was the strega free of her first two attackers, was Claudia before her, aiming her sword at the monster's heart.

The strega managed to side-step the attack and when Claudia attacked again, the strega grabbed Claudia's sword by the blade in one massive palm and used the other to backhand her.

The blow was brutal and sent Claudia staggering to the floor, tasting blood in her mouth.

But still there was no reprieve for the strega. Kas was there an instant later, lunging and slashing at the strega with her two silver blades.

The strega screamed when one of Kas's swords opened up a scorching wound along her front. A thick line of red reaching from shoulder to ribcage.

But before Kas had a chance to do more damage, or for Claudia to re-enter the fight, the strega summoned a powerful gust of wind that sent them all flying across the room. Claudia went crashing backwards into a bunch of prickly vines and branches that scratched at her skin.

When she regained her bearings, it was just in time to see the strega transform herself into a black raven and take flight out of the now open door, the remnant clutched in its talons.

"Fuck," she heard Kas say as they raced for the door at the same time.

Outside, Claudia realised they were no longer in a clearing. But in the middle of a wild forest, full of overgrown grass and ferns and towering trees with blackened trunks. The mist had faded, revealing a dusk-darkened sky.

There was no sign of the horses, but she did spot the strega. A black shape with frantically flapping wings, rising higher and higher, almost to the treetops. Cawing loudly, as if crowing about her escape.

Claudia could try to leap up and catch her. She was sure to be faster than Kas's crossbow.

But Claudia never got the chance.

A blurred figure leapt through the trees, snatching the strega out of the air with ease.

A dark cloak, almost the same colour as dryied blood, swirled and settled as the figure landed on the ground and Claudia thought her heart stopped for just a moment.

She knew that cloak. She knew that figure, clutching the squawking and struggling strega in her grasp.

*How? How could she have possibly found me here?*

With a quick and brutal motion of her hand, Ves pulled the strega's head from her body and allowed both to fall to the ground at her feet, before calmly bending to retrieve the remnant laying in the now bloodied patch of grass.

And as she did so, Claudia saw two new figures emerge from out of the gloom to stand near Ves. Both as instantly recognisable. Both making that cold blanket of dread sit more heavily upon her shoulders.

There was Orna, hunched over and face mostly covered by her curtain of hair.

And standing between Orna and Ves, dressed entirely in red and black to match her sleek black hair and gleaming red eyes, was Serisa.

The last time she had seen Serisa, she had been looking down on Claudia's bruised and bloodied form with disdain and disappointment that had hurt Claudia like a splinter to her heart. Even after the beating she had received from her, Claudia had still found it painful to think she had disappointed Serisa.

Now, she met Claudia's gaze with a triumphant curl of her lips.

"Hello, Claudia. I've been looking everywhere for you."

# CHAPTER 14
# KAS

KAS HAD ENCOUNTERED a few vampyrics in her years as a Slayer. Yet still the sight of them sent ice-coldness rushing through her veins like no other monster did. Every time she laid eyes on that pearl grey skin, clawed hands, and red eyes, she saw the three vampyrics that stole into her home ten years ago and slaughtered her family. She heard the screams of her brothers and sisters. Of her mother pleading with her to run right before one of the vampyrics sunk its fangs into her neck.

Kas had to force her body not to freeze up at the sight of the three vampyrics standing before her now. Had to will away the frightened remnants of her younger self and push her Slayer instincts to the forefront of her mind.

*You're not that frightened little girl anymore. You are a Slayer now. You know how to fight them.*

But it seemed that Kas wasn't the only one shocked into near stillness by the arrival of the vampyrics.

Beside her, Claudia had gone still as a marble statue and her grip on her sword had gone slack.

"Hello, Claudia," said the female vampyric with the sleek black hair. "I've been looking everywhere for you."

*So these are the vampyrics from her clan that she was running from,* Kas realised. *The ones who want to free the dragons.*

"Serisa," said Claudia, a crack in the calm tone she was trying to affect. "Orna. Ves. Nice to see you again. How did you—"

"Did you really think I wouldn't find you sooner or later," sneered the black-haired vampyric. "I didn't think you were so naïve, sister."

*Sister?* Kas's attention caught and held on that one word like a piece of fabric snagged on a branch. For a moment, Kas even wondered if she had heard correctly. It was difficult to imagine Claudia and this Serisa as siblings. She could see no resemblance between them at all. Looking at them was like looking at night and day.

Yet when she saw the way Claudia gazed at the other vampyric, she knew that Serisa spoke true.

Kas felt a flare of anger towards the half-vampyric but resolved to set that aside until later.

"Serisa," said the vampyric with long hair covering much of her face, her eyes on Kas. "I think that one there's a Slayer. Her blades are silver."

Serisa's eyes turned to her, and Kas saw such a deep, unfathomable hatred within those red irises. It was a hatred that Kas recognised lay within herself. Born of pain and loss.

"So it seems." Serisa's voice could have frozen rivers. "I think we need to have a talk about the company you keep, Claudia."

"You can have all the discussions you want with each other," Kas said. "*After* you return that to us." She gestured with her sword at the remnant being held in the tallest vampyric's hand.

"No." An unpleasant smile spread across Serisa's face. "I don't think you will be getting this back."

"We'll see about that."

Quick as she was able, Kas took one of the silver-bladed daggers strapped to the holster at her thigh and threw it with accuracy at Serisa.

But Kas had already come to learn that no matter how fast she was, a vampyric would always be faster. The trio scattered and Kas's dagger was lost to the forest.

What felt like a sudden breeze swept past her and then Kas saw Claudia in front of Ves, the cloaked vampyric. With a cut of her sword, she severed the hand holding the remnant. The vampyric cried out as the remnant and her hand fell to the ground.

Serisa flung herself at Claudia and Kas darted forward, both in hope of retrieving the remnant and aiding Claudia, when the silver-haired vampyric, Orna, appeared in her path.

She lifted one of her swords in time to block the vampyric's claws from slicing into her neck. The reverberation of it rang down to her wrist.

Orna struck out at her again with her other hand and Kas blocked it again with her other sword. This brought Orna in close enough that Kas took the opportunity to punch the vampyric in the temple and followed it up by slamming her elbow into the other side of her face.

The vampyric staggered and Kas chose it as her moment to run her through with a sword. The blade drove almost all the way through Orna's unprotected body, beneath her ribcage.

The vampyric let out a howl as the silver seared her flesh. A foul stench similar to charred meat filled Kas's nostrils.

"Kas, look out!"

The sound of a young girl's voice called her name at the same time Kas became aware of something coming toward her from above.

Releasing the sword she still had imbedded in Orna, Kas rolled out of the way before Ves could crush her skull in with the sole of her boot.

Kas only had enough time to rise from her crouch before Ves was speeding towards her with outstretched claws.

Claws and blade met with a clash of metal that rang through the air.

# CHAPTER 15

# CLAUDIA

CLAUDIA LANDED in a crouch along the side of a tree trunk. She was not allowed much of a reprieve, however. Already Serisa was hurtling towards her with a speed none but another vampyric could hope to match.

Claudia dropped to the ground only seconds before there was an explosion of shattering wood above her head as Serisa slammed into the tree where she had been a heartbeat earlier.

The collision was so fierce the tree gave a tremendous crack and groan as the trunk broke in two and fell to the ground with a shudder that ran through the earth.

As Claudia turned in the direction of the fallen tree, she was only just quick enough to react to Serisa appearing before her.

She aimed a cutting strike with her rapier at Serisa's unprotected neck. Serisa grabbed Claudia's sword in her palm, uncaring of how the steel edge of the blade cut through her skin.

Claudia tried to pull her sword free, but Serisa held tight. Her elder sister ran appraising eyes over the weapon.

"Hm, I see you still use the sword I gave you. And you've taken quite good care of it, too."

Gritting her teeth, Claudia struck out at Serisa with a kick. Her leg passed through a cloud of black smoke as Serisa vanished and then reappeared behind her.

Claudia leapt backward, putting a safe distance between her and Serisa.

She and Serisa stood across from each other. Behind her, Claudia was aware of the Slayer taking on Ves and Orna. She was also aware of Wolf, prowling close by, ready to leap to Claudia's aid should she need it. She did not want to think of what Serisa would do to Wolf if he attacked.

Serisa laughed. "And I see you still fight the way I showed you. You should have put those skills to use back at the castle. Maybe I would not have hurt you so bad."

"Sister, please," Claudia said. "Just stop this. Let me take the remnant away."

"I think not."

"The dragons should not be brought back to this world. Can't you understand that?" Frustration bled into Claudia's voice. "Allowing them to return won't change what has happened! And it won't bring your father back. Or mother, or—"

"I don't care!"

Serisa came at her so quickly, it was almost as if she were flying across the ground, her black hair streaming behind her.

Claudia jumped out of Serisa's path, lashing out with her sword and striking Serisa across the shoulder with the tip of the blade.

Serisa turned to face Claudia. Blood was blossoming at her shoulder where Claudia had cut her, and Claudia felt a pang at the sight of the hurt she had caused her sister—even if Serisa seemed to pay it no mind.

"Serisa," Claudia begged, "I don't want to fight you."

All the wicked mirth from before was wiped clean from Serisa's expression. "I don't care if unleashing the dragons on the humans won't change anything," snarled Serisa. "I *want* to do it. Because it's what they deserve, Claudia. And I will not hesitate to eliminate anything that gets in my way. Including you."

# CHAPTER 16

# KAS

Despite her bulk, Ves was just as quick as one would expect of a vampyric. And maybe even stronger.

More than once, Kas had to fight to keep her grip on her sword, lest it go flying after colliding with one of Ves's blows. Having one severed hand, still ribboning blood, seemed to do little to slow her down.

Kas struck out with her sword, aiming a decapitating blow at Ves's neck. Ves countered the strike by hitting the flat of Kas's blade with her elbow, knocking it out of Kas's grasp. In the opening that created, she grabbed Kas by the throat, lifting her off her feet.

Kas struggled in an attempt to break the strangling hold around her neck. It was an unthinking reaction. She knew she couldn't hope to match a vampyric's strength with her own. But with all of her weapons now out of reach, what else could she hope to do?

Ves bared her fangs in a grin. Kas could feel blood trickling down her neck where claws pierced skin.

The pounding of hooves and an angry whinny was all the warning they had before Bod slammed into Ves, knocking her down with kicking hooves. A girl—the werecat girl from Feldania, Kas realised with a start—was clinging tightly to his neck, struggling to right herself on the saddle.

To avoid being trampled by Bod, Ves dissolved into a cloud of black mist.

Knowing she wouldn't have much time before Ves struck again, Kas gathered up her fallen sword and searched about frantically for the dragon remnant, which she had last seen lying amongst the grass —there. It was still in the same spot, not far from where Claudia and Serisa were fighting. Darting and striking at each other with unmatched speed.

Scrambling to her feet and sheathing her sword, Kas darted for Bod's saddlebags. "You," she said to the werecat and pointed to the remnant. "Go get that. *Quickly!*"

Despite the wide-eyed terror on her face, the werecat barely hesitated before she leapt from the saddle and raced through the grass towards the remnant.

Just as she reached it, did Kas see the shroud of black mist that was Ves hurtling straight towards the werecat.

Kas slipped her hand into the gauntlet she had pulled from one of the saddlebags. She lifted her arm, palm up at Ves. The rune lit up and fire streamed forth and the smoke that was Ves swerved out of the way at the last minute.

"Girl!" Kas shouted to the werecat who had ducked to avoid the fire. "To me." She fired another stream of fire at Ves's mist form as the werecat ran towards Kas and Bod, clutching the remnant to her chest.

Kas had an idea on how to get away from these vampyrics, but they would need to move fast.

Then, she looked to where Claudia and Serisa were still battling. "Claudia!"

She only waited long enough for Claudia to look her way before she directed the gauntlet at Serisa who was preparing to attack again.

Only Claudia did something Kas never would have expected. Instead of getting out of the way of the fire and running to Kas's side, Claudia dove for Serisa, tackling her out of the fire's path.

For only a split second, Claudia and Serisa stayed wrapped up in each other on the ground. They could almost have been mistaken for two sisters sharing a playful embrace in the grass. At least until Claudia leapt to her feet as Serisa struck out at her with a clawed hand.

This time the fire had caught on the grass and was beginning to spread. Serisa dissolved into smoke, flying out of the way of the flames burning towards her.

*"Claudia!"* Kas's voice was more insistent. She noticed the black smoke form of Ves diving towards her again, and once again, Kas fended her off with a tongue of flame. "The stone!"

As Claudia dashed over to her, Kas noticed Serisa not far behind.

With her gauntlet, she directed more fire over Claudia's head at Serisa, and this time Serisa was shoved out of the way by Ves.

Once Claudia was close enough—along with Wolf who seemed to have appeared like a shadow at her side—she lifted her rapier and stabbed it towards Kas.

But Kas never felt the metal pierce through her body. Nor did she feel the wet warmth of her blood being spilled.

Because Claudia had not stuck her sword through Kas.

She had stuck it through the heart of the vampyric named Orna, who had snuck up behind Kas without her notice.

Claudia's sword had gone straight through Orna's heart, and when Claudia pulled her blade free, the vampyric fell forward at their feet and did not move again.

Beside her Bod was beginning to whinny and dance in fright as the oppressive heat of the fire began to close in on them.

"The stone, Claudia," Kas demanded over the roar of the flames. "Now. *Use it now!*"

Without a second more to lose, Claudia took the trastare stone from her cloak and flung it onto the ground between their gathered feet. It shattered on impact. As soon as it did, a plume of violet smoke rose up around them, blinding and consuming them and for a moment Kas knew no more.

# CHAPTER 17

# CLAUDIA

THE STONE DEPOSITED them in the middle of a dark and unfamiliar forest. Claudia fell to her knees in the grass and heard the sounds of impact as the others did alongside her. Kas's horse, Bod let out a startled cry as he fell on his side with a heavy thud, before promptly hefting himself up.

Claudia watched him, realising her own horse was nowhere to be found and thought dourly, *I'm going to need a new horse.*

Wolf was at Claudia's side before she could even stand, pressing his damp nose to her cheek, as if checking to make sure she was all right. She put a hand on his neck, pressing her forehead against the smooth fur of his head before she rose to her feet. The places on her body where Serisa had managed to land a few good hits, complained from the movement.

She spotted the werecat girl crouched on the ground, her mismatched eyes staring unblinkingly into the distance and her trembling breaths were coming out fast and loud. Claudia turned to where Kas was dusting herself off. She had cuts on her neck that were dripping blood onto her scarf.

"Do you have the remnant?" she demanded.

Instead of answering, Kas gave her a thunderous look. In three quick strides, the Slayer was in front of her, grabbing the collar of her shirt in a tight fist.

Beside her, Wolf growled and snapped his teeth, but Claudia kept her eyes, unflinchingly, on Kas, who was glaring at her furiously.

Her scarred lip curled into a snarl. "You never said anything about Serisa being your sister."

Claudia kept her face impassive. "I didn't see how it was any of your concern."

"Of course it's my concern, when I'm involved in this fucking mess of yours. If she is your sister, then how can I be sure you're really against her?"

"I fought on *your* side just now, didn't I?" snarled Claudia. This time she wrested herself from Kas's hold. "I've already told you; I want to stop Serisa from freeing the dragons. Haven't I made that obvious by now?"

"And yet I saw you save her," Kas pointed out. "You went out of your way to push her away from the fire."

"She's my sister. I won't see her killed."

"I saw the way she attacked you. She doesn't seem to have any qualms about seeing you dead. Or about being the one to finish you off herself."

Kas's words speared through her, painful and true. Serisa hadn't held back on any of her attacks earlier, and Claudia could feel the drying blood on her skin and clothes to prove it.

"She wasn't always like this," Claudia murmured, she touched the star pendant at the base of her throat. "She was—A lot has happened to her in the years she was gone. Loss and grief have warped her heart and mind. But I have to believe that she's—that the sister I knew is still in there. That I can still reach her. If I can just get rid of the remnant, maybe I'll have a better chance at talking her out of this need she has for vengeance."

Kas raised a condescending eyebrow. "How idealistic of you."

"Shut up," Claudia snapped. "I never asked for your opinion."

"Well, I fucking gave it anyway. There's no use pondering over your family issues tonight. I'm actually more concerned about where that stone of yours took us. And also"—she turned her glare on the werecat—"what in the hells *you* are doing here? Have you been following us since Feldania?"

The werecat, who had since gotten up to stand near Bod and stroke the horse's neck, returned Kas's glare with a defiant one of her own. "Well, it's a good thing I did. Or the two of you would have been cooking in a strega's pot, right about now. Or you"—she pointed at Kas—"would have been choked to death by a vampyric."

"I suppose that's true," Claudia admitted simply.

Kas only glowered.

The werecat took off her cap to scratch at one of her feline ears. "Would a mindless monster have helped you out like that, Kas of Veldenier?"

"I never said you were mindless. And how do you know my name?"

"I overheard them while I was following you. I overheard a lot of things, actually. Such as how you're trying to get this"—out of the pocket of her coat, she held out Ombral's remnant—"to your Slayers Keep, so you can destroy and keep the dragons imprisoned forevermore."

"Little sneak," said Kas as Claudia stepped forward to take the remnant from the girl.

Her satchel was gone, left behind in the strega's hut. She would have to find somewhere else to keep it safe on their journey. Most likely in one of Kas's packs.

"My name is Aara, by the way," said the werecat.

"I don't care. You shouldn't be here," said Kas, plopping herself down to lean back on one of the larger roots that protruded from the oak tree that stood near them.

Aara shrugged and flicked an ear. "Maybe. But I am here now and you won't be rid of me. I'll prove to you that I can be a Slayer, and I will do that by helping you save Vil Tresar and becoming a hero."

Claudia let out a mirthless laugh and said to Kas, "Looks like you are surrounded by idealists, Slayer."

They settled down where they were for the night, tending to their wounds by the light of the full moon, too weary and cautious of their surroundings to build a fire.

Claudia volunteered to take the first watch. While Kas and Aara slept, she sat upon a fallen tree, blanketed in moss. Wolf sat vigil at her side, while she stared down at the silvery scars like bracelets around her wrists. She looked at them and thought she could still feel the pain of the silver manacles locked around her wrists. Burning like nothing she had known before. Like it was melting through her skin and down to the bone.

Her memory also conjured up the ragged sounds of her own gasps and sobs for relief that never came.

With a harsh sound, she pulled her sleeves down, hiding the scars from sight.

After a moment, she reached into the inside of her cloak. Her fingers closed around what was tucked away in the pocket there, and she drew it out.

A pendant made of brass, almost identical to the one she wore. Except this one had a crescent moon carved upon its surface.

Claudia had bought them both when she was a girl. The star pendant for herself.

And this one for Serisa.

She could still remember the night she presented them to her older sister, and how proud she had felt when Serisa accepted it. She had always been so eager to make her sister happy back then. The attentive older sister who had taken Claudia in, when their mother was too overcome by grief over Claudia's father to do so. Who would sing her to sleep during her first days at the castle, who had played with her and taught her how to wield a sword. Her sister who had defended her from the clan members who wanted her banished from the castle and protected her from the ones who thought Claudia deserved a more gruesome end.

*"Nothing will harm you so long as I am near."*

For so long Serisa had been the sun in Claudia's lonely existence after her father died. Claudia thought there was nothing she would not have done for her sister.

Until now.

The night Serisa left the castle to search for her father, when Claudia was fifteen years of age, she had left behind a note for Claudia. Along with the pendant.

*I leave this here with you, as a promise I will return to you one day soon, little sister.*

Claudia closed her fingers around the pendant now.

*Maybe you might have forgotten about the promise you made me, Serisa,* she thought. *But I haven't. We will go back to the way we used to be. I'll make sure of it.*

Claudia allowed her eyelids to droop shut, succumbing to exhaustion. As sleep came up to meet her in a gentle rise, Claudia fell into a memory of her sister's voice, singing a familiar tune.

*Little bird, little bird*
*Break your chains and fly away*
*Don't let them catch you*
*Don't let them break you*
*Fly away, straight into my embrace . . .*

# CHAPTER 18
# SERISA

"Well," Ves said, "that could have gone better."

"Indeed," was all Serisa said.

She and Ves sat together on a hilltop overlooking an empty paddock. In the distance, Serisa could see the black shapes of a couple of houses. They had already made a quick stop at one of them as they passed by. Inside they had found an elderly human couple. Most definitely younger than Serisa's one hundred years and Ves's two hundred and eleven, yet next to the ageless vampyrics, they had looked nearly decrepit with their wrinkled and spotted skin and stooped figures.

Still, they had done an almost admirable job of putting up a fight—the man had actually managed to graze Serisa's leg with his pitchfork—even if it were in vain. For what could humans as old as feeble as they hope to do against two vampyrics?

Now the pair of them lay dead in the grass at Serisa and Ves's feet. Their bodies almost entirely drained of blood and their faces twisted into permanent expressions of horror.

"Maybe if we had focused on getting away with the remnant while we had it," said Ves, "instead of staying to fight, things might have turned out differently."

Serisa cast the other vampyric a sideways glare. Like Serisa, Ves's mouth was coated in blood, which had also dripped onto much of her front. The stub on her right arm where her hand had been had long since stopped bleeding and was already beginning to scar over.

"Are you scolding me, Ves?" Serisa asked her.

Unfazed, she answered, "Merely making an observation."

Serisa huffed a humourless laugh. She watched as a fox darted through the grass in the paddock. "The sight of that human—a *Slayer* —and with my sister no less . . . may have gotten the best of me."

It was true. Just the sight of a human these days made the blood in Serisa's veins pound with loathing. Stronger even than the desire to feed from them.

And Slayers were the worst kind of human. Hunting monsters for petty gold. Mutilating their bodies to either sell off like commodities or to make macabre decorations out of them. To hang them like trophies on their walls.

The image of her father's skull locked behind that glass cabinet, flashed before Serisa's eyes. She closed her eyes and tried to swallow back the fury.

Knowing that Claudia—her own *sister*—was working alongside one to thwart Serisa's ambition, felt like the deepest betrayal. Worse even than when Claudia had spoken against her at the castle. And it was no slight that Serisa would soon forget. Or allow to go unpunished.

"We shall regroup with the others," Serisa announced, rising from the rock she had perched upon. "And we will begin our hunt again."

"And how will we do that?" Ves asked. "Claudia and that Slayer could be anywhere in Vil Tresar, and that creepy fucking skull from the strega won't talk to us anymore."

"Well then, my dear Ves, we shall just have to pay old Brucca another visit." With a grin she added, "Maybe she can spare us another creepy fucking skull?"

Ves indulged her with a rare bout of laughter.

For the first time in what felt like an eternity, the black shroud of her sorrow did not feel so heavy.

# INTERLUDE

The first thing Serisa heard was singing.

*"Little bird, little bird*
*Break your chains and fly away*
*Fly over the treetops and fly over the mountains*
*Fly through the clouds and let the wind caress your wings*
*Little bird, little bird . . ."*

"I . . . know that song."
"Do you now?" said the singing voice.
"I used to . . . sing it to someone."
"Who did you sing it to?"
But the darkness pulled her under before she could answer.

The next time Serisa awoke, lucidness stayed to ward off the shadows that grasped at her mind. Few things were immediately apparent to her. She was lying in a bed, in a small, unfamiliar, shadowed room. A thick sheet of cloth was hung up over the lone window across the room. Acting as a protective veil against the sunlight, only the weakest traces managed to make its way through.

Something else that was immediately apparent to her was the

awful sting in her side whenever she so much as twitched. Memories came rushing forward to greet her; her fight with the Slayer, him stabbing her with a silver blade between her ribs right before he died, passing out from the pain of it in the middle of the forest.

And then, slower to come but harder to hit, was the reminder of her father. Of learning about his death and discovering a vampyric's skull that could only have been his in the Slayer's home.

Serisa clutched at the blanket over her body until her nails tore through the fabric. She wanted to sob. She wanted to scream and rage and break everything in sight, and then tear the world apart. She also wanted to see her father again. To hear him call her name with affection as he had always done, and to have him hold her in his arms.

The loss of both her parents rent open a chasm in her heart, deep and endless and painful, and she did not know how it could ever be healed.

The creaking of the door being opened almost had Serisa bolting upright. She turned her head against the pillow to see a woman enter. She wore simple peasant garb; plain skirts and a plain blouse. She had an olive complexion and long, golden-brown curls which were tied back with only a few stray strands left to frame her face. The woman looked as if she were around thirty years. In her hands she carried a bowl covered with a cloth.

"Oh, you're awake." The woman brightened when she saw Serisa blinking blearily up at her. "It's about time."

Serisa's brow furrowed as the woman came to stand beside the bed. "Who are you? Where am I?"

"Hm, I suppose I can't fault you for wanting to know that as soon as you wake up," said the woman, setting the covered bowl down on a nearby chair. "I'm Allegra and you are in my home. In my bedroom, more specifically. I found you in the woods two nights ago and doing a very poor job of keeping your blood in your body. So being the kind-hearted woman that I am, I brought you back here to tend to you."

Serisa lifted the blanket draped across her body. She realised she was without a shirt, and she saw only a glimpse of the bandaging wrapped around her waist before a stabbing pain in her side forced her to drop her arm with a hiss.

"Well, I managed to heal you somewhat," admitted Allegra. "I never have been a particularly talented sorcerer."

That was when Serisa finally noticed the amethyst amulet hanging from the woman's neck with a thin bronze chain.

Allegra must have caught her eyeing the amulet at her throat. "That being said, I can still manage to summon a great big ball of fire, if I wanted to. So don't get any ideas about using me as a drinking fountain."

Serisa's eyes drifted closed. She still felt weak and exhausted, and an uncomfortable pressure was beginning to build between her temples. "You talk too much," she muttered.

Her words were rewarded with soft laughter that was almost soothing to Serisa's ears. "So I've been told," Allegra said.

Serisa cracked her eyes open enough to see Allegra lifting the covered bowl.

"I imagine you need to eat—or drink—to keep your strength up," she told Serisa. "So I had this prepared for you."

She pulled the cloth away from the bowl and held it out to Serisa. For a disorienting moment, Serisa thought she was being offered some stew. It was her nose that caught on before her mind did, and told her that no, it was not stew, it was blood.

Saliva pooled in her mouth and any lethargy left in her fled as her body finally realised how thirsty she was. Serisa hadn't even realised she had tried to sit up until searing pain knifed through her and she gasped.

"Don't move so quickly," Allegra warned her. The sorcerer moved forward, putting an arm around Serisa's back, helping her to sit up without aggravating her wound.

"It took me almost all morning to catch enough rabbits for this." Allegra passed her the bowl of blood.

Had Serisa been in better shape, she might have wrinkled her nose at the idea of drinking animal blood—it did not have the same taste or nutrients as human blood, and most vampyrics avoided feeding off animals if they could. But right now, she felt starved, and she had no desire to test what the sorcerer might do to her if Serisa tried to take some of *her* blood.

So when she took the bowl in her hands, Serisa held it up to her mouth and drank. Ravenously.

It was thick and had lost much of its freshness. Still, every drop that passed along her tongue and down her throat felt like bliss. Like liquid healing pouring new life and strength into her veins.

When she had gulped down every drop of the rabbit blood, Serisa set the bowl down in her lap and realised that the sorcerer had already left.

ONCE THE SUN had gone down, Serisa wandered outside of the small, two-room cottage and found the sorcerer tending to a pen of chickens outside. But she was not feeding them. Instead, she was sitting on the ground while the creatures lay still beside her. She was singing.

*"Here in the meadow, lay down to sleep now*
*Surrounded by soft grass, flowers and old trees*
*The night will come, so lay down to sleep now*
*Dream of sweet and dream of peace*
*And when the dawn breaks, in the meadow*
*I will be waiting."*

"Why did you help me?" Serisa asked once Allegra was finished. "Not many humans would go out of their way to save an injured vampyric."

Allegra was stepping out of the pen, where her chickens remained dozing peacefully. Serisa had a fleeting thought that it did not seem safe for chickens to sleep out in the open at night, especially in the middle of a forest, but she supposed it was entirely possible Allegra had warded the pen to keep out foxes and other predators.

"I will admit," said the sorcerer, brushing off her skirts, "when I first came across you lying there, and I realised what you were, I did intend to leave you."

The admission came as no surprise to Serisa. What did surprise her was the brief prick of hurt. Keeping her expression impassive, she asked, "So what changed your mind?"

Allegra looked at her, both her brown eyes and her hair looked almost black in the dark. There was a sad smile on her face.

"I saw you were crying."

* * *

THE SILVER WOUND in Serisa's side took much longer to heal than was normal. For days, she often found it difficult to move without causing pain like she was being stabbed with the silver blade all over again. For much of that time she found herself confined to the sorcerer's bed, while the sorcerer slept without complaint on a couch outside the bedroom.

One night Serisa had wandered outside the bedroom to find Allegra curled up on the couch and snoring softly beneath a thin blanket. The curtains of the window above had been left drawn apart and silver shafts of moonlight lit the quaint little room and haloed the sorcerer's body. Limning strands of her hair in white.

Serisa stood there for a long time, doing nothing but watching Allegra's sleeping face.

When she finally did wander back to the bedroom, Serisa went to her belongings, which had been left by a stool in the corner, untouched for days now.

There she found the scale she had taken from the Slayer's house. Again, when she touched it, she heard the nightmarish roar, and saw flashes of great winged beasts breathing fire.

When the visions passed just as quickly as they came, like the last time, and Serisa found herself staring down at the scale piece, she was now convinced of what she held in her palms.

*Who would have thought?* she thought not without some wonder, rubbing her thumb on the hardened surface of the scale. *That I would be the one to find Ombral's remnant.*

The sorcerer didn't know of what was under her roof, could she? No, surely if she did, she would have made some sort of mention of it and would not have simply left it on a stool with Serisa's clothes.

Still, Serisa felt it best not to leave the remnant lying around in the open. Clutching it close, she looked around the tiny room, before settling with kneeling on the floor by the bed and lifted one of the loose floorboards with only the smallest crackling sound.

Serisa placed the remnant in the little nook in the floor before replacing the floorboard over it, satisfied that it would be well hidden there.

Now feeling worn and sore, Serisa climbed back into the bed. As she drifted into sleep, she realised it had never once occurred to her to attack the sorcerer while she was defenceless.

* * *

The more Serisa healed, the more she started making nightly excursions. Sometimes it was merely to stretch her legs by wandering the grounds close to the sorcerer's cottage—within the wards Allegra kept up to keep away unwanted visitors. Or to watch Allegra go about some nightly, mundane chores, such as sweeping, cleaning dishes, or singing a lullaby to her chickens.

One evening, Serisa even joined her while she stalked through the forest, hunting for more woodland critters she could feed to Serisa—sadly she was still quite adamant about not letting Serisa drink any of her blood.

Serisa could not remember a time in her life where she needed blood this constantly. Vampyrics needed only one or two good feeds a month. But with her body still trying to recover from that silver blade, she needed to build her strength.

"I must ask," she said to Allegra as they traipsed through the forest, thick with old oaks and prickly scrub, "what is a woman such as yourself doing living in seclusion like this?"

"Perhaps I simply like my own company," was all Allegra said. She had conjured a glowing orb of soft, white light that floated in the air ahead and lit the way for them—or for Allegra at least, since Serisa could see perfectly well without the light.

Serisa deftly stepped over a fallen tree branch. "And that of your chickens."

Silence stretched out between them until Allegra finally said, "I ran afoul of the wrong people a while back. I'd rather not meet them again."

She didn't elaborate any further and Serisa didn't pry. There were many things she still kept from the sorcerer; despite all she had done for her.

*Let her hold onto her secrets while I hold onto mine.*

Allegra's ball of light began to wane before rapidly flickering out of existence.

"Oh, damn it," the sorcerer muttered and Serisa could see her tapping at her amulet. "I knew I should have just brought a lantern."

Serisa opened her mouth to ask why Allegra even bothered using magic when she could hardly even keep a ball of light going for more than a moment or two, when she saw the woman stumble.

With the conjured light gone, Allegra could no longer clearly see the ground in front of her. But Serisa could. She saw the sharp dip in the earth before Allegra's feet. Saw Allegra take a step forward, expecting there to be ground where there wasn't.

As Allegra pitched forward, a startled cry on her lips, Serisa dashed towards her. Her arms went around Allegra, pulling her back and holding her firm against Serisa's own body.

She could feel Allegra's heart beating hard with her startled breaths, where her back was pressed to Serisa's front. With her chin rested upon Allegra's shoulder, Serisa could practically hear the quick beat of the pulse at her neck. It would be so easy; to turn her head and sink her fangs into the delicate skin. Taste the blood flowing through the warm body she now held in her arms.

She might have given into such a temptation, had Allegra not chosen that moment to turn her head and Serisa found herself looking into a pair of wide, brown eyes, and suddenly felt hopelessly and inexplicably captivated.

She felt curls of Allegra's hair brush against her own cheek in a way that sent pleasant shivers coursing down her skin. Allegra's parted lips were only scant inches away from her own now.

Serisa felt a new desire rise up within her.

"U-Um . . . thank you for that," Allegra murmured. Serisa could feel her breaths against her lips. "But you can let me go now."

"Right," was all Serisa said before unwinding her arms from around Allegra and the woman stepped away, creating a new distance between them. One that Serisa could not say she appreciated very much.

But then, Allegra's eyes flickered up to meet Serisa's again. She smiled. It was small and somewhat uncertain, but something about it made Serisa's own heartbeat quicken.

CHAPTER 19

# KAS

EVER SINCE KAS was twelve years old, there were nights where her dreams tormented her with the memories of her family's murder. Nightmares that would wake her up screaming when she was younger, and in cold sweats and gasping breaths now.

And it seemed that this was one of those nights.

Kas's dream started in the gardens of her family's manor house. On a gorgeous, sun-lit afternoon. She stood apart, watching her mother and father, who sat at the table beneath a white gazebo with intricate stonework that seemed to glow in the sunlight. They were smiling with each other and sipping tea from painted porcelain cups. Julus and Alvera bickered playfully. Lorenzo was on all fours in the grass, joining in on one of Ria and Givann's games. He was pretending to be a horse, making his younger siblings squeal with laughter with his snorting and exaggerated neighing sounds. They were all dressed in white.

"Kasanna," her father hailed her, a bright smile on his handsome face.

"Come join us, dear," her mother called out in her melodious voice.

Kas took a step forward, eager to join her family.

Then, the sun disappeared, like a candle being blown out, casting the world in grey shadow.

And out of the shadow came the monsters.

They swarmed all over the gardens, and the peaceful idyllic scene before Kas turned to one of horror. A gryphon descended from the sky and sank its talons into her elder sister's back, carrying her screaming, bleeding form out of sight. A pack of ghastlies swarmed Givann and Ria, tearing them apart like paper dolls.

Then came the vampyrics. Their faces were a blur to Kas, their only discernible features were their glinting fangs on display with too-wide smiles.

Kas found she could not move. Fear had grown roots from her feet that burrowed deep into the earth below her, keeping her in place. Despite her years of training, of slaying monsters, she was just as helpless to protect her loved ones as she had been that night ten years ago.

Out of the bloodbath, Kas saw her mother racing towards her. Her radiant smile was gone, now replaced by naked terror. Her white dress was dyed crimson, and her red hair had come loose from its chignon and trailed behind her like a flame.

*"Kasanna,"* she cried. *"Kas.* Help us! *Why won't you help us?"*

She reached a hand for her daughter.

Kas reached out for her in turn.

*"Mother!"*

If she could only take her mother's hand, perhaps she could save her.

Her mother came to a halt. Her body jerked with a sickening sound, and Kas saw a blade—no, a hand with claws like knives on each fingertip—had torn clean through her mother's chest, spilling an endless torrent of blood that turned the green grass scarlet.

Kas opened her mouth to scream but no sound came out. She watched her mother fall to the ground, revealing the killer who stood behind her.

A pale figure with long, glittering white hair, and pale blue eyes.

Kas felt a presence at her back. When she turned around, she only had enough time to see a giant, winged creature in the air, before a spiral of burning, blinding flame consumed her.

Kas awoke with a muffled shout, sitting up so fast, it made her head spin.

Awareness flooded back to her with dizzying speed. She wasn't in the gardens of her old family home, but in a forest. An old oak towering above her. There was no glimmering sunlight, or ominous grey skies, but instead the black-blue sky of night dotted with stars.

The werecat—Aara—slept in her cat form. Curled up on a thick tree root near Kas. Her side moving up and down in even breaths.

Claudia was kneeling at her side. Her hair looked as if it had been spun from one of the stars above them.

Kas had to force herself not to flinch away when she remembered Claudia and her white hair standing above the torn body of Kas's mother in her dream.

She also realised that Claudia had been calling to her.

"What?" she asked, her voice roughened with sleep.

"Something is coming our way," whispered Claudia.

The last dregs of sleep cleared from Kas's mind, and she was immediately on alert. "What? Where?" She reached for her sword which she kept tucked beneath her bed roll.

Claudia pointed to the nearby clearing, bathed in pale moonlight. There Kas spotted the black shape of Wolf. Sitting as still as stone, back turned to them, as if awaiting something.

"I've heard it coming for a while now," said Claudia. "At first, I thought it was just an animal, but Wolf had an . . . odd reaction when he heard it. He got up and just sat there and wouldn't respond to me."

"You don't think it's your sister and your other vampyric friends?" Kas suggested.

Claudia pointedly ignored the obvious jab. "No. I sense only one, and its movement is slow and lumbering. Definitely not a vampyric."

Kas looked over to where Bod was tied only a short stretch away, by one of the trees. As a Slayer's horse, Bod was trained to sense and alert Kas when a threat was near, whether it be monster or human. Yet he stood completely calm, head lowered in sleep and tail switching lazily every so often.

This eased Kas somewhat. Still, she took up her sword as she pushed herself to her feet and moved toward Wolf alongside Claudia.

They stood in the shadow of a tree line that stood before a small clearing, bisected by a stream dotted with smooth river stones. Over the gentle rush of the water, Kas heard the telltale sounds of someone —or something—approaching. The crackling of twigs and crunch of grass under heavy, languorous footfalls.

Kas crouched low to the ground, tightening her grip on the hilt of her sword. Out of the corner of her eye, she noticed Claudia echo her movements. She had her elegant rapier with its gold hilt patterned with roses, out at the ready.

First Kas noticed a shadow from behind the tree line across the clearing. Then it emerged out into the open and Kas saw it for what it was.

Her hold on her sword loosened, tension seeping from her body.

At first glance, it looked like an elk, with its two large antlers branching off from either side of its head. But after that first glance, one could soon realise that it was no elk. It stood far too tall, its body was shorter and bulkier, and instead of being covered in brown hair, what looked like long tangles of moss hung from its body, swaying with every step of its hoofed feet. The moss-like fur also hung from its antlers, and around its neck like a mane.

The most disconcerting thing about the creature, however, was its head. Instead of being made of flesh, all that was visible was bone, patched here and there with that same mossy fur that covered the rest of its body. It was reminiscent to that of a deer skull, with no visible eyes, only eye sockets, and an elongated snout that tapered off into a nasal cavity and canines like a mountain lion.

"It's an alderbeast," Kas said, keeping her voice low, only so as not to startle the creature.

Claudia gave her a look. "A what?"

"It's a forest guardian, of sorts. They're rare monsters. Very few of them still roam Vil Tresar."

The alderbeast walked further into the clearing, bending its long shaggy neck to drink from the stream.

"And it's not a danger to us?" Claudia asked, still not taking her wary eyes off the alderbeast.

"No," Kas replied. "Unless you mean to fell a tree or hunt an animal that lives in this forest, then that alderbeast means us no harm."

As if to help prove Kas's words true, Wolf stood and padded into the clearing, approaching the drinking alderbeast. Kas noticed Claudia go tense. She looked as if she were about to leap after the wolf and pull him back.

Kas placed a restraining hand on the other woman's shoulder— and felt the almost imperceptible jolt beneath her fingers. "Easy," she said. "Just watch."

Claudia's wolf was standing in the middle of the clearing with the alderbeast now. The alderbeast raised its head to regard Wolf. The two of them stood nose to nose in a quiet moment.

Kas felt Claudia relax, and then, realising that she still had her hand on the half-vampyric's shoulder, snatched it away.

"Have you ever had to slay an alderbeast, before?" Claudia asked her, still observing Wolf and the alderbeast.

Kas shook her head. "This is my first time seeing one that wasn't drawn in some monster encyclopedia at the Keep. Tsurra had to slay one a few years ago, after some villagers chopped down trees in its territory. She said it was one of the most formidable monsters she's ever faced."

"Tsurra? Is she your mother?"

Kas snorted a laugh. "She would like to think so. But no, she's my mentor. She was the one who found me after my family was killed by vampyrics when I was a child and brought me into the world of monster slaying."

Claudia looked at Kas with surprise in her pale eyes, that morphed into something more sombre. "I'm sorry to hear that. About your family."

The words spoken and the genuine sympathy behind them caught Kas completely off guard. Clearing her throat, all she found she was able to say was, "It was a long time ago."

"Who would have thought, Slayer? The two of us actually have something in common."

"Which is?"

"Dead family."

More speech that caught Kas by surprise. "You never did say what became of your mother and father?"

"I told you it was my father who raised me," Claudia said. "But when I was ten years of age, the Red Plague came to Trulio and my father was one of the many villagers who was claimed by it."

Kas had some recollection of hearing about the insidious illness that spread like wildfire through most of the south. She remembered overhearing a conversation between her parents and their friends one drizzly, grey morning. They had talked of a disease that seemed to live in the air and claimed its victims with scorching fevers and red boils all over the body before taking their lives.

"Thank the Saints, it's only in the south," an older woman whose name Kas could no longer remember had sighed.

To which, Kas's father had replied, "For now, at least."

But the Red Plague had never reached so far as Veldenier. A cure had been found before it could travel all over Vil Tresar.

At least Kas could say she had never had to experience the horrors of a plague first-hand in her youth.

In the clearing Wolf was leaping around the alderbeast, as if trying to entice it to play. However the alderbeast seemed content only to graze and rub its antlers against one of the nearby trees.

"Being half-vampyric meant that I was immune to the disease," Claudia continued. "After my father died, I went to find my mother and live with her. My father always told me that she lived high up in the mountains to the west of our village. But after learning of my father's passing, she fell into this pit of despair that no one could pull her from. Eventually, she took her own life. The only one who was really there for me after my father died . . . was my sister."

"The same sister who tried to kill us and wants to end the world as we know it?" Kas asked archly.

The remark earned her a half-smile from Claudia, but there was no humour behind it. Only thinly veiled sadness.

"She took care of me," said Claudia. "The other vampyrics despised me. They hated the idea that their leader would turn away from her husband and lie with a human and I was a reminder of that. I was *unnatural*. But Serisa never seemed to mind. She was more of a mother to me than our own ever was. Until she left and . . ."

Her words trailed off, but Kas thought she could guess the unspoken words.

*"And I was left alone."*

Kas's attention was stolen by the alderbeast in the clearing. Its head was tipped towards the sky. It was making a sound not too unlike the howling of a wolf, only deeper, and musical. Kas wondered if it was a call to the forest. To reassure it and all its inhabitants of its presence and its protection.

When it finished, the alderbeast shook its head, as if clearing away flies, and then plodded through the grass, crossing the clearing until it reached the next tree line, and disappeared from view.

With the alderbeast gone, Kas felt as if she had snapped out of some sort of spell.

*What in the hells are you doing? Talking with Claudia like that?*

She had shared more than she should have with the vampyric and learned more of her than she needed to.

That wouldn't do.

Continuing to talk with each other as they just did would only lead to familiarity.

It would lead to *sympathy*.

Wolf came lopping back to them. Claudia greeted him with a rub behind the ear before pushing herself to her feet.

"I believe I am due for some sleep now," she said, her tone airy. "Be a dear and take over the watch."

She didn't wait for Kas to respond before she sauntered back over to where they had been sleeping and claimed Kas's bedroll for herself.

Kas couldn't even find herself to be annoyed by it.

She was too busy being annoyed with herself.

*You're not going to get familiar with this woman—this* vampyric, she told herself. She stared out at the clearing, turned silver by the moonlight, where the alderbeast had stood. As she did, she remembered snatches from the dream she had awoken from. Of vampyrics coming to butcher her family. Of the one with white hair that looked so like Claudia, smiling as she cut down Kas's mother.

*You're not going to feel anything for her but indifference. She's a vampyric. She's a monster.*

# CHAPTER 20
# CLAUDIA

THEY CROSSED into the Verillino province three days later. They had left behind the dense forests of Nescoro and traded them for rolling green hills, vineyards and farmland dotted with windmills as far as the eye could see.

They were also fortunate enough to come by a village where Claudia was able to procure herself a new horse, a bay mare with a sweet disposition, and replace some of the items she had lost during their encounter with the strega and the Salvaclare vampyrics.

She had not been able to find a replacement satchel, however. So, the remnant stayed tucked away in one of Kas's saddlebags. Claudia found that the idea of the Slayer holding onto the remnant didn't bother her as much as it once did.

The horse was not the only new addition to their little company. Aara, the werecat, had refused to leave them, no matter how much Kas demanded—and at one point begged—she do so. The girl clung to them as stubbornly as moss to a stone. Aara also turned out to be quite the songstress, often filling their days on the road with her singing. Which so happened to consist of the same few filthy songs that one would expect to find in a seedy back-alley tavern.

"Saints," Kas groaned, interrupting Aara's ballad about a succubus and a high priest, "Will you shut the hells up already?"

Aara only sung louder.

As they travelled, the openness of their surroundings made Claudia uneasy. It would be far too easy for Serisa or any other monster to spot them like this. Any moment now, she expected them to fall under attack because they were out on the open roads with no forestation to obscure their journey from unwanted eyes. Of course, no such thing ever eventuated. Their travel along the winding roads was utterly tranquil and uneventful. Even the weather had been nothing short of perfect. The sun so bright and unobstructed in the sky that Claudia was forced to keep her hood up so her skin didn't become too irritated.

On the fifth day, they passed by a farmer toiling in a field of bright yellow sunflowers, next to a red farmhouse.

"Wouldn't be goin' down that a way, if I were you," he called out to them, in the gruff, rolling accent of the eastern provinces.

Kas was the first to bring her stead to a halt. "And why is that, good sir?"

"Been word the village a few miles up the road has been hit with a horrible illness. Fever and vomiting for days. Heard someone even died of it. Some worried it could be the start of a new plague. Sintiarn Lusin and the high priest put out a warning for no one to go near." The man spat out a seed from whatever it was he'd been chewing on. "If you keep goin' that way, you'll only find guards that will turn you away."

The mention of plague stirred unpleasant memories in Claudia. A dark and foul-smelling room. A doctor in a black mask, shaped like a crow's beak, trying to drag her away from her home, because she was healthy and should be kept far away from the village. Her father, deathly white where he wasn't covered in painful-looking red boils, and lying on sheets covered in bile and blood, no matter how many times Claudia tried to wash them.

"I see," Kas was saying. "I suppose we'll have to find another way to get to where we're going." She wheeled Bod around. "Thank you for the warning."

The farmer offered them a tip of his hat and returned to his work while they went back the way they'd came.

"So where do we go now?" Claudia asked, drawing her horse beside Kas's. "If I'm not mistaken this was our fastest way to Almora. And the only other road I know of is through the mountains and will add weeks to our journey."

"Not to fret," said Kas. "I know of another—quicker—way to Almora."

By midafternoon, they found themselves in the port town of Lyancoso. A modest-sized town, nestled between craggy mountain faces, looking out upon a vast stretch of ocean. The salty brine of the sea clung heavily to the air, and the raspy cries of seabirds could be heard even above the bustle of the town.

As they drew nearer to the docks, Claudia spotted a duo of burly men in sleeveless jackets, revealing heavily tattooed arms. They were manning a stall on the side of the road that was laden with animal pelts, curling deer antlers, and the ivory tusks of walruses. Poachers. One of the men was sharpening a wicked-looking hunting knife. When he noticed Claudia watching, he leered at her with missing teeth.

"So your plan is for us to reach Almora by boat?" said Claudia, once they reached the docks, which was playing host to a number of vessels of different shapes and sizes.

"It's either a few days at sea, or, as you mentioned before, we're up for a mountainous trek that could take us weeks," Kas replied.

"I've never been on a boat before," Aara said, leaping down from behind Claudia so she could get a better look at the sea. Its deep blue surface rippled and glimmered in the noon-day light. The breeze ruffled her hair and almost lifted her cap off her head. "I'm not sure if I'm excited or scared."

"You're always welcome to stay behind," offered Kas.

Aara scowled and poked her tongue out at the Slayer.

"You wait here with the horses while Claudia and I look for a boat." Kas said to Aara as she passed the girl her horse's reins.

"Why do I have to watch the horses? Why can't Claudia?"

"Because I trust Claudia alone in a street full of people about as far as I could toss one of those boats."

"But what is even the point of having those tree trunks for arms if you can't throw one little boat?" Claudia teased, which earned her an unimpressed glare.

"Oh, and I'll need some of your coin as well." Kas held her hand out to the werecat.

Aara took a step back. "Coin? What coin?"

Kas's face turned stern. "Don't start with me. I know you've got money in that bag of yours that you probably stole off someone else."

Aara opened her mouth as if to argue, before clearly thinking better of it. With a slump of her shoulders, she fished around in her pack and pulled out a ratty-looking coin purse that looked full to bursting.

"Do I have to give you all of it?" she asked mournfully.

"Do you want me to dump you in a grimy port town prison for being a thief?"

Aara handed over the purse. During the exchange, Claudia took out the remnant from Kas's saddlebag, tucking it through her belt at her back, where it would be well hidden by her cloak, before she left with Kas. It wasn't that she did not trust Aara alone with the remnant, she simply felt more confident in her own ability to keep it out of thieving hands.

"Most of these ships look like merchant vessels," Claudia noted after a while of silently walking together. "Not passenger boats."

"Any ship will take a passenger or two if you put the right amount of crowns into the right hands," Kas said, surveying the ships they passed.

"Speaking from experience, are you?"

"My mentor, Tsurra, lived in this town before she became a Slayer and shared a few words of wisdom."

It came as a surprise to Claudia that Kas would share even such a miniscule piece about her life, just as it had surprised her that night in the Nescoro forests, when the Slayer told her about her family.

Claudia could not help but feel as though something had shifted between them ever since that night where they had both opened up to one another about their pasts. She could not quite put her finger on it, but it felt like a burgeoning familiarity. It felt as though Kas was beginning to see her as something other than a monster.

While lost in thought, Claudia almost hadn't realised that Kas had come to a halt. Claudia followed her gaze to a modest-sized merchant vessel moored to the gangway in front of them. Its lowered sails were vermillion and the ship's beakhead was decorated by a bronzed carving of a mermaid; a beautiful human woman with a long, curling fish tail and flowing hair.

People that could only be the ship's crew were hurrying back and forth along the vessel, carrying cargo crates up the gangplank and shouting at one another. She could see no name on the ship from where they stood.

"I think this one'll do," said Kas. "They appear to be preparing to set sail, so it's perfect timing."

She didn't wait for Claudia's input before making her way towards the ship.

Wolf made a rumbling sound beside her.

"Buck up, Wolf. This will be an experience for you."

Following Kas, they approached a young man standing near the gangplank, stacking crates. He was without a shirt, displaying an upper body-physique covered with deep mahogany-coloured skin that Claudia found all too pleasing to look at.

"Preparing to cast off?" Kas said by way of greeting.

The young man clapped his hands together and turned his full attention to them. "Aye. Though it might still be a while yet before we can do so."

"I see. And you're headed to Almora?"

"That we are, miss. Helping to deliver some of the finest foods, wines and fabrics this side of Vil Tresar has to offer."

"What about people?" Claudia asked this time.

The young man's dark eyes turned to her and lingered for a beat or two. He looked as if he'd been clubbed over the head, an almost stupefied expression gracing his features. Ignoring Kas's exasperated look, Claudia offered him a wink and a smile.

He grinned. His teeth were startlingly white for a sailor. "No people this time around, no. My name is Linos, by the way."

"Well, Linos," Kas nudged herself back into the conversation, "we are also looking for passage to Almora. So would you be willing to add three passengers to your cargo?" She produced the coin pouch from her belt. "I can compensate you."

Linos offered them a rueful smile. "Ah, you see ladies, the decision isn't up to me. If you want to sail with us, you'll have to ask the captain."

"Fair enough. Then where might we have a word with your captain?"

Linos pointed them in the direction of the local tavern, *The Seven Cups.* A dingy building, with a lop-sided, slate roof crammed into the middle of a narrow street.

"All right," said Kas as they stood outside the tavern. "Claudia and I will find the captain. Aara, you—"

"Watch the horses, I know."

"And Wolf," Claudia added.

Inside, it was mostly dark, only the barest streams of daylight coming in through the shuttered front windows. Candlelight did the rest of the work. The room was crowded, with sailors looking for a last drink before they set off or enjoying their first since arriving on land. Further across the room, Claudia spied a bearded man sitting at a bench, speaking to a woman. He grabbed her by the wrist and swung her onto his lap, causing her to scream with laughter. Throwing her arms around the man's neck, she planted a kiss on his bristled cheek.

Towards the back was a rowdy group gathered around a table.

They all seemed to be paying attention to a woman who had her black, leather boots propped up on the table. She wore a dark coat and a captain's hat upon her shoulder-length, black curls. She took a long drink from her tin mug, and said something that made the men and women around her roar with laughter.

"That must be her," Claudia said, pointing out the woman to Kas.

"Captain Luisa?" Kas questioned as they approached the table. "Of *The Sea Saint*?"

Captain Luisa Lark downed her drink and set it down heavily on the table before turning a scrutinising, dark-eyed gaze on Claudia and Kas. "Who's asking?"

"Kas of Veldenier, and this is Claudia of Trulio. We'd like passage aboard your ship to Almora."

"We already spoke to a man named Linos, about it, but he told us it was a decision that needed to come from you," added Claudia.

Captain Luisa grinned. Claudia could see the resemblance to the young man they spoke to on the docks. "I raised a smart lad. You want to know how I did that?"

When neither Kas nor Claudia answered, the captain continued. "Because *I'm* smart. I keep my head down and don't ask too many questions. I know how to pick my fights and I know when someone looks like trouble. And you two, you look like trouble."

"Appearances can be deceiving," Claudia said.

"You tryin' to tell me your friend with the scars and the sword strapped to her back is actually some pacifistic priestess?"

"Actually, I'm a Slayer," Kas explained.

"Well, that proves it," said the captain. "You Slayers make a living off finding trouble."

"Could be bad luck to have you aboard *The Saint*," said the man sitting to the captain's left. He was missing two front teeth and had coloured beads hanging from his goatee.

There was murmur of agreement from the others gathered round the table.

*Is there such a thing as a sailor that isn't superstitious?* Claudia wondered.

Claudia expected Kas to either try to convince the captain to let them aboard, or to simply walk away. What she did not expect was for Kas to pull up her own chair at the table and hail the passing serving woman.

"Two cold ales," she said, handing over two crowns. "It's on me."

"You think you can convince me to let you aboard by buying me a drink?" Captain Luisa wondered with an arched brow.

"Not exactly," said Kas with an easy grin. "But you strike me as a woman who enjoys a good drink and good games, no?"

The unimpressed look on the captain's face morphed into one of intrigue. It was then that the serving woman returned, placing two tall tankards of frothy amber liquid on the table between Kas and the captain sitting across from her.

Kas lifted the tankard closest to her. "I propose a little drinking contest. If I finish first, you let us aboard your ship when you set sail, for half the price you would normally charge to take passengers."

"And if I win?"

"Then we bid you farewell and leave you with this." Kas tossed the coin purse onto the table. It made a heavy thud, and one of the crew let out an impressed whistle. "Double the number of crowns we would have paid, had you agreed to take us aboard."

Captain Luisa bared her teeth in what Claudia could only describe as a predator's grin. "All right, Slayer. You're on." She reached for the other tankard, as the group around the table cheered.

Claudia leaned down to murmur in Kas's ear. "Are you sure this is really a good idea? Risking so much coin like this?"

Kas shooed her away with a wave of her hand, as if she were an irritating fly. Claudia fought the urge to swat the back of Kas's head in return.

"Shall we begin?" Kas said to the captain.

"Prepare to say farewell to all those crowns."

They locked eyes with each other, before, moving at the same time, they lifted their cups to their lips and tipped their heads back.

The group surrounding them watched rapt, clapping their hands, thumping the table, and cheering on their captain.

Claudia watched on silently. Neither Kas nor the captain paused in their drinking once. Their throats bobbed rapidly as they gulped down as much of their ale as quickly as they could. Claudia supposed she had to commend them on that alone. She would have been choking on her drink by now.

A rivulet of dark amber trailed past Kas's mouth, down her jaw and slid down her neck, where Claudia's attention caught and held on the arch of her throat. A desire to touch her mouth to that spot pulsed through her. To taste the skin there. Scrape her teeth against it. Sink her fangs in—

Kas was the first to set her tankard down. Shortly followed by the captain. The metallic banging on the wood and the exclamations of the captain's group, shocking Claudia out of the stupor she had fallen into.

"Well, well," Captain Luisa announced, "there truly is a first time for everything."

"First time someone's beaten you in a drinking contest?" Kas asked, wiping the back of her hand against her mouth. Her face looked a little flushed.

"First time I've been beaten by a Slayer."

"So," said Kas, "about our agreement?"

Captain Luisa Lark threw her head back and barked a laugh that almost surpassed the rest of the noise in the tavern. "Aye you have a place aboard *The Sea Saint* when we leave tonight. I'm a woman of my word."

Claudia felt an unravelling of relief within her breast.

"A Slayer that can best the captain in a drinking contest might be good to have on board," said a woman with a blue bandana around her head.

"Could even be a good omen!"

*Saints.*

"You could be right," the captain said. She lifted her empty tankard. "How's about another round, to celebrate the Slayer and her companion that will be joining us on our voyage!"

The proclamation received a hearty cheer.

Four more rounds followed before Captain Luisa decided it was finally time to cast off. She and her crew headed off first, leaving Claudia and Kas to join them once they were ready.

Claudia, who had been sitting at the back, apart from the table of rowdy and tipsy sailors, approached Kas, who was still seated, her head pillowed on her folded arms on top of the table.

"How wonderful for you that your reckless little gambit paid off," said Claudia. "And you've even made some new friends. Delightful."

Kas replied with an unintelligible sound.

"Tell me, just how confident were you that you would win when you bet all those crowns?"

Kas turned her head in her arms and looked up at Claudia with half-lidded eyes, that were still so vividly green even in this dim lighting. Her mouth stretched up into a slow, satisfied smile. "I'm a good drinker."

Despite the slurred quality to her speech, she sounded so innocently pleased with herself, like a child waiting for words of praise and a pat on the head from their parent. Claudia couldn't even bring herself to voice some acerbic remark.

"I can see that," was all she said. And then, because she simply could not help herself while the Slayer's inhibitions were low, she reached out and tucked a piece of Kas's red hair behind her ear.

Claudia was sure that would have earned her hand a slap if Kas had been sober. Instead, Kas's eyes fluttered closed at the brief, feather-light touch. Claudia wanted to do it again, and let her touch linger.

*Enough, Claudia. Get a hold of yourself.* "We should be making our way back to the ship now."

"Claudia?" said Kas.

"Yes?"

"You may need to help me stand up."

WHEN THEY EXITED *The Seven Cups* with Kas's arm around Claudia's shoulders to keep her from stumbling over her own feet, they found the sky had darkened to a pinkish grey and streetlamps were already being lit. They also found Aara still waiting for them with Wolf and the horses.

"Well don't you look wasted," she said as soon as she saw Kas. There was some mischievous glee to her smile.

"I am hardly wasted," Kas protested. "Just a little bit tipsy."

Aara shrugged. "If you say so. Oh!" she reached into her coat pocket. "Look at what I found at one of the stalls on the streets!"

She held up a small bag made of moss-green felt. It hardly looked much bigger than her hand.

"Amazing," Kas drawled in a tone that showed she was certainly *not* amazed.

"But wait. There's more." Stepping over to Wolf, Aara took one of his front paws in hand and stuck it into the opening of the bag. Only it wasn't only Wolf's paw that was able to fit into the tiny bag. Aara was able to fit in his whole leg before he had enough and tugged his leg away.

"Now that is fascinating," said Claudia.

"Some woman was selling a bunch of magical items," Aara explained. "I thought this might be useful. You could use it to hide the remnant."

"Good thinking." Kas sounded a little stunned by her own admission.

"Wait." Claudia frowned. "We've had your money this whole time. How did you get this bag?"

The mischievous glint was back in her two-toned eyes. "Old habits sure do die hard."

"Maybe we should hurry and get on the ship," Kas said after a moment's silence between the three of them. "Before anyone comes screaming after us about thieving werecats."

## CHAPTER 21

# KAS

It would be a five-day voyage aboard *The Sea Saint*. Sailing along Verillino's coast until they reached Almora. Not an arduous journey, as Captain Luisa explained to them, and they would be within view of land the entire time.

"Do you ever have monster troubles when you're at sea?" Kas asked the captain and her son that first night.

"It's not unheard of for vessels to come into contact with the odd siren or merfolk," Linos answered. "But they rarely venture this close to land. The only monster we're likely to see are sea-imps, but they're harmless so long as you don't decide to go for a swim."

Kas, Aara and Claudia were each given a cabin to themselves—which was just as well seeing as the cabins were hardly big enough to fit *one* person. Their horses and Wolf were confined to the cargo hold. The captain had been reluctant to allow a wolf on board but had relented on the condition that he stay in the hold and on a length of rope.

This was not Kas's first journey by boat. She had a hazy memory of travelling by boat with her family to Tressino—an island off the west coast of Vil Tresar—where her aunt had lived. She wondered if her mother's sister, who once snuck Kas a lolly before bed, was still on the island.

And just as she had back then, Kas found herself growing restless while confined to a ship. But whereas back then, Kas had dealt with her restlessness by tormenting her siblings and exasperating her parents, she now had a better, less disruptive method.

Early in the morning of their second day out at sea, while the new sun was still rising and the sky was a canvas of soft shades of orange, pink, blue and lilac, Kas made her way onto the empty deck, with her sword in hand, and started practising her sword work.

Lunging forward, she struck at an imaginary opponent. The dawn light glinted off the silver edge of her blade.

These were moves she knew off by heart and had been practising since she was only a beginner swordsman learning the basics at the Slayers Keep. It was a simple set, but it helped to keep everything she knew about using a sword fresh in her mind and fresh in the memory of her muscles. And most importantly it helped wear down her restless energy.

The cool sea air against her skin and the briny scent of the ocean was surprisingly invigorating.

For a while the only witnesses to her practice was the endless ocean, the seabirds searching for their breakfast and a breaching humpback.

By the time Kas neared the end, the sun was higher in the sky and the crew of *The Sea Saint* were up and going about their morning duties. Kas had even garnered a small audience, and when she finally finished, they even offered her a round of applause.

"Remind me never to pick a fight with a Slayer," said one of the crewmen, a broad-shouldered man whose nose looked as if it had been broken once or twice before.

"Well, your monstrous mug might not help with that," Linos teased and there was a roar of laughter, infectious enough to make Kas grin as she wiped sweat from her chin.

As Kas went to lean her sword against the ship's gunwale and take a sip from her waterskin, she noticed Claudia approach her with an even and silent tread. Strands of her long hair drifted gently in the sea air and the pendant at the hollow of her throat winked when it caught the sun.

"You certainly know how to wield a sword," she said to Kas. An upward tilt to her lips.

Kas raised an eyebrow. "Is that so surprising?"

"Not at all." Claudia folded her arms and leaned her hip against the wale.

"I didn't even realise you were watching," Kas noted, pushing hair away from her damp forehead. "I thought you might still be in your cabin, getting as seasick as Aara." The werecat hadn't been able to keep her lunch down since they first set sail.

"Hardly," Claudia said. "I simply don't have much taste for the salty ocean air. All this sun is also irritating on my skin."

"Good to know," drawled Kas.

She would have gone on to ignore Claudia's presence, had the vampyric not spoken again.

"Seeing you practise like that gave me an idea."

"Should I be worried?"

"That depends. How do you feel about a friendly duel?"

Later, almost the entire crew had gathered on the deck. Even Captain Luisa had emerged from her quarters and was seated on the bottom of the steps that led to the bridge, grinning at something her first mate—the woman with the blue bandana—was saying. A pale-looking Aara had also made appearance, though she kept close to the side of the ship.

Kas stood in the middle of the deck, facing Claudia, her gold-hilted rapier in hand, and as Kas watched her, she wondered what exactly had possessed her to agree to Claudia's challenge? Perhaps it was a way of satiating the Slayer's need within her to fight the half-vampyric—partially at least, since this duel wouldn't end with Claudia's head rolling. Or maybe it was simply the challenging glint in Claudia's eyes when she proposed the idea. Kas had never been one to turn her back on a challenge after all.

Claudia eyed Kas's silver sword, though she did not look especially perturbed by it. Instead, she smiled as sharply as a knife point and said, "Try not to stab me through the heart, Slayer."

Kas returned the grin with one of her own. "Then I guess you better hope you're quick enough."

They came together in a quick clash of steel and silver before parting. Kas attacked again, her sword moving in a quick sequence of attacks.

Claudia countered each one. She teased Kas's blade with her own; only executing effortless flicks of her wrist and taps with her sword before moving out of range. She was quick on her feet, even without the use of her vampyric speed. She was hard to pin down and Kas felt almost like a bull trying to catch a spectre on the ends of its horns. She felt a begrudging swell of admiration for Claudia's skill.

It wasn't long before they'd gone down the deck and back up again. By then Kas could feel her breath starting to quicken and perspiration beginning to bead along her temples. Claudia, infuriatingly, was showing no signs of exertion at all.

"I would have thought you'd give me more of a challenge than this," Claudia said as they drew closer to the mast of the ship. Her teeth flashing in a haughty expression.

This time, when Kas attacked, she put all her strength and swiftness behind it. She had the satisfaction of seeing Claudia's blue eyes widen in the mere seconds she had to avoid taking the point of Kas's sword to her lithe neck.

Claudia's sword came up and met Kas's with a screech. She could practically feel every bit of strength Claudia was forced to call upon at such short notice so she could weather Kas's strike. Claudia's knuckles had gone bone-white on the hilt of her sword.

Kas's lips tugged into an involuntary grin. "Was that challenging enough for you?"

Now they were both fighting in earnest. Kas felt an odd thrill of delight at now having Claudia put in some of her best work. Kas was sure the grin from before had yet to leave her face.

"You *are* quite good," admitted Kas. She lunged forward.

"Was that ever in question?" Claudia responded. She parried.

Their swords rang against each other. Noise sounded from the rapt crew. All of that faded into the background for Kas. All her focus was on Claudia. On keeping up with her quicksilver movements. Claudia's sword work did not consist of any of the brutish, heavy-handedness she might have expected from a vampyric. Instead, she moved with the fluid grace of a dancer. Kas imagined it would have been mesmerising to watch had she not been on the receiving end of Claudia's attacks.

The bout was finally won by Claudia when Kas fell for a feint only to end up with the edge of the rapier kissing her throat.

There was silence for a time as they stood with Claudia's sword to Kas's throat, and just stared at each other. Kas's heart was a drumbeat in her chest and Claudia's breath was just as laboured as her own. A lock of hair was stuck to her flushed cheek with sweat.

There was something alive in those ice-blue eyes that had Kas lifting her hands into the air, and smiling as she said, "I yield."

CHAPTER 22

# CLAUDIA

"Saints, it was hard for my eyes to keep track of the two of you," said Aara from where she was sitting cross-legged on the cot in Claudia's cabin. "It was almost like trying to watch . . . two flies whizzing around each other."

"I couldn't have put it more poetically myself," said Claudia. She stood before the tiny, cracked mirror hung up on the wall as she pressed a damp rag to the back of her neck. Something rattled inside the chest where her belongings were stashed away. The waves outside had grown stronger and Claudia could feel their ebb and flow through the boards beneath her feet.

Aara made a sickened sound behind her.

"Are you all right?"

"I'm fine." The look on the girl's face said otherwise. Even her ears were pressed flat to her skull. "Where did you learn to wield a sword like that?"

"My sister taught me."

"The sister who wants to hunt us down and kill us all?"

Why did everyone feel the need to point that out? "Yes. I only have one sister, after all."

"Do you think—" An uncharacteristic shyness stole over Aara. Her tail flicked from side to side behind her. "Maybe you could . . . teach me how to fight with a sword?"

There was a hopefulness in Aara's eyes as she looked at Claudia that made her youth even more apparent. It also had Claudia wondering if that was how she used to look at Serisa.

"I—Yes," Claudia agreed. "When we're back on land, I'll teach you to use a sword."

A smile so wide and bright overtook Aara's face that it made Claudia's own lips turn up at the corners.

"Yes! I'd like to see Kas tell me I can't be a Slayer when she sees me use a sword as well as you can."

"It might take a bit of time before you're *that* skilled."

"You mean it might take me a few months of practice?"

Claudia, who had trained diligently with her blade almost every day since she was thirteen years old, said, "Yes . . . more or less."

"It's a good thing I'm a fast learner then," Aara said with a confident grin.

She left soon after—the captain's first mate had suggested Aara help out around the ship as a way to hold off her seasickness—and Claudia turned to face herself in the mirror once again. Her face was still pinked, and her thoughts kept returning to the duel from earlier. Of her sword against Kas's, of the wild look of enjoyment on the Slayer's face that mirrored the thrill pounding through Claudia's own veins.

It had been a long time since Claudia had sparred with someone. The last time she could remember was when she used to practice with Serisa in the castle courtyard. Under the blanket of night and surrounded by the long dead trees and overgrown gardens.

"You don't have claws of your own," Serisa had told her, the very first time she placed a sword in her younger sister's hands, "so perhaps this will do instead."

But sparring with Serisa had never been anything like sparring with Kas. Crossing swords with Kas had been exhilarating in a way she never would have anticipated.

It was—

Claudia doubled over. A pained gasp slipping past her lips.

The rag fell from her grip and onto the floor with a wet slap.

Pain burst in her middle and spread up to her skull and out to fingers and the tips of her toes. Like the way the surface of a lake rippled after having a stone dropped into it.

Then there was another painful pang, and a constricting pressure building between her temples. Everything tilted around her, though she knew it was not because of the boat. All of it at once was almost enough to make her retch.

*"Oh no,"* she gasped through a mouth that now felt much too dry. Her fangs had inched out of their own volition.

Dread settled in her gut alongside the pain flaring like hot coals brought to life.

It had been too long, she knew.

She had known it back in Lyancoso when she'd found herself gazing at Kas's neck.

But Claudia thought she'd have more time before she started to feel the effects.

She squeezed her eyes shut against another stab of pain, this one stronger than before.

Claudia sank to her knees and wrapped her arms around herself, as if that alone could stave off the agony she was about to endure.

CHAPTER 23

# KAS

THE DAYS WERE warm aboard *The Sea Saint* but the nights were cold once the sun dipped behind the horizon. On their fourth and final night at sea, Kas wandered onto the deck to take in the crisp, salty air. She could hear clearly the sound of the waves slapping against the ship's hull, and if she listened carefully, she could also hear the clicking of water imps beneath the water.

The deck appeared to be mostly deserted, many of the crew were down in the galley eating their dinner, but Kas did spot Aara, sitting atop a stack of crates, looking out over the dark expanse of ocean surrounding them, whistling a song Kas recognised from their time travelling together. She had taken off her cap and her triangular cat ears could be seen standing up from the mop of her unruly black hair.

"Do you only know lewd songs?" Kas asked, coming to stand beside Aara and look out at the water and the shadowy shapes of mountains visible in the distance.

"Well, they were the only songs I heard growing up," Aara answered. "My mum was the madam at a bordello. Most nights there would be singing and the girls didn't sing the Saints' hymns I can tell you that much."

"And where's your mother now? Don't you think she would be worried that you've disappeared to follow after Claudia and I?"

The wind picked up, ruffling Aara's hair. She was fiddling with something in her lap—a knife. "I doubt it. I haven't seen her in years. Not since she threw me out and told me never to step foot anywhere near her again."

"Was that when you turned?"

Aara was silent a moment, her ears turning back.

"That was when I told her I wasn't her son anymore."

Kas's brow lowered as understanding sunk in.

She studied the girl's profile, cast in the pale glow of one of the ship's lanterns. The rounded tip of her nose, the long lashes brushing the top of her cheekbone and the down-turned corner of her lips. For the first time, she looked not like a monster to Kas, but like a young girl.

Kas was not a parent, and she never intended to be one. Yet still she wondered how someone could turn their back on their child for choosing to live honestly and happily. Wasn't being a parent about loving one's child unconditionally?

She thought of her own mother and father, how they had never shown her anything but absolute love. She wondered at times if that love would have been so steadfast had they lived long enough to see Kas defy expectations for her to marry a nobleman from a good family and have children. Would they have been so accepting of her love for other women?

Tapping her finger against the flat of her knife, Aara said, "My ma, she—when I left, she said . . . well, she said a lot of things and it made me feel awful. Worthless. Sometimes I still feel that way. But maybe— maybe if I can just do something great in my life, something to prove that I'm *not* worthless, then I might stop hearing her words in my head."

"And that's why you wanted to become a Slayer? Why you want to help save the world? To prove your mother wrong?"

Aara nodded, not looking at Kas.

Looking up at her, Kas thought about what it must have cost the girl to come out with her secret to Kas, especially after Kas had been less than accepting of her being a werecat. Did she expect Kas to throw harsh words in her face like she had back at Feldania?

Like her mother would have?

"Well," said Kas after some time. "I think your mum doesn't deserve a single fucking thought from you. Let alone you going through this trouble to prove something to her. Hells, she doesn't even deserve to be able to call herself your mother. But I know what you deserve, and that's to have people around you who will accept and care for you just as you are."

The look Aara gave her was one of astonishment. "Even if I'm a werecat?"

"Hm. Well that's a different matter . . ."

"You arse. You're meant to say, 'yes, Aara, people should love and accept you even if you can turn into a big scary cat'," she said the last part in a deep and poor imitation of Kas's voice.

Despite herself Kas smiled. "I sound nothing like that. And you're not that big or scary as a cat."

"Big enough to take on a strega though."

"Big enough to take on a strega," Kas conceded.

Aara beamed in a way that made Kas feel a little wellspring of joy inside of her at the sight. For once that chastising voice didn't rise up to point out that Aara was a werecat—a monster and a danger to humans. For once Kas saw Aara as simply . . . *Aara*.

The girl hopped off her perch on the crates. She pocketed the knife and took her cap out and put it back on her head, hiding her ears away once more. "I'm going to get some food. Hopefully it's not all gone. Do you want to come with me?"

"I already ate. You go on."

She watched Aara scamper across the deck and disappear down the ladder that led belowdecks.

Now alone, Kas reclined against the side of the ship, tipping her head back to look up at the small scattering of stars, winking between the gaps of the sails.

The sound of voices caught her attention and Kas realised she was not as alone on the deck as she had thought. Further away from her she spotted the captain's son Linos, standing near the port side of the ship. Beside a familiar head of long white hair.

She didn't have long to be surprised to finally see Claudia out of her cabin after three days of refusing to open her door. As Kas watched the two of them, she saw how Claudia grabbed Linos by the shoulders, forcing him back against the wale.

Kas was already moving, her heart in her throat, when Claudia bared her fangs against the young man's neck.

CHAPTER 24

# CLAUDIA

CLAUDIA'S CONDITION had steadily been growing worse over the last few days she had spent locked away in her cabin. The bursts of pain in her abdomen had grown to an ever-present sensation like a knife twisting slowly in her gut. The throbbing in her head also refused to leave her, and she could now add trembling muscles and a cold sweat to the list of what was ailing her.

That night, Claudia decided to risk venturing out and onto the deck, hoping that the fresh air might make her feel better.

It did not.

Claudia was leaning against the gunwale, her head hanging over the side. *Get a hold of yourself, Claudia,* she told herself. *If Kas finds out about this, she'll—*

"It's a beautiful night, isn't it?"

Her senses were dulled enough that Claudia hadn't even noticed Lino's approach.

He stood before her in only a light pair of trousers, and a loose white shirt, rolled up at the elbows and open at the front, showing off much of his well-defined chest.

If Claudia had been in a better frame of mind, she might have been more appreciative of the sight. As it was, Claudia desperately wished he would leave her alone.

"I haven't seen you for a few days," Linos continued, his tone was easy. His smile good-natured.

"I . . . haven't been feeling well," Claudia said between clenched teeth.

"Is it your first time on a boat? It can take a while to find your sea legs."

The boat tipped beneath Claudia's feet.

No, not the boat. Only Claudia. She fell against Linos's solid frame, his hands coming up to steady her.

"Hey now," the humour was gone from his voice, replaced with genuine concern. "Are you all right?"

*No*, Claudia wanted to say, but the words would not come. She could not think of how to string together a sentence. All she could think about was Linos's steady, healthy heartbeat, too loud in her ears now that she was so close to him. The feel of it against the shoulder she had leaning on his chest. She was too caught up in the overpowering scent of him; tobacco smoke, and ocean salt, and . . . *blood*.

Claudia lifted her head to look Linos in the face but found her gaze catching instead on the barely imperceptible, yet utterly tantalising, beat of the pulse at his neck, right beneath his jaw. Proof of the blood being pumped through his veins.

Laid out right before her.

Taunting her.

Ready for her to take.

The last threads of her control snapped like the last threads on a frayed rope. Claudia felt as if she were moving through a red-tinged haze as she grabbed Linos by the shoulders and forced him back against the wale. She heard him voice his surprise, but as if from a distance.

All of Claudia's focus was on his neck. The dark skin that stretched over his bobbing throat. Skin that would give easily beneath the sharp points of her fangs. She could already taste the metallic blood that would hit her tongue. That delicious, *exquisite*—

Something grabbed her by the shoulder and wrenched her away from Linos. That red haze clouding her mind evaporated, bringing Claudia back to the reality of what she had almost done. Of Linos standing back against the wale, his eyes wide and his smile gone.

And of Kas standing at her side.

"I'm so sorry," said Kas, her light voice at odds with the bruising grip she had on Claudia's shoulder. "Claudia's been feeling just dreadful lately, and I think it's time I get her back to her cabin for some rest."

The captain's son seemed as if he were in a state of shock. His chest moved quickly beneath his white shirt. The way he looked at Claudia now was a far cry from the flirtatious looks he had given her previously. Now he stared at her as if he had seen a ghost.

Or a monster.

But he said nothing and made no move to stop them when Kas practically dragged Claudia belowdecks. Once they were alone in the narrow corridor, Kas slammed Claudia against the wall, her expression thunderous.

"What the hells were you doing back there?" she demanded. "You looked like you were about to—"

"About to drink his blood?" Claudia said—slurred. "I was." The pounding in her head was back, the quick burst of energy she'd had when she leapt at Linos was gone, leaving her feeling weak. As if she could barely hold herself up on her trembling legs.

Kas's nostrils flared. "You told me you didn't need to drink blood because you're only half-vampyric. Was that just a lie?"

"No. I never said I didn't need to drink blood, only that I can drink and eat what humans can. I still need blood, however. Not as frequently as other vampyrics, but I cannot go more than two months without it."

"And let me guess, the last time you drank some blood was more than two months ago?"

"Is it so obvious? I thought I was doing a rather good job of hiding it."

"Oh, yes, right up until you nearly ripped that boy's fucking throat out."

"I wasn't going to . . . kill him," Claudia said through chattering teeth. "I just needed . . . a drink."

Kas made a hissing sound between her teeth. "Put your fangs away."

When had they come out? "Can't," she mumbled. "'m too . . . thirsty . . . so thirsty."

She thought she might have heard Kas utter something along the lines of "fucking vampyric" under her breath.

Then she heard Kas say louder, "If you promise not to kill me, you can drink my blood then."

At first Claudia thought this sickness had gotten so bad she was beginning to hallucinate. It took a moment or two for her sluggish mind to realise that Kas really had uttered those words.

The Slayer was truly offering to let Claudia drink her blood.

Perhaps Claudia should have denied Kas and told her she could hold out until they reached the next port, where she could vanish into the woods and find a deer or a rabbit to drink from like a good little half-vampyric who would never dare to lay her fangs on a person.

But Claudia could feel her control slipping further and further. If she didn't drink any blood soon, well, she did not want to think too much about what might happen.

So, she told the Slayer, "Let's go somewhere else."

CHAPTER 25

# KAS

*Saints you are a bloody fool, Kas of Veldenier.*

Those words and others with a similar sentiment had been circling around her head all the way down to Claudia's cramped cabin, across from the equally tiny one Kas slept in. The ceiling was so low, Kas was forced to stoop. There were no windows to speak of, and the space was lit by a brass lantern hanging from a hook nailed to the wall. A narrow bed with a wooden frame took up much of the floor space. Along with a large chest pushed against the back wall.

As soon as they entered, Claudia practically slammed the door shut behind them. Kas watched as she leaned her head against the door for a moment. Her breathing was heavy, her body wracked by tremors, as if she were suffering from a vicious chill.

Once again, Kas silently demanded of herself what in the hells she was doing here? Why had she offered Claudia her blood? She was a Slayer. She killed monsters who were a threat to people. She didn't try to find them an alternative food source. And she certainly did not offer herself up as an option.

She should have cut Claudia's head off as soon as she saw the vampyric put her fangs near Linos's neck.

Yet something had stayed that impetus in her.

She looked to Claudia, who even now was trying to control her thirst. Even when Kas had given her permission to feed on her, Claudia was still trying to fight.

"I think I'd like to do this on the bed," said Kas, wandering over to take a seat on the edge of the mattress. It creaked alarmingly beneath her. "Since it is my first time and all."

She heard Claudia let out a strained huff of laughter. Kas shed her scarf and her jacket, so she was left in her grey, sleeveless tunic. With fumbling fingers, she pulled at the laces that held it close at the base of her throat.

Fucking hells. Why did she feel like a green youth about to have their first tumble? She may have been about to get in bed with another woman, but this would be nothing like all the other times she had done so. There would be nothing pleasurable about this.

By then, Claudia came to sit beside her, and Kas felt an irritating jolt of nerves. Long white strands of hair hung in front of Claudia's face, yet Kas could still see the strain on her face, along with a look of grim resignation. As if she were moments away from the executioner's block, knowing there was no way of escaping it.

Kas frowned. *She* was the one who was about to be gnawed on here.

"All right," she sighed. "Let's get this over w—"

Kas was forced to lay flat on the bed when Claudia took a hold of her by the shoulders.

She opened her mouth to voice her irritation at being manhandled, but the words never made it out.

Because Claudia chose that moment to sink her fangs into Kas's neck.

She gasped. Her eyes flew wide.

It felt . . .

*Incredible.*

It came with pain, as was to be expected, like being stabbed with a large, icy needle—or two. However, it was quickly overwhelmed by the *ecstasy* that flooded Kas's body from head to toe.

Kas thought she may have heard a sound escape her throat. She also thought she could hear sounds coming from Claudia; like moans of bliss, but she couldn't be sure. Everything felt . . . muffled.

She'd heard that being fed on by a vampyric could have a sort of paralysing effect. That it could dull one's senses. But she had not realised that the first-hand experience was so much *more*.

It felt as if every stress and strain in her body had melted away. Leaving her in a state of relaxation she wasn't sure she had ever felt before in her life. Every inch of her skin felt hyper sensitised, even to the clothing she wore, in a way that made her break out in gooseflesh and her toes curl.

Thoughts eluded her. A pleasant fog had blanketed her mind and barred anything but the pleasure she was feeling from entering. Anything else, except for Claudia.

Her open mouth against the side of Kas's neck. Feather-soft lips against sensitive skin. The occasional press of a warm tongue. Claudia's hands still gripping her shoulders. Fingers loosening and tightening at intervals. Her thighs bracketing Kas's. Claudia's chest pressed against hers.

Kas wanted to seek more contact with Claudia. She wanted to bring her arms up, wrap them around the other woman and pull her in until their bodies were flush with each other, and not even a whisp of air could stand between them.

She wanted more.

More of this euphoria.

More of Claudia—

The spell broke.

Like the shattering of a glass.

Claudia pulled away from Kas, taking with her that all-consuming bliss. Leaving Kas to come back to herself in stages.

She was breathing hard, and her skin felt overly warm and damp. As if she had just gone toe-to-toe with a monster. Not laid back while one fed on her.

Drowsiness lingered at the edges of her mind, threatening to take her. Kas felt as if the bed were tipping beneath her, but she couldn't be sure if it was dizziness or the rock of the boat. There was a stinging pain in her neck where she'd been bitten, but it was bearable. Nothing like how she would have imagined it to be.

Claudia's face was directly above hers. White hair, limned with amber lantern light fell around Kas's face. There was a flush of pink to Claudia's cheekbones, which stood out starkly on her pale skin. Her eyes were wide and overly bright, despite their pale colouring. She looked as if she had been imbued with new, radiant life.

A smear of red stained the corner of Claudia's lips.

Kas's blood.

Kas thought she would have been revolted or enraged by the sight of her blood on Claudia's lips—a symbol of what she had allowed herself to do—but instead, all she felt was a rising desire to reach up and wipe that blood away with her fingers. To touch the lips that had so recently been at her neck.

Kas hadn't even realised that she'd already lifted her hand until Claudia's was around her wrist.

"Thank you," said Claudia. "For . . . that."

Kas blinked. "Oh. You're welcome."

Claudia pulled away, the silky strands of her hair brushing past Kas's cheeks. She instantly and inexplicably missed the feel of having Claudia so close.

"You should stay like that for a while," Claudia told her in a soft, matter-of-fact voice. "I tried not to take too much, but you may still feel light-headed."

"Claudia—"

But she was already rising from the bed. "I'll bring you some water. And a damp cloth for your neck."

She left without a backward glance, leaving Kas all alone in the cabin.

And alone with a knot of confused thoughts and feelings tangling around inside of her.

## CHAPTER 26
# CLAUDIA

STANDING with her back leaned against the other side of the cabin door, Claudia could not believe what she had done.

She had fed on a Slayer's blood.

She had fed on *Kas's* blood.

And it had been unlike any she had ever tasted before.

It had taken an immense amount of willpower for her to pull away, and not only because of the thirst.

Even after she had stopped drinking, it had been difficult for Claudia not to dive back down. Not to feed on more blood, but to put her mouth to Kas's. To see if the taste of her lips was just as exquisite as the taste of her blood.

To hear more of those husky gasps Kas had made while Claudia had fed from her, and to feel them against her lips.

Claudia pushed away from the door and headed down the hall to the galley, to fetch that water and cloth.

She could still see Kas's face in her mind's eye, staring up at her with wide, green eyes, her face flushed, her breast heaving and the bloody smear at the side of her neck, and Claudia felt a pang of want.

"Of all the people in Vil Tresar," she muttered to herself. "It had to be a *Slayer*."

# CHAPTER 27
# KAS

THEIR FINAL DAY aboard *The Sea Saint* started as a grey one. Low-hanging clouds huddled close together, teasing rain. Mist blanketed the water's surface, adding an eeriness to the still, gloomy morning.

Kas could still see through the fog from where she was leaning against the port side, and into the distance where the dark shape of landmass was ahead of them. They would reach the main port of Almora by the day's end.

Kas for one was looking forward to setting foot back on land. Having such limited room to move about each day was beginning to wear on her. She longed for open spaces to travel across and to sleep beneath the open skies and stars instead of in a cramped cabin with a too small bed.

Last night, however, she'd woken up in a cabin that was not hers after a deep and undisturbed sleep. Not even the feel or someone cleaning blood from her neck and leaving a pitcher of water by her bedside had woken her.

Kas placed fingers against the side of her neck, where she now knew there to be two indentations, hardly bigger than pinpricks. A physical reminder of what she and Claudia had done last night.

*Fuck,* she thought. *I really let a vampyric drink my blood.*

She adjusted her scarf to make sure the wounds were hidden. What would Tsurra think? Kas shuddered to imagine it and resolved to never let her mentor find out.

"How are you feeling?"

Claudia had joined her as if summoned by thought alone and leaned her body against the wale beside Kas. She looked a far cry from how she had last night. Her fair skin was no longer a sickly colour or streaked in sweat, her eyes weren't bloodshot and animalistic, and her fangs were nowhere to be seen. Now there was a healthy flush to her cheeks, and she even looked at Kas with a relaxed sort of amusement.

"Terrific," Kas drawled. "Though my neck is aching, and I think I'm soon to have more scars to add to my collection."

Claudia craned her head forward to get a look at the bite mark. "Ah." She at least had the good grace to seem somewhat abashed. "Yes, I probably should have warned you about that. But as I'm sure you can remember; I wasn't quite in my right mind last night."

"I'll say."

"Perhaps you'll have to start growing your hair out. To hide the scar."

Kas made a face. "No thank you. I haven't worn my hair long since I was a child and even then I hated it."

"Really?"

"Yes. It was a relief the first time I picked up a knife and hacked it all off. Even if I did have a couple of bald patches afterwards."

Claudia looked as if she were trying to repress a smile. "That sounds absolutely disastrous."

"Tsurra tried to salvage it, but there was little that could be done but wait for it to grow back out. Some of the other Slayers spent days teasing me because of it."

"I tried to cut my hair with my father's sheep sheers once," said Claudia. "Not badly enough to give me bald patches, but I cut it shorter than I'd intended and when I looked in the mirror, I ran crying to him. I don't think I was even old enough to realise that it would grow back."

Kas caught herself before the image of Claudia as a child, crying over cutting her own hair wrong, could make her smile. She'd told herself before that this was not how she should engage with Claudia, that Claudia was not someone to share in easy banter or swap silly childhood tales with.

Kas cleared her throat. "Anyway, I won't be growing my hair out. I like it just the way it is, thank you very much."

Claudia made a humming sound. She turned to lean her elbows against the gunwale, mirroring Kas's position. A pair of seabirds soared past, skating the water, and cawing loudly.

Teasingly, she said, "Maybe I should have bitten you somewhere . . . less obvious."

Kas knew that Claudia was trying to rile her, and it very nearly worked. She thought of how it had felt to have Claudia bite her and thought briefly about how much more . . . intense it would have been if Claudia had had her teeth in a more intimate area—Kas wrenched her mind away from that line of thought. She would not let Claudia see her flustered.

So, instead she said, "What? Like on my big toe?"

Her response had clearly taken Claudia by surprise. Enough to startle a burst of laughter out of her.

It was such an uninhibited and genuine sound. Kas realised she had never heard Claudia laugh before or seen her smile. She had seen Claudia's mocking sneers and humourless smirks, but she had never seen this. It transformed her face, illuminating it with a youthfulness and an added loveliness that rendered Kas incapable of doing anything more than staring. She wanted to drink in as much of the sight and the sound of Claudia's chime-like laughter as possible.

The moment was interrupted when they were approached by Captain Luisa's first mate, Basta.

"Slayer Kas," she said. "Captain wants to see you in her quarters."

The captain's quarters were found behind a door below the stern of the ship. And they were quite comfortable quarters—unlike the cabins Kas and Claudia and Aara had been relegated to. The walls were painted black. A large, plush rug covered most of the floor. On one side of the room, two crossed cutlasses were hung up on the wall, on the other side was a portrait of Captain Luisa herself in her younger years as a captain, hung above a side table holding three crystal decanters of red and amber-coloured drink.

The present-day Captain Luisa was standing behind a large oak desk at the end of the room, smoking a pipe and filling the cabin with the scent of tobacco. She was looking out the frosted glass windows behind her desk.

"You wanted to speak with me, Captain?" said Kas.

"Indeed," she said, turning to face Kas. "Please sit."

Kas stepped forward and took a seat on the edge of one of the cushioned chairs before the captain's desk, adjusting the scabbard of her sword at her back, so she could sit comfortably.

The captain frowned. "Is my ship so hostile a place? Why must you carry your blade about everywhere?"

"When you're a Slayer it becomes second nature to keep your sword on your person."

"Hm, well, who am I to judge the habits of a Slayer?" Captain Luisa exhaled a puff of smoke. "Unless of course, they endanger the wellbeing of my crew."

Now it was Kas's turn to frown. "Captain?"

"I spoke with Linos earlier. He told me of the encounter he had with one of your companions last night. The white-haired one. Claudia, was it?"

Kas went still. *Fuck.*

"He said that she seemed ill, and while he was talking to her she tried to *bite* his neck," said the captain. "He also said she had *fangs.*"

"I see." Kas picked at a loose thread on her trousers. "That's quite the tale. Are you sure he hadn't had a bit too much to drink last night? I think I might have heard him slurring his words a bit when he spoke."

The captain shot her a venomous look. "My son does not drink. He has no tolerance for it and hardly ever sets foot in a tavern." She set her pipe down and rounded the desk to stand in front of Kas with arms crossed. "So when he tells me that he believes one of the passengers we took aboard might be a *vampyric*, I trust his word. Even if I do find it odd to think a Slayer would be in the company of a monster."

*Or two,* Kas thought drily.

For some reason, her mind brought her back to Claudia's smile and the bell-like sound of her laughter from before, and how in that moment, she could not have appeared as less of a monster.

"So tell me," said Captain Luisa, her dark eyes boring into Kas. "Is it true that you brought a monster aboard my ship?"

*Fuck, what am I supposed to say?* Kas could always lie. She could say that of course Claudia wasn't a vampyric, Linos must have simply been seeing things, but Kas got the feeling that the captain would see through any lie she tried to offer up like the smoke from her pipe. And where would telling the truth get her? Kas couldn't imagine that the captain would react well to confirmation that Kas *had* brought a vampyric onto her vessel, especially when she knew that vampyric had already attacked her son. At worst, it might end with Kas, Claudia and Aara all losing their lives. At best, they might be thrown overboard. Although Kas could not see an outcome where Claudia was simply allowed to go free.

Kas did not spare too much thought on why that bothered her.

"Well?" growled the captain, patience clearly wearing thin. "Are you going to give me an answer?"

"I—"

A yell went up from outside the captain's quarters. Followed by another.

"What in the hells?" said the captain, striding past Kas and toward the door. She took one of the crossed cutlasses off the wall as she passed.

Kas stood up and pulled her own sword from her scabbard as she trailed after the captain. Fast and heavy footfalls could be heard, and amongst the sudden commotion Kas thought she could also hear the cries of something distinctly inhuman.

The captain swung the door to her quarters open, and what awaited them beyond was a battle between the crew of *The Sea Saint* and humanoid creatures covered in iridescent, purple-grey scales, brandishing odd-looking swords and spears.

Of course, Kas knew what the creatures were straight away. Merfolk. Monsters that inhabited Vil Tresar's oceans. Fish-like scales covered their bodies, and they possessed webbed hands with fingers that tapered off into black claws and tails tipped with a single spike to help propel them through the water as well as to be used as a weapon. They had gills on the sides of their necks for breathing underwater, and two narrow slits for noses to breathe on land.

Something landed on the deck directly in front of Kas and the captain with a heavy thud, and it took Kas a moment to realise it was the body of the grey-haired sail master, his eyes wide and unseeing and his mouth bloodied. Crouched on top of him was a merfolk, a blood-slicked dagger in its webbed hand. It stared up at them with all-black eyes and hissed with its wide mouth full of fang-like teeth.

It was the captain who reacted before Kas even had a chance to. With a yell, she stabbed her cutlass through the merfolk's head, between its eyes. She barely waited for it to go limp before she pulled her sword back out and charged into the fray with Kas on her heels.

"Don't let the bastards take the ship!" shouted the captain.

The merfolk were climbing up over the sides of the boat in what seemed like an endless tide. As she hacked and slashed at the oncoming merfolk, Kas noticed Claudia in the midst of the battle. Her snowy locks almost like a beacon, as she moved about, cutting down merfolk with her sword—Kas could not say how or when she had been able to retrieve it—at an almost lightning speed.

Beside her, the captain dispatched another merfolk with a thrust of her sword. "Damn it all," she growled, wiping merfolk blood from her chin. "They've never attacked us like this before."

*That's because you've never been carrying a dragon remnant aboard your ship before.* And sure enough, when Kas looked towards the ladder leading belowdecks, she saw two merfolk making their way towards it.

Kas darted through the crush of moving bodies across the deck until she could reach the merfolk trying to make their way belowdecks. Where the remnant was hidden away.

She took the first one by surprise, stabbing it between the shoulders and driving her sword all the way through, where she knew a merfolk's heart was. It collapsed just before the second merfolk turned to face her, slashing at her with a jagged sword.

Kas parried its sword strikes and the merfolk leapt back to evade hers. She made to move forward, to close the distance between her and the sword-wielding merfolk, when she noticed another one rushing towards her out of the corner of her eye.

Kas ducked, narrowly avoiding having her throat sliced open by a clawed hand. The next time the second merfolk lashed out at her with its claws, Kas raised her sword and the merfolk's claws scraped along the silver of her blade.

The one with the sword was not about to give her space to focus solely on fending off the newcomer. It came at her again and Kas parried the blow and then immediately spun out of the way of the other merfolk.

It felt as though she spent some time doing nothing but fending off the attacks from the two merfolk, before she was finally presented with a window of opportunity.

She got beneath the first merfolk's sword, crouching low before lifting herself up again as she swung her sword in a downward arc that sliced through the second merfolk, carving it open from shoulder to hip.

Blood and innards splattered the deck at her feet as the two halves of the merfolk fell in opposite directions.

She turned her attention back to the other merfolk, which was already coming at her again.

Something launched through the air with a furious yowl, and it took Kas a moment to realise it was Aara in her cat form, throwing herself at the attacking merfolk before it could reach Kas. The merfolk fell on its back under Aara's weight and could do nothing but flail and make gurgling hissing sounds as Aara savaged its throat with teeth and claws.

Only when the merfolk stopped moving did Aara lift herself off of it. The brown fur of her face was covered in the merfolk's blood. The pupils in her two-toned eyes were narrowed to slits and she looked every bit a wild, untamed animal that it was almost difficult to believe this creature was also a young girl.

She gave Kas a look over her shoulder, as if to make sure she was all right before she raced off to attack more of the offending merfolk.

As much as Kas would have loved to watch Aara rip more merfolk to shreds, she noticed that even more of them were coming aboard. A group of them headed straight for Kas once they were over the side of the ship. Some carried swords and others brandished what looked like harpoons and Kas braced herself for even more fighting.

She was not about to let them get their slimy, webbed hands on that remnant.

## CHAPTER 28
# CLAUDIA

THE MERFOLK HAD all but taken over *The Sea Saint*. The deck was littered with their writhing, scaly forms and bodies of *The Sea Saint's* crew were interspersed between them as they fought to save their vessel from these monsters of the sea.

Claudia stabbed her sword through the chest of one merfolk and spun around to sheer the head off another. The merfolk were not particularly challenging opponents, their numbers made them more of a nuisance than anything, but for Claudia at least, they were relatively easy to dispatch.

Though it did not seem to be that way for the crew. She was just in time to save one man from being dragged over the side of the boat by two of the sea monsters. But too late to do anything but watch as Basta, was stabbed through the chest by a barnacle encrusted sword.

She caught sight of Aara streaking across the deck, felling merfolk and evading their attacks. Much of her brown fur was already coated in their blood.

Claudia heard a shout go up and spotted Captain Luisa a few feet away, brandishing her cutlass as she fought desperately through a group of merfolk surrounding her and a few of her men. There was a bloody rent in the shoulder of her coat, but Claudia quickly realised that her cry was not in response to her own situation. Across the deck Linos was fighting alone against the largest merfolk Claudia had yet to see. It must have stood at easily six feet, and it fought with no weapons but for its huge fists.

She saw the merfolk disarm Linos, pulling the young man's blade from his grip as easily as a grown man might rip a toy from a child, and with a blow to the stomach, it pinned Linos onto his back.

Claudia sped towards Linos and the giant merfolk. Past the other monsters that stood in between, too fast for them to even hope to block her path.

She reached them just in time to stop the merfolk from bringing its huge fist down on Linos's face. The steel of her blade flashed and pierced through the monster's hand, almost as easily as knife through butter. She tugged her rapier downward and cleanly sliced the merfolk's hand in half.

Thick streams of blood spattered the deck as the merfolk let out a garbled cry. Its black eyes found Claudia and it swung its mangled hand at her.

She ducked the blow and with a whip-quick cut of her sword, she opened up the creature's gilled neck from ear to ear.

Linos scrambled to his feet and out of the way as the now dead merfolk collapsed to the deck. He regarded Claudia for a moment with a mixture of wariness and astonishment. But Claudia thought she also saw gratitude in his gaze. When she picked up his cutlass and tossed it back to him, he nodded at her, the only kind of thankfulness he had the time to offer her before they both returned to the fighting around them.

Soon enough, it seemed to Claudia that their efforts were beginning to pay off. Fewer and fewer merfolk were still standing on *The Sea Saint*. It wouldn't take long for them to defeat the rest.

The ship gave a violent lurch, nearly catapulting them all into the water.

When Claudia righted herself after being thrown into the door of the captain's quarters, it didn't take her long to see it.

"Oh Saints!" she heard someone shout. *"What is that?"*

*What indeed,* thought Claudia, for she had never in her life seen such a thing.

It was draped across the front of *The Sea Saint*. Almost as large as the ship itself with grey flesh glistening with seawater.

And it had tentacles.

# CHAPTER 29
# KAS

Kas had never fought a crytan before, and she found herself grinning at the prospect of doing so now.

Like diavols, crytans were one of those monsters that looked like an amalgamation of different creatures. The front of their bodies looked like that of an octopus, with four long tentacles riddled with huge suckers on the undersides. While their bottom halves looked more reminiscent of an isopod, with a shell-like back and three armoured legs on each side.

Kas knew that crytans were often kept by the merfolk—as pets or slaves, no one knew—and that a full grown crytan could grow to twice the size of a ship like *The Sea Saint*. This one must have been a juvenile, as it was hardly big enough to encompass this merchant's vessel. But that did not make it any less dangerous.

Riding on the back of the crytan was a merfolk in some odd-looking saddle.

With a garbled cry from its rider, the crytan began pummelling the ship with its great arms. A sail was torn, crewmen were swept overboard, the wood of the deck splintered and broke and the mast cracked and groaned dangerously. A crew member that had taken to shooting merfolk with arrows from the rigging, was forced to leap off their perch before part of the mast could come down on them.

Kas rolled out of the way of a tentacle before it could crush her under its weight. When she looked up, she saw Aara leap at one of the tentacles lying against the deck and sink her teeth and claws into it.

Captain Luisa side-stepped another tentacle before stabbing her cutlass deep into the fleshy appendage.

A high-pitched squealing sound filled the air. Kas realised it was coming from the crytan. It jerked back the tentacle the captain had stabbed and lifted the one Aara was biting, so suddenly that it whipped Aara into the air.

But between one blink and the next, Claudia was in the air, catching Aara in her arms, and then she landed on the deck beside Kas.

"Well, Slayer?" she said over the shouts of the crew and the bellowing of the crytan. "Don't you have a monster to slay?"

Impossibly, Kas's lips drew into a wide grin. Seeing the way the crytan had reacted when its tentacles were attacked had given her an idea. But first, she would need to get the merfolk rider out of the way.

"Claudia," she said to the vampyric, "How long do you think it would take you to get rid of that merfolk on the crytan's back?"

Claudia looked briefly taken aback, as if it were so outlandish for Kas to ask for her assistance. Then she looked towards the crytan and its rider, considered them and said, "Not long at all."

No further words were needed between them. Only a look and then they were both off. Claudia towards the crytan on the prow of the ship and Kas for the still intact rigging on the starboard side.

Sheathing her sword, she gripped the sopping wet ropes and hauled herself up, having to press herself flat against it to evade a flailing tentacle.

Once she was almost to the top, she paused and looked down to see Claudia already engaging with the merfolk on the crytan's back. Claudia was quick as the wind and the merfolk stood no chance against her.

Taking the dagger sheathed at her thigh, Kas put the hilt of it between her teeth, and turned her attention to the crytan tentacle coming towards her.

Kas took a deep breath—*here goes nothing*—and grabbed onto the tentacle. The monster's flesh was slippery with water and some kind of slime, but still Kas managed to keep her hold, even as she was carried through the air, wind whipped through her hair and in her ears, deafening her to most other sounds.

She took her dagger in hand and plunged it into the meaty flesh of the crytan's tentacle.

Another high-pitched squeal reached her ears as Kas was whipped further through the air. Only when the crytan brought its injured tentacle closer to its body, as one might snatch a burnt hand to their chest, did Kas let go.

She landed on the crytan's head, in front of the saddle and between its eyes, at the same moment Claudia pierced the merfolk through the mouth with her sword.

As the merfolk's lifeless body crumpled, Kas took out her sword and plunged it right between the crytan's eyes, where she knew the brain was.

She buried the blade almost all the way to the hilt, bracing herself as the monster spasmed before going still. Its waving tentacles went limp, dropping into the water with almighty splashes and one collapsed across the ship's deck, forcing crewmen to scramble out of the way.

Kas pulled her sword out, wrinkling her nose at the foul-smelling blood and brain matter that came up with it—her sword was going to need a very thorough clean—before she felt the crytan's body beginning to shift and realised that it was sliding off the ship.

It was Claudia who grabbed Kas by the back of her collar and hauled her off of the crytan before it could take the two of them with it as it fell back into the ocean, almost tipping over *The Sea Saint*.

A great hiss and a plume of water went up as the carcass of the crytan disappeared below the waves. Kas and Claudia sat at the edge of the prow, breathing heavily and staring at the empty, ruined space where the crytan had been. In the silence that followed,

Claudia said, "Do you make a habit of slaying monsters in such a showy fashion?"

"Only when I have an audience to impress." She took in Claudia's disorderly hair and clothes stained with sea water and merfolk blood. "You look a mess."

"And you don't look much better yourself," Claudia said archly.

They stayed like that, staring at one another before, inexplicably, laughter bubbled up within Kas's chest. It wasn't long before Claudia followed suit and both of them, filthy and worn, were sharing a laugh as if at some joke that was unknown even to the two of them. And it felt *good*.

Something brushed against Kas's arm, and she looked down to see Aara. She looked up at Kas with round eyes, one brown and one green, and her fur matted by blood and meowed. Unthinkingly, Kas lifted a hand to stroke Aara between the ears and the werecat leaned into the contact.

They walked down the mostly intact steps and onto the deck, which was a mess of ruined wood, sea water and a scattering of bodies of dead merfolk and some crewmen, and those left standing were either having their wounds looked to or mourning their fallen crewmembers. Kas knew that this must not feel like much of a victory to them, not with friends dead and their ship in ruins.

The captain and Linos both came to meet Kas, Claudia, and Aara. Both mother and son looked quite worse for wear, with blood staining most of the left side of the captain's face and Linos appeared to be putting much of his weight on his right foot.

"It seems," said Captain Luisa, "that we owe you a debt of gratitude, Slayer. That crytan probably would have sunk this whole ship without your help. And you," she was speaking to Claudia now, "I saw what you did for my son. How you saved his life. For that, I owe you an even greater thanks."

"Then," said Kas, "our discussion from before . . ."

"Can be forgotten about."

Kas nodded, relieved.

"Your ship, can it still sail?" asked Claudia.

"She'll be a bit slow," Linos said, looking about sorrowfully at the damage, "but she should at least carry us the rest of the way."

"If we're not attacked by more merfolk, that is," added the captain.

Claudia replied, a touch sly, "Well if we are, at least there just so happens to be a Slayer onboard that can save us all."

Kas should have noticed it. It was inexcusable of her not to. A mistake that easily could have proved deadly. If she had been paying attention to her surroundings instead of allowing it to focus only on what was right in front of her, she would have noticed that not all the merfolk still aboard were dead. She would have noticed one behind her, struggling to its feet and taking up the spear it had dropped.

Would have noticed it aim the spear at her back and let it fly even before the shout of warning went up.

Maybe she might have noticed it before the spear was about to plunge through her chest.

Maybe she might have noticed it in time to stop Claudia from pushing her out of the way, and letting it pierce through her own body instead.

# CHAPTER 30

# KAS

THE POINT of the spear had driven through Claudia's shoulder, so while it was a nasty wound, it was not a mortal one. The merfolk that had thrown the spear had been killed, its body thrown back into the sea along with the rest and Kas and Claudia had retreated to her cabin so she could see to Claudia's shoulder.

"So I see being a half-blooded vampyric means you don't get those instantaneous healing abilities," Kas noted.

"I still heal faster than you." Claudia's tone sounded mildly defensive. "In a few more days this will be nothing but a scar. And after that, it'll fade completely."

They were sitting on the bed, with Claudia's back turned to Kas. She was bare from the waist up to allow Kas ease of access to stitch the wound. Her hair had been gathered over her uninjured shoulder, affording Kas with an uninterrupted view of her back. Apart from the bloodied gash in her left shoulder and the silver scars around her wrists, her skin was a canvas of fair and unblemished skin, unlike Kas's whose skin was a map of scars, freckles and darkened from endless days spent in the elements.

Kas heard Claudia inhale sharply, felt a barely imperceptible flinch beneath her hands before it was forcibly contained.

"Sorry," said Kas, pausing in her stitching.

"It's fine. You may continue."

So Kas did and after a while, she asked, "Why would you do that? Put yourself in harm's way for my sake?"

"I am not the type to stand idly by while someone is in danger," Claudia said.

*Aren't vampyrics the ones who usually endanger people?* Kas almost said. "You could have died."

"But I did not. And neither did you." She looked at Kas from over her shoulder. Something scrutinising in her blue gaze. "I am not the heartless monster you think me to be."

Kas felt as if her head was splitting open. The thought of Claudia, a *vampyric*, saving her life, getting injured in her stead and for no apparent ulterior motive was . . . it just didn't seem *right* to Kas.

She was a Slayer. She killed monsters because they killed people. She had learned that firsthand when she was only a child. Could still remember in excruciating detail the way those vampyrics had slaughtered her family, even her toddling younger siblings. And how they had done it with smiles on their faces.

Now here was Claudia, a half-vampyric, yes, but still a vampyric, who had been so reluctant to drink blood even though she was ill without it. Who had just fought alongside her to save a boat full of people, who had saved Kas's life at the risk of her own.

*"I am not the heartless monster you think me to be."*

*I know,* said a voice in her head, and she found she had no desire to shut it out.

Once Claudia's wound was sealed closed with a dark row of stitches that would probably be out by morning, Kas set the bloodied needle and thread down, and wiped the remaining blood away with a wet rag before applying some bandaging. Once she had done that, she rose from the bed.

"I'll leave you to get dressed," said Kas.

She made it no more than two steps towards the door when a hand reached out and caught her by the wrist.

"Kas, wait," said Claudia, and if the grip on her wrist hadn't stopped her, that voice would have.

Whatever Claudia had been about to say seemed to be caught in the vice grip of hesitation, and Kas found she could do no more than stare at Claudia.

She was beautiful, Kas had noticed that the first time she had laid eyes on her. But Kas's disdain and distrust had far outweighed any appreciation she might have had for Claudia's looks. Now it seemed that all she could focus on was the high cheekbones, the long, silvery eyelashes that framed her pale blue eyes, her full lips that Kas longed to trace with her thumb.

She also could not help but let her eyes wander further down, to the sharp arches of her collarbones and the large swells of her breasts, her pink nipples perked. Kas felt as if the air in the cabin had grown overwarm quite rapidly.

She felt as if she were caught up in that same spell from the night before when Claudia drank her blood. But Kas knew that this time, the pull she was feeling towards Claudia could not be blamed on loss of blood.

Whatever the moment was to turn into, was forestalled by a knock on the door. Kas pulled her hand free while Claudia reached to cover herself with her cloak. However, when the door opened, it revealed only Aara.

"Kas," she said, "the captain wanted to talk to you about something."

"Ah, right. I'll go see what she wants."

Without a backwards glance, Kas left the cabin. Left Claudia and hoped she could leave whatever new and dangerous feelings stirring within her behind as well.

Yet she knew it would not be so easy.

# PART THREE
# THE VAMPYRIC'S LAMENT

# CHAPTER 31
# SERISA

Dawn was on the approach.

Serisa could see its first rays of light reaching out from over the distant mountaintops that would lead them into Almora—the province where she knew the Slayers Keep to be. Where no doubt Claudia and that Slayer were headed. But daylight was still far off, and, for now, Serisa was safe in the darkness.

She stood at the edge of a lake; the lapping waves always shy of touching the tips of her shoes. A cool breeze played with the strands of her black hair and the dangling vines of a willow tree that arced over the lake's surface.

Serisa gazed down at the cracked amethyst amulet, nestled comfortably in the palm of her hand. Its faceted surface winked weakly up at her. The crack that ran the length of it was like a nasty scar. A glaring imperfection on an otherwise beautiful object. Serisa traced her thumb along the crooked line, wishing she had the power to make it disappear with touch alone. To rub away the tarnish on something so precious to her.

"I see you still have my amulet."

Serisa lifted her head and saw, standing at the edge of the lake only a short distance from her was a woman, with olive skin, and golden-brown, curling hair, fluttering in the breeze. She wore the same white blouse and long brown skirt that Serisa had seen her in so many times before.

Allegra.

Smiling, Allegra said, "I would have thought you would have left it lying forgotten somewhere by now."

"This is all I have left of you now," said Serisa. "How could I ever leave it somewhere to be forgotten?"

Allegra's smile lost much of its cheer, turning sombre at the edges. Serisa wanted to kick herself. She always hated it when anything dimmed Allegra's brightness, even when it was herself.

"Serisa," Allegra said, "why don't you stop this? This quest for vengeance you are on. It won't make things better."

"I can't," Serisa murmured. Her grip on the amulet tightened.

"I want you to find peace."

"I said *I can't*." The tip of one of Serisa's claws chipped the amulet, adding another scar.

Silence stretched out. The dawn's light was growing closer.

"I can't," Serisa said again, her voice calmer but no less dangerous. "Humans have taken everything from me. First, they took my mother. Then my father . . . And then they took you. There is far too much rage and hatred inside of me to stop now. So, I won't. I won't stop until this world knows even a taste of the pain I've known since the moment I lost you."

Allegra watched her from across the small space between them with a sad look.

*Don't look at me like that,* Serisa thought but could not say. *Don't make me feel—*

"Serisa."

This was a new voice. She turned to find Ves approaching her. Her typical impassive expression was fixed in place, only this time it seemed cracked with a look of concern.

"The sun's coming up," she said.

Sure enough, the sun had almost completely broken away from the horizon. The shadows were receding and Serisa could feel the beginnings of the new sun's warmth. Any more and her skin would burn.

When Serisa looked back to where Allegra had stood across from her, it was to find her gone. Not a trace of her to be found.

Of course there wasn't. Allegra was gone. Only able to visit Serisa in her dreams and the moments when her own mind wished to ridicule her.

The realisation made the yawning chasm of sorrow within Serisa grow ever wider. Followed by a spark of fury to fill that chasm. Strengthening her conviction to see her goal through to the end. Regardless of what apparitions of her lost love said to her.

Serisa secured the amulet back around her neck. The metal backing provided a comforting feel as it settled against the skin beneath her throat. She followed Ves back into the cave, where they would wait out the daylight along with Larnaz and Anirea, before they continued on their hunt for Claudia and Ombral's remnant, with the aid of the whispering skull, gifted by the strega.

*Soon, this chase will be over,* she assured herself. *Soon, it will* all *be over.*

# INTERLUDE

Four years.

That was how long Serisa had now spent with Allegra in the secluded little cottage in the woods.

Though it was not because of any lingering trouble with the wound she had received from the Slayer's silver blade, or some sort of payment the sorcerer was exacting from Serisa for the trouble she went through to nurse Serisa back to health when they met. No, she had a much better reason to stay with Allegra now.

Serisa returned to the cottage in the early hours of the morning. While the sky was still dark and studded with stars but was beginning to show threads of a red hue. The first sign of dawn.

She had spent much of the night travelling to a surrounding village to feed—although *surrounding* was a relative term. Even the closest settlement from Allegra's cottage would take a good two or three days to reach on foot. The journey was a much quicker one for Serisa, of course, when she could travel with the wind.

Upon entering the cottage, Serisa was quite literally hit in the face with a scrap of parchment. When she peeled the floating bit of paper off her nose, she realised that it was written on in Allegra's untidy scrawl.

***Meet me by the pond.***

Only a short walk away from the cottage was a small clearing, and in the middle of the clearing was a pond. A tranquil little spot that Allegra loved to frequent, for gathering water, washing her clothing, and oftentimes simply to sit and enjoy the peace and quiet.

Sure enough Serisa found Allegra sitting in the grass by the lake, a lantern perched on a nearby rock, bathing the clearing in a warm glow. The song of crickets hidden away in the grass filled the still night air. Almost as if they were joining in on Allegra's own song.

*"A strapping lad from across the way asked me for my hand*
*Father and Mother danced with joy*
*'Oh, daughter, won't you say yes? He's such a strapping lad.'*
*He offered me roses and dresses of silk*
*Even a sweet biscuit or two*
*He said, 'Oh, lovely girl, won't you say yes to me?'*
*But woe be me, my heart was already given to another*
*She gave me no gifts of flowers or silk*
*But she gave me sweet words and even sweeter kisses . . ."*

"I like it when you sing," Serisa murmured into Allegra's hair as she embraced her from behind.

She felt Allegra startle briefly before she relaxed and pressed herself back into Serisa's body. "Really? I never would have guessed since it's not as if you have told me plenty of times before."

Allegra turned to give her a smile. The changes in her appearance since they first met were small. The creases around her eyes and mouth were becoming more prominent and strands of silver had even begun to spring up in her honey brown curls. Never before had Serisa felt the rapid aging and short lifespans of humans so keenly.

Serisa leaned closer until their lips met and felt a slow unfurling pleasure in her chest that occurred every time they kissed. Even after all this time, Serisa would never get used to the simple pleasure of kissing Allegra.

When they parted, Serisa moved so she could sit alongside Allegra, their bodies close. She watched the surface of the lake and how it rippled occasionally in the calm breeze.

"When you sing," she said to Allegra, "it reminds me of my mother. She would sing to me all the time on sleepless nights when I was young. We vampyrics don't normally care much for human art, but my mother loved music. Once she even took me into a city so we could watch a play full of humans singing and dancing."

"And no one saw you? Two vampyrics watching their play?" asked Allegra.

"We stayed well hidden, of course. On a rooftop nearby."

"I see. And did that fondness for music rub off on you?"

Serisa was silent for a moment. "I . . . used to sing. I would sing to my sister sometimes, like mother did to me. But I haven't . . . not since my mother died."

She felt Allegra entwine their fingers. It was an odd sight. Allegra's hands were so . . . human, and seemingly fragile compared to Serisa's clawed hands. If she was not careful, she could easily slice through one of Allegra's fingers. But Allegra never seemed worried about that. She was always the first reach for Serisa's hands and hold them tight.

"I think you should. Try singing again, I mean," Allegra said. "Music was something your mother loved. Something that was special to her, just as I can tell it's special to you. You should keep the memory of your mother alive. Not quash it. So—" Allegra turned so she was facing Serisa directly. Her hands came up to cradle Serisa's jaw. "Will you sing? For me?"

Faced with those stunning brown eyes and sweet smile, Serisa found she was helpless to her lover's request.

She closed her eyes and took a breath. Drawing the words from a familiar song to the surface of her memory.

*"I listened to the wind, those words on the breeze*
*They said, 'I know you're lost come away with me.'*
*'I'll show you the path back to home.'*
*'Don't cry my dear come away with me.'*
*So I ran I ran*

*Fast and far*
*Through the woods past the rivers*
*I ran I ran*
*The words on the breeze they said,*
*'come away with me. I'll show you the path back home. Come away with me.'*
*I ran I ran*
*Straight for home*
*Where I belong*
*Right into your arms*
*Where I'll stay."*

The moment she stopped, she felt Allegra's arms around her.

"That was lovely my darling," Allegra told her.

"Really?" Serisa asked. "Or are you just saying that so I won't feel embarrassed by how out of practice I am?"

Allegra laughed, pulling away just enough that they could look at each other in the eyes. "I would never lie to you about such a thing. I think now I'll demand that you sing for me more often."

Serisa chuckled. "You sound like my sister."

Allegra's smile turned wistful at the corners. "Claudia," she said. "You speak of her often. I wish I could meet her."

"You could," Serisa told her earnestly. "I would never bring you to the castle, of course. But we could travel to Trulio, it's the closest village, and have Claudia meet us there."

"Oh, Serisa." Now the look on Allegra's face was one of sadness. As it always was whenever Serisa suggested leaving the cottage and the woods. "I wish we could, but . . ."

Serisa reached out and carefully tucked a stray curl of hair behind Allegra's ear. "Will you never tell me why you stay hidden from the rest of the world?"

She watched a conflict of emotions pass over Allegra's face, before an aggrieved sigh slipped past her lips. "You've stayed with me here long enough. I think it's past time you knew the tale."

Allegra seated herself more comfortably against Serisa. Her plum-coloured skirts were fanned out around her folded legs. Above them, the sky was beginning to grow lighter, the darkness in the sky was fading, but Serisa was not concerned, and instead focused her attention on Allegra's voice.

"In my younger days, when I was eighteen years or so, I . . . fell in with a bad sort. The Diavols—a gang that used to rule Spensiapore, my home city. And when I say they ruled, I do not mean so lightly. They held sway over everyone in the city, from street rats to wealthy merchants. Even the sintiarn was in their pocket. Back then I was a headstrong girl with loose morals and just happy to belong somewhere after spending a childhood alone on the streets.

"But my place in the Diavols unravelled when I fell for a baker. Jissen. But the son of the head of the Diavols . . . wanted me, and when he found out about Jissen and I, he went to his father, and they had Jissen killed. I was . . . heartbroken and angry don't even begin to cover what I felt. I decided that I would make the whole lot of them pay for what they did to Jissen. I came up with a plan, and one night, while many of them were busy sleeping off their ale after a celebration at the boss's estate, I set the whole place alight. It was the first time in my life I was able to conjure such a powerful spell. It was like watching a great serpent made of fire come alive to swallow the mansion. I stayed long enough to hear some of the screams from those trapped inside before I fled Spensiapore. But not everyone in the gang was at the estate that night. Not even a year passed before what remained of the Diavols managed to track me down. They started sending assassins after me, all of which I only barely managed to escape with my life.

"I knew my luck couldn't hold out forever, so I decided to disappear. I came out here into the deepest parts of the largest forest I could find and made a solitary little life for myself." Allegra's lips twitched. "Well, solitary until you came at least."

Serisa was frowning. "You mean to tell me you live secluded like this out of fear for some lowlife humans?"

"Oh, Serisa. Not all of us have your speed and your strength. If I'm run through with a sword, I won't start healing right away. I have my magic, yes, but I'm no powerful sorcerer." She touched the amulet at her throat and in a much quieter tone she added, "I do not want to die. I want to live until I am old. Until all my hair has turned to grey and my back aches even more than it already does. If I must remain hidden away from the rest of the world like a coward, then so be it."

Serisa watched Allegra's face, observing her serene expression as she stared at the pond, with its tranquil water and floating green lily pads. Strands of her hair had come loose from her braid to sway about her face.

She was so human . . . so fragile. But also so beautiful it made Serisa's heart twist.

Feeling a surge of protectiveness and affection, Serisa took Allegra into her arms once more. She buried her nose in those beloved curls, breathing in that familiar scent of pine and rosemary.

"You will live a long life, my love," Serisa told her. "And I'll be right there for all of it."

"Even when I am as wrinkled as a walnut?"

Serisa smiled. Her chest felt full to bursting with how happy and in love she was. "Even then. For I would set the world aflame if I had to. Just to stay by your side."

# CHAPTER 32
# CLAUDIA

Claudia's sword plunged straight through the harpy's chest.

The monster—winged, and humanoid and covered in greyish-brown feathers—ceased its struggling and shrieking and went still where it lay on the ground. Its beady eyes went blank, and the crooked, beak lined with needle-like teeth went slack.

Claudia drew her sword out of the creature's body with a sharp tug, spattering blood—even more of it—across the grass.

Across from her, Kas stood over the body of another harpy, bloodied silver sword in one hand and using the other to wipe blood from her face. The monster's body had been split cleanly in two, from hip to hip.

"Of all the monsters I've fought," Kas said between laboured breaths, "harpies are one of the most irritating."

"What are the others?" asked Claudia, as she bent to wipe some of the mess from her blade on the tall blades of grass.

"Imps," Kas responded, sheathing her own blade in the scabbard at her back.

"Did you get them all?" It was Aara. She was approaching them from a nearby copse of trees, in Bod's saddle while leading Claudia's mare by the reins. Wolf came lopping up to them as well.

"We told you to get away from here, Aara," said Claudia.

"Did you expect me to start making my way to the Slayers Keep without you?" She surveyed the four dead harpies spread out on the ground around them. "I don't understand why you wouldn't let me help you fight them?"

"Because you're not trained to fight harpies," said Kas.

"I killed merfolk on *The Sea Saint!*"

"Yes, but merfolk can't fly. Harpies can and they would have easily picked you up and carried you off to be a delicious afternoon meal for them."

Aara folded her arms, pouting. "I still say I could have been of help."

"But you did help," Claudia said, scratching Wolf behind one ear. "Without you, we would not have had anyone to get the remnant away from the harpies."

"Oh sure, pat me on the back for doing the boring part."

"Bratty today, aren't you?" Kas remarked as she took Bod's reins from Aara.

"Maybe we should have her walk behind us while we ride comfortably on horseback?" Claudia suggested as she mounted her own horse.

"Not that comfortable," said Aara, with a devilish little smirk that told Claudia she was only continuing to speak to get a rise out of them. "My bum is beginning to go numb from sitting in the saddle for so long."

"All right that's enough out of you, you little pest," Kas said without much real consternation to her words. She'd hoisted herself back into Bod's saddle, sitting in front of Aara. "I just had to fight off four harpies. I'm tired and I'm sore and I smell like harpy guts. All I want to do right now, is find the nearest body of water so I can take a dip in it. Not listen to you complain."

As she wheeled her horse around to find the dirt road they had been walking along before the harpies attacked, Claudia saw Aara pinch her nose.

"I can't wait for you to take a dip in a lake, too," the werecat muttered.

"Don't make me throw you from the horse," Kas said darkly.

It had been over a week now since Claudia, Kas and Aara arrived in Almora. The harpies she and Kas had faced earlier were only some of the monsters they had encountered since setting foot in the northern province. Drawn to the presence of the dragon remnant they carried with them. Two nights ago, they encountered a cockatrice—a monster that looked like a hybrid of a serpent and a rooster, and with a venomous bite—and the day before that, a pack of ghastlies.

They had also come across a travelling incubus, who had tried to simultaneously steal the remnant and seduce them. He had only reluctantly left them alone after Kas threatened his anatomy with her silver sword.

Almora was a wild province, full of dense, sprawling forests and lonely mountaintops and unexplored caves and ruins. Prime habitation for most monsters.

They still had yet to encounter Serisa or any of the vampyrics from Claudia's clan, however. Not since the confrontation outside the strega's hut in Nescoro. And Claudia did not know whether to feel relieved or worried about it.

She was sure, however, that it would only be a matter of time before they did meet her sister again, and once more, Claudia wasn't sure if she looked forward to it or dreaded it. She still had not given up hope that she would be able to reach Serisa. Talk sense into her and find the sister she knew through all the wrath and sorrow that held her captive.

But Claudia would be lying if she said that hope didn't take a battering each time she thought back to her last meeting with Serisa.

"Claudia's been teaching me how to use a sword, though." Aara was saying to Kas. They were still arguing about deciding to send Aara away when there were other monsters to fight.

"Only for a week." Kas huffed a laugh. "You're hardly close to being an expert swordsman."

Ever since *The Sea Saint,* Claudia had noticed a difference in the way the Slayer treated Aara. There was less wariness and disdain, more teasing and perhaps even some gruff brand of affection. Claudia thought she might even go as far as to say that Kas was growing *fond* of their young werecat companion.

"Ignore her, Aara," Claudia chimed in. "She's simply worried that you might become better at using a sword than she is."

Kas gave her a withering look. "That is not it at all."

Grinning, Aara reached up to pat Kas on the head. "Maybe one day *I'll* be the one having to teach our Slayer here a thing or two."

"You know, I almost wish more harpies would drop out of the sky and carry off right about now."

Aara laughed and Claudia found herself joining in.

When she looked back at Kas, she found those jade green eyes already on her. Almost as soon as their eyes met, Kas, appearing a touch flustered, looked away, turning her head instead to face the green and brown slopes of hilltops and valleys spread out below the mountainside path they rode along.

Claudia had felt Kas's eyes on her often over the past few days since their time on *The Sea Saint.* It was yet another change she had noticed in Kas. The Slayer always snuck glances at her when she did not seem to think Claudia was aware. But Claudia was always aware of Kas.

And it had nothing to do with her being a Slayer.

For there had been a change in Claudia as well.

There were times since they arrived in Almora, where Claudia wondered, perhaps absurdly, what it would be like if she and Kas could end this tentative dance they had started and be honest with each other. At times she had half a mind to put an end to it herself. But reality always put a stop to her.

Kas was a Slayer and Claudia had vampyric blood in her veins. Perhaps that fact didn't make half as much of a difference to her as it should. But she couldn't say the same about Kas.

Claudia may have an idea of where Kas's feelings towards her now stood, but could not be certain, and she would not settle for being the plaything of someone who would always see her as less than because she was not entirely human.

*The fate of the world is endangered by your own sister, and this is what you have to think about, Claudia?* she chided herself.

She refused to entertain any more thoughts of Kas and a possible courtship for the rest of the day.

Daylight was waning as they rode through what seemed like an endless expanse of lush, woodland, painting the world in soft hues of orange and gold. The forest was full of the sounds of birdsong and the gentle rush of a nearby river. They startled a herd of grazing deer. One sounded an echoing alarm call before they all turned up their white tails and fled out of sight. Wolf watched them with ears pricked forward but did not give chase.

It was one of the rare peaceful moments they had been given on this journey.

Then that peace was shattered by a scream.

Claudia and Kas brought their horses to a halt, only long enough to exchange concerned looks, before Kas was urging Bod in the direction of the scream, with Claudia galloping close behind.

Further up the road, they reached the end of the forest and the top of a steep hill. Below them was an open space, the ground scarred by a pebbled creek.

A carriage lay overturned in the creek. It was missing a wheel and standing only a few paces away from the carriage, was a *giant*.

Claudia had never seen a giant with her own two eyes before. Most likely because there were so few left.

It stood at what must have been more than ten feet tall, and seemed just as wide, especially in the breadth of its shoulders. It almost looked like a human man, with a dark, braided beard and tangled hair. It wore a collection of animal furs on its body, only the grey-brown skin of its face, arms, and bulging belly were visible. Its head appeared too small for its body, and its arms, thick as tree trunks, too long, fingertips almost reaching the ground. Two yellowed tusks protruded from its lower lip.

The giant was making its lumbering way over to the carriage, and Claudia thought she could hear screaming coming from inside.

A man stood on one side of the creek, yelling, and pelting the monster with rocks and sticks that he snatched up from the ground at his feet.

"You great, big ugly bastard," shouted the man in a trembling voice. He threw another rock. "Get away from there!"

The giant turned its head just in time for the rock to catch it in the eye. Roaring, the giant cast its baleful gaze on the man. Turning away from the carriage, it hefted a huge, crude-looking axe and charged at the man who seemed too stiff with fear to move.

"Shit," Claudia heard Kas hiss beside her.

Before either Kas or Claudia could spur their horses down the hill to save the poor man from the giant, a newcomer entered the fray.

A horse as black as a raven's wing came bolting out of the tree line below, carrying a rider in a red jacket and twirling a long, heavy-looking chain. The rider—a woman—raced up behind the giant, and once she was close enough, she let her chain whip fly, and its weighted end wrapped itself around the giant's massive wrist. The one that was holding the axe.

Yelling out, the giant came to a halt, looking at the silver whip around its arm, searing its flesh, and at the woman on the black horse who held onto the other end of the whip. When the giant pulled its arm, the woman, incredibly, held on and her steed stood its ground, bobbing its head and baring its teeth.

Growling, the giant yanked its arm forward with enough strength that the woman went *flying* out of her saddle.

Claudia expected that to be it. For the woman to slam into the ground with a sickening thud and never get back up. But instead, once she was high enough in the air, and directly above the giant's head, the woman released her hold on the handle of her whip.

She dropped and landed on the giant, clinging onto its shoulders. For a moment, it looked like some absurd mimicry of a child being carried on their parent's back.

The giant shouted and began shaking itself, arms swinging wildly in an attempt to dislodge the human from its back. The woman held on fast, however, and managed to manoeuvre herself further up the giant's back until she could swing both her legs over its shoulders.

Claudia saw a flash of silver as the woman took her sword out of the scabbard at her back and plunged the blade straight down and into the giant's skull.

The giant went still. Its axe fell from its hand and as blood began to ooze from the top of its head, the monster swayed and toppled to the ground with an earth-shaking thud that even Claudia felt.

The woman stood up on the fallen giant's back and pulled her sword out of the monster's skull.

"That was incredible," Aara whispered in awe, staring from over Kas's shoulder.

Claudia was inclined to agree. It was no small feat to best a monster like a giant and to do it so efficiently spoke to a remarkable skill. Claudia turned to speak with Kas about what they had just witnessed, but her words stopped in their tracks upon seeing the look on Kas's face.

Her eyes were wide and fixed on the woman and the now dead giant below. She would have looked completely shell-shocked if it weren't for the broad grin on her face.

"I can't fucking believe it."

Before Claudia even had a chance to question her, Kas's horse was galloping down the hill and it took a moment before Claudia followed.

Bod had barely come to a halt before Kas was off the roan and making her way over to the woman who was busy removing her silver whip from the fallen giant's arm.

"Tsurra!" she called, and the woman lifted her head.

*Tsurra.* Claudia knew that name. Kas had mentioned it enough times now during their travel. The woman who was Kas's mentor—and something of a mother figure, too judging by the way Kas spoke of her at times. So this woman who had single-handedly felled a giant was Tsurra of Lyancoso.

Tsurra took her boot off the giant's arm and Claudia took the opportunity to study her up close. She had dusky brown skin and curled brown hair pulled back into a loose tail. The grey in her hair and the lines around her mouth and eyes betrayed her middling years. She couldn't have been younger than forty.

"Well, if it isn't Kas of Veldenier," Tsurra's voice was booming, and her grin was wolfish. It reminded her of Kas's grin, even though as far as Claudia knew, there was not a drop of blood between them.

She and Kas embraced, and Claudia found it amusing that Kas was at least a head and shoulders taller than the older woman. Broader too.

"I never thought I'd see the day where Kas hugs someone," said Aara.

"It's a sight for the ages," Claudia replied.

"What are you doing here?" Kas asked of Tsurra.

"I was on my way back to the Keep when someone in a village I stopped at asked me if I could slay a giant that's been giving the people grief," explained Tsurra, jabbing a thumb over her shoulder at the giant in question. "I've been tracking this beast for shy of three days now. He was surprisingly elusive for a giant."

"How much was the bounty they offered you?"

"Eighty crowns."

Kas let out a low whistle.

"And yourself?" Tsurra's dark eyes passed over Claudia and Aara, but she still directed her question at Kas. "Are you headed to the Keep?"

Kas nodded. "Aye."

"Uh, pardon me."

The man Tsurra had saved from the giant had approached them and at his side was a young girl, with mousy blonde hair framing a ruddy round face. There was a smudge of blood on her forehead. Claudia surmised it was this girl she had heard crying out from inside the carriage.

"Thank you," said the man to Tsurra earnestly. "When that giant attacked us, I didn't know what to do. Our horse had run off and my daughter was trapped inside the carriage. I-I thought we wouldn't live to see tomorrow. But you saved us." The man reached into the pocket of his dirty trousers. "Here. I think I have—"

Tsurra held up a hand. "Whatever it is you think to repay me with, keep it. I've already got a reward waiting for me in the village north of here, and that's more than enough."

"In Sparthing? Ah, we're from there. We were on our way back when, well . . ."

"Do you have a lot of goods in that carriage?" asked Kas.

"Nothing we can't carry ourselves."

"Sparthing's still some distance away," Tsurra noted. "I'll escort you back. Make sure no other beasts attack you on your way home."

"Oh, Saints bless you." The man smiled and looked close to tears as he led his daughter back to the carriage so they could collect what they could from the wreckage.

"It should take until nightfall at the most to reach the village," said Tsurra, turning back to Kas. "What say you and your companions join me? Once I've collected my reward, we'll set out for the Keep."

"You wouldn't simply spend the night in the village?" Claudia said.

"Sparthing's only a small village with one inn and it's full of bed bugs," said Tsurra. "I'd rather camp out under the stars than stay in that place again."

Claudia realised that Kas was looking at her with a look that seemed to say, *Well?* Once Claudia had recovered from her initial surprise that Kas would be concerned with what she wanted, she returned Kas's look with a shrug of her shoulders that she hoped conveyed, *Why not?*

Turning back to her mentor, Kas said, "All right. We'll travel to the Slayer's Keep together."

# CHAPTER 33
# KAS

THAT NIGHT, they made camp in a grove not far from a lake they used earlier in the evening to wash away the days of journeying on horseback from their bodies.

As night settled, Kas, Claudia, Aara, and Tsurra sat around a fire eating the roasted meat from the rabbits Kas and Tsurra had caught earlier, as well as some stale bread and hard cheese from their packs. The horses were tied up nearby and Wolf dozed at Claudia's feet after having recently returned to them with his muzzle stained red from a kill of his own.

"And I told him"—Tsurra was in the middle of regaling them with her exploits from her recent travels across Vil Tresar—"I said hunting elk and bears isn't the same thing as hunting a wyvern. But of course, he wouldn't hear of it. Typical men. Refuse to believe a woman could know more than them. Even when that woman is a Slayer." Tsurra bit into her rabbit leg—perhaps with a bit more aggression than was needed. "But it was all worth it to see the look on his face after I had to save him from getting burnt to a crisp by that wyvern."

"Did he say anything else about being a more experienced hunter than you, after that?" asked Aara, who had been listening to the story with rapt attention.

"I wouldn't know. After I slayed the wyvern, I didn't see his face again. I can only assume his pride was much too wounded to face me again."

"Sounds like you've had quite the eventful few months," said Kas as she bit into her hunk of bread.

"Aye. I've certainly been kept busy of late." Tsurra finished off her rabbit and tossed her stick into the fire. She eyed Kas across the open flames. "And I have to say, I'm curious about what you've been up to, Kas. I've never known you to travel with others before."

Kas nodded to Aara. "This one wants to become a Slayer, so I thought I'd allow her to travel with me to the Keep."

Aara huffed. "Only after I spent weeks following you and saved you after you were caught by a strega."

Kas threw a twig at her.

Tsurra looked intrigued but turned her attention instead to Claudia. "And what of the young lady? Is she intent on becoming a Slayer?"

"I'm afraid not," Claudia answered with a small, diplomatic smile.

Tsurra rested her chin in her palm. Her elbow propped up against her knee. "Are the two of you lovers then?"

"*No,*" Kas said a bit too loudly. Near Claudia, Wolf came awake with a start.

While trying to dispel the memories of Claudia's body draped over hers with her mouth at Kas's neck in that cramped boat cabin, Kas added in a much calmer tone, "No, she and I are not like that."

Tsurra's gaze lingered on Claudia for long enough that it made Kas agitated, before returning to Kas. "Don't try to make a fool of me, girl. I've known you for too long and I know when you're keeping something from me. So out with it."

Kas opened her mouth to speak—there was no point in keeping the truth from Tsurra. Everyone at the Keep would learn about Ombral's remnant once they arrived—but Claudia beat her to it.

"She's not trying to keep anything from you," the half-vampyric said defensively. "It's simply not something that's . . . quite so easily explained."

Tsurra raised a brow. "Oh really? Well then, it's a good thing we have all night."

"I suppose it is," mumbled Kas.

She went on to explain how she came to meet Claudia, who was in possession of the dragon Ombral's remnant, and about Serisa and her clan who wished to use the remnant to free Ombral and the rest of the dragons.

The only part Kas omitted was Claudia being a half-vampyric herself. That, she thought would be best for Tsurra not to know about.

At the end of it, Claudia even produced the remnant, still bundled up in its white cloth, from the small, green bag to show to Tsurra. The older Slayer admired the broken off scale, with a look that was a mingle of awe and trepidation. Kas imagined it was probably much how she looked when she first laid eyes on it.

"And here I thought my hunt for the thirty-foot-long wyvern would surely be the most exciting thing that happened to either one of us." Tsurra's words came out jokingly, but the troubled frown never left her face.

"Sorry to steal all the glory," Kas said with her own attempt at some humour.

"And tell me this, Kasanna. You say that it's vampyrics that are trying to bring the dragons back. So how is it that you ended up travelling with one of them?"

The pause that followed was broken only by the chirping of crickets in the grass. Kas noticed both Claudia and Aara had frozen like deer that had scented a predator. They were staring at Tsurra with wide eyes and mouths hanging open. She didn't think she'd ever seen Claudia look so dumbfounded before.

Kas forced out a chuckle. "Wh-What makes you think that? Maybe—"

"I told you not to try and make a fool out of me," said Tsurra with a glare. "Oh, and I also know the girl's a werecat."

Aara made a choked sound.

"You need to do more than just wear a long coat to keep that tail hidden, my dear."

"How did you know?" Kas demanded, deciding to do away with pretence. "Even I couldn't tell that Claudia was a vampyric at first."

"That's because you don't have the experience that I do. When you have been a Slayer for as long as I have, it's not hard to spot a monster." Tsurra's dark gaze cut across to Claudia. "No matter how deceiving their appearances."

Kas had also been watching Claudia as Tsurra spoke, and she saw the way the half-vampyric's cool expression shook somewhat with Tsurra's words and the contempt coating them. A flinch. Hurt.

Anger flared through Kas and the words were pouring from her mouth before she could think to stop herself. "Well, regardless of what Claudia is or isn't, she's already done enough to prove herself a trustworthy companion. Including saving my life. Twice. I've made my judgement of her and that should be good enough for you. So watch your words, Tsurra. I won't have you speaking ill about her."

Now it was her turn to have everyone stare at her. Even Wolf was watching her.

Aara had a hand covering her mouth, as if she had just heard something scandalous. Tsurra regarded her with a raised brow, astonishment, and curiosity vying for a place on her expression.

Claudia's gaze felt the heaviest. Which was why Kas forcibly avoided looking her way.

Feeling suddenly stifled, Kas took up her sword and pushed herself to her feet. "I'm going to stretch my legs," she said, stepping around the fire. "Aara, watch Tsurra and make sure she doesn't try to slay Claudia."

She didn't have to walk for long before she was standing at the edge of the lake and looking out over the barely rippling surface. Moonlight reflected off the lake like a cluster of white gemstones. Across the lake was more forest, painted as black as pitch by the night.

Kas breathed in the fresh, woodland air before dropping her head into her palms, muffling the groan she allowed to slip between her lips. She felt ridiculous after her little outburst in response to how

Tsurra had spoken about Claudia. *Bloody hells, there was no reason for me to get so worked up.*

She had been feeling so out of sorts these last few days, ever since they had left behind *The Sea Saint*. Particularly where Claudia was concerned.

Kas wasn't so unaware of her own feelings that she did not know what had prompted this new feeling in her chest whenever she so much as looked at Claudia. Or caused her pulse to quicken when she thought back to the moments they had shared on the boat.

Somewhere along this quest they had embarked on, Kas had stopped thinking of Claudia as just a vampyric, as one of the monsters who had slain her family and haunted her nightmares for so many years. A creature she needed to be wary of at all times.

Instead, she had become someone Kas now felt impossibly drawn to, much like a moth felt drawn to a candle flame. Lured by its warmth and its brightness, unaware or simply uncaring of how it would burn if it got too close.

Did Kas care if she burned herself by getting too close to Claudia?

She thought she might already know the answer to that, and it unnerved her.

So lost in her own tangled web of thoughts, Kas almost didn't realise someone was approaching her until a familiar, soft-spoken voice reached her ears.

"I have to say, I am quite touched by you coming to my defence back there. Very gallant of you."

Behind her Claudia approached, her tread almost soundless. Kas thought that she was a bit like a cat in that regard.

"Laugh about it all you like," said Kas, reaching down to pick up a stone and threw it at the lake. It skipped along the surface three times before disappearing into the water.

"I'm serious." Claudia took up a position on a lichen covered boulder nearby. "It felt . . . nice. Having someone's support."

Kas skipped another stone. This time it only bounced twice before sinking. She turned to Claudia. "Is that not something you're used to?"

Shaking her head, Claudia said, "Ever since Serisa left when I was fifteen years old, I've had no one to count on but myself. Every success and every hardship, every cruel word spoken, and every abuse endured, I've had to face on my own."

Claudia had drawn her knees up against her chest, her arms wrapped around them. White strands of her hair drifted slowly in the breeze around them. Her expression was distant, as if she were lost in memory. Perhaps reliving the hardships she spoke of.

Kas felt a tightness in her chest. A longing to rid Claudia of that look and those memories.

Wordlessly, Kas crossed over to where Claudia was perched on the boulder and settled herself down beside her. There was enough room for Kas to sit alongside her comfortably, but only if she pressed herself against Claudia. She felt the shock of the contact ripple through Claudia before she carefully repressed it. Kas forced herself not to think too closely about the feel of Claudia's arm pressed against hers. Her thigh against Kas's.

"I'm sorry," Kas said softly.

"What for?"

"That you had to be alone for so long."

Her words must have taken Claudia by surprise. So much so that the other woman didn't have time to hide it from her expression before Kas saw it.

The quiet between them stretched on before Claudia finally spoke. "Kas . . . how do you feel about me?"

Now it was Kas's turn to feel caught by surprise. "What—Why do you ask?"

"I feel your eyes on me. Quite often. And it's been that way since our time on *The Sea Saint*. I can also tell that the way you look at me is the same way I look at you."

"And what way is that?"

"You want to fuck me," Claudia stated without hesitation.

The bluntness with which she spoke almost knocked Kas off her seat. She fiddled with her wyvern tooth earring. "Well, that's—"

She wanted to say *I think it's more than that,* but the words felt wedged on her tongue. Saints, she felt as green to all of this as she did at sixteen.

"But if I allowed you to," Claudia continued. "If I told you of my feelings and then allowed you to take my hand and lead me into your bed, is that all it would be? A night of sex before you go back to seeing me as just another monster?"

"What are you trying to say?" asked Kas with a frown.

"I know what I am Kas. And I know what you are, too. I know anything between the two of us could be difficult. Perhaps even near impossible. And I know that my kind have taken from you and hurt you deeply in the past. But even so, I won't allow you to use me. I won't be the pretty face you can use for your own satisfaction while you go on treating me like something dangerous or like your dirty secret." Claudia looked her straight in the eye. "Is that how things would be between us, Kas? Or could you offer me more? Could we be more, despite what we are?"

Words dried up on Kas's tongue like a drop of water under scorching sun. In that moment, the question Claudia posed seemed like an impossible one. She knew Claudia was not the untrustworthy vampyric Kas might have first thought her to be. But then she thought back to everything she had learned and experienced as a Slayer.

She remembered the sound her father's head made as it was ripped from his shoulders.

She heard the screams of her brothers and sisters.

She could still see the way the life had fled her mother as a vampyric drained her of blood.

When Kas finally did find her words again, all she could bring herself to say was, "I-I don't know. I'm a Slayer and you're—" *a monster.*

Kas kept her gaze fixed on her lap. Unable to bring herself to look at Claudia and see the hurt or the anger or both on her face.

But Claudia's voice gave nothing away when she spoke. "And that's answer enough for me."

Claudia slid off the boulder and Kas immediately mourned the loss of her touch. She listened to Claudia's almost soundless tread until she could hear it no longer, and Kas was alone at the lake. Alone with only the sounds of the chattering nocturnal beasts of the forests and a hollow ache in her chest.

# CHAPTER 34

# CLAUDIA

"We were just in a village the other day," Kas was saying. "Why didn't you think to get one while we were there?"

"Obviously it slipped my mind," said Tsurra.

"How could it have slipped your mind?"

"Old age is creeping up on me, Kas. So be careful with how you speak, because it might happen to you too one day and you don't want me there rubbing your face in it when that day comes."

"If you're even still around," Kas muttered petulantly.

"What was that?"

"You didn't hear that? Maybe old age is starting to take your hearing too."

"Girl, don't think I can't still tan your hide just because you've grown taller than me."

"Do you think they'll ever shut up?" Aara sighed. She was riding with Claudia, her cheek rested on Claudia's back and her arms wrapped around her waist. "They're starting to give me a headache now."

Indeed, Kas and Tsurra had been having a back and forth for much of the morning after Tsurra announced they would need to make a detour to the nearest town, which, according to Tsurra's map, was

Gorsa Té. The reason for this being that Tsurra was in need of a new whetstone for her sword.

"Can't you just wait until we get to the Keep to worry about sharpening your blade?" Kas had asked.

"We're still days away from the Keep," Tsurra had retorted. "Plenty of time for us to encounter more monsters, and I do not want to be hindered by a dull sword."

And so, their small party had spent most of the ride to Gorsa Té with Kas and Tsurra arguing and Claudia and Aara riding behind them in exasperated silence.

Claudia also spent most of the time with her eyes on Kas ahead of her. As much as she tried to look elsewhere, her gaze kept returning to that broad back, just as her thoughts kept returning to her conversation with Kas the night before.

Each time she remembered she felt a pang of disappointment anew. Maybe even a little bit of hurt. Yet she could not bring herself to feel any resentment toward Kas, even if she wanted to.

*It was your fault for allowing your hopes to get the better of you,* she scolded herself.

Still, she had made sure to keep a distance between herself and Kas since their lakeside conversation. One that Kas had never once tried to close, and Claudia could not help but feel saddened by it.

It wasn't much longer before they reached their destination. Gorsa Té was a mining and farming village built beneath the shadow of a high cliff face and nestled amongst a forest of pine trees.

If it weren't for the smoke rising above the treetops, Claudia thought it would be an easy village to miss, and perhaps that was the point. After all, villages such as these ones had no walls or town guards to defend them. If they were attacked by bandits or even monsters, then it would be up to the people themselves to defend their homes. Keeping the village as shielded from outsider's eyes as possible would be in the villagers' best interests.

Wolf left them to go his own way just before Claudia and her party rode over a low bridge that arched over a rushing stream. Nearby a woman with a small child on her hip watched on as a young girl gathered stream water into a clay jug almost half her size. The woman looked up as they passed over the stream, and instead of casting them a wary glare, as Claudia might have expected of someone from a secluded village, she smiled and nodded before returning her attention to the girl with the jug.

Once they were over the bridge, they found themselves on a main road that splintered off in different directions and wound around the small buildings with thatched rooftops that dotted the village.

They found their way to the village square and discovered it bustling with people. Everywhere Claudia looked, stalls were being set up, coloured ribbons were being tied to fence posts. A large, wooden statue of the Divine was being erected in the centre of the square. Alongside another statue of a man with a long beard, head bowed and holding a rose to his chest. Saint Aumecere, the Saint of good harvests.

"It looks like they're getting ready for a party," Aara noted.

A booming voice sounded from across the square.

"Tsurra of Lyancoso!"

A man dressed in the white and black robes of a high priest was striding towards them, arms spread wide.

Tsurra dismounted from her black stallion. "High Priest Edvichi," she said, greeting the priest with a broad grin and a little bow.

The priest waved his hands at the formality, the loose sleeves of his robes flapping. "Oh, please, Tsurra. We've known each other for some ten years now. Come here."

The pair embraced, kissing each other on both cheeks. Claudia noticed some people nearby stop to stare. Kissing on the cheek in greeting was nothing uncommon among friends and family, but it was certainly not the way one greeted a high priest.

Though this High Priest Edvichi certainly did not look like one of those priests who stood on ceremony and affected an untouchable air when amongst the common people. In fact, he looked more like he belonged out in the fields, tending to crops, with his somewhat unkempt black beard, spliced with grey, and a weathered, sun-tanned face.

"Preparations for the summer harvest festival are coming along well, then?" asked Tsurra looking at the activity around them.

"Indeed it is," said Edvichi, clapping his hands together. "I heard the harvest this year will be a big one."

"A harvest festival?" Kas said now to Tsurra. "Is this the real reason you had us come all the way here? To attend a festival?"

"I planned on coming to the harvest festival before returning to the Keep," Tsurra explained. "Though if you're in such a hurry, Kas, you can always go on without me."

"Oh, no, can we stay for the festival, Kas, *please?*" pleaded Aara.

And simply because some petty part of Claudia felt like being defiant towards Kas, who looked as though she was about to argue, she said, "I think I would also like to enjoy the delights of a harvest festival. One night should hardly make much of a difference, don't you agree, Kas?"

It was a challenge to keep the smile from showing too plainly on her face at the sight of Kas looking so disgruntled.

"Fine," she relented with a sigh.

"Splendid!" said the high priest. "The more the merrier."

Edvichi personally showed them to the village's only inn, which was merely a handful of cramped rooms above the tavern. Afterwards, Claudia, Kas, and Aara were sent to see the village seamstress, who also happened to be the high priest's sister, and who would give them proper clothes to wear for the night, free of charge.

"I made sure to bring that red dress along when I came here," Edvichi had said to Tsurra, as the pair prepared to go their own way. "In case you decided to come this year."

"I'm surprised you kept it after all these years," Tsurra said.

"Of course. After all, I thought you looked quite stunning the last time you wore it."

Watching them walk off arm-in-arm together, Claudia got the distinct impression that Tsurra and High Priest Edvichi were more than mere acquaintances. When she turned to see what Kas thought, she found the other woman had the kind of sour look on her face that

Claudia imagined most might wear when confronted with their parents' romantic escapades.

They found the seamstress's home near the centre of the village. Her name was Quitone, and she looked to be only a few years younger than her brother, and with the same short and portly stature.

Quitone brought the three of them into the back room of her shop, where an array of clothing was folded up onto shelves or hung up on racks.

"I'm fine with just wearing what I have," said Kas. "It's not that dirty." She chose that moment to start scratching at a dark stain on her sleeve that could have either been a bit of mud or dried blood.

"I forbid it," Quitone said with all the sternness of a mother. She pulled a dress off one of the shelves. Yellow, with a ruffled skirt. "I have many exquisite dresses for you to choose from that I made myself—"

"No dresses," Kas said with conviction.

If Quitone thought it odd that Kas would refuse to wear a dress, she did not show it and simply pointed Kas over to the men's wear.

She found Aara an ivory dress that laced up at the front and came with a peach-coloured short jacket. When the garment was presented to her, Aara looked at it with something akin to reverence and touched the soft fabric in the way someone might touch a precious gemstone.

Claudia wondered if perhaps the dress was the nicest piece of clothing Aara had ever been given to wear. Or was it the first time Aara had ever worn a *dress*?

"My dear, if you would please come with me for a moment?" Quitone asked Claudia, before leading her back out to the main room while Kas and Aara changed their clothes.

The seamstress brought her up a staircase and into what was clearly her bedroom, but also seemed to be used as a second workstation. The small room was overbrimming with crates containing bolts of cloth. A mannequin in one corner wearing an unfinished jacket. Scrolls of parchment with clothing designs drawn upon them blanketed a small table by the bed.

Quitone headed straight for the oak wardrobe opposite the foot of her bed. "I do believe I have the perfect dress for you."

Claudia stayed by the door as the older woman opened the doors of her wardrobe and began rifling through the many fabrics there, before finally selecting one and holding it out for Claudia to see.

Presented to her was a long, satiny dress. The colour of it was so dark it looked almost black, but Claudia could tell it was a deep purple. It had no sleeves or straps, though the bodice looked tight enough to stay in place without them. Two dark gemstones were sewn into the bodice on either side.

It was simple, yet elegant, and probably far too fine to wear for a harvest festival.

"What do you think?" Quitone asked, her tone hopeful. She seemed quite eager for Claudia to wear this one dress. "I made it years ago as a gift for my niece when she went to live in the city, but she took ill and passed away before I could. I've kept it hidden away since then, but now I think I would like to see it worn."

Claudia stepped forward and ran a finger over the fabric. It was velvety soft beneath her touch.

"I think it's perfect."

Sometime later, Claudia exited the seamstress's room, donning the satin dress, and a pair of long, black gloves that reached past her elbows. She kept her newly cleaned boots on beneath the dress.

As she made her way down the stairs, trying not to fiddle with the way the dress left no room for imagination about her shape beneath the fabric, she thought about how she looked more as though she ought to be attending some grand ball at a noble's luxurious mansion, rather than a village festival.

Kas and Aara now stood in the main room with Quitone. Aara was wearing her ivory dress and short jacket—she still wore her dusty cap —while Kas had donned a simple pair of grey trousers, calf-length black boots and a plain white tunic with loose sleeves and a high collar. She had left the top lace undone and the hollow of her throat and the upper part of her chest bared.

It was the first time she had seen Kas in anything other than her black Slayer gear and blue scarf, and Claudia allowed herself a fleeting moment to admire how attractive Kas looked. She had always found Kas appealing to the eye, even when she couldn't stand the woman, and the fine clothes she wore now only seemed to enhance that.

*Oh, that is most unfair,* thought Claudia.

Quitone looked up from where she was adjusting the sleeve of Aara's jacket. A delighted smile breaking across her round face when she saw Claudia.

"Oh, I knew it! That dress looks simply splendid on you."

"Thank you. It fits perfectly," said Claudia, even though most of her attention was focused on only one other.

Of course, she had not failed to notice the way Kas had looked up at her. Or the way her eyes rounded before sharply turning her head away. Perhaps Claudia would have felt hurt at that, if she hadn't been able to catch the hint of red on Kas's cheekbone and the tip of her pierced ear.

And despite everything, Claudia felt a thrum of pleasure at being able to inspire such a reaction in the Slayer.

"The sun's almost down," announced the seamstress. "The festival will be about to begin."

## CHAPTER 35
# KAS

Gorsa Té was teeming with people, colour, music and laughter that night.

On the streets there was a man who juggled three flaming torches, twirling them around so quickly they created bright patterns in the air. He made it seem so effortless. They passed a puppet show at the end of one street with an audience mostly made up of children. From what Kas could tell, it looked like it was a performance about a Slayer battling a wyvern. She hung around to watch some of it.

There was also food aplenty, much of it produced from the village's last harvest of the year. There was buttered corn to be eaten, as well as sliced tomatoes on freshly baked loaves of bread. Hunks of cheese paired with thinly sliced cuts of meat and drizzled in olive oil and sprinkled with herbs. Kas made an effort to enjoy as much of the food that was on offer as she could—especially since much of it was free. She was also particularly keen to try some of the apple and blueberry ciders.

She eventually found Claudia and Aara standing by a stall where two elderly women were cutting up and giving out slices of panettone. Aara appeared to be enjoying her panettone so much that she was taking great, hurried bites, raining sugary crumbs and bits of dried fruit all over the front of her dress.

"Should I go get you a bib?" said Claudia, taking it upon herself to wipe away the crumbs with a cloth given to her by one of the women.

The sight brought a smile to Kas's lips, reigniting a memory of when her elder sister, Alvera, had scolded Kas for her own messy eating, while doing her best to clean the food off her skirts. *"What man will want to have you as his wife when all you do is drop cream and crumbs all over yourself?"*

She had been embarrassed and annoyed with her sister at the time, but now Kas could only look back fondly on the moments when Alvera would coddle and scold her.

*I wouldn't know about men, sister, but I've done quite all right with women.*

Until now at least.

Kas's gaze wandered to Claudia.

She found it was doing that a lot tonight. And it was partly because of that damn dress she was wearing. The bodice of it hugged her frame so tightly, giving ample attention to the curves of her waist and breasts. It was far too distracting.

Why couldn't the seamstress have given her something frumpier to wear? Although Kas was sure that Claudia could have worn a grain sack and still looked like a piece of art deserving of being admired by the masses.

The three of them eventually found their way to the village square, where a group of minstrels were playing by the statues of the Divine and Saint Aumecere—now decorated with ribbon and garlands. There was a gathering of people there who were dancing in time with the music, cheering and clapping at intervals.

They settled together by a low stone wall, watching the dancers. Braziers had been set up and lit around the square, warming the air and casting everything in a warm orange hue. It wasn't long after that Aara left them to dance with a boy about her age.

Which left Kas and Claudia alone and Kas was all too aware of how they hadn't been alone since the night before by the lake, and how they had hardly shared a word with each other.

They stood together in oppressive silence until a giggling woman came stumbling into Kas. She might have even fallen flat on her face, had Kas not caught her by the waist.

"I'm so sorry," said the woman, who looked a little red in the face. "I think I might have had a bit too much cider to drink."

Kas offered her a smile. "It's all right. I've tried some and it is very delicious cider. Hard to resist."

The woman laughed, leaning into Kas for perhaps longer than was necessary.

When she finally pulled away, she was gazing at Kas with a heavy-lidded look that Kas knew all too well. "I better get going. Maybe I'll bump into you again?"

"Maybe."

"Well, what do you know?" said Claudia after the woman had gone. "Women really do trip over themselves in front of you."

"I think it was more the cider making her stumble, but I appreciate you feeding my ego."

"Hm," was all Claudia said. The look on her face was as opaque as a statue's.

"Are you jealous?" Kas could not help but ask.

"Of your ability to make women swoon into your arms? No."

*That wasn't what I was talking about.* Instead, Kas said, "I suppose you have no trouble with that yourself."

"Now who's feeding who's ego?" There was an upward tilt to Claudia's lips. A long lock of hair had fallen over one shoulder and Kas had to wrestle back the longing to brush it away and skate her fingertips along that smooth white skin.

"So, you like women?"

"That wasn't already apparently obvious?" There was an amusement in Claudia's voice that made Kas's cheeks heat. "But yes. Men as well. I enjoy the variety."

Kas would have said more, but her attention was snared by a

familiar voice. Standing among the minstrels in the centre of the square was Aara. And she was singing some toe-tapping tavern tune.

*"I met a boy at the bar*
*A farmer's son from afar*
*A pretty face with an empty head*
*I let him lead me up to bed*
*Aaand well, the rest was history!"*

"Of course." Kas said with a laugh despite herself.

"You must admit," added Claudia, "she is quite a good singer."

A young man with blond hair and a dimpled smile approached them and held out a hand to Claudia. "Would you like to dance with me?"

Claudia looked a bit taken aback and Kas had the notion to refuse on her behalf, but dismissed it just as Claudia responded, "All right."

She slipped her gloved hand in his. The man beamed and led her off into the throng of dancing people.

Kas stood there alone against the wall; her eyes trained on Claudia's white head from amidst the dancers. Watched the way Claudia smiled as she was led through the steps, and the way the young man never took his eyes off her.

The jealousy in her chest was hot and strong.

"If looks could kill."

Tsurra had joined her, leaning against the wall next to Kas.

She had her hair down and was wearing a red dress, the colour of wine with a black bodice and an open neckline. The dress showed off the puckered mess of scar tissue between the join of Tsurra's neck and her right shoulder. It was a vicious scar and one she'd had for as long as Kas had known her. Yet even after all this time, Kas did not know how Tsuraa had come by it. She always told Kas that it was from a werewolf bite when she was young, though Kas knew that to be a lie. One couldn't be bitten by a werewolf and not turn into one themselves.

Tsurra was carrying two tin cups of what appeared to be some darkly-coloured ale.

"I don't know what you are talking about," Kas said.

"Sure." Tsurra held out one of the cups. "Here."

Kas accepted it, took a sip and then spat it out while Tsurra laughed.

"Ugh, that is vile," Kas said, wiping her mouth. "I feel as though I've drunk horse piss."

"It's got a strong taste, that's for sure," said Tsurra and took a drink from her own cup. Hanging from her shoulder, was the small, green bag spelled to carry a limitless supply. Where Ombral's remnant was hidden inside. Tsurra had been adamant about being the one to keep an eye on the remnant tonight.

Kas grimaced and set her cup on the wall's ledge.

She looked back to the dancers and realised she had lost sight of Claudia. She scoured the moving gathering, almost feverishly, until she spotted what could have been a flash of Claudia's snowy head on the other side of the square, but it was hard to be sure when other bodies kept blocking her view.

"Trying to keep an eye on the vampyric girl to make sure she doesn't maul anyone, are you?" asked Tsurra.

Kas frowned. "She wouldn't do that." And she meant it.

A sigh. "If you say so."

Tsurra took another gulp of her disgusting ale and Kas went back to keeping an eye out for that familiar head of long, white hair. Though hopefully not so obviously this time around.

"I know I haven't been with your little party long, but you and the vampyric—Claudia," Tsurra amended, catching Kas's look, "are not exactly subtle about whatever is between the two of you."

Kas felt her cheeks go hot at the thought of Tsurra being able to tell what was on her mind when she looked at Claudia. And, of course, there was the stirring of nerves at what Tsurra might think. Would she be angry and denounce Kas as a Slayer? Would she be disappointed?

Kas opened her mouth to speak, but Tsurra continued.

"I know that you're no longer my responsibility. You are a grown woman and what choices or mistakes you make are your own. But some annoyingly sentimental part of me will always see you as that little girl I pulled from the river and brought back to the Keep because while she could face the idea of fighting monsters for the rest of her life, she couldn't face the idea of returning to her home without her family."

Kas had nothing to say to that.

"I only want you to be careful about the choices you make. Especially in regard to this Claudia of Trulio."

"That's it?" asked Kas. She could hardly believe it. At the very least, she had expected a warning or even an order to cut all ties with Claudia after they reached the Slayers Keep. "You're not going to hit me over the head and call me a fool? Not going to warn me off getting entangled with a vampyric?"

Tsurra shrugged. "It's as I said, your choices are your own. It's not my place to try and control you."

Tsurra finished the rest of her drink and told Kas she was going to get another one. "Want me to get you one, too?"

"Don't you dare."

Left alone again, Kas was given the chance to ponder. In her odd and indirect way, Tsurra had just given Kas her blessing to pursue a romance with Claudia if she so wished.

*Only Claudia might not wish to,* Kas mused, thinking back to their conversation at the lake.

The minstrels started playing a new song. This one louder and more upbeat and the dancing grew faster. People moving in a dizzying whirl of brightly coloured skirts and tunics.

And something about it compelled Kas to step forward and join in.

It was easy enough to fall into the rhythm and pick up the steps, it wasn't the first time Kas had participated in a group dance such as this. She could remember a fair few of them done with her siblings and friends when she was a child.

Dancing partners changed at a rapid pace. She had started off dancing with one of the older women who had served her panettone, and the next was the blond man who had asked Claudia to dance.

Every one of them was smiling, laughing. So full of life and joy that it was infectious, and Kas soon found herself laughing along with them.

She spun away from the little boy she was dancing with, and almost tripped over her own feet when she found herself faced with Claudia.

Claudia seemed just as surprised to wind up dancing with Kas. But only momentarily. She gave Kas that challenging smirk that once would have had Kas's blood boiling, but now lit something completely different inside her.

The words of the minstrels' song were loud in her ears.

*"Oh, my love*
*Watch her dance in the starlight*
*Have you ever seen a sight*
*More enchanting?*
*More delightful?*
*She sends my heart running fast—"*

The brief time that Kas got to hold Claudia in her arms was . . . wonderful. A feeling of exhilaration and comfort. As if there was nothing in the world more natural than being able to hold Claudia. She almost couldn't bring herself to let go of her once it was time for them to break apart, but somehow, she managed to.

*"—Mother said to me*
*Hold her tight*
*Never let go*
*Treat her like she's made of gold—"*

Her eyes stayed on Claudia. Watching her hair, loose and long and wonderful, twirl around her bare shoulders. Her movements so fluid and elegant and she wore an expression of such carefree exhilaration that it lit up her face. Claudia's beauty was heart stopping.

*"Oh, my love*
*My love*
*She's as pretty as a flower*
*As stunning as the sea*
*I'd stare at her all day*
*And never tire of that beauty*
*Oh, she's my love."*

And Kas realised she had been a fool because what she wanted could not have been any plainer.

The song and dance came to an end, and the people around Kas broke into applause. Kas did not join in. She strode purposefully through the crowd until she was in front of Claudia, a hand loosely wrapped around her wrist as the other woman looked up at her questioningly.

"Come with me?" she said breathlessly into the small space between them.

Claudia nodded and that was all the permission Kas needed to lead her away.

She found a secluded corner for them, in a space between two small, brick homes. It was further enough away from the festivities that only the barest traces of light managed to reach them.

"Kas?" Claudia asked once they were alone. "What is it?"

Kas had her backed up against one of the walls, her arms caging Claudia in on either side.

"I was an idiot," said Kas in a rush. "The other night when you asked me if there could be anything between us, and I said I wasn't sure, I was so bloody foolish. And I was foolish because I was afraid. Of what Tsurra and others might think. I—I let what happened in the past with my family get the better of me. But why should I? Why the fuck should I allow some monsters from my past ruin my future? I won't do it. I won't let them take another good thing away from me."

Claudia stared up at her with eyes that were wide and made her look startlingly young. "Have you forgotten," she whispered, "what I am? What *you* are?"

"No, but I don't care. All I care about is the way I feel for you. And that you are brave and witty . . . and perhaps the most gorgeous woman I have ever laid my eyes on."

Claudia arched one delicate, silver eyebrow. "So my looks are what is most important to you?" But Kas could tell it was said in jest.

"Did you not hear what I said before that?" Kas was smiling and beginning to allow herself to draw irresistibly closer into Claudia's space. "I could go on, but we might end up being here a while."

Claudia smiled and took Kas's face between her hands. "I suppose the night could be better spent than here in this alleyway. But first . . ."

She brought Kas's face down to hers and their lips collided.

Kas had kissed many women before, but none had made her feel quite like how it felt to *finally* be kissing Claudia.

It felt right in the way it had to dance with Claudia. It was heart-wrenching, and breath-taking and as intoxicating and addictive as the finest, strongest mead Kas had ever tasted. Perhaps even more so.

In her eagerness for more—more of the kiss. More of Claudia— Kas was the one to turn a chaste kiss into something hungrier and open-mouthed. Claudia seemed just as enthusiastic to taste more of Kas. Soon enough, their kissing had lost all finesse, and they were panting into each other's mouths. Claudia's fingers were curled in Kas's hair so tight it bordered on painful and Kas had one palm against Claudia's hip and the other splayed against the small of her back.

Kas never wanted the kiss to end. She thought she would be more than happy to truly spend the entire night outside in the dark, pressed against someone's house, and doing nothing but kissing Claudia.

Claudia's teeth sank into her bottom lip, hard enough to draw blood and Kas let out a low groan.

She felt Claudia's smile against her lips, and then her tongue was on Kas's lip, licking away the blood she had drawn.

It was so alluring Kas thought her knees would give out. She felt suddenly overwhelmed with the idea of all the things she wanted to do to Claudia. She did not know if she had enough of a hold on her inhibitions to stop her from doing so right then and there.

But against her mouth, Claudia said in a husky tone, "Let's take this somewhere else, shall we?"

Kas could only nod.

Now it was her turn to be led away.

## CHAPTER 36
# CLAUDIA

IT WAS a quick walk back to the inn. Apart from a cat with a bushy tail cleaning itself on the front counter, there was not a soul to be seen.

Not that it mattered much to Claudia and Kas. They were only intent on each other and reaching the privacy of a room. Once they did and the door was shut firmly behind them, Claudia pounced on Kas. Arms around her neck and mouth pressed insistently against hers.

Claudia felt consumed by a desperate want—*need*—for the other woman and she was well pleased to note that Kas seemed just as eager for her. If the hands groping at the bodice of her dress and the open-mouthed, biting kisses were anything to go by.

Without breaking their kiss, their hands roamed each other's bodies, frantically attempting to divest the other of their clothing. Claudia even opened up a tear in the fine linen of Kas's white shirt as she hurried to pull it over the other woman's head.

Kas growled, "I hope *you're* planning on paying for that when we return to the seamstress tomorrow."

Claudia grinned devilishly against Kas's lips. "Or I could just make it up to right now?" she said, nipping at the Slayer's bottom lip.

It elicited a groan from Kas and Claudia relished it. Skating her open palms along Kas's firm back and stomach, caressing the scars she encountered there just as she had envisioned doing so, Claudia pressed her lips against the underside of Kas's jaw.

She heard Kas release a soft sigh as she tilted her chin up, giving Claudia more access. She trailed her lips tantalisingly down the side of Kas's neck, over her beating pulse, until she came to the two smooth scars at the base of her neck. The scars Claudia herself had left there when Kas had allowed her to drink her blood during their voyage to Almora.

Kas inhaled sharply when Claudia licked at the raised bits of skin. Remnants of *her* fangs. *Her* mark on the Slayer. The thought made her inordinately pleased. Unable to help herself, she grazed the scar with her teeth. Only lightly, yet it was enough to make Kas shiver.

"Sensitive, are you?" whispered Claudia.

"Just a draft," Kas responded haughtily. "I suppose you wouldn't feel it. Still being clothed and all."

Claudia pulled back so she could look at Kas directly in the eye. "Then undress me."

She spoke the words with the barest hint of a challenge and Kas raised her eyebrows in response. Claudia expected Kas to reach for the back of her dress. To peel it off her with the same urgency she had done to Kas's shirt.

She didn't.

Instead, her hand travelled up Claudia's arm, taking hold of the edge of her glove. Then, with an almost agonising slowness, she pulled it down, down until the glove was all the way off and Claudia's arm was bare.

Kas lifted her hand, holding it lightly by her fingers, and bent her head over it. Placing one of the softest kisses to the back of Claudia's hand.

Something so small and simple should not have made Claudia's heartbeat speed up the way it did. Should not have made her feel like there were hundreds of butterflies with silk-soft wings flitting about beneath her skin. And yet, it did.

Such tenderness was not something she had expected from Kas. It made her feel . . . treasured. And that was something new.

Kas removed the glove from her other arm, allowing it to fall soundlessly to the floor. This time, she feathered a kiss against the inside of Claudia's wrist. Lips against her scarred flesh.

"I do believe you're getting sidetracked," said Claudia, her eyes heavy-lidded.

Kas lifted her head, gazing up at Claudia from beneath strands of red hair that fell into her eyes. Her mouth was curled into a rakish grin. "You think so?"

"Yes. I told you to undress me."

"I am undressing you." Another kiss, further along the inside of her arm. This one with a hint of teeth.

"You've taken off my gloves," Claudia pointed out. "That hardly counts."

"All right then, since you're so impatient."

They were kissing again as Kas's hands made their way to the back of Claudia's dress, undoing the laces there with surprising adeptness. Claudia belatedly realised that she was also being herded backwards when the backs of her legs bumped against the side of the bed.

She found herself lying flat on the blankets, and by that time Kas had undone her dress enough that it now hung shockingly loose against her body. It was no effort at all for Kas to—*finally*—strip it off her.

It took no time at all to rid themselves of the rest of their clothing. No time at all before Kas was lying on top of Claudia, and they were exchanging, hungry, hurried kisses while their hands slid across each other's naked skin.

Kas's hand stroked an enticing path between her breasts and down her stomach.

Claudia pressed kisses to the arm that was braced on the bed beside her head. She thought she would be content to spend an entire day doing nothing but tracing her lips over the swells and slopes of Kas's muscles. *Saints, it's almost as if this woman was carved from stone.*

Kas's body atop Claudia's was a welcome weight. The feel of Kas pressed against her with no barrier between them lit sparks along her skin. Claudia hitched one of her legs up, wrapping it around Kas's waist and pulling her in even closer.

"Fucking hells," Kas breathed. Her lips on one of Claudia's breasts. "How is your skin this soft?"

Claudia laughed. "Jealous?"

"No. I'm enjoying it. It makes me want to . . ." She trailed off as she moved further up Claudia's body.

Claudia gasped at the feeling of blunt teeth biting into the side of her neck.

Kas had bitten her.

Above the ribbon of her pendant, in almost the exact same place where Claudia had done to her. Where she now bore two scars.

Of course, Claudia would bear no scar of her own, but Kas had certainly bitten her hard enough that she wouldn't be surprised if there was a mark.

"Payback," she thought she heard Kas murmur.

Something ignited in Claudia. Allowing some of her vampyric strength to take the reins, she took hold of Kas by her broad shoulders and in one fluid motion, flipped their positions. Now Claudia straddled Kas's waist while the Slayer stared up at her with a look that was part bewilderment and part arousal.

What followed after that was frantic. Hot. No more words passed between them. The only sounds to leave their lips were breathless moans and bitten off cries.

"*Fuck,*" Kas ground out when Claudia buried her fingers between Kas's thighs.

She arched her neck until the tendons stood out. Her chest rose and fell with her rapid breaths. The sweat that had built up along her skin shone in the dark amber glow from the lights outside. Her hair—much like Claudia's—was sweat-slicked and mussed from having Claudia's fingers twining through and gripping the strands repeatedly.

She looked a wreck and Claudia drank up the sight of it, the way someone dying of thirst would drink up every drop afforded to them. The way a vampyric would drink a human's blood.

Even as she moved inside Kas, trying to find the right speed and angle that would give her the most pleasure, Claudia couldn't tear her eyes away from Kas's face.

She wanted to see every expression. Every flutter of her lashes and shift of her brow. Did not want to miss the way Kas's teeth dug into her lower lip at the same time she tightened around Claudia's fingers.

When those green eyes, heavy-lidded and darkened with want, looked up at her, Claudia felt her heart stutter in her chest.

Kas had said that Claudia was the most beautiful woman she had ever seen. Many others had voiced similar sentiments in the past. But in that moment, Claudia couldn't believe that she—or anyone for that matter—could ever come close to matching the beauty that was the woman beneath her.

Kas of Veldenier.

*"Claudia,"* Kas cried out as she reached her peak.

The sound of her name spoken from Kas's lips with such want and desperation would be her ruination.

As she allowed herself to become lost in the sight, sound and feel of Kas, Claudia thought that if this was what her mother and Serisa had found, then she could almost understand them.

*If I were to lose this, maybe I too would give up.*

*Maybe I too would burn the world down.*


AFTER, they lay on the tangled bedding in each other's arms and talked. Claudia told Kas the story of how she rescued Wolf when he was only a pup from a hunter's camp, while Kas recollected moments from her childhood as a daughter of house Lelvinare. Including one tale of her father taking her for her first ride on horseback, which ended with Kas in tears and with a fear of horses that had lasted until she began her training as a Slayer.

When Claudia mentioned her age, she laughed at how shocked Kas seemed.

"How old did you think I was?"

"I don't know. A hundred maybe? Vampyrics live such long lives, it hardly ever occurs to me that they might be as old as I am."

They spoke to each other of the dark days that had followed the deaths of Kas's family and Claudia's father. Sharing the pain of grief that would never truly leave them.

"Tell me," said Claudia, "What made you choose to become a Slayer after your family died? You came from a noble family. Surely there was no shortage of those who would have taken you in?"

At first, Kas merely hummed absent-mindedly as she toyed with a lock of Claudia's hair. "You're right. There were a number of people who I could have gone to live with," she said. "My grandfather and my grandmother. An aunt. Friends of my parents. Hells, I'm sure even an ordinary townsperson would have been keen to become the guardian of the sole survivor of the wealthiest family in Veldenier."

"So what made you want to give up that life of luxury?"

"I—When I first begged Tsurra to take me with her to the Slayers Keep, I thought I was being noble. That by leaving behind everything I had ever known to become a Slayer, I could stop what happened to my family from happening to other children and their families." Kas smiled wistfully. "But of course, I realised that such a thing is impossible. And as time went on, I also realised that maybe I just . . . didn't want to go back to my old life without my family. That doing so would have been too painful, and it would have been easier to start completely anew. To leave behind Kasanna Lelvinare and become Kas of Veldenier."

"And was it easier?" asked Claudia.

Kas stared up at the ceiling. Her expression gave nothing away. "No. I still miss them every day. Sometimes I think about how I can't exactly remember what my younger siblings' faces looked like, or what colour my father's eyes were, and it—it hurts."

"I feel the same way about my father," Claudia said. "He was the best man I had ever known. He did not deserve to die the way he did."

"What about your mother? You don't miss her?"

Claudia took a moment to consider. "I never got the chance to know her all that well. Before my father died, the times where she would come to visit us were few and far between. And then when I came to live with her and the rest of the clan, she was too consumed in her own grief for me to come to know her any better before she died."

Claudia thought back to the night her mother was found dead. The shock of it and the shock she felt at her own reaction—or lack of. Her *mother* was dead, and she could not find it in herself to feel as broken-hearted about it as she had when her father died. Claudia had felt more sorrow on Serisa's behalf at the time.

It had been the first—and only—time she had seen her strong, unbreakable older sister cry and it had felt like any physical wound might.

*Did she cry the way she had cried over our mother when her lover died? Or when she found out her father was also dead?* wondered Claudia. *If I had been there for her as I had been back then, would things have still turned out this way?*

The sound of Kas laughing quietly snapped her out of her sombre musings. "What is it?"

"I was only thinking about what a sad pair of orphans the two of us make."

"We make a good match then, don't we?"

Kas smiled, stretching the scar on her face. "I suppose we do."

The warmth and affection in Kas's eyes made Claudia's chest tighten pleasantly.

Shifting, she brought an arm around Kas's waist, fitting herself against her side at the same time Kas twisted around to wrap both her arms around Claudia. They fit against each other as if they had been carved from the wood of the same tree. Kas rested her head atop Claudia's, while Claudia pressed her forehead against the jut of the Slayer's collarbone and inhaled the scent of her. Old soap and a hint of horse.

Having Kas's arms around her made her feel safe and comforted in a way that had begun to grow foreign to her. When was the last time someone had held her like this?

But it did not matter. She had it now and Claudia thought that if she could stay like this for the rest of her life, warm and safe in her lover's embrace, then she would be quite content.

# CHAPTER 37
# SERISA

They never noticed her.

Perhaps Claudia might have sensed her if she weren't so enraptured with the Slayer.

Shrouded in the dark, away from the lights and the humans enjoying their silly little festival in the streets below, Serisa stood on a thatched rooftop. Looking in through the windows of the neighbouring inn. More specifically, through the window of the room where Claudia and that red-haired Slayer lay relaxed in each other's arms.

In their own little world of newly minted affections and delight.

Serisa seethed at the sight.

*How could she? Not only a human but a Slayer?*

A Slayer like the one who had killed her father and had almost killed her.

She heard Claudia's soft laughter in response to something the Slayer whispered in her ear.

Serisa curled her hands into fists, so tightly she heard her own knuckles crack.

It was as if Claudia was taunting her. Flaunting her new little romance with the Slayer. But it was also more than that.

*Why? Why does Claudia get to have the warmth and happiness of love when it was ripped away from me? Why should she be able to enjoy having her lover's arms wrapped around her as they whisper sweet nothings to each—*

And that's when it struck Serisa.

She had come here planning to find a way to steal the remnant out from under Claudia's nose.

However, now she had a far more interesting method of getting what she wanted.

Serisa hadn't even realised she was smiling.

She would get the dragon remnant.

And she would shatter Claudia's happiness as she did so.

Serisa would make her come to regret ever allowing herself to give her heart to a Slayer.

Turning her back on the unsuspecting couple, Serisa vanished into the night.

# INTERLUDE

Serisa knew something was not right, even before she made it back to the cottage. She could feel it in the air like the ominous stillness that descended right before a storm.

She had spent the night out feeding, as she did every once a month. Now that the night was nearing its end and her thirst was thoroughly quenched, Serisa soared high above the treetops. As a streak of dark smoke, barely visible against the dark sky. Many of the trees were still bare of leaves from the harsh winter. The landscape below her rushed past in a grey and white blur.

Only when she was near enough, did Serisa notice it. The plume of smoke rising above the trees. Right where she knew the cottage to be.

*Allegra.*

Serisa hastened and landed on the ground only a few paces away from the cottage . . . only to find that it was no more.

What was left in its place was a smouldering ruin and a dying fire that had left the air hot and so thick with smoke and ash it nearly choked her.

The nearby coop of Allegra's beloved chickens was empty, though untouched by the fire. Only a few stray feathers lay among the ashen snow.

Serisa stared, unable to fully comprehend what she was seeing for a moment. How could this have happened? What caused such a fire? And where was Allegra? Surely she hadn't been claimed by the blaze?

Serisa's panic was stopped before it could fully take root, by the sound of voices—unfamiliar voices—only a short way away.

Between one breath and the next, Serisa found herself near the pond in the small clearing, where she had spent many cherished moonlit moments alone with Allegra.

But it was no secluded spot now. Six humans, five men and one woman, all dressed in ragged, travel-worn clothing, stood gathered around one of the trees.

Serisa might have wondered how, after all these years, a group of strangers managed to find their way here, how they had managed to get past Allegra's wards. She might have demanded to know *what* they were doing here.

But Serisa was robbed of her speech. Robbed of her ability to think.

All she could do was stare at the body dangling from one of the lower branches of the tree the strangers stood before.

When Serisa had bid her farewell earlier in the night, Allegra's cheeks had been flushed and her hair rumpled from the pleasure they'd so recently given each other. She had been beautiful and sweet and smiling as Serisa kissed her.

That beloved smile was gone now. All that remained was a slack, haunted look on a face bruised almost beyond recognition. Her golden hair was in disarray around her face and neck which was bound and distorted by rope. Her body was limp beneath her torn and blood-stained dress.

Serisa was only dimly aware of the strangers speaking.

"She took longer to die than I thought she would."

"Good. After the way she betrayed us and how long we had to spend huntin' her down. Why should her death have been a quick one?"

"She always was a shitty sorcerer. She hardly even put up much of a fight!"

*"What have you done?"*

The words were torn from Serisa's mouth, ragged and painful, and the strangers finally became aware of her presence.

"Who's this?" said one with a greying beard.

"I thought Allegra was all alone out here?" the woman remarked. She had a sorcerer's amulet around her neck.

They didn't know she was a vampyric. They couldn't tell with the hood of her cloak up and the darkness obscuring her grey skin.

One of the men ambled towards her. A sneer curling the corner of his mouth. "What are you doin' out here all alone, missy? Don't ya know there's dangerous folk about—"

The man's words were cut off with a wet choking noise.

Serisa's claws had pierced through his throat. All the way in until the tips could be seen sticking out the back of his neck.

Blood poured over Serisa's hand, hot and slick.

The man wasn't smirking anymore. His eyes were wide, his jaw slack and dripping blood.

He lifted his hands as if he could bat hers away, but as soon as Serisa pulled her hand back, the man collapsed. He was already dead.

"What the fuck?" shouted the one with the greying beard, drawing a blade.

Serisa attacked him too. Faster than he could raise his weapon in self-defence. Faster than he could shout in terror or plead for mercy.

It was like the night when she had fought the Slayer who murdered her father. Where her rage took a hold of her body, dulling her senses so she was hardly even aware of the blood being spilt all around her. Of the screams, or of her claws cutting through flesh and bone.

It moved her forward to tear open the stomach of the sorcerer, like ripping open a sack of grain, and propelled her to rip out the throat of another with her fangs.

All she could think about was Allegra.

Allegra, her kind and gentle lover.

Allegra, who loved to sing.

Allegra who was far too good for this world.

Allegra who was now dead.

Dead.

*Allegra was dead.*

When Serisa came back to herself, she was drenched in blood and the bodies of the six strangers lay strewn along the ground around her. The red of their blood mixed with the white of the snow. One dismembered body lay close enough to the half-frozen pond for their blood to seep into the icy water.

She crossed the clearing, entirely uncaring of the gore she stepped in along the way, until she reached Allegra. Her bare, purpled feet hung directly in front of Serisa's face.

She hardly even remembered cutting Allegra down. Everything felt like a daze until she was laying Allegra's body slowly, gently on the ground.

Serisa knelt with her. She cradled her face, brushing hair away from it and some of the blood that had dried around her mouth and temple. She did it all with the softest touch she possessed. As if Allegra were so breakable. As if Serisa could do anymore harm to her now.

Warm tears of blood spilled from Serisa's eyes, blurring her vision. They landed on Allegra's still face.

"Allegra . . ." Serisa whispered, because what else could she say? A small, foolish, part of her wondered if she just called out to Allegra, if Allegra heard her voice, maybe she would awaken? Maybe this was some sort of illusion Allegra had managed to cast? Maybe it could be undone, and all could return to as it was.

But no matter how many times Serisa uttered her name, no matter how Serisa apologised for leaving her alone, or told her that Serisa needed her, so she *had to come back*, Allegra did not wake.

Her eyes remained glassy and unmoving. Her body stayed limp and grew colder by the second. Serisa could feel no heartbeat.

Allegra's life was gone. Snuffed out like a candle flame. Only there was no relighting it.

As the enormity of it settled around her like a cold, piercing wind, her grief swelled. Growing into a hard, painful thing that wracked her body with violent tremors, and she felt sure it was going to tear her apart. Rip her into grisly pieces like the bodies around her.

Instead, it freed itself in the form of a tortured scream from Serisa's lips. The scream turned to sobs that choked her and felt never ending. Serisa clutched at her chest as if that might stem the tide of this agony, so hard her claws pierced through her clothes and drew blood. But she hardly felt it. The only pain she could feel was the one inside of her.

One she was sure would never go away.

When her tears and her cries finally ran dry, Serisa lay there in the snow, curled as tight as her body would let her. Beside Allegra. She stayed like that for a long time, until snow began to settle on her. Alone with the dead and the stench of it.

When finally, she did move, Serisa noticed for the first time what lay discarded in a snow pile nearby.

Allegra's amethyst amulet.

It must have been torn from her neck, Serisa realised as she picked it up and saw the chain had been snapped. There was a crack in the stone, as well.

A renewed surge of anger spilled over her. How dare they. How dare these people—these *animals*—come here to take and destroy what they had no right to. To ruin another's happiness.

*But that is the way of humans, isn't it?* she said to herself.

They ruin all they touch.

Humans had taken her mother, coming between her and Serisa's father until he was driven away. Then when the human had died, her mother did as well.

They had killed her father and put his bones up for decoration.

And now . . .

Now they had stolen Allegra from her. They had ripped Serisa's heart from her.

She clutched the amulet tightly, until it was in danger of cracking further.

If humans would see Serisa's happiness and loved ones taken from her, then Serisa would do the same to them.

She rose to her feet and strode from the clearing.

If she had to endure this torment, then she would see it returned to the humans tenfold.

Serisa was standing before the ruin of the cottage—the home she had shared with Allegra these past few years. A place where they had shared so much laughter and love.

Picking around charred wood, blackened stone and the ashen remains of what had been carpets and furniture, Serisa made her way to where once had been their bedroom.

She lifted what little remained of the bed and flung it aside, uncaring of where it landed or the splintering crash it made.

The floorboards below hadn't been spared by the fire but were mostly still intact. Even if they looked as though they would crumble to dust with even the lightest touch.

Serisa tore at them anyway, ripping up bits of the frail wood and uncaring of the splinters that tore open her palms.

Until finally she found it. Still in the exact same place where she had hidden it beneath a loose floorboard when she had first come here all those years ago. Not that she had been worried otherwise. She would have felt it if it was missing. Never was there a moment where she wasn't aware of the remnant's presence.

Taking it into her hands and wiping away bits of ash and debris, Serisa noticed that the broken dragon scale was undamaged. Not by the fire and not by the passage of time.

Maybe another time she would feel thankful to her past self for keeping the remnant close.

For now, all she could feel past the hollowness within her, was a hardened conviction.

If she was to get her vengeance on humankind, then this was how.

She would unleash their most feared monsters. She would watch as the dragons brought fire and death down upon them. She would rejoice in their fear and savour their anguish.

She would see them all burn for taking from her what she loved most.

"*I would set the world aflame if I had to. Just to stay by your side.*" she had said to Allegra once.

*I can no longer stay by your side,* Serisa made a silent vow. *So instead, I will have the world burn for daring to take you from me.*

# CHAPTER 38
# KAS

"Watch your stance." Tsurra's terse instruction rang through the air. "You'll never do any good in a real fight if you're unsteady on your feet."

"I wasn't *feeling* unsteady," said Aara, but she nonetheless readjusted the placement of her feet as she worked through the set exercises with the sword Tsurra had given her.

"Well, you'll certainly feel it when your enemy is easily able to knock you down. You must be mindful where you put your feet as well as your sword," said Tsurra. "It could make the difference between whether you live or die."

Kas stood under the warmth of the sun, watching Aara train with Tsurra's guidance. As they rested their horses, Tsurra had decided to spend the time giving Aara a quick lesson.

Kas couldn't help but smile as she watched Aara discover that Tsurra could be a ruthless teacher. Hearing Tsurra point out flaws and call out commands that Aara tried desperately to keep up with, brought back memories of Kas's own time training under Tsurra. Countless hours spent practising the same exercises until she was dripping in sweat, sore all over and fantasising about pushing Tsurra off the Keep's battlements.

Behind Kas, Claudia sat beneath the shade of a birch tree. The sun was particularly warm and the clouds in the sky were few. Kas knew that days such as this could be taxing on Claudia, yet she never complained. Wolf sat tall by Claudia's side, a long pink tongue hanging from his open muzzle.

Kas finished up brushing the tangles out of Bod's mane and retreated to the birch tree and sat herself down in the shade beside Claudia. When she did, Claudia tipped her head to the side, resting it atop Kas's shoulder. Kas brushed her lips against the crown of Claudia's head and inhaled the faint floral scent from the soap she'd used the night before.

"Would you like me to tip some water down the back of your neck?" she murmured. "It'll help you cool down."

"Oh? Are you sure it's not just an excuse to get my shirt wet so then I might have to take it off to dry?"

Kas huffed a breath of laughter. "Surprisingly no. But I wouldn't complain about that outcome."

She felt Claudia tremble with laughter against her. "I'll pass. The warmth isn't so unbearable."

They stayed like that for a while, watching Aara and Tsurra. The pair trained near the edge of a cliff and beyond them was the open view of blue sky and mountains. And somewhere within those mountains they would find the Slayers Keep, and at the Keep they would find the sword *Velane* and use it to rid the world of Ombral's remnant and any chance of freeing the dragons from their prison.

"We should arrive at the Keep by night tomorrow," said Kas. "After all this time our journey will finally be over."

"Mm," was all Claudia said, her tone clearly distant. Distracted.

"Is something wrong?"

Claudia hesitated. She pulled her head away from Kas's shoulder, sitting up straight, and her hand went into the long fur of Wolf's back.

Finally, she said, "There's been no sign of my sister. Not since Nescoro. It makes me nervous. As if this is simply the calm before the storm."

"Is there any chance she could have decided to give up on her plans to bring death and destruction to Vil Tresar?"

Claudia looked as if Kas had just told her something mildly amusing. "As much as I would like to believe that," she said, "I know she would not give up on this so easily."

"After we reach the Slayer's Keep," Kas said, "and Ombral's remnant is destroyed, what do you plan on doing with your sister?"

"I will keep trying, I suppose. To get through to her and make her abandon her quest for vengeance."

"That didn't go so well the last few times you tried."

Claudia said nothing.

Kas chewed on her lip, wondering if it was wise of her to speak these next words. She did not want to hurt Claudia, but she did not want her to be naïve when it came to her sister, either.

Kas took a breath. "But maybe she's too far gone now. Maybe . . . we might have to—"

Claudia's words were firm but soft as she said, "She is my sister."

Kas watched her. Claudia's eyes were fixed ahead of her and while her expression was unreadable, Kas saw the way her fingers gripped Wolf's fur. Not tightly, but it still looked as if she were trying to ground herself. And that was enough to give Kas even a hint to the kind of turmoil Claudia must be feeling.

So, Kas decided to let the conversation lie. For now. They still had to bring Ombral's remnant to the Keep after all. Everything else could wait until then.

Carefully, Kas brought her arm up around Claudia's shoulders, pulling her back against her side. Claudia went willingly, nestling her head against Kas's throat and breathing out a sigh.

*"As if this is simply the calm before the storm,"*

* * *

THE PARTY of four settled down for sleep in a pass between two mountains, beneath the shelter of one of the towering pine trees that

255

grew there. The night was a cacophony of crickets, owl hoots and the distant screeching of bats.

Kas could even hear the echoing yowl of a mountain lion when she shook Claudia awake, took her by the hand and whispered for her to follow. Claudia did, with no hesitation. Wolf stayed sitting by Claudia's bedroll, like some shadowy shape in the dark.

Kas didn't feel guilty as she abandoned her watch, she knew that due to the lack of any snoring, Tsurra was still awake.

"Where are you spiriting me off to?" Claudia asked as they walked down the hill they had climbed hours earlier.

Kas squeezed Claudia's hand in hers. "Patience," was all she said.

"You woke me up in the middle of the night. I don't have patience." There was teasing in Claudia's voice.

It didn't take long before Kas brought them to her intended destination. At the base of the two twin peaks, all other nighttime sounds were drowned out by the rushing of a waterfall that descended into a river. Its bed was littered with chunks of rock and reeds. They had passed this way during the day. There had been dragonflies droning around the reeds then and a heron hunting for fish.

"The waterfall?" Claudia looked at Kas with an arched brow. "It's a lovely sight, but I did already see it."

Kas smiled and tugged on Claudia's hand. "But did you notice this, I wonder?"

She brought Claudia right to the edge of the bank and up to the waterfall. Close enough that she could feel the spray of tiny water drops on her face. When Kas put a foot in the water, she felt Claudia tug back on her hand.

"Oh, come on. You trust me, don't you?"

Claudia didn't answer, but she did not pull away either and Kas took that as confirmation enough. This time when she moved forward, Claudia followed.

The water only came to Kas's ankle where she stepped. She felt the unyielding hardness of stone beneath her foot. Closing her eyes, she stepped through the waterfall, feeling her hair and clothes become sodden in seconds. Claudia's hand remained in hers the whole time.

When she next opened her eyes, it was to find they were standing in a small cavern. The damp, craggy walls and floor were overrun with moss and purple petalled notte sera orchids. Their sweet, herbal aroma mixed with the odour of wet soil and rock.

When Kas looked back at Claudia it was to find her as soaked through as Kas was and with her mass of wet hair falling all over her face. Kas couldn't help it. She burst out laughing, the sound of it bouncing off the stone walls.

"Stop laughing at me you buffoon," complained Claudia as she pushed her hair back.

"I'm sorry," Kas said though she couldn't strip the smile from her face. She stepped forward to move a few more stray strands from Claudia's face. She brushed away a water droplet dangling from Claudia's chin. "You're all wet now."

Claudia gave her an unimpressed look. "Yes, thank you. Is that why you interrupted my sleep? To see me half-drowned?"

"You're not half-drowned. And actually, I thought it would be fun to explore this cave with you."

"Hardly much to explore." Claudia stepped past Kas and further into the cavern. "You could walk all the way around it in ten paces."

Kas stepped into Claudia's space. Her front to the other woman's back. Her arms twining around Claudia's waist, and her nose against the top of Claudia's head. She murmured, "It's cosy, though, don't you think?"

Claudia let out a little breath of laughter that lifted Kas's heart to hear. It seemed her plan to lift Claudia's spirits was working. Claudia turned in the circle of Kas's arms and Kas was presented with that alluring smile and those arresting eyes that were such a delicate shade of blue, framed by lashes the colour of silver.

Would Claudia's beauty ever not rob her of breath?

"You are insatiable, Kas of Veldenier," Claudia whispered right before she pulled Kas in for a hard kiss.

It was as if they had found themselves on a cliff's edge and they had now decided to take the plunge together. That first kiss became a series of longer, more desperate kisses. Hands wandered and grabbed and began tugging on clothing.

As a Slayer, Kas should be aware of her surroundings at all times. Never to let only one thing capture all her attention. Yet when she was with Claudia like this, she could not bring herself to withhold any part of herself from her.

When they were both naked, Kas lay Claudia down against the soft moss and orchids. Kas couldn't help but think how particularly beautiful she looked like this. Her lithe and pale body against the dark greens and purple of the bed of flowers. Her lily-white hair fanned out around her like a halo.

The sight was like a fist around her heart. She wished she could brand the way Claudia looked right then into her mind forever. If she were an artist, she might have felt inclined to find some way to capture Claudia through brush and paint. If she were a poet, she might compose sonnets to immortalise Claudia's beauty. But since she was neither of those things, the only way Kas found she could pay homage to the woman beneath her was through worshipful kisses and reverent caresses.

"Kas," Claudia breathed when her lips wandered between pale thighs. "*Kas.*"

The sound of her name on Claudia's tongue was as heady as a glass of Wyvern's Breath Whiskey. Heady as the taste of her.

Kas wanted to give her everything. Every piece of herself. For she knew that Claudia would treat them as nothing less than precious in return.

Before long, the little cave was filled with the sounds of their lovemaking. Kas found herself whispering broken words that were Claudia's name alongside a string of endearments, into those delicate collarbones.

If this really was their last moment of peace, then Kas was going to savour it.

## CHAPTER 39
# CLAUDIA

THE AIR WAS a chill against Claudia's naked skin, yet she felt no compulsion to reach for her clothing which lay scattered on the cavern floor around them.

Kas lay sleeping peacefully beside her amongst the moss and notte sera orchids. Claudia would need to wake her soon; they couldn't spend the whole night away from the others. Still, she wanted to spend a few more quiet moments with only her and Kas in this secret little cave, shielded from the rest of the world by a curtain of water.

She sat up, the moss rustling softly beneath her. Drawing her knees up against her chest, Claudia gazed at the sheet of water falling over the mouth of the cave, turning the colour of silver and white under the light of the moon.

She let her mind drift and it wandered, as it had been doing of late, to her sister. She thought back to the day she had first come to the Salvaclare clan's castle.

Claudia had never thought she could know loneliness as she had in the days after her father died and she had fled Trulio, the only home she ever knew. But then she had stood inside that vast castle, expecting to be taken into her mother's embrace, only for her to turn away from her daughter so she could be alone in her own grief over her lost love. Leaving Claudia alone with vampyrics who loathed the sight of her. Who might have killed her, had it not been for Serisa.

The sister she had never met before, had appeared, parting the encroaching vampyrics as effortlessly as if they were water. Her presence was commanding and her beauty as striking as a blade. Yet when she had knelt in front of Claudia to brush some mud from her cheek, her touch and the expression on her face had been utterly gentle.

*"It's wonderful to finally meet you, little sister."*

Nights later, when one of the vampyrics had attempted to kill Claudia in her bed, it had been Serisa who came to her rescue. Claudia could still see clearly, her sister covered in blood, standing over the torn apart body of the Claudia's would-be murderer. A gruesome and terrifying sight for any child to behold, but Claudia had felt no fear. Only relief and admiration for her saviour.

She'd thrown herself into the safety of her elder sister's arms and listened as Serisa made her a promise.

*"Nothing will harm you so long as I am near."*

But then Serisa had left. Disappearing into the night and leaving Claudia to fend for herself.

And since she returned, she had done nothing but try to harm Claudia.

If Claudia focused, she thought she could still feel the echoes of pain from the wounds Serisa herself had given her on the night she had returned to the castle. All because Claudia had spoken against her wishes to free the dragons to wreak havoc on humankind.

Those wounds may have long since healed, but there was something inside of her that Claudia was not sure ever would.

*It's not her. Not really,* Claudia reminded herself. *She's lost. But I can bring her back.*

Creeping up like a weed from the ground, doubt whispered to her, *But can you really?*

A wordless sound from beside her, and Claudia looked to where Kas was still sleeping. She had shifted onto her side, drawing closer to Claudia. As if seeking her out even in her sleep.

Smiling, Claudia lay herself back down, her position mirroring Kas's. She reached out and traced a gentle line down the aquiline bridge of Kas's nose. Then she ran the tips of her fingers over the scar that carved across Kas's cheek, making sure to keep her touch as light as a moth's wing.

Kas stirred but did not wake. Her expression remained peacefully smoothed out in sleep. Claudia allowed herself the delight of observing Kas like this, so close and unguarded. Affection fluttered in her chest.

Her melancholy from moments ago was chased away by the closeness of Kas, and the reassurance her presence brought to Claudia. Who would have thought that amongst everything happening, she would have found this? This warm, and bright and wonderful thing.

Without her even realising it, Kas of Veldenier had carved her name upon Claudia's heart.

Claudia nestled in closer to her lover and allowed herself to focus on nothing else.

CHAPTER 40
# KAS

The Slayers Keep was made entirely of grey stone and blended in quite well with the craggy grey rock of the mountainside it was built into.

Sprawled out beneath the Keep at the base of the mountain was the city, Rosille, the birthplace of the first Slayer, Lyar. They had to cut through Rosille to reach the Keep, and even though it had been a little over a year since Kas had last returned, these streets had lost none of their familiarity. She still knew which turns she'd have to make to reach the tavern she had often snuck out to visit in her adolescent years. Still recognised the alley next to the blacksmith's, where she had kissed the daughter of a travelling merchant.

Rosille was more familiar to her than Veldenier had ever had a chance to be.

"It looks like a castle," was the first thing Aara said as the Keep loomed above them.

"Not a castle," said Kas. "A fortress."

And like any fortress, it looked large enough to host an army of hundreds. Though it was only home to twenty, and they were never all within the walls at the same time. It was made up of battlements that ran the entire perimeter of the Keep, and turrets with pointed rooftops that overlooked the surroundings. She saw a group of sparrows take flight from the east guard tower as they neared.

"It's certainly nothing compared to the actual castle I lived in," Claudia said.

"The castle infested with vampyrics?" said Kas.

"Maybe don't mention anything about that once we are inside the Keep," said Tsurra. "Unless you want the others to try and mount your new lady friend's head on our walls, Kas."

They had to cross over a bridge to reach the gate, its portcullis already pulled open, which was not an unusual sight, and soon enough they rode into the Keep's courtyard. Nothing about it had changed since Kas had last set foot in the Keep. Perhaps the grass had grown longer, but the beaten-looking training dummies still stood in a row to the west side. The same broken chunk of battlement lodged in the earth by the gate, that had supposedly been there for decades.

They left their horses inside the stable near the gate. There were already three other horses and Kas recognised the bay stallion missing half an ear as Caisus's.

"I'll see you again in the morning, boy," she told Bod, stroking his nose. "I think your hooves could use a trim."

"It's so quiet here," Aara remarked, as she stood in the middle of the courtyard, taking in the Slayers Keep from up close. She had to crane her head back.

"Very rarely is the Slayers Keep full," Kas explained. "Usually there might only be a small handful here at a time, while the rest are out travelling, looking for monsters that need killing."

Aara gave Kas a querying look. "Do all Slayers live in the Keep?"

"Not all," it was Tsurra who answered. "There are plenty of Slayers who live in their own homes. My father grew up in Gravende and didn't set foot in the Slayers Keep until he was twenty and already a seasoned Slayer."

Kas noticed Tsurra eyeing Claudia who stood a little apart from them with Wolf at her side. She was also looking around at the Keep, but where Aara's gaze was full of wonder, Claudia's was with trepidation. It hit Kas then that Claudia was a monster thrust into the stronghold of monster slayers. Aara was as well, but a werecat would have little to fear from a group of Slayers. A vampyric, however, was a different story. She imagined that Claudia may feel a little like a deer that had found itself in the den of a bear, and that to Tsurra, it might feel wrong to bring this vampyric she still barely knew and did not trust, into their home. Their sanctuary.

Kas however felt a thrill at the sight of Claudia standing within the walls of the Keep. A thrill that came with sharing parts of oneself with a new lover. She went over to Claudia's side and laced their fingers together.

Claudia looked startled by the display of affection, but she did not pull her hand away. Instead, she leaned closer, and Kas was delighted at the faint dusting of pink on the other woman's cheekbones.

They climbed the stone steps that brought them to a set of towering double doors that would lead them into the main entrance.

The creaking of the great doors echoed loudly through the empty hall with its vaulted ceilings and stone floors, patched here and there with rugs, some woven together with fabric and others made from animal hide. Braziers scattered about the place had been lit, warming the air, and keeping the encroaching darkness of night at bay.

Windows and archways leading into other parts of the Keep lined almost every inch of the walls, but directly ahead of them was another set of doors that Kas knew led into the dining hall. It was like a communal place for the Slayers of the Keep, and Kas could recall many meals shared with Tsurra and the other Slayers in the dining hall, in front of a blazing fire in its massive hearth. Stories being traded in voices that echoed across the room. On rare occasions there had even been song and dancing.

Kas could not deny that she was looking forward to sharing such moments with Claudia and even Aara.

"Kas," Claudia's urgent whisper broke through her imaginings of a dinner shared with the other Slayers, regaling them of her journey while her cup stayed full, and Claudia lounged in her lap.

"What?"

"Something's wrong here."

"Wrong? What—"

There was a furrow between Claudia's brow as she said, "I can smell . . . blood."

Blood? Kas wanted to say that wasn't unusual. Slayers often arrived at the Keep injured or still covered in the blood and muck of the last monster they killed. Sometimes monster parts were brought to the Keep to be studied or hung up somewhere within these walls.

But the look on Claudia's face ignited an abrupt sense of foreboding within Kas.

"Kas, Claudia!" Aara called out to them. She and Tsurra were already halfway toward the dining hall doors. "Hurry up. You can kiss each other after. Preferably where we don't have to watch."

It was Claudia who moved first to catch up with Aara and Tsurra, leaving Kas with little choice but to follow. Claudia's words of warning and her own new unease pounding like a drumbeat inside of her.

Tsurra reached the doors first and pulled them open.

The body suspended right above them from the rafters was the first thing they saw.

Chains were coiled around the arms, holding them straight above the head.

The body wore a plain linen shirt and brown trousers, now torn and stained almost entirely with dark red. Beneath all the blood on the face, Kas recognised the square jaw and round cheekbones. *Safora,* she realised with a shock. A Slayer she had known almost as long as Tsurra.

Blood still dripped from her corpse. Stemming from a torn open throat.

When Kas could finally drag her eyes away from Safora, she realised that hers was not the only body on display.

The dining hall was a mess. The long tables and chairs that had stood in rows on either side of the hall were all overturned, some were no more than a heap of broken wood and splinters. A window had been shattered and shards lay strewn on the carpet. The steel chandelier now swayed by a single chain. Kas saw a sword lying on the floor amidst a spatter of blood.

And around the hall, hung the bodies of three other Slayers. They were held up as Safora was, with chains and even rope tied to the rafters of the ceiling, their bodies covered in ragged and bloody wounds. Kas thought they looked like macabre marionettes.

Kas recognised each one of them. There was young Oracio, who had only come to the Slayers Keep the year before, wanting to follow in the footsteps of his grandfather.

Teres, who hailed from Veldenier just as Kas did, and who's body now looked as though it had been mauled by some vicious beast.

And at the head of the hall, above the fireplace in the wall that was carved to look like a dragon's open mouth, was Caisus, whose horse Kas had recognised in the stables. Who had taken her on her first monster hunt and had taught her how to use a crossbow.

*What happened here? What could have done this?* Were the questions that raced through Kas's mind, until she saw the figure perched atop the hearth. One leg dangling over the stone dragon's snout and one propped up, with her elbow rested on the knee in a casual manner.

When Serisa saw the new arrivals, she smiled. "Finally. I was beginning to wonder if you would ever show up."

Rage sang through Kas. Her blood turned molten and there was no thought behind her as she drew her sword and lunged forward. A shout went up and she wasn't sure if it belonged to Tsurra or Aara or Claudia. She caught movement out of the corner of her eye, and Kas's world went black before she could even react. For the briefest of moments, she felt as if she were in a waking dream. Only there were no visions, only darkness, yet she could still hear and feel and smell; a metallic stench, a rough hand gripping her like a weighted iron. Laughter.

When her vision returned, Kas found she was now by the cold hearth at the other end of the hall. On her knees and with an ice-cold hand around her neck. Claws dug uncomfortably into her skin. Somewhere along the way she had also lost her sword.

Holding her down was the vampyric she had faced last time they encountered Serisa.

"Move one muscle," Ves said lowly into Kas's ear, "and I'll crush your neck."

Beside her, Kas noticed Tsurra and Aara were also being held down by two other vampyrics that Kas did not recognise. Keeping Tsurra pinned to her knees as Kas was, was a male vampyric in a gold doublet and with grey sideburns.

Aara was pinned flat on her stomach by a vampyric with long-straw coloured hair tied into plaits and wearing a ruffled pink dress that made her look almost child-like. The too-wide grin and the blood all over her face was anything but, however.

Only Claudia stood free at the opposite end of the hall. Wolf's growling was loud in the hall.

"Serisa," Claudia called out, "Leave them be!"

With a laugh, Serisa landed on the floor beside Kas and Ves. "I wouldn't move if I were you, Claudia. Unless you're willing to risk the lives of your companions here."

Claudia did as her sister said and stayed where she was, though Kas could practically feel how much willpower it was taking her to do so.

"I knew you would listen," Serisa said smugly. "After all, I'm sure you would hate to see something happen to your precious lover here." She reached out and ran the tip of one claw lightly over Kas's cheek.

Kas wanted nothing more than to jerk away from the touch. But with Ves's threat still lingering in her ears, she forced herself to remain still. *How the hells could she possibly know about Claudia and I?*

Dropping her hand, Serisa turned her full attention back to her sister. Her tone took a more serious edge as she spoke. "Now, Claudia, the time for games is over. Give me the remnant, or you can watch as I open your precious human up from neck to navel. And then I'll get started on the other two."

"Try it you murderous piece of—" Tsurra snarled before her face was slammed to the floor.

"Shh," hissed the male vampyric leaning over her.

Claudia looked torn. "Serisa, I know you are grieving," she said. "I know you're in pain and I understand it. We both lost our fathers and we both lost mother. We could share in that pain and stand by each other as sisters should, if you will just stop this."

"I think you will find, sister, that I don't want to stop."

"And what do you think will happen when you free the dragons? They will burn this world so they can rule over the ashes. Humans will die and then what will you—all of you—feed on? And if starvation doesn't kill off the vampyrics then I'm sure living in a world on fire will."

Serisa and Ves were unflinching, but Kas noticed the other two vampyrics look perturbed by Claudia's statement. Clearly such a thought had never occurred to them before now, though Kas was unsure if it was enough to sway them from Serisa's side.

"The remnant, Claudia," said Serisa. "I will not ask again."

But Claudia did not move. Only continued to stare defiantly at Serisa from across the ruined hall.

Serisa sighed.

And between one flutter of Kas's eyelids and the next, Serisa was in front of Claudia, striking out at her with a fist that sent Claudia sailing into one of the toppled tables at the side of the hall.

Kas watched as Claudia righted herself, wiping blood from her lip before she charged at Serisa, this time with her rapier drawn.

When she was close enough, Claudia struck out with her sword, but before her blade could even touch Serisa, she dissolved into black mist, and rematerialized behind Claudia.

A clawed hand cut across Claudia's shoulder and blood blossomed through the torn fabric of her clothing.

Claudia stifled a cry as she spun around, this time aiming a strike at Serisa's leg. In a motion that was too fast for Kas's eyes to track, Serisa sent the sword flying from Claudia's hand and aimed a kick to the younger vampyric's ribs that sent her stumbling.

She didn't give Claudia a chance to recover. Serisa struck her hard across the face. When she went to do it again, Claudia's hand shot out and grabbed Serisa by the wrist, halting the second blow.

A manic smile spread across Serisa's face as she used her free hand to crush Claudia's wrist.

Claudia cried out and Kas felt her heart clench painfully at the sound. She hadn't even realised she was struggling until Ves's hand on her throat tightened its grip, threatening to cut off her breath. Kas gasped, her eyes watering.

"I told you not to move."

The next time Kas looked for Claudia, it was to see Serisa pinning her flat to the floor with a boot between her shoulder blades.

"I thought we had already settled this more than once," sneered Serisa. "You are no match for me. And certainly not while you're still holding back."

Claudia struggled, but could not break Serisa's hold.

Wolf came charging across the hall, teeth bared and a wild sound tearing from his throat. Always ready to leap to the defence of his beloved mistress.

Kas wished desperately that she could have done something to stop it, but she was powerless to do anything but watch as Serisa batted the wolf away as if he were no more than an irritating insect.

*"No!"* Claudia cried out at the same time a pained yelp was ripped from Wolf.

He went careening through the air where his body impacted harshly with the stone wall before falling limp to the floor.

Wolf did not get up.

"Why?" Claudia demanded through gritted teeth. "Why are you so adamant about doing this? You already killed those responsible for the murder of your beloved, you don't have to punish all of humanity for it."

"Yes. I do. Because all humans are the same." Serisa's voice had taken on a feral edge. "All they do is take and destroy. I lost my father and my mother because of your despicable human father. And Allegra . . . Allegra just wanted to *live*. I was supposed to stay with her for years to come. But humans just couldn't allow that, could they?" She cast her wild gaze towards Kas. "And Slayers are the worst of all. Do you know how many of us they've killed? And yet you lay with one.

Do you think she won't someday mount your head on a wall, Claudia? Do you think you're safe just because you gave her a taste of your body?"

Fury surged through Kas anew. She wished to be free and wished for her sword so she could take it up and drive it through Serisa's vile heart.

"Stop," Claudia growled as Serisa snatched up the green felt bag she carried.

Serisa upended the bag. Kas's coin purse fell to the ground, as did several articles of clothing, some food, Kas's whetstone . . . and Ombral's remnant. The cloth it was wrapped in loosened as it hit the floor, revealing the smooth, black-red surface of the broken scale.

With a satisfied smile, Serisa plucked it from the ground, then leaned over Claudia and spoke so lowly that Kas almost couldn't hear the words.

"I'm sure the dragons will be hungry after all those centuries imprisoned. Perhaps I'll bring them your darling Slayer. As an offering."

"No," Claudia said, voice full of horror. Of pleading. "Serisa, *please.*"

Kas was being hauled to her feet.

"Serisa, *please stop!*"

Claudia's cries were the last thing Kas heard before everything turned to shadow.

# CHAPTER 41
# CLAUDIA

CLAUDIA WATCHED the smoke rise from beyond the walls of the Slayers Keep. From where she sat at the top of the front steps, she had a perfect vantage point.

Tsurra and Aara had taken the bodies of the four dead Slayers beyond the Keep to a little grove at the base of the mountains to give them their funeral rites. Claudia had felt it best to stay behind. If Tsurra of Lyancoso had not liked her before, she certainly held no warm feelings for her now that Claudia's sister had slaughtered her friends and stolen Ombral's remnant. Along with Kas.

But Claudia also wanted to be alone. Alone with her thoughts and her melancholy and the pain from bandaged shoulder, bruised ribs, and splinted wrist. Physical injuries dealt by her sister to go with the emotional ones she had left as well.

She wished she could have Wolf beside her. Feel his calming, quiet presence and run her fingers through his shaggy coat. But she couldn't. Because Wolf was—and it was her fault.

*"Because all humans are the same. All they do is take and destroy."*

*"I lost my father and my mother because of your despicable human father."*

*"Slayers are the worst of all. Do you know how many of us they've killed? And yet you lay with one."*

Claudia had been a fool, such a *fucking fool* all this time. She thought she would be able to save her sister. That somehow Claudia could get through to her, dispel all the warped grief and anger that had taken hold of her, and that they could go back to the way they had been before. Even when Serisa had beaten and imprisoned her for speaking out against her. Even when Serisa had tried to kill her outside the strega's hut, Claudia had still foolishly held onto that hope.

That she would get her big sister back.

*"But maybe she's too far gone now."* Kas had said that to her only yesterday, and Claudia had refused to heed those words. To even entertain the idea that her sister was beyond saving.

How wrong she had been.

Now, everyone would pay the price of her stupidity.

And Kas would be the first.

*Kas.*

*"I'm sure the dragons will be hungry after all those centuries imprisoned. Perhaps I'll bring it your darling Slayer. As an offering."*

Anger entwined itself with Claudia's misery, followed shortly by the beginnings of a new resolve.

She would not let Kas die by Serisa's or some damned dragon's hand. Claudia had already had so much taken away from her, she would not let Kas be another name to add to that list.

Standing, Claudia strode back inside the Keep.

It was eerily quiet, not a single soul to be found within this vast fort now except for Claudia herself, and she traipsed up staircases and through hallways with all the soundlessness of a wraith.

Kas had told her of the library, with its vast collection of books and where Kas had been forced to spend many long hours studying about monsters before she could become a Slayer.

Claudia finally found it on one of the upper floors, behind a set of heavy, oak doors. It was just as big as Kas had described. Row upon row of shelves filled to the brim with books and scrolls, high enough that a ladder would certainly be needed to reach the topmost shelves.

Long tables ran the centre of the room, some with sheets of parchment and open books still on them. The skeleton of a wyvern hung on display from the ceiling, its bones the colour of old parchment.

And on the wall across the room was a broadsword, with a long obsidian blade with veins of silver, polished to a shine. The hilt was as red as a ruby and the silver crossguard had been carved to look like a pair of wings. Dragon's wings. It had to be *Velane*. The sword that slew the dragon Morvelth.

Claudia did not spend as much time taking it all in as she might have under different circumstances. Instead, she set about combing through the shelves, pulling out book after book and dropping them carelessly to the ground when she saw they weren't what she was looking for.

Before long the library was a mess of books strewn along the floor, but Claudia could not bring herself to care what the repercussions might be for ransacking the Slayers' library. Hells, she would decimate the whole Keep if she thought it would help her get Kas back.

Just when her frustration was beginning to boil over, Claudia finally found a book that made her stop short. It was a massive, leather-bound tome the length of her forearm. Written in faded black lettering on the front read the title; **DRAGONS: Rise & Defeat.**

Claudia leapt down from the shelf she had climbed and brought the book over to the nearest table. Setting it down, she flicked frantically through the yellowed pages, only coming to a stop towards the end of the book when a particular sentence caught her eye.

*. . . When Morvelth failed to be imprisoned by the spell that had captured the rest of his brethren, Lyar waged a fierce battle against the dragon on the peak of the mountain, Va Serote.*

Va Serote. The place where the last battle between the dragons was waged. Where they had been vanquished from this world.

And where Serisa would be taking Kas.

Leaving the book, Claudia strode over to the map of Vil Tresar hung up on the back wall. She ran her finger over the lines segregating each province, over the inked curves of mountaintops and the written names of cities and villages. Then she found it, *Va Serote*. It was right here in Almora, to the north of the Keep. It looked like it would only be a two or three-day journey.

Having found what she needed, Claudia left the library.

SHE FOUND Aara and Tsurra in the courtyard, just having returned from the base of the mountain. The acrid stench of smoke clung to their clothing. It was the first thing Claudia noticed about them.

Tsurra noticed her first and as soon as she met the older woman's gaze, Claudia spoke without preamble. "You've seen to your dead. Now prepare to set out. We are going after Serisa."

"Claudia," said Aara quietly. "I'm not sure we're ready yet to—"

"And I'm telling you to get ready."

"Just like that?" Tsurra asked, eyebrow raised. "You think you can command us—command *me*—to follow you with a snap of your fingers?"

Claudia kept her chin held high. "I'm giving you the chance to accompany me. But I'm more than willing to see to this on my own."

"Because I'm sure that will work out any better than it did earlier," scoffed Tsurra.

Aara winced and Claudia felt her upper lip curl away from her now protruding fangs.

Tension simmered in the air before Tsurra sighed, rubbing at the back of her neck. "I'll join you, all right? I'll be damned if I just let some vampyrics get away with what they've done."

Claudia nodded and moved to head back into the Keep when Tsurra's voice stopped her in place.

"But know this, Claudia. I plan on killing every one of those vampyrics for the Slayers they murdered here. Including that sister of yours."

"You won't lay a finger on my sister," and in a steady voice, Claudia added, "Because *I* am going to be the one to kill her."

# PART FOUR
# THE DRAGON ON THE MOUNTAIN

# CHAPTER 42
# KAS

KAS HAD ALWAYS WANTED to visit the place where the first Slayer Lyar had killed the dragon Morvelth and sealed away the rest. The place that had been the backdrop for one the historical events she had studied in her lessons to become a Slayer, and for the last story her mother had ever read to her.

However, she had never intended to visit it under these circumstances.

Daylight had still yet to fade from the sky, meaning that the vampyrics were confined to the cramped mountainside cave until night could set in. Kas sat at the lip of the cave, staring out at the vast sea of treetops and mountainous protrusions against a pink and red sky dusted with imminent nightfall. And from there, Kas could see it.

Va Serote.

The mountain where the dragons had been imprisoned.

And where Serisa now intended to free them.

So desperately did Kas wish to attempt an escape. Perhaps she would have if she wasn't bound by rope pinning her arms to her sides and rubbing uncomfortably against her wrists and ankles, with all of her weapons gone, and inside a cave that stood a good few feet from the ground. The only thing trying to escape might grant her now was either a plummet to her death or to break every single bone in her body. Neither of which proved very helpful. So all Kas could do was sit and wrack her brain for some way out of this, as she had spent much of the past three days doing.

Unbidden, the gentle tenor of her mother's voice came back to her. *"When you are in trouble and can't think of a way out, be sure to send a prayer to the Saints. They'll offer you their guidance."*

*And where were the Saints you always prayed to on the night you and your husband and children were killed, Mother?* Kas thought bitterly. She had not sought the Saints for help in years and she would not do so now.

"Nice and comfortable all tied up and helpless, Slayer?"

Kas forced herself not to react to Serisa's taunt as the vampyric came to stand at the mouth of the cave across from where Kas was huddled. She made sure to keep within the shadows the cave afforded them.

Kas wished the shadows would recede and that the lingering sunlight would burn her.

"But don't worry," she said, gazing out at the mountain. "You'll be put out of your misery soon enough."

Kas studied the vampyric before her, the hungry look in her red eyes as she watched the mountain, where she would bring her dark ambition to fruition. It was almost impossible to believe that she and Claudia were sisters by looking at them. And it wasn't merely that Serisa looked wholly vampyric whereas Claudia looked wholly human. Or that Claudia's hair was the colour of clouds on a summer's day—or starlight depending on what light you were looking at her in —while Serisa's was the colour of spilled ink.

When Kas looked at Claudia, she saw the woman she wanted to take into her arms and shower in kisses, and perhaps even spend the rest of her days with. Claudia was a sunshine after a bitter storm. Rain after a dry season. She was warmth and tranquillity and shelter that Kas wanted to bask in every chance she was able.

But looking at Serisa now, all Kas could feel was a jagged stone of loathing lodged painfully in her chest. When she looked at Serisa she could still see Claudia in pain beneath her sister's boot. Could still hear the cruel, deprecating words Serisa had hurled at her. She saw the malicious delight Serisa had seemed to take in hurting Claudia.

"Just how badly do you want to torment Claudia?" said Kas. "You had no reason to take me. You don't need to give the dragons an offering. I'm only here because of some twisted thing you have against Claudia."

"Maybe." Serisa's tone was airy. "Or maybe it has to do with you being a Slayer, and of all the humans Slayers are the ones I hate the most." Her smile was unpleasant as she cut a sideways look at Kas. "Oh, how I enjoyed slaughtering those Slayers at your little hideout. I can still hear their screams as they died. Can still taste their blood."

Kas ground her teeth together but kept her expression unreadable. She wouldn't let Serisa have the satisfaction of seeing how her words bothered Kas. Still, it was an effort to keep her voice steady as she said, "You speak about humans as if you hate us all so much. Yet you fell in love with one, and just look at the lengths you've gone to avenge her death."

The mirth drained from Serisa's expression. "Shut up, filth."

But Kas would not be silenced so easily. "And despite everything you've done to her, Claudia still cared about what happened to you. So, you must have cared about her to some extent in the past, even though she's half-human."

"I said *shut up*."

"I wonder . . . what would your human lover think of you now? I wonder if she would be ashamed of you? Do you think she would regret ever giving her heart to a vile monster like y—"

Serisa was in front of her faster than Kas could draw breath. A fist knotted in her hair and Serisa slammed the back of Kas's head brutally against the cave wall. Not hard enough to crush her skull in, but enough that the pain left Kas boneless and blacked out every other thought or feeling for a moment or two.

The next thing she knew was Serisa holding her by the throat, very nearly cutting off her airways.

"Keep the mention of Allegra out of your mouth," Serisa hissed, her face only inches away from Kas's. This close, Kas could see dark veins beginning to stand out beneath the skin around Serisa's eyes. Red creeping into the whites of her eyes.

"The woman I love was the *only* thing worth preserving in this wretched world. But she's gone now. Because of humans. Because of their petty grievances."

Serisa's hand tightened, and Kas struggled to breath. Futilely, she tried to squirm out of Serisa's hold.

"You humans think you can just destroy whatever and whenever you please. So I am simply going to show you that your actions have consequences."

Serisa stepped away and Kas slumped forward, coughing, and gasping in the air her lungs had been deprived of.

When she looked up at Serisa, she saw the vampyric examining a bit of blood on the nail of her thumb. It was only then that Kas felt the sting of broken skin on the side of her neck.

Keeping her eyes on Kas, Serisa licked the blood from her claw, something triumphant in her gaze.

Kas felt a fresh surge of hatred and this time she didn't bother to keep it from showing plainly on her face.

Serisa looked outside of the cave. "The light's gone," she remarked as one might remark on a sunrise or new spring blooms.

To her dread, Kas realised that Serisa was right. The setting sun had dipped completely behind the horizon, leaving only the barest traces of pale light against the ashen sky in its wake.

Serisa said, "It's time."

# CHAPTER 43
# SERISA

THE CLIMB up the mountain would have been a long and treacherous one, what with all its jagged edges and sheer drops. Fortunately, Serisa and the others needn't make such a trek when they could simply soar all the way up to the top in a matter of minutes. The peak looked like any ordinary mountaintop, dotted with boulders, and covered in tall blades of grass and wildflowers that shifted in the night breeze.

Standing in the middle, looking as though it didn't quite belong, was a tall stone archway. It was chipped and cracked in places, weathered by time and the elements. Lichen and creeper weeds were doing their best to overtake the white stone.

But that was not all that caught their attention. Lying not far from the archway was the great skeleton of what could only be a dragon. The last remains of Morvelth, the greatest and most feared of the dragons.

Like the archway, Morvelth's skeleton looked as if it was in the process of being swallowed by the earth. Much of the bones were overgrown with moss and untamed grass. Serisa could not even quite make out its huge, horned skull because of the vegetation consuming it.

Stepping up to the archway, Serisa placed her palm against one of the columns and felt only the roughly hewn stone and patches of lichen. There was nothing to suggest that this was anything but an ordinary archway. One could be forgiven for thinking it only a remnant of some long-ago structure. Not realising that it was so much more. That somewhere beyond that invisible veil in the arch lay the prison of the dragons. The once conquerors of Vil Tresar and the originators of monsters such as vampyrics. Such as Serisa herself.

*Finally,* she thought, staring up at the structure. Finally, her vengeance on the world of humans was at hand. This world would become nothing but a fiery wasteland of ash and despair.

Then, Serisa would rest.

She sensed Ves's approach before the other vampyric took her place at Serisa's side.

Ves held out Ombral's remnant from where she had kept it tucked away beneath her cloak. "We're ready when you are."

Serisa reached for the remnant.

"Hold on."

She looked to where Larnaz and Anirea stood beside the bound Slayer near the dragon's skull. "You have something to say, Larnaz?" Serisa forced the impatience out of her tone. "Speak."

"Once you free the dragons and they take over Vil Tresar, the humans—they'll die."

Serisa couldn't help but laugh. "Astute observation. Since when do you care so about the wellbeing of humans?"

"It's not that. Less humans means less blood for us to drink."

"And the dragons," Anirea spoke up this time. "They breathe fire. They'll turn this world into a fire pit. Which doesn't sound so good to us."

"You've all known of Serisa's plan for months," said Ves. "And you only now raise these questions?"

"Claudia did bring up some good points back at that Slayer's fort," admitted Larnaz with a shrug. "We thought the dragons would just cause some havoc and let us have our fun while they do. But how do we even know that they'll be willing to share this world and its spoils with us?"

Serisa hissed, fangs bared and annoyance on full display. "What happens to this filthy world of humans is of no concern to us!"

"It is when we just so happen to live in this world, too," Anirea snapped.

"Watch your tone," Ves warned her.

"Just because you've given up on your life because of some silly little human lover of yours," Larnaz growled, his red eyes boring into Serisa's, "does not mean the rest of us want to do the same."

Serisa would have killed him for that. She would have killed them both—it was not as if she needed them now, anyway—but it was forestalled by a familiar, if unexpected, voice carrying through the air.

*"Serisa!"*

There, toward the other end of the mountaintop, Claudia was striding purposefully towards them. Her long white hair turned almost to silver in the light of the full moon.

*Oh,* Serisa thought with some amusement, *she looks quite angry.*

She couldn't help but let her gaze travel to the Slayer, who, like the rest of them, was watching Claudia with astonishment. Her scarred lips formed the shape of her sister's name.

"Hello Claudia," Serisa called out. "You took your time. I was beginning to think you might have developed a bit of sense and realised when to give up."

"Put an end to this now," Claudia said, her voice commanding. "Before you regret it."

Serisa's laugh was high and shrill. She laughed so hard that it almost knocked her off balance. "We've done this all before Claudia," she said wiping at a non-existent tear. "Haven't you by now realised that you're no match for me? What could possibly make you think that now is any different?"

"Like you said before, sister." Claudia's mouth curled into a grim smile. "I was holding back."

Something rushed through the air. So quick that Serisa had no time to figure out what it was until the arrow pierced her shoulder.

The burning that followed told her it was tipped with silver.

Ves caught her before she could topple to the ground. The remnant falling from her grasp.

As Serisa tore the arrow from her shoulder and viciously tossed it aside, she cast about for the unseen attacker and spotted someone standing upon a nearby boulder behind where Claudia stood. It was the other Slayer woman from the Keep. Her dark hair caught in the wind. She held up a crossbow, pointed at Serisa.

"There," Ves hissed, noticing the other Slayer at the same time she did. Then, to the other vampyrics, "Kill them."

It seemed their new distrust of Serisa's plan was not enough to rival their hatred of Slayers, and Larnaz and Anirea turned to attack Claudia and the Slayer without hesitation.

Larnaz dove for Claudia with a yell while Anirea rushed at the Slayer.

As she did, the Slayer dropped her crossbow and unfurled a whip curled at her belt. She leapt deftly off the boulder before Anirea could reach her. As she did so, the Slayer twisted around, bringing her whip with her. The whip lit up, fire licking along its length as it struck Anirea across her back.

As soon as the flaming whip touched her, Anirea went up in a burst of fire, her piercing screams soon drowned out by the flames.

"Shit," Serisa cursed. She said to Ves, "Go handle it."

Ves only nodded before she turned to black smoke and fled to join the fight herself.

Serisa turned her attention to looking for Ombral's remnant. It didn't take her long to spot the dark scale lying in the grass before her.

Ignoring the burn in her shoulder, Serisa reached out for it.

Before even the tips of her claws could brush the remnant, something crashed into her. Hard enough to lift her off her feet and slam her back against one of the columns of the archway. She cried out as it caused a flare of pain in her shoulder.

With one hand she grabbed Claudia by the throat, forcing her off before slamming her against the ground, hard enough that cracks splintered in the earth.

"I'm starting to lose patience with your interference," said Serisa.

Claudia punched Serisa in the throat. Not hard enough to snap her neck, but with enough force that she was robbed of breath.

Using her momentary distraction, Claudia was able to free herself from Serisa's hold. Rolling out from under her, Claudia launched herself at Serisa once more. She had her sword in her hand, its tip clearly aimed for Serisa's heart.

Serisa lifted her hand right before the sword could pierce her breast. Instead, it cut straight through her palm, and she allowed her hand to slide along the length of the blade until she could grab the ornate hilt, forcing Claudia to come to a halt.

They stood face-to-face and Serisa grinned. "What's this? You actually mean to kill me now?"

"It's what you want, right?" spat Claudia.

"Is it?"

The corners of Claudia's lips curled into an expression that was not quite a smile. "Perhaps you would like me to send you to mother and your father?"

The words sparked something within her, igniting her ire.

"Or maybe I'll send you to your wretched human father instead."

Serisa turned to smoke and carried Claudia off her feet, and over the mountain's peak.

Dropping her over the edge.

# CHAPTER 44
# KAS

KAS COULD DO nothing but struggle in vain to free herself while Tsurra and Claudia fought with the vampyrics.

Tsurra had already reduced one of them to a smouldering corpse with her whip, but now she was facing Ves and the male vampyric, Larnaz, alone. While Claudia was grappling with Serisa by the archway.

Kas refused to stay trussed up like this while others fought.

Unfortunately, refusal was not enough to free her. Her bonds were too tight and there were no sharp rocks close by that she could use to cut herself free. Maybe if she could find a way to scale the dragon's skull and reach its horns—

She felt someone sidle up beside her and looked up to see a familiar face looming above her with a pair of mismatched eyes and a grin that showed off feline fangs.

"Aara." The name rolled off Kas's tongue in a breath that was part surprise and part relief. She never would have thought she'd be so relieved to see a werecat.

"Kas," Aara returned. She held up a sharp-looking dagger. "Need some help?"

"Just hurry up," Kas said even as Aara was already in the process of cutting through the ropes around her arms, then her wrists.

Once Kas was finally free, Aara drew a sword from the enchanted green bag and handed it to Kas. "We thought you might be needing this."

Kas took the sword gratefully. It felt good to be with a weapon again.

"Thank you," she said. "Now you should get—"

She cut herself off when she noticed that, by the archway, Serisa had turned to black smoke and was carrying Claudia through the air at a break-neck speed. All the way to the edge of the mountain side where Claudia fell.

Kas's heart seized, and without thinking of anything besides the sight of Claudia falling off the mountain, she ran for where Claudia had already disappeared from her view.

Halfway there, she was brought to a halt when more black smoke rose up in front of her, quickly coalescing into none other than Ves.

# CHAPTER 45
# CLAUDIA

THE FALL WAS NOT AS great as Claudia had anticipated. A jut of rock caught her fall partway down, so instead of meeting her end at the bottom of the mountain, she had the breath knocked out of her and sharp pain spiked through her body as she hit hard stone.

As Claudia got to her feet, Serisa materialised on the side of the mountain above her.

"You say you want to try and kill me?" Serisa shouted down to her. Her eyes were entirely red now, the skin around her eyes turned the colour of charcoal. "To send me to the same place as my loved ones? Well fine. Do your best, sister."

Gone was the feeling of sadness when she looked at her sister now, and the desire to save Serisa from herself. Now, all Claudia felt was anger and betrayal. There was no more hope that she could get her sister back. Only the iron-hard resolve that if she wanted to put a stop to Serisa's madness, she was going to have to kill her, here and now.

Claudia and Serisa rushed towards each other.

And when they met the impact was like a thunderclap as they exchanged blows. Claudia to Serisa's jaw and Serisa to Claudia's stomach.

They were blown apart, Claudia's feet scraping against the

mountainside before she was finally able to bring herself to a halt. When she looked up, it was to see Serisa already lunging for her again, a fist aimed towards her head.

As they fought, they both poured all their vampyric strength into their hits and utilised their speed to dodge as many of the other's attacks as they could.

Serisa clawed across Claudia's chest, opening up four long gashes in her skin—shallow fortunately.

Claudia in turn, drove her knee into Serisa's face, knocking her flat to the rock.

It didn't keep her down for long. Screaming like a wraith, she grabbed hold of Claudia and reversed their positions. Now Claudia was the one with her back against the ground.

Before Claudia could even gather her bearings, Serisa started raining blow after blow upon her face.

As Serisa pulled her fist back in preparation for another, Claudia slammed her own, with as much strength as she could muster, into Serisa's injured shoulder.

Serisa yelled her pain and Claudia used the distraction to wrap her arms around Serisa's middle and pushed forwards, propelling them both over the edge.

Again, there was no fall to certain death. The side of the mountain was jagged with jutting stone ledges to break their fall.

When they hit one such ledge, Claudia's hold on Serisa came undone and the two of them flew apart as they rolled down a steep incline, before coming to a stop.

Claudia coughed as she staggered to her feet.

"What's the matter?" Claudia looked up at Serisa, sauntering towards her. There was no trace of fatigue to be seen on her. Even the wound from a silver arrow hardly seemed to be slowing her down. "Is pretending you are even half as strong as a full-blooded vampyric beginning to wear you out?" Serisa laughed nastily. "The blood of your weak human father letting you down, Claudia?"

Claudia snarled, baring her fangs. She gathered every scrap of her strength and launched herself at Serisa. Beginning their battle anew.

# CHAPTER 46
# KAS

KAS WAS REWARDED with a cry from Ves as her sword cut open the vampyric's shoulder—the first wound she had managed to deal since she and Ves first started their violent dance.

Ves moved out of reach before Kas could inflict any further damage. She leapt into the air, high enough that Kas almost lost sight of her. As soon as she saw Ves diving back towards her, Kas ducked and rolled out of the way.

The ground where Kas had stood only seconds ago, splintered with deep cracks upon Ves's impact. A plume of dust went up and hardly a moment later Ves appeared from out of the dust cloud and was headed straight towards Kas.

Kas ducked Ves's claws aiming for her head. The vampyric's attacks were a flurry of movement from then on, so quick that Kas was forced to do nothing but evade and block.

Ves managed to get past Kas's guard, and those dagger-sharp claws tore across Kas's side, along her ribs.

The sudden burst of pain made her falter, her sword grip wavered. It was only for a moment, but it was enough for Ves.

She grabbed Kas by the throat, lifting her off the ground before flinging her aside like a wet rag.

Kas rolled across the grass, and she felt the edge of her sword slice across her own arm as she did. But she refused to relinquish her hold on the weapon.

As soon as Kas came to a stop, Ves was there to pin her flat before she could get back up. The vampyric's lone hand went back to her throat in a choking grip and a boot stamped on her sword arm, keeping it pinned to the ground.

Distantly, she heard Tsurra calling her name, but she knew she could not rely on Tsurra to come save her now.

"You won't get in our way," said Ves, fangs on full display as she spoke down to Kas. "It's time those of us who have suffered and lost at the hands of Slayers and all humans were paid their due. It is time my son was avenged."

She leaned closer, mouth open and fangs poised to sink into Kas's neck. No matter how much she struggled, she could not free herself from Ves's hold. Her strength was no match for a vampyric.

A shout broke free from Ves, part surprise, part pain. It took Kas a moment to realise that *Aara* was clinging to the vampyric's back, and with one hand she was holding onto the handle of her knife which was imbedded in Ves's wounded shoulder.

She'd also taken things a step further by *biting* the vampyric. Her own fangs were sunk into Ves's other shoulder.

Aara's assault had the effect of forcing Ves to let up her hold on Kas, and she didn't waste a second in pushing herself up, lifting her sword and driving it through Ves's chest.

Aara fell from Ves's back just as the sword went in. Kas now knelt with her face inches from the vampyric, and she watched as Ves's expression changed from anger to a blend of shock and agony, as the silver blade burned inside her.

Blood ribboned down her mouth, but Ves did not turn to a blackened corpse as vampyrics tended to do when a killing blow was struck. That's when Kas realised her aim had not quite been close enough to pierce Ves's heart.

*Fuck.* She drew the sword back out of Ves's body. As soon as she did, Ves turned to smoke, and flew up into the night sky, and out of sight.

Kas stood with her sword at the ready, waiting for Ves to show herself again.

But the moments dragged on, and there was no attack from Ves. No sign of her at all.

"Is she gone?" Aara asked somewhat tremulously. She was holding her dagger at the ready.

Perhaps Kas hadn't needed to go for the heart after all. Maybe the blow she had struck had been enough to end Ves.

Kas heard a shout from Larnaz and a fiery crack from Tsurra's whip. There was no use waiting around for an enemy who might never show themselves when there was still one right in front of her that needed to be dealt with.

Kas ordered Aara back to the hiding place she had found among Morvelth's bones before and went to lend a helping hand to Tsurra.

# CHAPTER 47

# CLAUDIA

CLAUDIA ALWAYS KNEW Serisa was stronger than her. Even when she was young and the two of them would spar in the castle courtyard as part of her learning how to wield a sword. The only times Claudia had managed to best Serisa was when her sister went easy on her.

Still, she had hoped that this time, things would be different.

It was beginning to appear that she had hoped in vain.

Her body cried out from every wound she had been dealt thus far.

It diminished her strength and speed. Slowed her reactions.

Serisa meanwhile, was barely even out of breath.

A blow to the chest sent Claudia careening into the wall of rock behind her. As soon as her back hit the rock, Serisa was in front of her pinning her in place with an arm against her neck.

"Had enough?" There was a manic glee in Serisa's voice and expression. Clearly enjoying seeing Claudia struggle.

Claudia slammed her fist into Serisa's sternum and felt the bone there crack. The grin slid off Serisa's face as she choked on a pained gasp, momentarily stunned.

Claudia used it to her advantage, heaving both her legs up and planting the soles of her boots against Serisa's stomach in a kick that sent her sister flying off of her.

Claudia went tumbling downward, her body hitting pointed rock, making new spots of pain blossom along her body.

She lay there for a moment, unable to make her body move. There was blood in her mouth, and Claudia spat it out as she fought shakily, to raise herself onto her hands and knees.

She sensed Serisa above her before she even saw her.

"You're showing your breeding, sister," said Serisa, amusement in her voice. "Even if you are a vampyric, you're also just a human, and that makes you nothing compared to me."

It was a battle just to get enough air into her lungs, and a monumental effort to raise her head enough to look up at Serisa.

"And you're showing *your* weakness," said Claudia.

A flicker of annoyance crossed Serisa's face. "What?"

"All this . . . because the world took from you. As if you are the only one who's ever lost something dear to you."

"Not just something. I lost everything."

"But you didn't!" snapped Claudia. "You didn't lose everything, you still had me. But I wasn't enough for you, was I? Even though to me you were—" She bit her lip hard enough to draw blood. Her heart hurt. Just as much as the wounds on her body. It made her want to return that hurt to Serisa, but she knew no physical hit would be enough.

Keeping her eyes on Serisa, she said. "They would be ashamed, you know? Of this pathetic outburst of yours."

"What was that?" Serisa snarled, a dangerous edge creeping into her voice.

"Mother would be embarrassed by you. Your father too—"

Serisa grabbed hold of Claudia by the forehead, in a grip so tight Claudia thought her skull would split. Serisa slammed the back of her head into the ground, and Claudia heard the ground crack beneath her, even as the pain nearly obliterated her consciousness.

Then she was being hauled upright once again, only for Serisa to knee her in the stomach.

Claudia's mouth fell open, but no sound came out. No gasp or cry of agony, only a glob of blood.

"I. Have had. Enough. Of. *You!*" Serisa yelled, each word punctuated with a punch, a kick or a scratch to Claudia's body.

They came too hard and too fast for Claudia to even try to avoid them. Her bones were not so easily breakable as an ordinary human, but beneath Serisa's ire, she felt them break like porcelain. Her collarbone. Her arm. Her knee. Her ribs.

*I really am no match for her.*

She stumbled on shaky legs, as yet another ruinous hit caught her in the face and sent her falling down a steep incline. Only when the rock beneath her evened out onto a plateau, did Claudia come to a halt and lay sprawled on the ground.

Pain raged through her like wildfire, but still, she tried to pull herself up. A strangled cry escaped her when she put pressure on what she now knew to be a broken wrist and a few broken fingers.

Through the hair that fell around her face, Claudia saw Serisa coming towards her. Not rushing towards her with breath-taking speed, but leisurely down the rocky slope. Like a predator slowly, but surely closing the gap between itself and its prey before it went in for the killing blow.

And Claudia felt a pulse of true fear. Because she knew she could not fight Serisa. Knew she could not escape her.

*So this is it?* She wondered bleakly, wearily. *This is how I die?*

# CHAPTER 48
# SERISA

Serisa would kill her.

She would kill Claudia as she should have done many times before. When Claudia first opposed her at the castle. When they fought in Nescoro. At the Slayers Keep.

So many opportunities and she had wasted each one of them.

But she would not waste this one.

This time Serisa would kill Claudia, and finally rid herself of a nuisance that had been standing in her way all this time.

She descended the slope slowly, taking her time as she approached Claudia, who could barely even lift herself onto her hands, panting and trembling like a newborn lamb as she made the attempt.

It would be no effort at all.

Killing the younger vampyric would be as easy as crushing a brittle leaf in her palm. Just like all the lives Serisa had taken up until now.

And once Claudia was gone, she would finally—

Something cracked beneath her foot.

The sound was so unexpected and surprisingly loud in the stillness that it startled Serisa.

She paused and lifted her foot to see what it was she had stepped on.

A brass pendant that gleamed weakly in the moonlight.

She reached down, picking it up by its black velvet ribbon.

A crescent moon was carved into its surface, along with a crack made from Serisa's boot.

At the sight of it, Serisa felt a memory rushing up to meet her.

* * *

Serisa remembered *what felt like so long ago now, a young girl with hair as white as a daisy's petal.*

*"Serisa!" The girl was racing through the hallway. The hour was growing light, many of the vampyrics of the castle had already retreated to their chambers to sleep through the daylight hours.*

*"What is it, Claudia?" Serisa asked of her younger sister. "Where have you been all night?"*

*"Out."*

*"Clearly. You're too young to be leaving the castle on your own, or without telling anyone, you know?"*

*Claudia rolled her pale blue eyes. Serisa had to fight to keep herself from smiling, it wouldn't do for her sister to know how much she enjoyed her childish defiance. It would only lead to her taking advantage of Serisa's affection—more than she already did, at least.*

*"I'm thirteen years old. I can look after myself," said Claudia. "And it's not as if anyone would be too bothered about my being gone. I'm sure even mother never noticed I was not around tonight."*

*She could tell Claudia was trying to pass the statement off as if she didn't care. But Serisa knew better.*

*"I care," she said, gently tapping the girl's nose with the tip of her nail. "Now, are you going to tell me where you were, and what it is you are holding in your hands? Or are you going to make me stand here all day?"*

*The smile was back on Claudia's face. Her round cheeks flushed with delight and in a way that made her look so human it was almost difficult to believe she was a vampyric at all.*

*"I went to Trulio," Claudia explained. "Tonight was their spring*

market, when merchants from all over come to sell things in the village. I used to love it and I haven't been since—well—anyway, I-I bought you something."

"You bought me something?" said Serisa, surprised.

Opening her hands, Claudia revealed a brass pendant. Hanging from a black ribbon, and a crescent moon carved into its centre.

"And I bought myself one, too." Reaching into the pocket of her cloak, Claudia produced another brass pendant. This one with a star carved upon it.

"I thought—the merchant said they're matching pendants," Claudia said. "And that they should be worn by two lovers or two friends, and I asked him, 'what about two sisters?' and he said yes, so I thought, maybe we could wear them? But if you don't want to—"

Serisa cut the girl off by pulling her into a hug.

"It's lovely," she spoke the words into the top of her sister's hair. "Thank you."

The pair of them stayed that way for a while. Serisa could hear the way Claudia's heart sped up in delight.

"Come on," Serisa said, taking Claudia's hand and tugging her down the hall. "I want you to put this pendant on for me."

"All right," Claudia agreed, beaming. "And will you put mine on for me?"

"Oh, please, Claudia, do I look like a servant to you?"

"Serisa."

But even as Claudia slapped her arm playfully and whined loudly enough that her voice might have disturbed the rest of the vampyrics of the castle, Serisa could not bring herself to care.

Never could she have imagined holding such affection for another within her heart.

Serisa would do anything to keep her little sister from harm. Anything to keep that smile on her face and happiness in her dear heart.

* * *

Now, that same little sister she had always thought she would protect was on her hands and knees. Bloodied and bruised and struggling to stand.

And it was all Serisa's doing.

*Serisa* had created those wounds.

*Serisa* had spilled that blood.

*Serisa* had *tried to kill her sister.*

And not for the first time.

Sickness rose up hot and fast in her throat and Serisa thought she would bring it up on the rocks at her feet, but it never came.

Instead, she felt two hot lines carve down the skin on either cheek. Saw the dark drops fall to the ground.

Serisa looked down at the cracked pendant in her hand, closed her fingers over it, and then clutched it to her chest.

She closed her eyes and gasped, *"What am I doing?"*

# CHAPTER 49

# CLAUDIA

One moment Claudia believed she was about to die by her sister's hand. She had been filled with more rage than Claudia had ever seen her—had ever seen in any vampyric—and Claudia knew she was not strong enough to beat Serisa. Knew that Serisa would not let up until Claudia was dead.

And the next . . . it had all stopped. And it was all because of that pendant. The one she had bought from a market to give to her older sister what seemed like a lifetime ago.

The pendant that was a sister to her own.

The pendant she had found alongside a note in her bedroom the night Serisa left.

The pendant she had carried with her for all these years in the hopes it would bring her sister back to her.

*"What am I doing?"* she heard Serisa say, clutching her old pendant to her heart. Streaks of red spilled from her eyes. Serisa was *crying.*

And then she was on her knees. Still holding the pendant in a fist against her breast. She must have been holding it tightly enough to draw blood because Claudia saw it falling from her sister's closed hand.

"What am I doing?" Serisa repeated in that choked, trembling voice. "What am I doing? I—My sister. How could I do this to . . . *my little sister?*"

And that was when Claudia knew, blessedly, remarkably that Serisa—*her sister*—was back.

Standing was slow and painful, but Claudia managed to do it. Managed to push herself upright so she could drag her shaking legs across the jutting rocks and sink to her knees in front of her weeping older sister.

"It's all right," she whispered, even though she knew it was a lie. Nothing Serisa had done up until now was all right. But right then, Claudia could not bring herself to care.

She bent her head close to Serisa's, hushing her and stroking her dirt and blood-stained hands through the whisps and tangles of Serisa's hair. It was so reminiscent of the time she had consoled her sister on the night their mother died.

"It's all right. It's all right."

Serisa finally raised her head. Her face was twisted into an expression of utmost pain. Claudia wiped one of those bloody tears away with her thumb.

"Claudia," Serisa said, "Please . . . end it."

The words rocked Claudia. "End it? What—what are you saying?"

"End me, Claudia. Finish what you came here to do."

"No." Claudia shook her head. "No, no."

"Claudia, please."

"No, I said, *no.*" When Claudia came here tonight, she had resolved to kill her sister. But she thought she would be killing the stranger parading as Serisa since they had reunited at the castle months ago. Not the sister Claudia loved and admired from her childhood.

"Claudia—Sister, please listen to me." Serisa had a hold of her by the shoulders, keeping her in place when she tried to back away. "You have seen what I've tried to do. What I've done to you—"

"That doesn't matter!" Cried Claudia. "I can forgive you."

"Well, I cannot! And Claudia, I—I can't go on like this. Even after I released Ombral, I wanted to—" The tears were falling again.

"Please," Claudia begged. "Don't ask me to . . ."

"I want it to stop. This pain that's like a knife in my heart that I can't get out. I want to—I want to be with mother again. And my father . . . and Allegra. That's all I want. I don't want to live long enough to forget their faces."

*But what about what I want?* Claudia's own eyes burned with tears. She wanted to go on refusing. To scream that she could not do this. To curse Serisa for even asking it of her.

But when she looked at Serisa now, she thought she had never seen her look so wretched. So broken. Not even on the night when they discovered Mother's lifeless body in her chambers. For the first time, Claudia saw the damage loss and grief had done to Serisa, the suffering she was enduring.

Claudia loved her sister. Despite everything, she still loved her. So how could she deny her the mercy she asked for?

Finally, Claudia allowed her own tears to fall.

"It wasn't supposed to be like this . . . I was supposed to save you."

Something flickered across Serisa's face, as if the knife she spoke of being in her heart had twisted. She took her hands from Claudia's shoulders and placed them on either side of her younger sister's head and pressed their foreheads together.

It was something Serisa would do often when Claudia was a child. And even though it made Claudia sob, it was as comforting now as it was then.

"I'm sorry," Serisa said to her. "I am so sorry for everything, little sister."

They stayed close like that for a long, drawn-out moment.

How Claudia had longed for a moment like this with Serisa. How she wished she could make it last for an eternity.

Softly, Serisa hummed a tune that Claudia immediately recognised as belonging to the lullaby Serisa would sing to her as a child.

*Little bird, little bird . . .*

It took every bit of strength she could muster for Claudia to raise her hand.

And plunge it through her sister's heart.

Serisa gasped. Her body jerked once, and then again when Claudia pulled her fist—now trembling and coated in her sister's blood—back out of her chest.

Serisa's eyes were blown wide. More red tears welling up at the edges. She looked at Claudia, her mouth opening, and Claudia was sure she was about to say something.

But she never got the chance. Her pearlescent skin began to darken to the colour of burnt-out wood. Her flesh sinking in and withering the way a dying flower's petals withered. Her lips pulled back, revealing her fangs and all of her teeth and the red of her eyes vanished, leaving only two pits of black.

All that was left of Serisa was an ashen corpse that looked as if it had been pulled from a fire. It fell backward with a crisp thud.

And for what felt like a long, long time all Claudia could do was stare at it.

Her mind refused to comprehend that it was the body of her sister, who had just been alive, talking to her and holding her. That her sister was truly dead.

Dead because Claudia was the one who had killed her.

Claudia could still feel the touch of Serisa's hands on her shoulders. How their foreheads had pressed together.

The brass moon pendant lay in Serisa's open palm.

The cracked amethyst amulet glinted up at Claudia from where it rested against Serisa's charred and still chest.

And when her mind did comprehend it, all Claudia could do was fold in on herself and cry.

And cry.

CHAPTER 50

# KAS

LARNAZ JUMPED over the fiery lash of Tsurra's whip. When he landed, Kas rushed towards him from behind.

The vampyric twisted around and caught Kas's sword with his own cutlass. Their blades pressed against each other in a battle of strength, both willing the other to back down first.

Larnaz grinned unpleasantly at Kas as his strength quickly began to outmatch hers.

Almost as soon as it appeared, the grin slid from his face. Replaced by a grimace as he cried out. Kas spotted the hilts of two of Tsurra's silver daggers imbedded in the back of his calf.

Behind him, Tsurra attacked with her whip once more. Larnaz turned to smoke before the whip could even touch him. He launched into the sky, and they lost sight of him.

"I hate it when they do that," Kas growled as she and Tsurra moved to stand back-to-back, shoring up each other's blind spots.

They stood like that for what felt like a long time, watching, and waiting for Larnaz to strike.

Only the subtlest shift in the air—something so little that one who hadn't had the years of training she and Tsurra had, would never have noticed—betrayed the vampyric's surprise attack.

"Above us!" Kas called out and she and Tsurra sprang apart just as Larnaz descended on them.

He evaded Tsurra's whip and shot straight towards Kas.

As luck would have it, Kas noticed his movements were beginning to slow and his attacks were beginning to lack in that ferocious strength. Perhaps the battle was finally beginning to wear on him? Maybe it had been too long since he last fed and was not up to full strength? Whatever the case, Kas was determined to use it to her advantage.

When he stabbed at her with his cutlass, Kas fell to her knees. Avoiding his attack at the same time she moved into position behind him to slash her sword across the backs of his knees.

He fell forward onto his hands and knees with a cry, blood already soaking through his trousers.

Tsurra was in front of him before he could make another move, letting her whip fly.

"*No,*" Larnaz cried right before the fire of Tsurra's whip made contact.

His shouts were drowned out as his body went up in a burst of searing bright flames.

It didn't last long, and when the fire dissipated, Larnaz's blackened corpse collapsed to the ground, still smoking.

Kas let out a breath now that they were alone. "Aara?" she called out in time to see the girl scamper out from behind Morvelth's skeleton.

"I'm all right," she said. "Are you both?"

"None the worse for wear," said Tsurra, looping her whip to hang it from her belt.

"Claudia," said Kas in a rush. Now that her own imminent danger had passed, all she could think about was that she had last seen Claudia being thrown from the mountain. "I have to find her—"

The world lit up. Blindingly so.

And the still, mild air of only moments ago turned to a hot gale.

Shielding her eyes with her arm, Kas saw the colours of twilight had vanished and instead, the world around them had turned to the orange and red of an inferno.

*Saints, what is happening?*

She didn't have to wonder for long.

Looking to the archway, Kas saw that it was lit up with what looked like a fiery whirlpool between its stone columns. Outlining the hunched over silhouette of Ves standing before it, her cloak billowing around her.

The archway was open.

Ves had opened the gate to the dragons' prison.

"No!" she heard Tsurra shout over the roar in her ears. Tsurra took off towards the archway and Kas and Aara followed.

By the time they reached it, Ves was slumped over on the ground. Kas could just make out the dark stains of blood on her cloak and around her mouth. She might have thought the vampyric was dead, had she not looked up to regard them with a tremulous smirk.

"I told you . . ." Her voice was barely audible. "You wouldn't stop us."

Kas responded by beheading Ves with her sword.

She didn't pay further attention to the now dead vampyric after that. All her focus was on the opening archway before her.

The remnant hung suspended in the middle of it. As if Ves had used it to pierce through the invisible veil like one might with a knife through a curtain.

A trembling started beneath their feet. The distant cry of a creature she had never heard before echoed through the archway, sending a spear of cold dread down her spine.

"What do we do now?" Aara was saying, her eyes wide and her hair whipping about her face wildly. "How can we close it?"

There was only one course of action Kas could think of. To Tsurra, she said, "The remnant opens the gate, but maybe it can also close it, if we just remove it?"

Tsurra nodded and stepped forward.

Reaching up, she took hold of the broken end of the remnant. A hiss of pain twisted her features as soon as she did, making Kas realise it must have been hot to the touch. But Tsurra did not let go. Instead, she firmed up her grip and pulled.

The rumbling grew stronger, and Kas almost expected the earth to split open underneath them with the force of it.

She thought she could see shadows through the archway now. Large shapes growing closer.

Tsurra pulled on the remnant with what Kas could tell was all the strength she had to spare. When she released it, it was only because her hands slid off. Kas could see shiny patches of seared skin on her palms.

"Fucking Saints," Tsurra cursed. "It won't budge."

The thunderous sound of what could only be the roar of one of the monsters sealed away behind the opening archway pierced the air.

And it sounded as though it were right in front of them.

"Kas." She felt a tug on her arm and turned to see Aara, holding out the little green bag to her. "I brought it with us. The sword—in case we needed it."

"Sword?"

"*Velane.*"

At the utterance of the name, Kas plunged her hand inside the bag, until she felt the grip of a sword hilt and its pointed crossguard. Wrapping her hand around it, she pulled and out came the famed sword that had once slain a dragon on this very mountaintop. The blade was almost as long as Kas was tall and the weight of it was already beginning to put a strain on her arm. Someone with a lesser sword arm would not have been able to bear its weight.

Holding *Velane* firm in both hands, Kas marched towards the archway. Coming to a halt directly in front of the remnant hanging suspended.

She lifted the sword.

And brought it down on Ombral's remnant.

It made a sound like striking solid stone in an empty, echoing chamber. She felt the reverberation of it up her arms and through her skull. Unpleasant, but it did not stop Kas from raising *Velane* over her head and hacking at the remnant again. And again.

Her arms and shoulders were already beginning to scream in protest. New beads of sweat formed along her skin. But she would not stop. Not when Tsurra urged her to, telling her it wasn't working. Not when she was sure the blade was beginning to dull.

And certainly not when she noticed what looked like glowing cracks beginning to form along the surface of the remnant.

Kas struck it again. Harder this time.

A sound like an explosion above their heads shattered Kas's eardrums. A great, horned head had burst forth from the archway. It seemed as if it was straining against whatever force still wouldn't quite let it through.

The beast opened its jaws and loosed a roar that Kas might have thought could be heard across the continent. That could rattle a person's bones and shake the earth.

Kas swung the sword again. The edge of it rang against the remnant and those bright fissures grew longer, until they almost encompassed the whole of it.

"Kas." She heard Tsurra speak her name with urgency over the deafening sounds around them. Though whether she was urging Kas to come away or to hurry what she was doing, Kas did not know.

The head of the beast above them seemed to have inched further out, revealing an armour-plated neck.

Gritting her teeth harshly enough to crack her jaw, Kas lifted *Velane,* and with a yell to rival a dragon's, she brought it down on the remnant once more.

This time when the sword hit, the remnant shattered.

Pieces of it went flying at the same time a white light flared from within the archway, blinding Kas.

She heard what sounded like stone cracking. Heard the monster from the archway let out one last roar before Kas must have caught her heel against something. Her feet went out from underneath her and the last thing she knew was her head striking the ground painfully.

CHAPTER 51

# KAS

"Kas . . . ake up . . . Kas . . ."

*"Kas!"*

Kas's eyes flew open to find herself surrounded by rubble, a dusty-looking Aara and a bloody and battered Claudia.

"Easy," Claudia told her as she sat up. There was concern in her eyes and Kas briefly wondered how Claudia could look worried for Kas's wellbeing when she looked—well, at least she was alive.

It was then that she noticed the body lying unmoving beside them.

"Tsurra," Kas gasped, reaching for her.

The entire right side of Tsurra's face was slicked in blood, all stemming from a ragged gash across her eye. She didn't even stir when Kas gripped her by the shoulder.

"It's all right," said Aara. "She was still breathing when I checked. I think she was hit by the debris."

"What happened?" asked Kas. "The archway—"

"Kas," Claudia interrupted, though her eyes were elsewhere. "Look."

Following her gaze, Kas looked to where the old, stone archway had once stood tall, but now lay among them in a shattered ruin. But what was more eye-catching than that, was the beast before them.

The head of a dragon.

Kas felt her heart leap into her throat, until she realised it was only that. A head. Severed from a body that was nowhere in sight and leaking a pool of blood on the ground around it.

Getting to her feet, Kas picked up *Velane* from where it lay on the ground beside her. She stepped warily closer to have a better look at the dragon head.

Its scaled head was huge. Taller even than Kas was and far longer. It reminded her of a wyvern, with its long snout and slitted nostrils. Its mouth lay open, revealing rows of curved teeth as long as Kas's arm. Its eyes were blown wide in the way of all dead things. It was slit-pupiled like a cat, with no whites to be seen. Only yellow with veins of a darker shade, creating tracery through the iris. Like the veins on marble.

"So this is what a dragon looks like in the flesh," breathed Claudia, sounding equal parts awestruck and terrified. Kas felt the same mixture of emotions.

But this dragon could do no harm. The only thing it would do now is become food for the ravens. Its bones to be devoured by the earth just as Morvelth's were.

Kas breathed a sigh of relief. The tension seeped from her body.

The earth shuddered beneath them with enough force that Kas and the others almost toppled off their feet.

A sudden gust of wind tore past them, and with it, a voice.

"I did tell them to wait. But Nalzaar always was the most impatient one."

Kas turned towards the rumbling voice. *Saints, no. It can't be.*

But there was no denying what stood before her.

If seeing the head of a dead dragon had been impressive, it was nothing compared to witnessing one that was whole and very much alive.

Covered in red-black scales, the dragon stood taller than a building. Its four legs looked thicker than tree trunks. It had a long, serpentine neck and tail and its head was maned by longer scales that sharpened off into dagger-like points.

Kas noticed one of those longer scales on the underside of its jaw was missing the tip, as if it had been broken off. It did not take her long to realise. *This must be Ombral.*

Ombral lifted her head towards the sky, inhaling the air. "Ah," she said with a satisfied sigh, "I have waited for this moment. Waited to be free again for far too long."

Kas shifted her foot, an involuntary movement, almost unnoticeable. Yet it was enough to draw Ombral's eyes—like fire captured behind glass—on them.

Kas felt like a fox caught by a hound, and she barely dared to breathe as the dragon lowered its head until it was almost eye level with the three of them.

"I wonder if I have you to thank for my freedom?" Ombral mused. But then those luminous eyes fixed solely on Kas, the pupils narrowing. The dragon's scarred mouth curled into what could only be described as a sneer. "No. I do not think so. For you, flame-haired one, carry the same blade as *her*. That insolent pup, Lyar of Rosille. The one who imprisoned me and my kin."

Ombral raised herself to full height and Kas could feel a new anger coming off the dragon like heat from a bed of coals. She tightened her grip on *Velane*, even though, in the face of Ombral, the sword felt no better than a toothpick in her hand.

"It saddens me that I never got the chance to tear her flesh from her bones," said Ombral. "So, I will just have to make do with you."

Ombral lunged forward, jaws open and Kas knew right then that she could not hope to stand against a dragon.

Kas turned towards Aara, grabbed hold of the girl and threw themselves out of the way of Ombral's path.

They landed hard on the ground. A pained grunt went up from Aara. Kas looked back to where she had last seen Claudia and Tsurra. To make sure they were out of harm's way, but all she saw was Ombral, her flame-like eyes fixed on Kas and burning with loathing.

This time when Ombral opened her maw, Kas saw a light building in the back of her throat, and that light quickly turned into a stream of fire pouring from the dragon's jaws and roaring towards Kas and Aara.

It was coming towards them too fast. She wouldn't be able to get out of the way in time. She—

"Kas!" was all she heard before the wind was knocked out of her and she was lifted off her feet by a strong grip around her middle as the world sped past her. When Kas finally recovered her bearings, it was to realise that both she and Aara had been moved, further down the mountain, away from Ombral and her fire. Claudia stood with them, holding Tsurra's limp body beneath one arm like a sack of flour.

"We need to get away from here. *Quickly,*" said Claudia.

She was breathing hard; her face was leeched of colour and had a pained set to it. Kas wanted to go to her, to take Tsurra from her arms and ask her where she was hurt and to what extent. But there was no time for that.

A sound from above alerted Kas to Ombral in the air, and she was quickly bearing down on them.

"Run," she told the others at the same time she reached for the motionless Tsurra's weapons belt and plucked two daggers.

She had no illusions about what such weapons could do against the dragon. *At the very least, I can hope I can do something to slow it down.*

As Aara and Claudia hurried down the hill with Tsurra, Kas stood her ground, waiting for Ombral to draw closer. As soon as she could clearly see the fiery glow of Ombral's eyes, Kas let the daggers fly from her hand. She aimed them at the dragon's left eye, in an attempt to hinder her vision. Perhaps she would have been successful too, had Ombral not ducked her head at the last moment. Instead of the knives hitting her eye, they bounced harmlessly off the hard scales of her head.

"Fuck," Kas swore before she turned tail, running as quick as she could down the mountain.

She heard what sounded like an explosion behind her, followed by a scorching heat against her back and an orange glow lighting up the rocky terrain around her. Kas didn't have to look back to know that

Ombral was breathing more fire at her. Or that it was swiftly gaining on her.

The ground fell out from under her, and Kas went tumbling over a rocky ledge. The fall was not long enough to be dangerous, but enough that pain sang up her hands and knees when she hit the ground below.

Moving quickly, Kas gathered up *Velane* where she had dropped it, before pressing herself back against the wall of rock behind her, keeping as much of herself tucked beneath the edge that stuck out over her head as she could, just as Ombral's fire washed over her.

The sound of it was deafening and the heat excruciating, suffocating. Even though the rock protected her from being directly hit by the fire, she still feared that she would be burnt alive.

But as quickly as it came the fire passed over. As did the dragon.

"Kas! Over here."

At the sound of her name, she looked around and spotted Aara, standing in what looked like the narrow gap of a cave entrance to her left.

Kas looked over to where Ombral was wheeling back around in the air, her huge, dark body blending in almost seamlessly with the night sky.

Kas didn't hesitate, she scrambled to her feet and darted towards Aara.

As she made her way over, she noticed Ombral coming back towards her with startling speed. She managed to reach Aara and the crevice in time, slipping between the rock as the dragon's cry echoed through the air and more fire blasted the ground where she had just been.

Aara led her through the tight squeeze of the passageway, the rough edges of protruding rock jabbed her in the hip, in the shoulder and caught and pulled on the threads of her clothes. From somewhere up above, moonlight filtered down, giving Kas a chance to see where she was stepping.

Finally, the space they were in opened up into a wider tunnel, where Claudia waited with Tsurra propped up against one of the walls.

As soon as she saw them, Claudia threw her arms around Kas's shoulders and Kas instinctively returned the hold with her free arm. For a moment she allowed herself the simple joy of holding Claudia close and luxuriating in the knowledge that they were both alive, that she could feel the breath from Claudia's lips against the base of her neck.

The moment was interrupted however by a shaking beneath their feet and in the walls around them.

"Where are you?" Ombral's voice thundered from outside. "Do not think you can remain hidden from me, vermin."

"We need to go," urged Claudia, pulling away from Kas.

"This tunnel must lead to somewhere," said Aara. She pointed at the way ahead of them. "I can feel air coming from down there. And at least this way the dragon won't see us escaping."

As Claudia moved away, Kas stood her ground, looking back the way she had come. Then she stared down at the sword in her hand. *Velane.* The sword that had been wielded by the first Slayer, created to slay a dragon. It had been used to protect the world. Was Kas truly going to run away with it now? Would she forgive herself if she did?

"You go," she told the others. "But I stay here."

Claudia turned to look at Kas as if she was being ridiculous. "Kas, now isn't the time to—"

"To what? Play at being a hero? It is," she said simply. "Ombral needs to be stopped here and now, otherwise who knows what havoc she'll wreak. This is what the last few months have been about after all. Trying to stop the return of the dragons. Maybe we failed to stop one, but that doesn't mean we need to give up. A dragon was slain on this mountain once before. It can happen again."

"But it doesn't need to be you. Someone else could—"

"There's no time. Do you remember how I told you that I once thought I could protect other children from what happened to me by becoming a Slayer? I know I can't protect everyone from every monster. But I might be able to save everyone from *this* monster."

There was a distressed look on Claudia's lovely features that told Kas she understood what she was saying, but that she did not like it one bit.

Kas reached out, stroking her fingers along Claudia's cheek. "Go with Aara. She can't carry Tsurra away from here on her own."

"No." Claudia's tone was bordering on frantic. "No, I'm not leaving you to fight alone. I'll go with you. I—"

"Claudia. You're hurt. Too hurt to fight against a dragon. And if its fire gets too close to you, you'll—" Kas didn't want to finish that sentence.

Claudia shook her head. "That doesn't matter." Her protest was weak.

"Yes, it does. It matters to *me*." She softened her voice and tilted Claudia's chin up so the other woman would meet her eyes. She wanted to look at those beautiful blue eyes one last time. "Please, Claudia. Get them to safety."

In all the time she had known her, Kas did not think she had ever seen Claudia cry. Kas's heart felt like it was tearing at the sight of tears barely held back. And knowing she was the cause of them.

*I'm sorry, I'm sorry.*

"All right," Claudia finally said in a voice so low Kas almost didn't hear it.

Another tremor shook the tunnel walls, loosening some stones from above.

*"Come out and face me."*

"Kas."

Tsurra was awake, though she looked as though she hardly had the strength to lift her head.

"If you're going to face a dragon," she said, "You need the right weapon. Aara . . . the bag."

She held out an unsteady hand as Aara handed her the bottomless green bag. Reaching inside of it, Tsurra pulled out a chain. Her silver whip.

She held it out for Kas to take and she did so almost hesitantly.

"You may have *Velane,*" Tsurra said, her voice strained. "But you don't have a sorcerer to hold down the beast for you while you strike as Lyar of Rosille did. The whip . . . might be able to weaken it enough for you to find the right opportunity."

"Thank you," Kas said through the constriction building in her throat. "I'll do my best to return it to you."

"Hang that," Tsurra growled. There was blood on her teeth from where it had trickled down from the mess of her eye. "Just do what you can to make sure *you* return."

Kas only nodded, not trusting herself to say any more. She took the little green bag from Aara, to stow *Velane* away until the time was right to use it.

Aara put Tsurra's arm around her own shoulders and hauled her to her feet. As she led Tsurra further down the tunnel, Aara paused to look back at Kas. "If you die out there, I will be so cross with you."

That startled a smile out of Kas. "I'll try not to then." Finally, she turned back to Claudia.

She stood there, looking small and hurt and alone and Kas's chest tightened to see such vulnerability from Claudia.

"I don't want to lose you," Claudia breathed when Kas stood close. "Not you too."

Kas's only response was to take Claudia's face in her hands and kiss her. Hoping it was enough to convey all her feelings of affection and the promise she would try with all her might to keep.

Far too soon for her liking, Kas pulled away. Her fingers lingered on Claudia's cheek for a heartbeat longer before she turned away, heading out to face the dragon while the others made for safety. It took everything within her not to look back, so she could stay focused on what was ahead.

When Kas stepped back out into the open, she saw no sign of Ombral. Had the dragon grown tired of searching for them and flown away? Was she already far from Va Serote, preparing to unleash fiery hell upon some unsuspecting village? Before Kas could begin to let such thoughts panic her, a large shadow passed over and she looked up to see Ombral perch atop the stone peak of the cave Kas had just appeared from. Bits of rock rained down from beneath the dragon's weight.

"Did you tire of your own cowardice?" she asked of Kas. "Have you truly come here to face me alone?"

"Someone has to," said Kas. "It might as well be me."

"It would have been wiser of you to have chosen to flee instead," Ombral sneered.

"Maybe. But I'm a Slayer. We slay monsters, even if it means getting killed in the process. And that's what I intend to do, right here and right now." Kas let the whip in her hand unravel. It hit the ground with a metallic clatter.

Ombral barked out a laugh like a thunderclap. "And you truly think you can slay me?"

A feral grin split Kas's face. "Well, I won't know unless I give it a try."

She lifted the whip and with a rattle of its chains, sent it soaring through the air, straight for Ombral.

Ombral leapt out of the way before the silver whip could strike her.

In the air, Ombral breathed fire upon her and Kas was forced to retreat and take shelter behind a nearby boulder.

The fire ran its course, but once it had, the dragon did not allow Kas much chance to gather herself. Ombral was already directly above her. Kas was forced to dash out of the way once more to avoid being caught up in her snapping jaws.

When Kas next turned to face the dragon, she found her already bearing down on Kas with a massive talon.

Kas lifted the whip and this time it made contact, scoring a long, burning line across the underside of Ombral's talon.

The dragon roared, snatching her burned talon back. Ombral moved with a surprising swiftness as she used her other talon to bat Kas away. Like one might do to an irksome fly.

The attack was so quick, Kas had no recourse to block or dodge. The back of Ombral's talon struck her, knocking her off her feet and sending her soaring through the air. When she hit the ground again, it stole the breath out of her. Pain exploded through different points of her body, as she rolled down the mountain, only coming to a stop when the ground evened out, and she found herself lying on a rocky plateau. She thought she might have even heard the internal snap of the bone in her shoulder.

Trying to get to her feet again was torture. Everything hurt, and she struggled to catch her breath. But still, she did it. Clutching Tsurra's whip in her hand the entire time, imagining that she could draw strength off it, like she might if her mentor were here now, and fighting alongside her. How she desperately wished that could be true.

Ombral landed on the plateau in front of her, with such a tremendous thud that it nearly shook Kas off her feet again.

Ombral could have moved in for another attack, but instead the dragon merely watched her, as if seeing Kas struggle even to stay standing brought the monster great amusement.

Spitting blood out of her mouth, Kas lashed out with the whip. But the move was sloppy, her injured shoulder robbing her of finesse. Ombral easily evaded the attack.

Kas was forced to throw herself backwards, to avoid being caught under Ombral's claws. The ground where Kas had just stood, cracked, and shuddered beneath the force with which the dragon brought down her talon.

Her feet gave out underneath her and Kas landed on her back on the hard ground.

This time, she feared there would be no getting up in time.

*I'm sorry Tsurra. Aara . . . Claudia.*

"And here I was hoping you'd prove more of a challenge," Ombral mused. "But perhaps that was foolish of me. You are just a human, after all. A pitiful little mortal, not even worth the dirt under my claws. You are nothing. Your entire race is good for nothing more than feeding and serving my kind."

Kas closed her eyes, hoping whatever end she was about to meet would be quick.

In her mind's eye she saw Tsurra's face. *"Just do what you can to make sure you return."*

*She would never forgive me if I let it end like this, Kas realised. And if we ever meet again in whatever afterlife awaits, she'd give me such a thrashing, I would probably be dead twice.*

Then, she thought of Claudia. She wanted more time with her. To hold Claudia in her arms, to hear her voice and learn of all the ways to make her laugh. What they had been through so far together didn't feel like enough. It absolutely was not enough time.

*I need more time with her. I need to make it back to Claudia.*

She cracked her eyes open to see Ombral opening her jaws, whether ready to swallow Kas whole or breathe fire on her, she did not know—and nor would she wait to find out.

Kas tightened her fingers around the handle of Tsurra's whip.

Gathering every last ounce of speed and strength she had, Kas rolled her body out of Ombral's reach.

In the same fluid motion, she raised herself onto her knees, spun around to face Ombral, and lifted the whip into the air.

And this time her whip hit its mark. Landing a blow directly in the dragon's eye.

Ombral cried out and cursed, wrenching herself backwards. Smoke was rising from the burnt and bloodied tear Kas had made in her eye.

"My eye—*It burns!*" She shrieked, limbs and tail flailing. The tip of her wing scraped against the side of the mountain.

Kas had to press herself flat to the ground to keep from being hit by Ombral's spiked tail. When she got back up again, Kas struck out at her hind legs with the whip, opening burning lines in Ombral's scaled skin.

With a cry, Ombral spun around to try and face her, but Kas made sure to remain in the dragon's new blind spot.

She kept up her attacks in a quick succession. Each strike of the silver whip opened up new, bloodied, smoking wounds along the dragon's hide.

Ombral's roars pierced the air. Roars of agony and fury. Because now the dragon was the one at the mercy of *her*.

"*Enough*," shouted Ombral, and spread her great wings.

Ombral lifted herself off the ground, trying to flee into the air.

But Kas was not about to let that happen.

She spun the whip about herself, before she hurled it at one of Ombral's outstretched wings.

The thin, leather-like skin of the dragon's wing had no protection and when Kas's whip collided with it the wing tore, almost entirely in half. It was like watching a hot fireplace poker tear through parchment.

With a cry of pain, Ombral's wing gave way, and she went toppling back to the ground, rolling off the edge of the plateau and down the mountain.

Kas didn't hesitate. She threw herself over the edge as well. Skidding and sliding on the uneven rock as she followed after the dragon.

They had almost reached the base of the mountain when Ombral's descent came to a halt. The dragon lay on her side, struggling to right herself, the silver wounds and her ruined wing clearly causing her great pain.

Kas was all too pleased to use it to her advantage.

Kas halted her own descent, by planting her feet firmly on a jut of rock, just above where Ombral lay. It was a perfect vantage point.

Somewhere along the way, Kas had lost Tsurra's whip, but she couldn't bring herself to feel shameful for it now. She plunged her hand into the green bag at her hip and withdrew *Velane*.

Ombral's remaining good eye finally spotted her and Kas tried not to feel unnerved by the terrible fury she saw in the dragon's fiery red eye. Instead, she firmed her grip on *Velane's* hilt and stepped off the rock.

"You . . . *miserable piece of filth*." Ombral bellowed as Kas fell towards her.

While she was in the air, Kas managed to manoeuvre herself away from Ombral's open maw. Heading instead for the wide, black scales that armoured the underside of the dragon's neck.

Kas twisted the sword in her grip so she could plunge the point of the blade through the dragon's scales. She managed to drive *Velane* in almost all the way to the hilt and Kas put all her weight and waning strength behind dragging the sword down.

Ombral let out a blood-curdling cry as Kas tore open her neck almost all the way to the chest. A thick torrent of blood burst forth, washing over Kas as she released the sword and fell back to the ground.

Her leg took the brunt of the fall and bent painfully beneath her weight. Kas screamed. She felt as though something had cracked and torn through muscle and skin in a way that made bile rise in her throat.

She was aware of Ombral writhing and roaring above her as impossible amounts of blood spilled from the long, deep wound in her neck.

"No . . . no," Ombral growled weakly. Blood spilled from between her teeth. "This cannot be. I . . . Not to a human . . . Not like . . . Morvelth. No."

She tried to fly, as if she might find safety and healing in the sky, but with her torn wing, all Ombral succeeded in doing was flipping herself over onto her back.

She made one last wet growling noise, as if she were choking on her own blood, and then her face went slack, her eyes dull and her body limp. The dragon Ombral did not move again.

The world fell into stillness.

From where she lay half-sprawled in the dirt, Kas kept her eyes fixed on Ombral. She half expected the dragon to blink her eye at Kas or bare her teeth in her own version of a smirk as she got back to her feet. But she didn't.

Ombral was well and truly dead.

Claudia and Tsurra and Aara and the rest of the unwitting world would be safe.

Whatever energy had lent itself to her to allow her to defeat

Ombral was beginning to recede, like the tide at dawn. Her injuries were beginning to make themselves known again and she found she could not even so much as hold herself up on her elbows any longer.

Kas collapsed onto her side. Darkness moved in from the edges of her vision and she could do nothing but let it overtake her and pull her under into oblivion.

# CHAPTER 52
# CLAUDIA

IN THE END, Claudia could not leave.

The walk through the tunnel had felt endless as every part of Claudia's being screamed at her to turn back and go after Kas. But she resisted. Kas had wanted her to go with Aara and Tsurra, so she had. She had seen them to where they'd left the horses at the bottom of the mountain, tied to a tree, when they first arrived at Va Serote. Once she had, Claudia charged back up the mountain.

She had already left Serisa upon that accursed mountain. She wouldn't leave Kas too.

It took some time of wandering and following the signs of battle—scorched earth, the jagged wounds of giant claws in the rock, and Tsurra's whip dangling from a protruding branch—before she found them.

On a plateau toward the base of the mountain, she discovered the dead body of Ombral. Her red-black scaled hide crisscrossed with lashes like burns that could have only been made from silver. And there was a long grisly gash in her neck that had spilled a profuse amount of blood.

But other than that, Claudia paid little heed to the dragon.

"Kas?" she called out, surveying the area for any sign of her red-headed Slayer. "*Kas.*"

She saw the sword, *Velane,* covered in blood and lying on the ground near one of Ombral's outstretched claws. So where was Kas?

Then Claudia spotted her. Some distance away from Ombral's body Kas lay motionless. And covered in blood.

Claudia was falling to her knees by Kas's side in an instant, turning the other woman onto her back so Claudia could cradle her upper body in her lap, uncaring of the blood that seeped into her own clothing. Only caring about how much of it was Kas's own.

"Kas," Claudia breathed, running a hand down the side of Kas's face, hoping her touch would wake her.

But Kas's eyes remained closed, and Claudia's heart faltered.

Beneath the blood, Kas's face was ashen. There was rent in her side, not only in her clothes, but in the flesh beneath. Her left shoulder protruded unnaturally, and Claudia could see *bone* sticking out from beneath the knee of her right leg.

"Kas, please," she whispered, leaning over Kas and gripping her tighter as if she could shield her from further harm. "It's over now. You can open your eyes."

Still, she stayed unresponsive, and Claudia prayed, for the first time since she was ten years old, clutching her father's hand while he lay pale and feeble in bed, his breathing growing weaker and weaker. The Saints hadn't listened to her then, but maybe they would now.

*Please don't take her from me. Please don't let me have to lose someone else I love tonight.*

Claudia bent her head, pressing her ear to Kas's chest.

She closed her eyes.

And listened.

# EPILOGUE
## THREE MONTHS LATER

THE SUMMER DAYS were coming to an end. Bit by bit, the air was turning colder, trees began to shed their leaves and night cast its shadows earlier. But today it seemed as if summer wished to give a last hurrah before surrendering itself to the harsher months ahead.

A warm breeze swept in through the open windows in one of the top chambers of the Slayers Keep.

Kas stood in front of her bed pulling up her trousers.

It had been nearly three full months since the battle with Serisa and her vampyrics on Va Serote and the slaying of the dragon Ombral. In that time Kas had been confined to the Keep, bedbound for the first few weeks as she recovered from the injuries she had sustained that night. Her shoulder had popped out of its socket but had since healed nicely. The shattered bone in her right leg had given her the most grief, however. Even now as she fitted it through the leg of her pants, she felt a twinge of pain.

But she was not about to let that stop her from finally venturing forth into the world again.

She heard the drawn-out creaking of the door hinges as it was opened. Kas didn't need to turn around to know who it was. The near silent padding of feet against the tiled floor had become all too familiar to her after so many days and nights spent together.

Gentle arms snaked around her newly clothed waist. A warm and welcome body pressed up against her back.

"Need some help?" Claudia whispered into her ear.

"I'm not incapable of dressing myself you know?" said Kas. "Unless you mean you want to help me with getting *out* of them, then I could be persuaded."

Claudia pressed a quick kiss to the edge of the scar on Kas's cheek, before settling her chin on Kas's shoulder. "Tempting, but I think we should be going, don't you?"

Kas made a disappointed sound. "Fine."

Claudia slid her slim, pale fingers through her opened collar, touching Kas's bare skin.

"I thought you said you didn't want to have sex right now?" There was teasing in Kas's voice.

Claudia made a relaxed humming sound, burying her nose into Kas's shoulder. "Just wanted to feel you."

Kas smiled, feeling hopelessly and utterly endeared towards her lover.

She took Claudia's hand away from her chest and brought it up to her lips, so she could press them against Claudia's open palm.

Claudia had been a steadfast presence in the time it had taken Kas to recover. She had hardly left Kas's side, always around to fetch her some food or water, to tend to her wounds with salve and bandages. To keep Kas company during the days and through the nights when sleep was difficult.

And Kas had tried to be there for her in turn. Claudia's wounds had healed within days after the battle with Ombral, but not so quickly healed were the wounds Kas could not see.

She knew that Serisa had died that night and that it had been by Claudia's hand. There were nights where Claudia would awaken calling for her sister, like a lost child. Only the other day Kas, had found Claudia on the balcony of her rooms, staring out at the view with tears trailing down her face. Kas had not needed to ask what the tears were for.

Despite all Serisa had put her through, Claudia clearly still grieved her sister, and Kas did what she could to help her through that grief.

For didn't Kas know better than most what it was like to be the last of one's family?

Claudia parted from Kas to allow her to finish dressing. She walked around the bed, toward the pool of sunlight spilling in through the open balcony doors and the black mass curled up on the floor there.

"Come on, Wolf. It's time to go."

Wolf peered up at Claudia with a look that seemed to say he very much did not wish to move from his spot.

Claudia stroked one of his pointed ears. "Being left in this keep for so long has made you lazy."

But when she turned away, Wolf rose up, stretching languidly and yawning wide.

Kas had been relieved, after returning to the Slayers Keep, to discover that Wolf had survived his encounter with Serisa. Only suffering broken ribs that Claudia herself had set back into place. He too had spent much time recuperating, becoming almost as good as a pampered house dog, with Claudia and even Aara at times, bringing him all his meals until he was able to walk without pain again.

Kas had just secured the scabbards of her two new swords onto her back, when Claudia asked her, "Are you ready now?"

"Yes."

With their belongings in hand and Wolf loping ahead of them, Kas and Claudia made their way into the Keep's courtyard. There they found Aara, practising with a sword on one of the beaten-up sack dummies.

"You're getting quite serious about your Slayer training now, aren't you?" said Kas.

Aara lowered her practice sword. Sweat gleaned on her brown skin and her black hair had grown long enough now to be pulled back into a scruffy knot on the back of her head.

"About that," Aara said, fiddling with the straps on the wooden sword's hilt. "I wasn't quite sure how to bring this up to you after everything, but . . . I have decided that I don't want to be a Slayer anymore."

"What?" Kas felt more stunned by the admission than she should have been—and maybe an ounce of disappointment. "What changed?"

"I just think that the Slayer life might not actually be for me. After these last couple of months, I think I've had my fill of battling monsters and dancing with death. Also, I . . . don't feel like I have anything to prove to people anymore. Not to my mother, not to you, Kas, not to anyone."

"So, what are you going to do now?" asked Claudia. "Do you want to come with us?"

Aara shook her head, a strand of hair slipped free of the knot. "No. I'd love to, but I already know where I'm headed next."

"And where's that?" Kas said.

"Back to Verillino, where I'll meet up with those minstrels from the summer harvest festival in Gorsa Té." Aara was beaming. "They asked me back then if I wanted to be a part of their group and that if my answer was yes, I could find them in Verillino."

"You're going to become a bard?"

"Hm, Aara the Bard does have a nice ring to it," said Claudia with a quirk of her lips.

"I've even been thinking of a song of my own. Inspired by our adventure. I'm thinking of calling it *A Ballad for Slayers and Monsters*."

Claudia hummed. "Not bad."

"I don't know," said Kas. "I'd keep working on your song titles, if I were you."

Aara gave her a sour look.

"But if you're not interested in being a Slayer anymore, then why are you still training?"

"Because I think it's a good idea that she does." Kas looked over her shoulder to see Tsurra making her way towards them.

Like Kas, Tsurra had spent much of her time here at the Keep of late. Her right eye had been too damaged to be saved after the battle at Va Serote and had to be removed.

She now wore a black patch over her right eye, held there by thin leather straps. A still healing scar, snaked out from beneath the patch, to carve a crooked line almost to her jaw.

"If she's going to be travelling on her own," Tsurra went on, "then it can't hurt for her to know how to defend herself. Especially if she's going to be subjecting the masses to her singing."

"In that case you should be building up her speed to run away from irritated locals," Kas remarked.

Aara tried to whack Kas's good leg with the flat of her sword, but Kas quickly danced out of reach, coming to stand beside Tsurra instead.

"A Slayer training a werecat," Kas remarked. "Will wonders ever cease?"

The older Slayer eyed Kas's gear. "All set to leave then, are you?"

Kas nodded. She swatted at a dragonfly that came too close to her head.

"You sure it's not too soon?" Kas noticed Tsurra's eye flick down to her leg.

"I've been lazing around the Keep for three months. Besides, there are still monsters out there that need killing."

"You'll be the one getting killed if you're not healed up enough."

Smiling, Kas nudged Tsurra in the shoulder. "Is the old lady worried about me?"

The skin around her eyepatch crinkled as Tsurra's expression twisted into a scowl. "Well, I'm certainly not going to miss that disrespectful mouth of yours. Or finding you and Claudia doing things in places you shouldn't."

"How were we supposed to know you'd also be coming into the library?" Kas muttered.

Tsurra placed her hand on Kas's shoulder. A firm grip that always managed to instil a sense of ease in Kas, ever since she was twelve years old.

"Take care of yourself out there." Tsurra told her.

"And you as well," Kas replied. "When you head back out again."

They embraced.

When they released each other, Kas turned to where Claudia was saying her goodbyes to Aara. Wolf sat in between the two of them, demanding some final chin scratches from the werecat.

"I just wanted to say," Aara said to them both when Kas joined them, "before you left, that . . . I'm really grateful that I got to meet you both. If you hadn't come to Feldania I'd probably still just be a half-starving thief with nothing to really look forward to, except surviving to the next day." She gave them a bashful smile, showing off a cat-like tooth. "But you gave me an adventure and helped set me on the path to figuring out who I want to be . . . so thank you."

Kas opened her mouth to speak, to give voice to the swell of fondness she felt for the young werecat, but all that came out was a winded sound as she soon found her arms full of the girl.

And then Claudia was pulled into the embrace as well by Aara.

"What's this?" said Claudia. "You're not going to weep on us now, are you Aara?"

Aara shook her head, but kept her face hidden against Kas's chest.

Kas let out a breath of laughter. She placed her hand atop Aara's head. "Even if your path doesn't follow one of a Slayer, you know you are always welcome at this keep. And maybe one day our paths will lead us right back to each other again."

WITH THEIR GOODBYES SAID, Kas and Claudia left the Slayers Keep. Kas saddled on Bod and Claudia mounted on her mare. Wolf raced down the hill ahead of them, off to chase a rabbit hidden in the sea of tall grass and wildflowers.

Bod tossed his head, flicking his mane, and pawed at the ground. Kas rubbed a hand up and down the side of his strong, curved neck.

"Are you glad to be on the road again, too, old boy?"

Bod nickered his affirmation.

Kas took a moment to breathe in the mountain air, to feel the warm breeze against her skin and admire the vast stretch of land ahead of them. All of Vil Tresar lay before them. Full of monsters to slay and mysteries to stumble upon. The prospect of what awaited them filled her with excitement.

Kas of Veldenier was not made for a sedentary life. She was meant to roam and dive head-first into adventures great or small.

And the thought of getting to experience all that with Claudia by her side filled her with a delight words could not describe.

"So," Claudia said after a moment. "Where are we off to?"

Kas looked at Claudia, at the way her long hair caught in the breeze, lifting it off her shoulders, and the curve of her lips as she looked at Kas in turn. It made Kas want to reach over, take the reins of Claudia's horse, and draw her closer until Kas could lean over and kiss her.

Instead, she said, "Why don't we just see where the road takes us?"

# Acknowledgments

It's a little surreal to think this book is really finished after so many years of it being an ever-growing idea in my head. The feminist *'The Witcher'* story I came up with for a creative writing class. The sapphic love story between a monster hunter and a monster I longed for and the fantasy adventure with an all-female cast that I'd love to see more of. It's been quite the journey, Ballad, and I'll leave you now with a piece of my heart tucked between your pages.

As always, this book would not have been possible without the hard work and support of others who deserve their honourable mentions. I'd like to start off by thanking my lovely editor Kai, who helped me shape this story into what it is today and for all her encouragement. Thank you, Talli and Ash, for being Ballad's first readers and for your enthusiasm for this story and its characters. And a big thank you to my cover artists, Miriam and Annalise. I could not be more pleased with the absolutely gorgeous covers you both came up with.

I also owe a thank you to you, dear reader, for deciding to take a chance on my book. Your support is invaluable.

# About the Author

Rita A. Rubin is an Australian born author who currently resides in Melbourne and is living their best introvert life. When not writing, Rita can be found with their nose in a book, or gaming console in their hands or making up songs to sing to their dog and cat.

Follow Rita on Instagram @ritarubin9, and on Twitter, Bluesky and TikTok @ritacoolbeans.